Three warm and entertaining novels by Joyce Dingwell, a favorite author from Harlequin's Romance Library

The Boomerang Girl... Clancy Clyde had no convincing explanation for her change of heart—and Guy Osman would not have listened anyway. He questioned her motives for returning to Australia and Clancy despaired that he would ever forgive her first failure. (#1160)

September Street... To Clair, alone after her mother's death, Mrs. Henry's offer to hire her as a companion on a cruise to Italy seemed like a blessing. But her status was that of a servant; even worse, her ultimate humiliation was witnessed by the lordly Enrico Montales. (#1566)

Nickel Wife... Sandy Lawford was captivated by the colorful beauty of the empty vastness of Australia's desert. And in spite of the arrogant Stone Wetherill, she began to feel as much at home in the world's last frontier as he did. (#1589)

**Another collection
of Romance favorites...
by a best-selling Harlequin author!**

In the pages of this specially selected
anthology are three delightfully
absorbing Romances—all by an
author whose vast readership all over
the world has shown her to be an
outstanding favorite.

For those of you who are missing
these love stories from your
Harlequin library shelf, or who wish
to collect great romance fiction by
favorite authors, these Harlequin
Romance anthologies are for you.

We're sure you'll enjoy each of the
engrossing and heartwarming stories
contained within. They're treasures
from our library...and we know
they'll become treasured additions
to yours!

The fifth anthology of 3 Harlequin Romances by

Joyce Dingwell

Harlequin Books

TORONTO • NEW YORK • LONDON
AMSTERDAM • PARIS • SYDNEY • HAMBURG
STOCKHOLM • ATHENS • TOKYO • MILAN

Harlequin Romance anthology 83

Copyright © 1977 by Harlequin Enterprises Limited. Philippine copyright 1984.
Australian copyright 1984. All rights reserved. Except for use in any review, the
reproduction or utilization of this work in whole or in part in any form by any
electronic, mechanical or other means, now known or hereafter invented,
including xerography, photocopying and recording, or in any information storage or
retrieval system, is forbidden without the permission of the publisher, Harlequin
Enterprises Limited, 225 Duncan Mill Road, Don Mills, Ontario, Canada M3B 3K9.

These books by Joyce Dingwell were originally published as
follows:

THE BOOMERANG GIRL
Copyright © 1962 by Joyce Dingwell
First published in 1962 by Mills & Boon Limited
Harlequin edition (#1160) published November 1967

SEPTEMBER STREET
Copyright © 1969 by Joyce Dingwell
First published in 1969 by Mills & Boon Limited
Harlequin edition (#1566) published February 1972

NICKEL WIFE
Copyright © 1970 by Joyce Dingwell
First published in 1970 by Mills & Boon Limited
Harlequin edition (#1589) published May 1972

ISBN 0-373-20083-8

First edition published as Harlequin Omnibus in December 1977

Second printing September 1978

Third printing April 1979

Fourth printing April 1984

Printed in Canada

Contents

The Boomerang Girl

Homesickness sent Clancy back to England after her first emigration to Australia. Then, belatedly, the magic of that new country took effect, and she knew she had to return.

Her path back was made surprisingly easy. She became Australia's "Boomerang Girl"—an example to other immigrants who might have a change of heart.

Only Guy Osman questioned her motives and disapproved of her celebrity status. But why should it matter what he thought about her?

CHAPTER 1

"So you are the Boomerang Girl."

Although the man sitting at the purser's desk spoke without expression, although he did not look up, for the first time in three months, for the first time since she had made her fresh decision, Clancy felt a cobweb of doubt.

Before this moment everyone had been so kind, so unbelievably kind—*undeservedly* kind. Not one had said to her: "But why? Why return to a country you came away from? Why go through all again that obviously you found distasteful before? You must have found it distasteful, otherwise you would not have come back to England. Why do it all once more?"

Instead she had been smiled upon, encouraged, welcomed. At Australia House where quite hopelessly she had ventured her *second* enquiry regarding immigration, fully aware that the general rule was that migrants could receive an assisted passage only once, the answer, after some official heads-putting-together, had been the astounding "Yes, we will make an exception of you, Miss Clyde, in spite of the fact that you stopped long enough in Australia the first time *not* to refund the Government's contribution to your fare.

"We will do it," the officials had smiled, "for two reasons. One is because we regard convinced applicants, in other words applicants who know what it's like out there, know to what they're going, as good bets when it comes to citizenship.

"The other reason" . . . the officials had looked approvingly upon Clancy, then wisely at each other . . . "is that you will be our come-again migrant, our second-timer . . . our Boomerang Girl."

Clancy had not needed to question, "Boomerang?" She knew that the boomerang was a bent missile used by the natives of Australia, balanced so that it returned towards the thrower. She had seen boomerang-throwing at La Perouse, in Sydney; she had heard Australians say ruefully when something recoiled on them: "It did the boomerang on me."

That was what the officials had meant, what another country might have termed "full circle." She had been a boomerang, she had gone her distance, and now she was going back.

"Thank you," she had murmured gratefully . . . and that had started it all.

From somewhere a man had appeared with a camera. He had flashed Clancy as she signed her application, and that night she had looked, a little dismayed, at herself on the front page of a London newspaper, and beneath the photograph three words: "The Boomerang Girl."

It had not stopped at that. When next she had called at Australia House to go through more details there had been another flash.

The clerk who was dealing with her had smilingly shown her some Australian newspapers. There had been the first photo, the same tag, "the Boomerang Girl."

Jokingly Clancy had complained that she was getting nothing out of all these free flashes.

"I think you are," the clerk had pointed out, "in spite of a waiting list that could fill a book, *you* are down for the next ship."

She had gasped at that. She had recalled how long she had waited the first time. But then, of course, she had been in a group, and that might have made the difference, now she was by herself. "I suppose," she had laughed, "they want unattached singles."

"More like it," the clerk had complimented, "they want their Boomerang Girl."

Whether this was true or not, Clancy had found her path back particularly easy.

Papers had been got through almost miraculously; the Customs drill about no Hides and Musk-rats and Parrots and Snuff that always sent emigrants either into peals of laughter or moods of deep confusion had passed her by;

the money question of ten pounds had been as uncomplicated as handing out a bus fare. Much sooner, far easier, shades smoother than she had thought possible, she had learned that she would depart on Tuesday week.

It never had struck Clancy that this was exceedingly fast even for an unattached single . . . it never had occurred to her later aboard the *Loch Maree*.

She had been a popular passenger, but then all single young women were popular on a ship . . . or so she had believed. Even when the Captain had chosen *her* to dance with on Open Night she had found no significance. She was no millionth migrant, no migrant with an imposing list of degrees, no member of a very large family, she was nothing exceptional at all, just a girl who had changed her mind and come back.

Come back. That was what a boomerang did. How was Clancy to know that that group of Australia House officials responsible for immigration, responsible for the forty-eight per cent British side of it, had seized on her return with verve?

The next "by chance" photo . . . or so Clancy had ignorantly thought . . . had been when the ship had sailed, and it had appeared with the caption: "Goodbye, says Boomerang Girl."

Later it had been the Mediterranean. . . . Clancy in cool cotton and rope sandals, and saying something like "I'm going back for a place in the sun," which, of course, not even knowing this time she was being photographed, Clancy had not said at all.

She had learned she had said these things, though, when she had been shown newspapers at Perth, Western Australia . . . she had learned what she had said also at Aden . . . at Ceylon.

She had laughed a little dubiously . . . knowing from a bitter experience what a newspaper can concoct . . . then she had forgotten her unease in the warm smiles of those around her. Not just the smiles of fellow immigrants, but the smiles of Australians coming back from world tours, the smiles of Australians on the Fremantle and, later, Melbourne streets.

This was a good country, she had thought, smiling back, one poised for greatness, even leadership. It had no pettiness about it, it did not frown on someone like herself who had faltered on the immigration road—rather, like the prodigal son, she was being *rejoiced* back.

It had encouraged her to smile more radiantly then than ever when the cameras had clicked busily at each Australian port, it had persuaded her not to object to the tag she had earned. When she had been informed that in England she was being used as an alternative poster to "Emigrate to Australia for £10" she had accepted that, too, with a smile.

She had smiled when the camera had clicked only a few moments ago—"Just there, Miss Clyde . . . backdrop of the Sydney Harbour Bridge . . . must have the Bridge in it."

And she had smiled when she had entered this room.

On her first voyage, on the *Olwen*, the immigration relations man had taken over the purser's office. It had never occurred to Clancy when the reporters had finished with her to go elsewhere.

She knew she was to be interviewed, they were all interviewed; she knew she was to be welcomed, they were all welcomed . . . but was that deep inscrutable look on the face of the man sitting at Mr. Reynolds' desk a welcome? For a moment Clancy paused.

She felt the cobweb of doubt. It really *was* a cobweb. It was like walking in a fair garden and suddenly brushing something alien and intangibly strong.

The man looked up now and she saw that his eyes were blue ice, nothing warm about them. There was nothing warm but all the reverse of warm in his voice as he repeated coldly, "So you are the Boomerang Girl."

CHAPTER 2

WHAT was there for Clancy to say?

A frank "Yes, I am" would have sounded abominably self-satisfied, and yet a negation would be absurd. So she said nothing.

Silence did not suit Ice Eyes, however. He glanced up, sharply this time, and reminded her, "I asked you a question."

This time Clancy mumbled, "Yes, I am the Boomerang Girl."

He had taken out the makings of a cigarette, and now he was rolling it.

"Nice of you," he drawled at length.

"Nice of them," said Clancy inadequately, and she felt herself flush.

"Them?" The sharp way he asked it made her answer sound unpardonably rude and boorish, and she had not intended that.

"The—migration people; everybody." She knew she was scarlet now, and she disliked him for having embarrassed her like this.

"I suppose I should complete the circle," he drawled, "by saying nice of you to say nice of them."

Again she was silent.

"However," stated the man at the desk, still not asking her to sit down, "it's *you* making the circle, isn't it, though I must remind you that the boomerang only returns towards the thrower; only upon occasion and when the throw is expert does it come right back."

"Perhaps this will be one of those occasions," she said, for something to say.

"I doubt it," he answered at once, "considering your previous performances." He exhaled.

13

She stood silent again, silent and uncomfortable. She wished he would get through what had to be done.

Her sense of waiting must have reached him. His blue ice eyes glanced upward again in rather irritable enquiry. "Did you want me?" he asked.

"I—I thought you wanted me."

"Perish that thought," he replied.

This was going too far. What had she done to this man that he should treat her like this?

Words rushed to her lips, hot indignant words, but, wisely, she stopped them. She was the immigrant; he . . . apparently . . . was the citizen. There was a world of difference between the two; she had found that out before —not unkindly, but nonetheless definitely. Although these Australians held out their arms so wide they could have embraced the earth, they were still the possessors. It was their land. The dweller against the newcomer, she recalled, the old hand against the tenderfoot. And perhaps it was only right that the tenderfoot should tread with extra care.

So quietly, humbly, then, Clancy said, "Last time, on the *Olwen,* I was interviewed in the purser's office."

She could not have said a worse thing, it seemed. The black brows above the blue ice eyes, surprisingly black for eyes of that colour, met in one disliking line.

"Oh, yes," he said, "the last time." Then he said no more.

Somewhere in Mr. Reynolds' office a clock ticked. Absently Clancy counted the rhythmic beat. Why did this man dislike her so much? It was not just that straight disliking line of brow, it was every gesture, every word, every blue ice glance.

She had expected criticism from many quarters, she had expected people to remark pointedly, "Odd that you didn't return to England until your agreement of two years had exhausted itself, until you were sure you didn't have to repay your Australian-bound fare." She had expected a sly, "If you had returned earlier than two years you would have had to make up your out-passage, wouldn't you, less, of course, the ten pounds which was all *your* share." She

14

had expected, "Isn't it strange that you felt no compulsion to return to England under the stipulated time?"

These were what she had braced herself for. These were what she had not received. Until now.

Not in words as yet, but in every fibre of this accusing man sitting at the purser's desk and regarding her with more dispassion than Clancy had ever met in anyone before.

He was speaking again, idly, almost as though it did not interest him.

"Yes, the last time. . . . You have a pattern of procedure to fall back upon, haven't you? Nice for you."

"I believe," said Clancy tautly, "you said that before."

That did it. That pierced his armour of tight control. This time he was not icy, he was hotly furious, he pulled no punches with his words.

"I said it and I meant it. I think it's *very* nice for you. I think it would be nice for anyone to have their globe-trotting financed, but when the finance is showered on someone so totally unsuitable, so completely undeserving, so sadly ill-advised, I think it's extremely nice for them indeed."

Clancy said in a bleak little voice, "What do you mean?"

"Dray Hill Chronicle," he replied. Then he leaned back in Mr. Reynolds' chair and exhaled once more.

Clancy was not aware that she was clasping and unclasping her hands. Not that, she was thinking in misery, not Terry Kent's editorial in his little free weekly rag.

For rag the *Dray Hill Chronicle* was and always had been. In the world collection of local newspapers Clancy knew that Terry's would have earned last place.

It had nothing to it, for Terry was bone lazy, too lazy to cover the village affairs that villagers love to read about, only interested in the shilling-a-line ads that supplied him his inn wants that Dray Hill long had recognized as Kent's sole wants.

Years ago, when she first had worked for him, Clancy had regretted Terry's lack of ambition. In a few weeks she had accepted like the rest.

However, no one ever read the *Chronicle.* Years of its

15

inferiority had taught the locals only to leaf over the front page to see who was selling what in the Classified on the second and final sheet.

When she had returned from Australia and gone again to Dray Hill, Clancy had had cause to be glad of this.

For Kent, back from the inn one night just before weekly publication, had called to Clancy, "Clan, my love, I'm going to let myself go. I *can* write. You didn't know that, did you? Well, I feel like writing now."

"Good for you, Terry. Got a subject?"

"No, tell me one."

"The big oak in the square that the council wants to remove."

"That's old stuff . . . woodman, spare that tree. A tree takes years to grow and minutes to destroy . . . all been done before. No, Clan, give me something to get my teeth into, preferably something I don't really believe."

"Don't believe——?"

"Yes, at school I always chose to be on the debating side I didn't believe in, I found I could tear my opponents to shreds. Now what will it be?—Ah, *you*, Clan. And this will be the leader:

'NOTHING'S ON THE *UP* DOWN UNDER'
'EX-MIGRANT SPILLS THE BEANS ON THE
PSEUDO SUNSHINE-LAND.' "

"Terry, you can't——"

"Give me pen and paper."

"It's so untrue."

"That won't matter, no one in this forsaken town reads me, anyway."

"I won't let you."

"All right, I'll exhaust myself back in the Swan, then, and you can put the paper to bed."

"You know I can't do that."

"Then pen and paper," Terry had said.

It had come out the next day, as vindictive a column, Clancy knew, as she ever would see.

Terry was inordinately proud of it. "If I can do that on

16

something I don't really believe, just think what I could do on something I did."

"It's mean, it's untrue, it's unkind, it's horribly exaggerated!" she protested.

"I admit that, Clan, but what the heck? I just passed Dobson's and they're wrapping their fish and chips in it. No one reads me in this forsaken place."

No, no one did. And yet someone must—how otherwise did this blue ice man sit back now and remind her briefly but sufficiently, "Dray Hill"?

Perhaps it had been written up in a London paper . . . reached some syndicate. No, she could not think that, otherwise she would have heard of it before. People would have written to her, enquired of her . . . some, undoubtedly, would have accosted her. But nothing like that happened. Only kindness had happened. She had become the Boomerang Girl.

"How did you . . ? I mean . . ." She looked at him miserably.

"How did I find out? I read it, of course."

"How did you read it?"

"The same way as English people, I should think, with my own two eyes."

"How did you get the paper?"

"I collect local newspapers. As a matter of information to you I am writing a book on local newspapers."

"Including the *Dray Hill Chronicle?*"

He did not reply to that. He sat silent. She sat silent. She did not know what he was thinking about, but she hoped abysmally that it was not the same that she was.

She was seeing Terry's wretched:

"NOTHING'S ON THE UP DOWN UNDER"
"EX-MIGRANT CLANCY CLYDE INTERVIEWED
AFTER HER RETURN FROM AUSTRALIA TELLS
US WHY SHE CAME BACK."

Then it had all poured out . . . not just innocuous things like the heat being hotter than Australia House promised, the cold being slyly and tellingly, colder, but exaggerated hostel conditions, antagonisms, preferences, lack of culture, colonial snobbery, wrong values . . . even squalor.

"*Down* Under is right," Terry had written, and then he had let himself go.

"I can explain it all." Clancy heard herself answering the man as in a dream. Her voice was lacklustre, she was acutely aware of that, she knew it was unconvincing.

"Of course you want to try," he agreed, "*now*."

"Now?"

"Now that there's a reception committee outside, now that they're waiting for you. The Minister for Immigration has a golden key for your hostel room, no doubt; no doubt there'll be a bouquet of flowers from a little frilly girl."

"They—don't know?"

"Obviously."

"You'll tell them?"

"I will not. I am one of the majority here who sees the Australian Migration story as a modern saga. I'm not going to spoil that saga by one miserable mean little chapter by a vindictive and miserable girl."

"I didn't write it."

"You were the inspiration."

"I was not!"

"Then," he asked, lighting a fresh cigarette, "you're *not* Clancy Clyde?"

"Yes, I am."

A silence, a significant silence on his part.

He broke it idly with an entirely different question.

"How come *Clancy?*" he said.

"What do you mean?"

"Is it an assumed name, the Clancy part I mean, is it affected for this occasion?"

"Why should it be?" she said indignantly.

"Because it's as Australian as the Snowy River. 'Clancy of the Overflow' was the song of one of our best-loved poets. He was A. B. Paterson, the Snowy River man."

"Clancy," she said tightly, "was my mother's name."

"Irish?"

"Do you object to the Irish as well as the English?"

"Look here," he said, putting down the cigarette, "let's get this straight. I only object to *you*.

"I'm as keen on the forty-eight per cent British intake as I ever was, with one exception. Because publicity about that one exception could affect future intake I intend to hold my tongue about Dray Hill."

"Your tongue, but not your feelings?"

"You held neither in leash, remember, when you returned to your home town."

"I——"

He paid no attention. He got up, and Mr. Reynolds' swivel chair swung violently round. He was tall and wide-shouldered, she saw through hot tears, and he looked as hard as rock.

"Don't keep your public waiting," he advised. "You'll find the reception committee on the boat deck."

She still paused a moment. "You won't let me explain?"

"I'd know the text in advance . . . over-exuberant editor exaggerating a few disparaging remarks."

"They were not even few," she appealed. "I said nothing, I simply returned to England because——"

"Because?"

She hesitated. "Because I wanted to go back. You wouldn't understand that. You wouldn't understand the longing just once more to . . . to . . . Oh, what's the use?"

"No use at all," he agreed, "no use to explain."

He crossed over and flung wide the door.

"Never let it be said," he smiled thinly, nodding her out, bowing derogatively, "that I delayed the homeward flight of Australia's Boomerang Girl."

CHAPTER 3

THERE was a little crowd gathered on the boat deck.

Before, Clancy would have stepped forward light-heartedly, now, she shrank back.

To no avail, though. Iron fingers were suddenly under her elbow. Firmly she was impelled towards the group. "Go and do what's expected of you," hissed Ice Eyes in her ear.

At once officials took over. It was very like what *he* had told her to expect. A little frilly girl came forward with flowers, someone thrust the usual furry koala in her arms. She was introduced to Australia's millionth migrant, a charming 1955 bride from Yorkshire now well established in her new land. She met the parents of the largest British family yet to arrive.

Then the Minister for Immigration was congratulating her, and his wife was handing over a silver boomerang.

Everyone clapped.

Everyone, Clancy knew, except one. *He* stood in the shadow of one of the lifeboats, and she did not need to turn to see the thin smile on his lean dark face.

The Minister for Immigration was speaking of balanced intakes to meet the wants of the Australian work-force. For what rôle am I suitable, Clancy wondered bleakly, apart from accepting silver boomerangs, koala bears—and long despising looks?

One of the Good Neighbours came over. Clancy remembered these people before, no starry-eyed idealists but realistic Australians devoted to the objective of a united *all*.

She stood talking to the Good Neighbour until the cameras stopped whirring and the V.I.P.s smiled and left.

Then she smiled, excused herself and left, too. She wanted to say goodbye to those of her shipboard friends who were not proceeding with her to the British Hostel at Bunnerong . . . friends travelling under their own steam,

20

unneedful of assistance, some with houses already waiting for them, with rooms, until they could find a house, with relatives or friends.

Then there were the tourists' hands to shake . . . the Captain's . . . the hand of Mr. Reynolds, the purser, into whose room she had barged, to find not Mr. Reynolds but a stranger.

She rushed through them all . . . especially she rushed Mr. Reynolds, which was a pity, for she had liked the *Loch Maree* purser. Then she went down to her cabin and fastened her small bag.

When she came out on the deck again a hand took the bag.

"No need," Clancy said coolly. "It's not heavy, the big stuff is still in the hold."

"A pity to have gone to all that trouble," the man remarked, in spite of her objection taking away the bag.

She did not ask, "What trouble?" for by now she knew what his reply would be.

He would remind her that she could have left the bulk of her things back here, seeing she was only to return again . . . he would say it in that despising voice.

She did not look at him, she looked instead to the skyline, that Sydney skyline she had found so stimulating last time, could have again . . . if he were not here. She saw the London bits of it, the New York element, the hints of many continents, yet over all that distinctive line that was Sydney's own.

She looked to the harbour. She saw the blue shellac of it, throbbingly alive with its beetling ferries, tramps, colliers, liners . . . Pinchgut in the middle of it all like a medieval rampart.

"Quite a charming ceremony just now," he remarked conversationally, forcing her out of politeness to turn her eyes from the shining blue.

"Why," she enquired bitterly of the ceremony, "why me? I'm nothing unusual."

"No," he agreed hatefully.

"Then why?"

"Could be that the Immigration people are anxious to

21

keep up the present yearly sixty-five thousand British arrivals."

"That sounds a great many."

"It includes returning Australians," he reminded. He added inevitably, "It also includes migrants who came, went back, came again . . ."

"You're really meaning——" she began.

"Yes," he said.

"You like to keep a thing alive, Mr. ——" Her voice trailed off.

He did not tell her his name. Instead he said, "And *you* would sooner kill something, wouldn't you, Miss Clyde, you would sooner dam that sixty-five thousand that we have hoped we could swell, hoped at least we could keep stable, to a far smaller number."

"No," she objected.

"You made it read like that," he said.

She had no answer. Even if she could have found one, what would have been the use?

"Why are the numbers dropping?" she asked. "That is" —reddening—"apart from me?"

"It's natural," he shrugged. "Just now prosperity is everywhere, why bother to leave one's own green field for another field whose verdure you have yet to prove? Also, the war wounds are healing, England is beautiful again."

"Yes . . ." she said, suddenly homesick. Then she glanced at him in surprise. "*You* can say that?"

He stopped, and stopped her with him.

"Look," he told her, "when I said what I did in Reynolds' office it was as much in sympathy as protest."

"For what was the sympathy?"

"For *whom*," he corrected. "For the English for having had you again in their midst."

Clancy started off again. "It seems I'm not needed in either place," she said.

"These ideas are strictly my own," he shrugged. "You have seen how other people feel, you have encountered it just now."

"But that's only because I've come back—something like Immigration desired."

"Yes. But it's also very satisfactory to them no doubt that you are not male, not elderly. A young, pretty, photogenic female boomerang. What else could any empty but ambitious country desire?"

"Thank you," she returned.

They came to the gangway. He put the bag into her hand.

"Goodbye, Miss Clyde," he said.

She watched him go along the deck. He had not travelled out, of that she was sure. It had been a full ship, one thousand five hundred migrants, and then there had been the freelance travellers, the globe-trotters, the crew, but she knew he had not travelled out, first class or second class, any class in or out of sight. She knew she would not have been unconscious of an enmity like his.

The Public Relations man was bearing down on her.

"Ah, Miss Boomerang" . . . Clancy winced, but summoned a smile . . . "Ready to push off?"

"Yes. Are the others in the bus?"

"They've gone."

"Gone?" She looked at him blankly . . . and then she understood.

Of course there was to be more fanfare yet, more press and T.V. interviews, this time at the British Hostel where she would arrive no doubt not by bus but by car. No doubt, too, the Bunnerong personnel officer would greet her . . . another silver boomerang? . . . The cook probably had been instructed to bake a cake. Or he would be carving an English roast, perhaps, and be photographed handing her the first slice. Oh, heavens, thought Clancy, I'm becoming sarcastic and disillusioned—like *him*.

"Yes," smiled the Public Relations man, "there was no need to wait for you because you're coming with me."

She looked enquiringly at him and he explained, "You're not going to Bunnerong, to the Hostel this time, Miss Clyde. You're going to live, until you find somewhere of your own, with the Stantons."

"The Stantons?"

"I'm Dick Stanton. My wife is at home eagerly waiting your arrival."

"But——"

"You're disappointed?" He looked anxiously at her.

"I couldn't be disappointed," she admitted, "but I am dismayed. I don't want to be different, Mr. Stanton, you must appreciate that."

He nodded seriously. "I know how you feel. However, this is not just to be 'different', Miss Clyde. It's essential."

"Essential?"

"There is no room for you at the Hostel. You might recall that your papers went through exceedingly quickly, that really you were an 'extra.' "

"Yes," she admitted, "but I still feel I should be housed with the rest, as before."

"Come now," he laughed, "was it all that enjoyable?"

"Perhaps not," she admitted honestly, "and yet on the other hand it was by no means *un*enjoyable."

—It hadn't been, she thought back. The Hostel had been full to capacity but never cluttered. There had been sufficient playing space, breathing space. A few miles eastward had stretched the lovely Pacific coast, though to reach it, admittedly, there had been factories to pass, tall power stacks, a hospital, a gaol. The glorious, the short of glorious, it had all balanced up—and that was why she was a little worried now. She would have liked to have talked with her fellow immigrants, tell them things she had learned, tell them not to be discouraged, that in the end it would be all right.

—And who should know better, she could imagine a sarcastic voice, than you who have gone through it all before?

That was true, she had gone through it. Gone through the initial dismay at the size of the place, the instinctive dislike of impersonal common rooms instead of familiar corners, the absence of little home gardens, that first horror of eating with hundreds of others that changed later into monotony—the monotony of cafeteria living. She had gone through it and because of this she wanted to tell the others to be of good heart.

They would find, as she had found, that even the food at first seemed different. She remembered little Sam who had complained bitterly, "Aussies eat rabbit stuff. Can't we ever have kippers again, Mum?"

Even a cup of tea at first would seem different. The butter. The marmalade. But after a while they would have the same taste.

She wanted to tell them this . . . Other things . . . How the Hostel was not perfect, how it had grown in a hurry to be used in a hurry, that it never had been intended for a permanent home, that it was only a springboard to better things to come.

Yes, she heard that imagined voice again, *you* made it a springboard, didn't you, a springboard for a trip back.

She wanted to tell them that although housing was hard in Australia, still it was ultimately possible. Only a small sum to be raised. In time a quite charming home. You had to wait for it, admittedly, you had years ahead of you paying for it, but your own four walls, lawns, all the lovely, lovely flowers that this country grew in glorious riot were the reward.

There was hard work, she wanted to tell them, but the end was well worth the journey.

You tell them this! You!—Again she heard the imagined sneering voice.

"Well, Miss Clyde?" Mr. Stanton was beaming.

"You're sure your wife——"

"My wife is a Welsh girl, only six months in Aussie; I'm from Suffolk myself, but five years here for me."

"Oh." She smiled.

"You'll see your friends again," he reassured her. "You're an old hand, you know your way out to Bunnerong."

"Yes, I know my way," she answered, and she stood back as he picked up her bag.

She glanced up to the *Loch Maree* as they came on to the dock. She remembered glancing up to the *Olwen* the last time and wondering what lay ahead.

Well, she *knew* this time . . . knew that the heartaches would be balanced by the happinesses, knew that it would all even out in the end.

She squirmed as she heard that imagined voice again,

this time sneering, "Of course you know, Miss Boomerang, you've gone through all this before. You told it to the *Chronicle* at Dray Hill, didn't you? *Of course you know.*"

Squaring her shoulders, firming her lips, shutting her ears to those carping reminders, Clancy stepped bravely out along the wharf.

CHAPTER 4

THE Holden was parked at the end of the dock.

Dick Stanton looked at the tangle of traffic, and shrugged.

"We'll have to be in it to win it," he resigned himself, and having settled Clancy he backed out and joined the complicated web.

Now was no time to question him, so instead Clancy sat back and questioned herself. How often, she thought, in the last few years have I questioned myself?

She had questioned herself before she emigrated the first time. Do I want to go to this new land, to this Fifth Continent, to Australia? she had demanded. Yes, had been the reply.

I have no ties, she had added to her answer, no one to keep me here. It would be stodgy of me to refuse adventure just because I'm settled and have an easy post.

The next questionnaire had been after that first arrival. Do I like it?—Yes, I like it.

What about the things I *dis*like, the casualness, the breeziness, three sharp changes of weather in as many hours, the irritating way Australians assume that I find life infinitely better here, what about being called a Pommie?—I still dislike them, had been her answer, especially Pommie, even though it is short for pomegranate cheeks, or so they say, and therefore a compliment, yet even disliking I still *like*.

The next self-examination had dismayed her. It had been some months after, and she had been at the Hostel.

Do I want to go home to England? had been the question, and her answer had been, "Yes, yes, yes."

Why had she wanted to go? Just as on the ship, talking to *him*, she had had no explanation. Could a tug at the heart ever be expressed in words?

27

Mrs. Gilroy at the Hostel had expressed *her* tug as Christmas. Christmas was cold weather and plum pudding, not cicadas shrilling in gum trees and free and easy dinner eaten cold on a blazing beach.

Little Marion had said it was rock. "I'd like some rock like at Brighton, but they don't have it here."

What had the tug been for Clancy? She had thought rain, the silveriness of it, not this frantic down-pouring, then sun ten minutes after . . . She had thought friends. I've friends here, but my old ones are there. Old friends are the best.

So she had hung on for two years and then she had left.

No rancour to it, not even a real complaint to speak of, certainly nothing like what Terry Kent had concocted for his weekly rag.

Then soon after her return she had found herself probing again . . . facing up to things . . . knowing that rain was the same wherever you were, that it still wet you, knowing that in the years between most of her friends had married or moved off.

Do I want to go back to Australia? she had asked, and once more her answer had been yes.

A different yes this time, though, not just based on the resolution not to be stodgy, not to turn away from adventure, but the yes of deep thought and steady conviction, of wide-open rather than starry eyes, of being two years older, of possessing two more years' maturity.

If they'll have me I'll go and I'll *stop,* she had said.

They had said they would have her, and now she was here.

That was all there was to it. There had been none of the things *he* had suggested, there had been only a tug at the heart, a tug which another migrant, a family migrant, might have resisted, lived on with, but which she, unattached, had found too big.

She had been very young, she had been unsure, she had looked back and seen golden windows, but now she knew that all the golden windows of the world were equally distributed, she knew that if one had the right approach all places were fair but that some places suited some people

28

better, and she sensed intrinsically that this place suited her.

And that was all.

Dick Stanton was out of the snarl. The traffic was still heavy, but he was moving along at a better pace. They were climbing up to the southern approach of the Bridge.

There were two miles of bridge, and from its two-hundred-foot deck Clancy picked out the *Loch Maree* looking like a child's toy ship. "I'm glad you live on the north side," she told Dick. "I'll like being here."

"Reserve that till you see it," he grinned. "We're in an emergency settlement awaiting Our House. We think of it as that, Our House. It won't be long now, we hope."

"I shall be an inconvenience," Clancy frowned. "Emergency settlements don't run to house guests."

"This one does. It's an old army hut, we've plenty of space."

"Mr. Stanton——"

"Dick, Clancy. It can be Clancy, can't it?"

"Of course. Dick, why are you having me? I mean apart from there being no room at the Hostel which I don't really believe. *Why*, Dick?"

He said, "I would pick the wrong bridge queue, can't change now." Then, "Frankly, we're having you, Clancy, to keep you in sight."

"In sight?"

"You're valuable publicity, we don't want you to get away." He glanced at her apologetically. "You have a talent for getting away."

There it was again, but kindly now, said with a smile.

"As you know," resumed Dick, "with British migrants there are no stipulations. You're not confined, you're not directed to a job at which you're bound to serve for two years as with our European intake. You're freelance. You can move about. At the Hostel, which is very large, you might do just that, move about, and that's what we don't want. We want you under our eye."

"Why?" she asked again.

He had left the bridge and was climbing the northern

29

approach. "Because," he said simply, "you're the Boomerang Girl."

"What does that mean? I mean apart from the koala and the interviews and the applause?"

"It means that we . . . I'm speaking as an Australian, Clancy, which I am now . . . intend to call upon you in the future to help the British Migrant Drive, and I think you will agree that we're entitled to do that."

Again the reminder of her two cheap passages, her two welcomes, but kindly once more, different, coming from *him*.

"Yes," said Clancy, "and I shall be glad to, but I wouldn't have run away from the Hostel, Dick, I've had all the running round I want."

"Indeed you have not, young lady. We've lots more lined up for you. And never think we're blaming you, my dear, there's not one migrant ever arrived here in Australia who wouldn't have gone back home within a week."

She looked at him eagerly. "You, too?"

"Me, too. Another thing, Clancy, these Australians . . . most of them, anyway . . . understand that tug."

The tug again . . . the tug of white Christmas, Brighton rock, soft rain, old friends. Good to think that Australians understood . . . most of them. But one, Clancy knew, would never understand.

The Holden was skimming the northside suburbs, leisurely, favoured suburbs, and Clancy asked Dick if Our House was to be here.

He shook a rueful head. "Latecomers can't be choosers. This city is bursting its seams, and it's probably on the furthest seam of all that you'll find the Stanton brood. There's to be a brood, Clancy, and that's why Bronnie is particularly eager to have you. Having your first Australian is a bit hard on a Pom."

"Does she mind being a Pom?"

"No use in minding. Australians have names for everybody. When the first European intake began they came under the collective though erroneous 'Balts', but that didn't suit the Aussies. *Aussies,* Clan," Dick laughed. "See how soon you do it yourself! Anyway, the Aussies allotted individual names to them all, impertinent in many cases though probably meant quite companionably, but eventually they tired of that and banded them together as New Australians. *You* are privileged, then, to be a Pommie . . . think of it like that, anyway. The rest are New Aussies, though I do believe that will rapidly become archaic, the children and the children's children will see to it.

"We turn off here," he added.

They left the Pacific Highway and skimmed more beautiful homes until suddenly, quite without warning, the elegant residences stopped.

Before them stretched army huts, rows of army huts, a few of them Nissen huts, bare unpainted walls, tin roofs.

"It was a services pre-posting camp," explained Dick. "Australians first, later Americans, later British, all were stationed here. Now it's a waiting post again, but this time a peace-time waiting, waiting for a house."

"Our House," Clancy smiled.

"Our House—musical chimes, push-up windows, a proper fireplace, plenty of cupboards—or so Bronnie dreams.

"Meanwhile, no chimes, narrow casements, a radiator, but a *welcome* for you, my dear."

He put his finger on the Holden horn and held it there. A girl came to the door of the converted hut and waved a greeting. Then she came out on to the narrow road.

"Bronwen Stanton," said Dick, "mother-to-be of our first Aussie, and darling, this is Clancy, our Boomerang Girl."

Dick's wife was unmistakably glad to see her. She had tea waiting and they sat down at once.

"I came straight here to Braefield when I arrived," Bron told Clancy. "At least"—she laughed—"straight after the wedding. It was nice to have a place of your own, even a place like this, but it meant that I was cut off at once from my own people. I had to find my feet all alone."

"I was here," reminded Dick feelingly.

"My *woman* feet," said Bron.

"It looks," commended Clancy, surveying the hut, "as though you certainly found them. The home you've made

31

of this couldn't have been achieved without tramping many shops."

Bron smiled. "All our houses are nice here, in fact we try to outdo each other. Oh yes, I found my feet, but I don't mind telling you, Clancy, that many days I've longed to be at the British Hostel, not this housing waiting centre, if just to be able to talk."

Dick said feelingly again, "Darling, what is it you and Mrs. Tibbett do over the back fence?"

Bron giggled, "Talk."

She became serious again, and leaning over, took Clancy's hand. "I am going to enjoy you," she said.

Clancy looked seriously back. "Even though, unlike you, when I felt that way too I didn't fight it, I didn't last out, I simply went back?"

"Clan, so would I have, without Dick."

"Ah," said Dick, "I'm recognized at last."

"And now, Bron," asked Clancy, "now how do you feel?"

"Now I am completely happy . . . that is, I shall be when I have——"

"Our House."

"Oh, so you've heard of Our House. As it's Saturday Dick's off duty, so we intend to scout round this afternoon and choose us a likely district."

"You can do that?"

"Not exactly, but the housing projects are in different areas, and you can express a preference. I thought we'd go after lunch. You'll come, won't you?"

"No, Bron, though thank you. I've a lot to do . . . unpack. And I'd like to get my bearings, too."

"Of course."

Clancy's little room was unpretentious but charming, Bron had done a lot with flowery chintz. "To think," Clan smiled, "that I told Dick I didn't want to be different, that I wanted to go to Bunnerong."

"If it had been your first time perhaps it might have been wiser," said Bronwen thoughtfully, "just as it might have been wiser for me. However, I settled down in the end. If you've finished that bag, come out into the garden and keep the other bags till this afternoon."

Clancy's first arrival had been in mid-winter, a winter more unkindly than Australia House had promised—sunshine, admittedly, but a wind that blew through to your bones. The grass had been a threadbare brown, the only colour in discouraged gardens the scarlet of poinsettias. But now it was different, it was September, Australian spring. And Australian spring, Clancy remembered, was extravaganza.

Here in the waiting settlement the waiters had only gone in for annuals, but in the elegant houses not far up the road Clancy could see the rioting japonicas, the spilling azaleas, the wreathing wistarias, masses of colour, colour, colour.

Bron had contented herself with bulbs . . . "we can lift them when we move to Our House" . . . and daffodils and narcissi—and one English bluebell—stirred in the sweet, faint breeze.

Clancy looked around at the huts.

"They won't be here for ever," said Bron. "Braefield is too endowed a suburb to throw to house-waiters, it's to be strictly residential like up there." She pointed to the lovely homes behind the japonicas and azaleas. "Besides being in a good area it's a very pretty area. There's a river down there, the Lane Cove."

Between the huts Clancy caught a sight of it. In contrast to the blue shellac of the glittering harbour this morning it was a deep leaf green.

"You must go down there," advised Bronwen. "The top of the river has been dammed up and a National Park laid out. It's really very charming."

They had lunch outdoors under a striped umbrella.

"I hardly think," smiled Clancy, "that when the services had this unit they ever thought that someone one day would sit outside it and eat asparagus soufflé and tossed salad under a striped umbrella."

"Stew, more likely," said Dick, recalling his own experiences, "but the salad would be tossed all right."

The Stantons left after lunch on their project inspection,

calling out to Clancy to make herself at home, raid the cupboard. "Just so long as there's a slice of bread for tea," laughed Dick.

Clancy came indoors again and finished another bag. She pressed a few blouses, put around a few of her personal things. Then she made a cup of tea and went and sat in the Stantons' makeshift "lounge" . . . a daybed with bright scatter cushions, several cane bucket chairs, a bowl of daffodils, a shelf of books.

She looked through the books, mostly beloved volumes brought by Bron from England, though here was one that Dick must have given her on her arrival in Australia. He had inscribed it: "To Bronnie, Wishing her happy returns of her first day."

The volume was *The Wide Brown Land* and it was a book of poems.

Clancy sat down and leafed over it.

Then she remembered something and looked down the index to A. B. Paterson. She went past *The Man From Snowy River* to the poem *he* had mentioned, had suggested she had borrowed from to establish herself this time as an *Australian* Australian. *Clancy of the Overflow.*

She found the page and read with interest, even finding in *her* a little of the nostalgia that she knew a city Australian from the bush would always find.

"I had written him a letter which I had, for want of
    better
Knowledge, sent to where I met him down the Lach-
    lan, years ago;
He was shearing when I knew him, so I sent the letter
    to him,
Just on spec, addressed as follows: 'Clancy, of the
    Overflow.' "

And then:

"And I somehow rather fancy that I'd like to change
    with Clancy,

34

Like to take a turn at droving where the seasons come
   and go,
While he faced the round eternal of the cash-book and
   the journal——
But I doubt he'd suit the office, Clancy, of the Overflow."

Suddenly shut in even in this uncluttered room Clancy
put down the book, went out of the house and down to
the green Lane Cove.

CHAPTER 5

It was not Australia here, it was parts of England she had loved, deep, sweet, cool. The trees might be eucalyptus, but the softness was of the northern hemisphere, not of Down Under. When I have My House, Clancy thought, I would like it on this quiet Lane Cove.

She smiled at the thought. What chance had she, a later-comer than the Stantons, of getting such a near and very beautiful Sydney seam?

She descended to the river. Small boats were riding the upper reaches which had been enclosed within a weir. Of course, she remembered, it's Saturday.

She left the family parties boiling billies in the stone fire-places, the subtle tang of woodsmoke mingling with the river smell, and crossed the causeway to the banks of the lower unenclosed Lane Cove. She knew this flowed out into the harbour because once last time she had taken a harbour cruise; she knew it lost its green tranquillity as it went east, became instead a busy place of shipyards and wharves, instead of the sough of wash and ripple, the shrill and toot of tender and ferry.

But just now it was still a corner of England, green, woodsy, soft, caressing. She even saw some buttercups with bright, alive faces, and climbed over a low fence to pick herself a nosegay.

She heard a soft plop on the water, then glimpsed the taut wet sheen of a fishing line. She turned to retrace her steps . . . fishermen did not care for interlopers . . . but a voice hailed her.

"It's all right, I don't believe there's any fish here, any-way . . . why, Miss Clyde!"

"Mr. Reynolds!" She greeted the *Loch Maree* purser with warmth.

He wound up the line and came across to her.

"What are you doing here? Don't take that as anything but delight, please. I was rather put out at the cursory way you bade me goodbye in the ship this morning."

"Yes, I'm sorry about that, I—I was rather in a hurry."

"So I gathered. But I never gathered you were in a hurry to come *here*. I rather thought of you at Bunnerong."

"That's where I should have been, but it seems I was an extra and there wasn't room, so I'm to stop with the Public Relations officer instead."

Mr. Reynolds smiled pleasantly. "Nice for you," he said.

Someone else had said, "Nice for you," but not nicely, as this was meant.

"Yes," she agreed, "it is."

She looked around her and saw that a flagged track led upward from the river's edge. "I must be on private property," she frowned.

"You are."

"Your house, Mr. Reynolds?"

"No—unhappily."

"Then I must go, of course."

"Of course you must not. You're coming up with me."

She raised enquiring brows and he said, "Greenmarley is my friend's property, I'm spending the day with him. In case the accent hasn't sunk in, Miss Clyde, I'm one of your breed."

"A Pommie!" She laughed. "It had sunk in," she then assured him, "but there are so many resident accents here I thought this property could be yours."

"It could be if envy achieved anything," he admitted ruefully. "It's certainly my idea of a perfect place."

"Yes, it's lovely." Clancy looked up through the deep tapestry of trees and saw a terraced garden, beyond the garden a half acre of formal shrubs, beyond the shrubs a wide lawn. Beyond all she glimpsed the delicately carved columns of an old Italian-style stone house. It was a beautiful yet somehow saddened house. Clancy wondered why.

"Greenmarley," Mr. Reynolds told her. "Around this district there are several old Italian houses; some hundred years ago craftsmen were brought from Italy, and this is one of the glorious things they left behind."

"Would it have a history?"

"For Australia, steeped in history. Everything apart from the Italian masterhand was convict labour. The red bricks of the kitchen which I'm going to show you when we get up there were hand-made on Sydney's Brickfield Hill, now a large emporium. The original oven-surround is still in position."

Mr. Reynolds had taken Clancy's hand and he was impelling her up and forward.

"But the owner——" she protested.

"Guy Osman."

"Mr. Osman might not like an unannounced visitor."

"I intend to announce you at once," Mr. Reynolds assured her.

Not unwillingly Clancy obeyed the pressure of the fingers. That terraced garden, those shaped shrubs, that sweep of lawn, those carved columns attracted her very much.

"This Mr. Osman, of course, must be a family man. A house like this would need family living," she stated.

"That's what I tell Guy," shrugged Mr. Reynolds. "The house is lovely, but it's inert, it wants steps on those stone courts, laughter under its century-old trees. No, he's not married, Miss Clyde."

"A pity."

"Well, he's still fairly young, so there's still hope. Who knows, a lovely young lady like yourself might do the trick." Mr. Reynolds gave her arm a nudge.

She laughed at him, then warned, "You stop yourself at announcements, Mr. Reynolds. Not one step further . . ." then she stopped in her step herself.

For a man was pouring sundowners on the paved verandah. He was turned away from them, but not for one moment was Clancy unsure of the identity of the tall, rock-hard figure. She had not watched him stride away from her along the *Loch Maree* deck not to have marked him . . . and his enmity . . . indelibly in her mind.

"I don't think there's any need for an announcement," she said in a low uncertain voice.

Although she spoke softly the words must have carried

38

over the lawn. The man straightened, wheeled round, then bowed stiffly.

"No need, Tim," he agreed. "I've met Miss Clyde; she has met me. She didn't know my name, but I have no doubt she knows it now."

"That's right," said Tim Reynolds cheerfully. "This is Guy Osman, Miss Clyde, the owner of Greenmarley. Guy, I brought Miss Clyde up for a sundowner as well."

Even before he had finished speaking a third drink had appeared on the marble-topped table, mosaic marble, very old marble.

Clancy sensed more than saw, since her eyes were down, the chair that was held out for her. Not raising her glance to the holder, she sat down.

The two men sat down as well and took up brandies. "What have you given Miss Clyde?" asked Tim Reynolds. "Something persuasive, I hope."

"Persuasive?" Guy Osman was estimating his brandy, his blue ice eyes narrowed on the burnt-gold.

"Must persuade her to stop this time," smiled Tim, "mustn't lose her again." He held up his glass. "Here's to our Boomerang Girl."

But Guy Osman did not drink to that. "Here's to persuasion," he amended drily.

They both looked at Clancy, and, flushing, she held up her glass. Boldly, deliberately, meeting the blue ice eyes now, she said, "Here's to the yearly sixty-five thousand."

He reminded significantly, "And one."

Tim Reynolds glanced at each in turn. He looked a little puzzled. There was something between these two, he thought, and it was not the usual man meets girl.

A really lovely young woman, too, which made it more puzzling, for Guy, though never a lady's man, had good taste there. Tim recalled being introduced to Dallas Wyse.

Dallas was a beauty . . . yet so was this girl, in a finer-cut way. He liked that ash hair, those gold-green eyes, more golden-green still because of their sooty setting, he liked the winged brows.

He became aware of a silence and hurried to the breach. "Miss Clyde is a neighbour of yours now, Guy. Instead of being housed at Bunnerong she's staying with Dick Stanton."

The blue eyes had narrowed. In the keen slits Clancy read a lot of things: she read stricture, objection, dissent, denunciation, sharp dislike. But all Guy Osman said was what he had said before.

"Nice for you."

"I didn't arrange it," she told him, "I was quite willing to go out to the Hostel."

"Of course," he agreed falsely, "home sweet home again, the old familiar ways."

Again the uncomfortable silence . . . again Tim Reynolds breaking it up anxiously.

"Have you a position yet, Miss Clyde?"

"Surely her former one would be available," suggested Guy blandly.

"I don't anticipate any trouble there, Mr. Reynolds," Clancy answered. "The Immigration always places us if we can't place ourselves. I rather thought I'd try to do it on my own this time." She glanced quickly at Osman, then glanced away again.

"Good for you," applauded Reynolds. "Got a *Herald* at Stanton's?"

"I don't know."

"Then take old Guy's, he won't want it any more. There are pages and pages of Positions Vacant in Saturday's *Herald*." Without asking Osman's permission, Tim took a bulky paper from one of the chairs, turned to the appropriate columns, took out his pen and ticked off a few ads.

"There's some probables for you, Miss Clyde," he said.

The silence was looming up again.

Hurriedly Tim Reynolds said, "I promised to show our visitor the kitchen, Guy." To Clancy he said, "Like to come now?"

The old kitchen was at the rear of the house, the brick oven-surround was still in position, as Tim had said, but the oven was not of course in use.

"What would be the good," pointed out Tim, "even if it was operable, with only one to be fed in the house? Greenmarley needs a family, needs it badly, the stone

40

courts need footsteps, the lawns need laughter. As I said, the place is inert."

When they came back to the carved pillars a car was drawn up on the drive.

"I'll run you back, Miss Clyde," Guy Osman said.

"I can walk."

"I'm not doubting that. Nor am I doubting that you *will* return to the Stantons, for after all, though it's an emergency settlement, it's still preferable to where you *should* have been."

"In that case———" she began stiffly.

"I'm simply saving you," he continued shortly, "also saving the Stantons any worry over a late return. Our days are not long yet, so it would be dark by the time you walked back." He did not wait for any other objection, he called, "Coming, Tim?"

"I'm going to have another brandy," said Reynolds. "Goodbye, Miss Clyde . . . I'll see you on my next trip."

Guy Osman said what Clancy knew he would not be able to resist saying.

"If she's still here."

She smiled at Tim Reynolds, but did not answer Osman. She did not speak until he had swung out of the drive and started along to the settlement.

She said conversationally, in the dim hope of diverting his attention from herself, "I read your poem today."

"My poem?"

"A. B. Paterson's, I should say, *Clancy of the Overflow.*"

"Oh." He negotiated a bend. "I should have said that it was *your* poem."

"Because of the name?" She thought of the restlessness even she had felt reading it, and remarked, "But it's Australian, every line."

"And you," he remarked, "are not."

"Which makes it not my poem," she argued.

"You're right, as ever."

"Am I that?"

"Evidently the Immigration authorities believe so. All right, Miss Clyde, here we are."

She got out of the car . . . then for a moment more she still tried.

"I liked the poem."

He nodded coolly. "No doubt you liked the idea of place-changing; place-changing is a pastime of yours."

She wanted to cry out, "Give me a chance . . . call off your dogs. Just try me . . ." but the blue ice eyes were glaciers now.

"However, as Banjo said——" he resumed.

"Banjo?"

"That was what he was called, Banjo Paterson . . . he said he had *doubt* that the *change* would *suit*. Remember?"

She stepped back from the car. What was the use?

"Thank you for returning me, Mr. Osman. You have a very lovely home. Goodnight."

CHAPTER 6

Bron and Dick were arguing amicably over the future location of Our House.

"She fell in love with the name of one of the housing suburbs," groaned Dick, "she wants me to apply for it even though it would be over an hour's journey to work."

"Well, I don't want Simpsonville," said Bron. "It sounds dull."

"But Simpsonville was where you saw the house washed pink with the stepping stones instead of concrete paths."

"I want a cul-de-sac," yearned Bron. "I always planned I'd live in a house called End of the Lane."

"There are few lanes in Australia," discouraged Dick, "certainly not many in any of the planned housing settlements. Clancy, break up this family row and tell us what you've been doing. Pretty well for yourself, by the look of that car."

"It's Mr. Guy Osman's."

"Greenmarley," breathed Bron, enraptured. She looked at Clancy. "I suppose now that's Your House."

Clancy's quick denial did not even reach her lips. Against her wish she saw the lovely old Italian home again, the columns, the flagged court.

Instead of refuting Bron she said inadequately, "It would be handy to town."

This understatement sent them all into peals of laughter, laughter that Clancy broke up by saying feelingly, "Well, I must begin to consider that. I simply must find a job."

"The Department of Labour and Industry will fix you up," reminded Dick.

"I know, and I'll go along if I don't find something myself. I believe there are lots of posts offering, though. Mr. Reynolds ticked off a few probables and I intend to go

43

through them." Clancy smiled. "You two can help me pick which one."

After tea they did.

"What are you, Clan," asked Dick, "tinker, tailor, soldier, sailor?"

"You should say teacher, nurse, typist, clerk, actress, model," corrected Bron.

"Well, I suppose I could settle for typist," decided Clancy. She told them about working on the *Dray Hill Chronicle*. As she did so she felt that old dismay all over again.

"Made to order," acclaimed Dick, pointing to an ad. "Reynolds must have thought so, too, he's marked it off."

He read the vacancy aloud.

"Typist, for Jarrah Publications; good English an advantage; satisfactory wages, conditions. Apply Monday, Macquarie Place."

"How does it sound, Clan?" asked Bronwen.

"It sounds the very thing," said Clancy, pleased. She wrote down the details and put them in her bag, glad to have settled so soon on her first job-application.

They played Scrabble after that, and over supper Bron told Clancy that tomorrow they planned to go straight from church on another housing prowl.

"You'll come this time?"

"I'll come when it's Our House," promised Clan. "Thanks for including me, but I'd rather like to go out to Bunnerong and see how the gang are settling down. But may I join you at church?"

* * *

St. Chad's was of red brick, but you could see only patches of red, for the rest was hung in ivy. In the soft interior as well as the light through the stained glass windows there was the light of flowers, banks and banks of flowers, daffodils, guinea golds, nodding poppies.

There had been smiles for Clancy when she arrived, and during his sermon the Reverend Mr. Flett welcomed "one of us who left us, now back with us again." Smiling eyes turned to Clancy and she smiled back . . . except at one pair of eyes that were not smiling. Blue ice eyes. Whose but his?

She tried to avoid Guy Osman when church was over. It was useless. The congregation had gathered around and Bron was flourishing Clancy with pride, introducing her to everyone she saw.

"You know Mr. Osman," Bronwen beamed.

Clancy said formally, "How do you do."

"Wasn't it nice for Clancy to be welcomed by Mr. Flett?" bubbled Bron.

Guy Osman nodded politely. "Yes," he echoed, "nice for her."

Clancy escaped at last.

She had told the Stantons she would go straight out to the Hostel, so she slipped down a side street and hurried along to the railway. She was glad when she looked round that there was nobody she knew in sight.

There were spring flowers on the station, too, more garden plots really than railway functions. Clancy bought her ticket and waited for the train.

It was a pretty journey into the city. When the flowers and trees stopped, the harbour began. Once more she crossed the Bridge. She went up to Elizabeth Street and waited for the Matraville bus.

When she got in it, it seemed to Clancy that she had never stopped getting in, that she had not paused in her round of travelling to and from the Hostel into work to return, instead, to England. I'm taking up the threads, she thought in satisfaction, taking them up almost as though I never put them down.

It was not a short trip, but today she did not find it tedious. That was because she was looking out for landmarks that she used to know before—the sweep of Hyde Park, the busyness of Oxford Street, the Courts, the Showground, the clusters of suburban shopping centres.

And then she was back . . . almost as though she had never gone away.

She saw the columns of buildings that housed and fed

eleven hundred British people . . . "eleven hundred and *seventy*, miss," as old Lucas had always said.

She wondered if Lucas was still about. She was vague about his position here, a sort of janitor general factotum she had thought, but he had had a lot of sense. He had not liked her coming to the Hostel. "Better for young ladies to get together and take a flat some place," he had frowned. "This is for families, don't have many singles. You'll find it lonely, you'll want to clear home."

That showed how wise Lucas had been, for she *had* cleared home.

It was true you could count the singles, this was predominantly, as he had said, a family place. Young women *did* migrate to Australia, but usually they migrated in sets of friends. They did not go to the Hostel, they clubbed together and took a house, an apartment, shared a room. When you divided expenses rents were not so impossible, but how could she, a lone hand, have afforded her own place? Admittedly she had left England in a group, but the others had disembarked at Melbourne and she had come on to Sydney quite alone.

As she walked through the gates Clancy knew now that had she had someone her own age she would have stopped on. But going to her little single room of a night when others around were going to their family flats had made her believe she was lonelier than perhaps she really was.

So, she said, passing one of the two dining-halls, I simply gave in.

She saw that dinner was still on, so she sat outside and waited. She could have gone in; she recalled the easygoing manner in which meals had been conducted, cafeteria style, no stringent checks made to make sure the Hostel was not feeding an interloper. As though anyone would interlope, the hostellers had grinned.

She remembered the family tables. She had eaten with the Quinns. She wondered where the Quinns had got to. They would be out of the Hostel by now. When you arrived you were asked to get somewhere else by twelve to eighteen months, you signed for no longer than two years.

I, thought Clancy, took the stipulated two years and then I went back to Dray Hill.

Some of the diners were coming out of the hall. Clancy watched them, then saw her special shipboard friends the Gillespies. She hurried across. More *Loch Maree* passengers joined them, and they all found a spot near the children's playground.

"Well?" Clancy asked.

She knew all the answers before they told her; she believed she knew *all* the answers to *all* the intakes. The littlies . . . apart from an absence of rock . . . would settle in immediately, the teenagers would have no regrets, neither would the young adults, but the oldsters frankly would find it hard going, they would miss their old friends, their old ways. The in-betweens, perhaps, would have the most heart-flutterings of all, they would worry about future housing, about the higher cost of living. Clancy said, "Well?" again and waited to hear.

She heard it, as she had heard it before.

"I like it, Miss Clyde, they have nice sweeties here."

"And good pop."

A teenager said, "Coo, no washing up, you do your own rooms but the Hostel looks after the other chores."

Her mother, one of the worried in-betweens, said, "It's not good for a young girl not to have to wash up, it's bad training."

"I wanted a dog," regretted a little boy, "but the rules say no dogs in rooms."

His brother added knowledgeably, "And no firearms."

"I'm worried about our fees here," said a father. "They sound very steep."

"Don't worry," assured Clancy. "They're concessionary; families pay less; families on a lower income are conceded less again. It will be all worked out, you'll see."

Another in-between voiced the housing problem. "I know we were warned about it," he said, "but Government-built houses seem the only ones with reasonable rentals, and they have a waiting list as long as your arm."

"That's what I'm going to miss," said old Mr. Felix, "the Arms. I used to go there every night . . . just one jug and a game of darts. I went to a pub here yesterday evening . . ." He ran his hand through his thin silver hair. "Different, all right," he proclaimed. "Terrible lot of noise." Then he said, "But good beer."

That started a few more good things . . .

"Nice-looking girls, the chaps call them sheilahs here, you know."

"Lovely fruit."

"Good wine."

On the whole Clancy felt confident, felt pleased she had come.

She went with the Gillespies into their family flat, then afterwards strolled with them up to the tramline that ran to La Perouse. This was almost the last tramline in Sydney; buses had taken over. It was a long run from the city but only a moderate distance from Bunnerong. Clancy had gone to La Perouse regularly . . . last time. She had considered the sudden blue shout of Botany Bay well worth the rather discouraging trip past power stack, hospital and gaol.

When she got there she was pleased to find the snake man out again, the lubra displaying her little shell shoes as she had two years ago, the smiling aboriginal boy displaying his boomerang skill in the hope of selling some of his boomerangs, boomerangs that Clancy knew tourists would take home and throw to no avail.

They crossed the green and gold hill, golden with cape weed, to that little part of Australia that was French territory. Jean la Perouse had done this for his country when he had arrived so soon after Captain Phillip.

Clancy stood by foreign soil, an English migrant to Australia, and read again "Erected in the name of France."

She and the Gillespies turned their backs on the Pacific and took the tram again, the family to the Hostel, Clancy for home. At least her temporary home. Like that troubled father, for a moment Clancy was troubled, too. Where am I going, she thought, where am I bound?

Bron and Dick knew where they were going. It might not be Bron's "End of the Lane", Dick's easy distance to town, but it would still be "Our House" for all that.

48

But what about a single migrant, with not enough money even with Australian wages to rent an apartment unless someone else shared with her, what about Clancy Clyde?

And even if somebody did share, would she be entirely happy with what she got? Clancy thought with sudden dismay.

Now she had seen—Greenmarley?

CHAPTER 7

CLANCY was up early the next morning.

"Darling," Bron complained when she came sleepily out to find Clan already bathed, breakfasted, dressed, "didn't Australia House tell you that there's not enough girls to go round?"

"Not in those words," smiled Clancy. "They said for a single girl there were good opportunities."

"Then——"

"But I'm not taking any chance. This job sounds just the one I could handle. I'm going to be first in the queue."

"Could be there is no queue."

"Better still, then, he'll *have* to give me the job."

In spite of Bron's protests she left almost at once.

"If you'd only wait Dick would drive you," Bron called out to her retreating figure.

"The head of the queue," resolved Clan over her shoulder.

When she reached Jarrah Publications in Macquarie Place she saw that she could have dallied after all. The office end of Sydney was still yawning after the week-end, it was barely awake.

She marked which building of the small handful of buildings housed her quarry, then wandered across to the pocket handkerchief park. It was a pretty, leafy place, said to be the site of Governor Phillip's tent after the first landing at Farm Cove in 1788. She looked at the Obelisk from which main road distances throughout New South Wales were measured, then she sat down opposite the handsome Wool Exchange and waited for the hands of the clock to creep round.

At five to nine she went back again to stand at the Jarrah door. At nine a typist arrived and opened up. She gave Clancy a surprised look.

"I've come in answer to the advertisement."

"Well, one thing, you're not late, are you," said the girl companionably. She pushed the door, flung open the windows, found Clancy a chair.

"Which is more than I can say for the others," she added reprovingly, looking at her watch. "Monday is always the same, talk about laggard feet. Ah, here they are now."

Five of them came in . . . but no applicant, noted Clancy.

She heard the other Jarrah door open further along the corridor, though, and wondered if a queue was waiting up there.

However, several applicants joined her by half past, and ten minutes later the first typist said cheerfully, "You can pop in now if you like—that room on the left."

Clancy "popped." She decided it must be because it was a publishing firm that rules were so relaxed. There had certainly been more formality when she had worked last time for Howard and Ross, Accountants.

Last time . . . there she went once more. When would she teach herself to forget her inglorious beginnings, persuade herself to step out fresh and new again?

Never, it seemed. Never while *two* people lived in the same state of Australia; New South Wales was simply not big enough for Clancy Clyde—and *him*.

For there at the desk he sat—Guy Osman. When would she stop running into him, finding her fate dependent on his state of mood?

She had taken not one step forward after the initial step in which she had made her dismaying discovery. It must have irritated him. "Come in or go out," he said sharply, "but don't just stand there."

"I'll go out," she decided, and she wheeled round.

"Miss Clyde." His voice clear and authoritative stopped her.

She half turned.

"Come back," he said.

"You said to come in or go out."

"Before you go out I have something to say."

"I don't want to listen."

"If you didn't intend listening why did you apply for

51

this position? I'm presuming this is an application, not just a social call."

"It *was* an application, Mr. Osman, but when I applied I was not thinking of you."

"Apparently," he said. Then he said, "Sit down."

She sat down because her knees were trembling. She would have liked to have swept out of the room, but just now she realized she could not have managed a step, let alone a sweep.

"I must apologize," he said drily, "for what must seem our haphazard methods here. By rights your name should have been taken and given to me——"

"Whereupon you would have sent out a definite refusal," said Clancy, her trembling now subsiding.

"Not necessarily," he said.

She raised her brows at that, and the man noticed against his will how delicately arched they were, like fine wings.

"Although I don't run my firm formally," he said, "I do like the best that my money can buy. Determination to have that would have prompted me at least to interview you, give you a test."

"You intend to do that now?"

"Why not?" he said.

"Why not——?" She stared at him disbelievingly. *Why not,* after all he had said. 'Look here,' she remembered hollowly, 'I am as keen on the forty-eight per cent British intake as I ever was, *with one exception.* I see the Australian Migration story as a modern saga . . . I'm not going to spoil it by one miserable mean little chapter by a vindictive and miserable girl.'

He read her thoughts. He said coldly, "This is business."

"I didn't think it was sentiment," she came back.

She went to rise. Again he stopped her. "A moment, Miss Clyde."

The trembling was on her once more. What was there about this unpleasant person that had the power to upset her like this?

Stiffly she said, "I'm not interested in your post."

"You must have been to have applied for it. Why did you apply for it?"

"It was in the paper Mr. Reynolds had ticked for me, it was one of his probables."

"If you had looked closer you would have seen that his ticks were inked. I marked this myself. In pencil."

"You did?"

"I invariably check a paper when I've inserted an ad. It was my paper you took, you might remember."

"Yes," she said.

"You haven't yet told me why you applied—that is, apart from Reynolds' supposed recommendation."

"It—it looked likely at the time."

"It doesn't now?"

She did not answer that.

"I suppose it would attract a person of your experience," he said thoughtfully. "I suppose as well as supplying the *Dray Hill Chronicle* with its leaders you even did a little freelance."

"Yes," she said, "I worked on the paper."

A few moments went by.

He was taking something from his drawer, Clancy was waiting for the trembling to stop, after which she would get up and get out—as steadily as she could.

"I want you to go out to Miss Cooper, fill in this form, then attend to the next page, a small questionnaire I have prepared which will decide me which applicant would suit me best."

"No, thank you."

"Don't be a fool," he said.

"There are other jobs." She remembered Bronwen and added, "There aren't enough girls to go round."

His brows had met in a straight line. "Did you find the reverse when you went back to England? Is that why you returned here?"

Now she looked at him directly, and presently she spoke directly.

"Mr. Osman, why do you dislike me so much? I mean apart from that—that mistake. I mean why do you dislike me so *personally?*"

"There's nothing personal about it."

"Oh yes, there is."

She thought he was going to argue her question, either that or ignore it, pass it over, but suddenly he must have changed his mind. He bent across the desk and spoke in a low, hard voice.

"Perhaps it has been personal . . . I'll tell you why. My best friend had a friend coming from England, the same way as you."

"You mean assisted." *Her* voice was clipped.

"Yes. I wanted to bring her out at once . . . oh yes, the friend was a woman, a young woman . . . but Peter was stubborn, he was also intolerably independent. He was also again hard up. So he had to wait."

"*She* had to wait, too, presumably," said Clancy.

"The trouble is she couldn't," he answered shortly. "While she waited while other people came and couldn't make up their minds, so they went back——"

"And came again," reminded Clancy.

"You've said it," he nodded remotely. "While she waited like that—she died."

It made it all the more stark that he said it so expressionlessly. All at once Clancy was aware that her handkerchief was tied into tight little knots, she was aware of the traffic beneath them in Macquarie Place, muted, as in a dream.

"He can't blame me——" she half whispered, half whimpered.

"No, he can't," he agreed. "He was killed in an accident . . . it was called an accident . . . early this year.

"Well, that's the simple little story. Not a very nice story, is it? Here at Jarrah our fiction editress likes happy endings, so certainly the story would not suit her.

"Where are you going, Miss Clyde?"

"Away, of course . . . I'm sorry I can't go a long way away, to another state at least."

"That would be a very bad throw of the boomerang. You left from New South Wales, so you must return here."

Again the trembling. Why was she weak like this?

"I propose," said Guy Osman, "to consider your application, I propose that you submit yourself to the test. I want the best my money can buy, you undoubtedly want the best

54

your wits can earn. We would be fools to look upon a purely business matter in any other light. Well, Miss Clyde?"

She sat silent a long moment. She had a lot to lose if she did not submit to a test as he recommended, she would have had a morning lost. And a lost morning when you have very little money and no definite position is foolhardy. Undoubtedly she would not get this post, all things, she thought, being obviously *un*equal, but not to avail herself of the opportunity was, as he had said once more, bad business indeed.

"I shall take the test," she said.

He handed it over and she went out to Miss Cooper . . . Miss Cooper was the first friendly typist . . . and was given a desk.

By the time she had finished the paper there were about eight applicants in all.

She folded the sheets and gave them to the friendly girl, who smiled conspiratorially and whispered, "I hope you pull it off."

She could not say back, "I hope I don't." It would have sounded absurd.

So she just smiled and thanked Miss Cooper and went down to Macquarie Place again.

She left her name at the Public Services Bureau, at several other institutions, then she walked for a while where she had loved to walk last time . . . *last time* . . . *last time* . . . There she went again.

It was round old Sydney . . . St. James's Church, the Law Courts, the few balconied houses left in Macquarie Street.

She bought some sandwiches and sat in the Gardens . . . but when she opened the packet she found she could not eat them. What had he said?—"While she waited—she died."

She closed her eyes on the spring riot of flowers and the pigeons wondering at her quiet came to perch at her feet. She opened her eyes again and began tossing a largesse of crumbs and ham to them. Sparrows joined the pigeons. Some slow old doves. She sat on until the warmth of the spring day was over, until the tree shadows lengthened and the city lost its sun and seemed to be built instead of blue air.

She came home to Braefield just as the emergency settlement lights were spangling out bright and golden . . . and there was Bronwen at the gate, smiling in British pride.

"Smart girl! You did it—one up for the Poms!"

"Did what?"

"Got the job. Mr. 'Jarrah' phoned this afternoon for you to start tomorrow. Clancy, did you know that Mr. 'Jarrah' was Guy Osman when you applied?"

"I didn't, but I know now."

Bron Stanton said, well satisfied, "And you've got the post now."

She put her arm around Clancy and together they went into the house.

CHAPTER 8

THE next morning Clancy travelled in with Dick. She had not enquired about the office hours, but the three of them had decided it would be the usual nine to five, time out for lunch and cuppas, no Saturday work.

Dress had created more of a problem. Bron had glanced across at Clancy and said tactfully, "You know, Clan, Australian secretaries look the world."

"I know," Clancy smiled back.

She remembered her first impressions at Howard and Ross . . . that the girls took their dress very seriously. No merely neat skirts and spotless blouses for them but beautifully cut dresses, fine suits. Of course, the climate had been conducive to dressing up, but even in the cold July and August days a standard had been set.

Clancy felt relieved now that the winter-into-spring weather made it a little early for a summer frock; she felt relieved because the suit she had bought in London before she left was the very latest as well as a superb cut.

Bron cried out in approval when Clancy came out in the soft laurel green that did the right things for her gold-green eyes and ash hair. Dick whistled.

The ride into town was a test for any driver. Clancy marvelled that any of the cars finally got to their destination, but they did, Dick did, by tortuous weaving, wreathing, taking advantage of occasional clear runs.

"Good luck, Clan," Dick called at Wentworth Avenue on the city side of the Bridge. "I'll pick you up after five."

He was off before he could be booked for standing.

Clancy took the same lift up as three of the Jarrah girls. She could remember them from yesterday. They half-smiled at her as though they remembered, too, and when Miss Cooper, first in again, introduced her as they came

57

through the door they smiled all the way at her and established first names at once.

"Jean, Adrienne, Claudia, I'm Janet, and you're"—Janet Cooper hunted out a paper—"Clancy."

With one voice they greeted, "Of the Overflow."

"Not with that clear, soft voice," said Janet. "Say something in English for them, Clancy."

> " 'I had written him a letter which I had, for want of better
> Knowledge, sent to where I met him down the Lachlan, years ago——' "

began Clancy, and they circled her, laughing, asking how a new chum could recite Banjo Paterson in so short a time.

She made friends with the others when they arrived . . . let Daphne make a sketch of her suit, assured Glyn that Glyn's father was wrong when he said that Australian girls touring England were more nuisance than tourists—(Glyn was leaving for England in November.)

"It will be cold," warned Clancy.

"It will also be cheap," smiled Glyn cheerfully. "It's a Boomerang trip, they call them that, you get very reduced fares because you go out of season."

"I gather you must come back," said Clancy.

They all laughed. "You know what a boomerang is, anyway."

"Yes, I know." Apparently, deduced Clancy, rather relieved, they did not know about *her*.

She joined the Tea Club—"Biscuits every day except Friday and then we splurge on a cake."

She joined the Enjoyment Fund—"We have a dinner out once a month and at Christmas we go to a show as well."

By lunch break Clancy felt that she had been here for years.

She did copying all that day; evidently Mr. Osman had told Janet what he wanted from the new girl. It was straightforward work, so she had no need to question him. Once when Janet went into his room for a file Clancy noticed that his chair was empty, so even if she had required his direction none would have been forthcoming.

Five o'clock came round before she knew it, and she was descending with the rest of the girls, saying goodbye in the lobby, hurrying up from Macquarie Place to Wentworth Avenue.

Dick picked her up, moved off smartly, joined the snarl across the Bridge, then made better pace as the traffic began to unravel itself into a long moving snake along Pacific Highway.

Bron was waiting for her folk, the dinner was waiting, everyone exchanged notes . . . Dick his day's experiences, Clancy her day's impressions.

Then it was clear up, wash up, Scrabble. Then bed.

It was not until the end of the week . . . "Cake Day," rejoiced Daph . . . that Clancy saw Guy Osman again.

She had learned that he was in the country. "He goes to the bush quite a lot, gathering data, getting colour, he's on a Thing now."

"Yes," Clancy said. To herself she added, "Local papers, including the *Chronicle* of Dray Hill." But she said nothing to the girls.

She had found that Jarrah Publications was a small but prospering firm.

"Mr. Osman publishes in all branches," said Janet, "not a lot, but the best of each category." She had passed over a selection of Verse, Belles Lettres, Biography, Fiction. They were very attractive books, Clancy unwillingly conceded.

"Take this one and read it," said Janet, and she handed over a slim volume. It was bound in green and it looked smart, apt and sophisticated. The author was a Dallas Wyse.

"She's like the book," said Janet succinctly.

"Read it tonight," they all said.

It didn't take very long to read . . . it was slick, brittle, it ran easily, it was quite clever. It was also cruel and malicious.

When the girls asked her how she had liked it Clancy

hesitated and said, "Well——" and they all looked at each other.

"How did you like it?" Clancy asked of them.

"Well——" they said back.

"It's that sort of book," stated Janet.

"She's that sort of woman," stated Glyn.

"It's selling well," observed Adrienne.

"Is that why Mr. Osman accepted it?" asked Clancy, "because of its selling properties?"

"Guy is no fool," said Janet. "Naturally he has to be first a business man."

"Yes," agreed Clan. She was remembering firm lips as a man had stated, "I want the best my money can buy."

"However, he will still stand a loss if a manuscript particularly appeals to him. He's not all business and no soul."

"Or if a *woman* appeals to him," insinuated Daph.

"He doesn't look a woman's man to me," observed Clancy feelingly.

"It all depends on the woman," Glyn sniffed.

Janet said loyally, "All this sounds very bad for Guy, Clan, who is, and we all say this whole-heartedly, a very *nice* guy."

The girls eagerly concurred.

"Also, although Guy and Dallas Wyse are like that"—she clasped her hands together—"I still think Guy had wide-open eyes when he published *Yesterday and Tomorrow*."

"Sales agree with that," nodded Adrienne again.

"Well," accepted Clancy, "he is at least human and not a machine."

They all looked surprised at that. "He's certainly not a machine," they agreed.

Clancy endeavoured to explain herself. "I really meant that I hadn't considered him a married man, or a man a woman could find interesting."

"If he was married," interrupted Jean acidly before Clancy could elaborate her point, "Dallas Wyse wouldn't be around like she is."

"Or perhaps she would," disliked Glyn.

"I haven't seen her this week, have I?" enquired Clan.

"Mr. Osman," pointed out Claudia shrewdly, "hasn't been here either."

"He arrives today . . . Cake Day." Daphne had a sweet tooth.

"What's Guy been after in the bush, Janet?" Glyn enquired. Janet appeared to do most of Mr. Osman's work.

"Not kangaroos or sheep as you might think, but *papers,* local rags. He's doing a Thing on them. I'm filing some of his notes now." For a few moments Clancy's breath came unevenly. "There are some hilarious bits. One is a tiny northwest paper, three full columns of wedding description, church, gowns, speeches, honeymoon, but no identity of the bride or groom."

They all laughed.

"But," said Clancy, remembering the *Chronicle,* "do people *read* their locals?"

"Yes," drawled a voice at the door, "some do."

The speaker came right into the room and greeted each girl in turn before he came to Clancy.

"*Some* read their papers, Miss Clyde," Guy Osman informed her.

He did not address her again, not even during the tea and cake break. But just as she was putting the cover over her typewriter for the night he buzzed her bell.

She hesitated, then took up her pencil and steno pad and went into his room.

"No need for those"—he nodded to the dictation equipment—"Janet takes for me. I just wanted to set your mind at rest."

"My mind?"

"Or should I say conscience?"

"I don't understand you, Mr. Osman."

"I will not be using," he said stiffly, "in fact I have destroyed, the *Dray Hill Chronicle* of several months ago."

She should have thanked him for that, but instead she blurted accusatively, "You didn't destoy it, Mr. Osman, you filed it away in your mind."

"What makes you think I would want to keep such a distasteful thing?" he replied coldly.

"Because that would be you," she came back.

"You haven't a good opinion of the Australian, Miss Clyde."

"You haven't a good opinion of the English."

"Of *one*," he amended.

She stood silent.

"Come," he said sarcastically, "surely you can be as generous in return."

"I like Australians," she proffered. "Some I already love."

He raised his hateful brows at that. "Of course," he smiled blandly, "sweet romance . . . inevitable when there are not enough girls to go round."

"I didn't say that."

"Pardon me, Miss Clyde, they were your exact words."

"I mean I didn't say romance," she blurted.

"No? Too soon, perhaps? And yet you appeared to me to be a smart worker. This copy"—he tapped a pile of her week's work—"appears quick and efficient. Also"—he had taken out his cigarettes—"you've never wasted too much time in one place, have you?"

"Is this what you summoned me in for—just to repeat yourself?" asked Clancy.

"No, I called you in to reassure you. You appear to be on good terms with the girls. Far be it from me to alter that amicable state of affairs."

She nodded stolidly. "A good business depends on a contented staff?" she suggested.

"Exactly, Miss Clyde." He gave her a cursory nod which she took for dismissal. She turned and went to the door.

"No Saturday work, I presume you knew that; I'll see you, I also presume, on Monday again."

Clancy said the only thing she felt capable of saying.

"Yes, sir."

But she saw him before Monday. She saw him Saturday night.

Dick came home with tickets . . . and the Migration's first request of Clancy. Would she attend the Grand Concert for the British Migrant Drive at the Sydney Town Hall tonight?

"It will be good . . . the best artists are performing. You'll have a seat on the dais."

"Oh, Dick, must I?"

"It would help."

She stood silent and miserable, hating this position because *he* had made it wretched.

"Clancy, they all love you, just as we love you," persuaded Bron. "There won't be one in the audience not happy over their Boomerang Girl."

Yes, that could be possible, thought Clan, without *him* somewhere in the hall, and there was no reason she could think of that he should be there.

In the end she became as excited as Bronwen over it all.

She pressed her soft pink chiffon, let Bron clasp round her neck her own precious string of pearls.

"No flowers, Clancy. You're sure to have some presented when *you're* presented."

"Oh, no, not that as well!"

"You'll love it when you get there . . . the lights, the music, the applause."

And Clancy did love it.

The millionth migrant was present again, the parents of the big family, the Good Neighbours—why, she was among old friends.

Then across the footlights she found her own eyes being drawn to another pair of eyes. It must have been the lack of warmth when everything else was warm, the absence of light when everything else was light, that drew her like this.

Guy Osman sat there, a cold little smile on his firm, long mouth. Clancy tried to turn her own glance away. But she found herself looking again . . . hoping that some of the ice had melted? . . . and when she did she noticed the girl.

Not girl, woman. A remarkably attractive woman. She had one gloved hand tucked under Osman's arm.

When she stood up at the end of the performance Clancy saw she was tall, rather like a poppy. A red poppy. She was dark-haired, crimson-mouthed, she had quick, smoke-black eyes.

Then to her dismay she saw that Guy Osman was guid-

63

ing the woman across to her. She looked to right and left, but saw she could not escape.

"Dallas, this is Miss Clyde," said Guy Osman. It might have been because Miss Wyse was the senior that Osman presented Clancy, but the man gave Clancy the bland impression that it was because *she* was the lesser of the two.

"So I just learned," nodded the tall girl. She inclined her head to the dais. "Quite a nice cosy get-together up there."

If she had been going to say something more, and by the slyly malicious look in the smoke-black eyes Clancy believed this probable, she did not have the chance.

"And this is Dallas Wyse," concluded the man.

He took Dallas's hand, bowed stiffly to Clancy, and led his companion out of the vast hall.

CHAPTER 9

THE next few weeks went very quickly for Clancy.

Perhaps this was because Dick, on behalf of the British Migration, had come forward with a string of social but objective invitations. "Do accept them, Clan," Bronwen had cajoled. "I love going out with you, and if I don't go now I soon won't be able to go."

Clancy had laughed. "All right—for you, darling, I accept."

"For Bron, for England, for future Australia," Dick had sealed with a grin.

Perhaps the weeks went quickly, because Clancy found her post at Jarrah Publications both pleasant and stimulating. Admittedly *he* was something to be taken with the work, but Clancy found Guy Osman not such bad medicine as he might have been. He met her on a strictly business basis and because she was an efficient worker all their encounters were quite equable, very smooth.

Perhaps the time went on fleet feet because the season was spring.

Oh, this lovely Australian spring, not so delicate and enchanted as English spring perhaps, but lavish, brimming over. Clancy would look at the flower-laden trees with ruffles of wind in them, the bright careless plum, the drifts of peach, the cream and the rose of the apple. The heady fragrance of it all.

One of the Migration invitations had been to attend an Empire Ball, another to address a youth centre, a third to help judge at an English baby show.

"If they wait a few months I'll judge for them," said Bron when Clancy complained of her inexperience in this last category.

"You'd be a biased judge," pointed out Clancy, "you'd give the championship to Baby Stanton."

"Well, isn't he or she?" laughed Bron.

Clancy had been out several times to the Hostel. Each time something or some condition had changed. Except one thing, and to Clancy's worry and regret. For instance the Willards had moved out within three days. They had been destined to be the lucky ones. They chanced on a roomy, attractive, very reasonably-priced house.

The young Masons, too, had found a flat, not a cheap flat by any means, but with Paul making good money in the building trade and Pam well ensconced in a departmental store they should be able to manage and save.

Not everybody was as sanguine, though. Rob Milford, schoolteacher, had been appointed his first Australian school. "Fifty-three pupils," he groaned to Clan.

"It won't be always," she cheered.

"The thing is, will I still be here when it won't?" he grieved. "Fifty-three boys, age eleven. I'll fall by the wayside, Clan."

"Not you. The wages are satisfying, aren't they?"

"Yes, they're good," grinned Rob.

Others had cares, but they were as fairly well adjusted to them as the new schoolteacher.

All—except the Gillespies.

It was the Gillespies that caused Clancy the worry and regret. The worry was over their obvious unhappiness, the regret was because, the way things were going, the Gillespies simply wouldn't last the two years.

Everything went wrong with the Gillespies. They were the sensitive type of people to whom community living could never be something to resign oneself to, to abide, to plough through until such time as something better happened.

The Gillespies in a way were molluscs, thought Clancy. Like little brown snails, if you touched them with a harsh finger they crawled into their protective shell. But where was their shell? All they had was a shell that sheltered one thousand and seventy others. They were not thin-skinned, they were simply Gillespies. If only *they* had snared the house instead of the easy-going Willards everything might have been all right.

66

But nothing went right, not from the very first meal when little Lyndall had stared at her knife and fork and then burst into tears. From then on it had been worse.

Mr. Gillespie was a carpenter and had been found a job at once.

"But he came home so upset, Clancy," said Mrs. Gillespie. "His workmates told him he was working too hard, to take it easier."

"They meant it kindly."

"Jack took it that they resented him, that they thought he was trying to put them in the wrong."

"Mr. Gillespie was over-sensitive. Perhaps he *was* working too hard. You do that in the beginning because you're over-anxious. As for taking it easier, Mrs. Gillespie, these Australians might appear to do that, but the work obviously gets done."

"The children, too, have had troubles," Mrs. Gillespie went on.

"Yes, I noticed Lyndall was not eating well."

"Young John has been a worry. He had some words at school with one of the boys, and this lad said, 'Anyway, it's our country. Why, my great-great-grandfather came out here,' and John said something dreadful back."

"Yes, Mrs. Gillespie?"

"He said, 'I suppose he was a convict.' When John told me I felt so ashamed. John's no angel, Clancy, but he's never been rude and hurting like that. Why, you're smiling!"

"I'm *laughing,* Mrs. Gillespie, it's so funny. Tell me, did the boys finish with a fight?"

"No, the curious thing is they still speak to each other, in fact I'd go as far as to say they're friends."

"You see," said Clancy, "mountains out of molehills. No doubt the boy appreciated John speaking back in the same strain, he knew at once he was the same species as himself."

"But I don't want John to be tough."

"Don't you want him to be reliant?"

"Yes, but——"

"Mrs. Gillespie," said Clancy, "that's not the real thing that's worrying you, is it? It's not Mr. Gillespie and his few words with his mates, it's not Lyndall off her food, it's not young John. They're all settling, slowly perhaps, but *settling*, and you know it. Mrs. Gillespie, it's *you*."

The woman had nodded dumbly.

"What is it, Mrs. Gillespie?"

"Everything's different. I hate eating in there, I—I——"

"You won't always be there, it's only for a waiting period. You might chance on something at any moment—look at the Willards."

But Mrs. Gillespie had only looked at Clancy.

"Even if we got the Willards' luck we wouldn't take it, Clancy. We all want to go back."

"You mean *you* want to go back."

The woman had wrung her hands.

"I thought that you at least would be sympathetic, you went through all this before."

"Yes, but I was alone, I had no one with me. If I'd had someone, Mrs. Gillespie, I wouldn't have returned. And I'll tell you something else—if I had my first time over again I wouldn't do what I did."

Mrs. Gillespie had turned her head away. Clancy might have left her with her last statement to think about had she not seen the woman's trembling lip.

She knew that the mother was the heart-beat of a family. If Mrs. Gillespie refused to become acclimatized the rest would refuse. On the other hand if she could be prevailed upon to give it a trial Clancy had no doubts that the family would settle here. Already she suspected that young John was halfway to becoming an Aussie.

Something else worried Clancy, too. Money. If Mrs. Gillespie was determined not to find new roots, if she insisted upon going home to England before her term in Australia was up, then she would have to pay back their outward fares as well as their return passages. And Clancy did not think that the Gillespies had that sort of money. Besides, what sort of return to the Mother Country would it be, with nothing in the purse after they had paid back what they owed, had paid for their home journey?

"At least, Mrs. Gillespie, you must try to last out if only for your finances' sake," she pleaded.

But at that Mrs. Gillespie had broken down altogether.

"Even if we can last out can——can *Mother?*"

So that was it, had deduced Clancy, that was Mrs. Gillespie's "tug." Not a hot Christmas instead of cold, not an absence of rock, not the softness of English rain, but something tangible and human . . . *somebody*. Mrs. Gillespie's mother.

"She's old. She stood at the station and waved us off. She said, 'Course I won't miss you. I have my friends . . . there's telly . . .' But I know she does miss us. I know she's breaking her heart for us. And I can tell you this, Clancy, I'm breaking my heart for her."

"Bring her out, Mrs. Gillespie."

"Bring her out! Do you realize how long *we* took to come? Oh, no, you wouldn't realize. You got through very soon, you were the Boomerang Girl."

It was not meant unkindly, Mrs. Gillespie was too absorbed in her own grief to be unkind, but it stabbed Clancy to the heart.

What have I done? she thought. As well as take the place of a girl who 'while she waited——died', I'm taking the place of Mrs. Gillespie's mother.

Suddenly totally inadequate, Clancy had patted Mrs. Gillespie's arm and said lamely, "Well, do try a little," and had gone slowly out of the Hostel gates.

She had almost run into Guy Osman before she saw him. He had stepped out of his car and opened the door beside the driver's seat for her.

"I was out this way," he said carelessly, "and I thought it possible I might run into you and be able to save you your trip back. You look very desolate. What's wrong, Miss Clyde? Migrants getting you down?"

For a moment she was inspired to confide in him, but what would have been the use?

Put in bare words the Gillespies' story sounded a rather selfish little story . . . certainly it rang hollow and weak.

"You know, I think you take too much on yourself," stated Guy Osman. "You were destined to be a Boomerang Girl, not a Hostel Mother. Let the new chums fend for themselves."

"Perhaps—perhaps some can't."

"No, *one* couldn't, could she?"

"Must you always bring it back again to me?"

"I'm sorry, I said I'd destroyed the evidence and I have. If I recall it at times, it's just because it has stuck in my gills. But I'll not pursue that now, Miss Clyde. I'll not pursue your faint-hearted immigrants either; I'm going to show you a heart that was *not* faint."

He closed the door on her, came round to the driver's seat, and started the car.

"Ever been to La Perouse?"

"Of course."

"I forgot . . . you were here previously."

She bit her lip.

"Have you been to Kurnell?"

"Across Botany Bay . . . where Captain Cook landed? No, I haven't, but I've always wanted to," Clancy said.

"We'll go. Now that there's a road through from Cronulla the launch doesn't have a regular run, but I've ascertained that it will be running this afternoon."

He started off.

He parked the car at La Perouse and they went down to the pier, past the lubra with the shells, the aboriginal boomerang-thrower, past the little plot of France.

"It can be a rough crossing," said Guy Osman, "but I think we'll have it smooth today."

Presently the launch chugged in and the passengers clambered aboard.

They set off at once and were soon on the open sea and dipping rhythmically with each oncoming wave. Even on a calm day like this spring day there was a considerable swell.

But it was all very lovely, the waters of the vast bay reflecting the blue of the sky and the dipping wings of gulls, Kurnell looking like a dream-place from the distance, a world of colour and light, transparent, unreal, and then taking shape, the shape of yellow beach, sweeping lawns, dignified old trees.

They got out of the launch, walked down the long jetty, then crossed the grass to the Obelisk.

Here was hallowed ground, here James Cook, one of the

greatest sailors the world had known, had stepped ashore to a new country. And he had been a wise as well as a great man, he had established friendly terms with the natives, he had brought his men through long months of ordeal safe and sound.

Yet not all. There was a lonely grave. The name, Clancy read, was Forby Sutherland, and he had been the first white man to die in this Fifth Continent.

All at once it seemed inordinately sad to Clancy that a young sailor, a son of the sea, had been encompassed by solid earth. She wondered if Captain Cook had thought that, and when he had left these shores looked back and grieved.

She found a little grieving in herself, and turned sensitively away, but even as she made the impulsive gesture Guy Osman turned her back.

He said, abruptly, so that she realized at once he had read her foolish sorrow, "Come and we'll have tea."

As they had it in the kiosk underneath the immense Norfolk Pine she felt she almost could have liked him.

Another man might have shrugged at her little sadness over a lonely grave, but Guy Osman just plied tea and talked in a quiet relaxed way until Clancy, too, relaxed.

The easiness remained with them on the trip back across the bay, on the journey home in the car. There was no mention of boomerangs, of playing the Hostel Mother, no barbs, no sarcasms, only a companionable silence until Guy Osman said a quiet "Goodnight" at the Stanton gate and Clancy gave her grateful "Goodnight" back.

CHAPTER 10

AUSTRALIAN springs were short.

Barely had the soft petals begun to fall than leaf harvest set in, and among the trees, on the first really hot day, the cicadas began their shrill notes.

They were called locusts here, and their stridency was considered a song, and little boys pursued them mercilessly, collecting varieties known as Greengrocers and Yellow Mondays. Collection was done in an entirely kindly spirit, but doubtless, confined to a grubby pocket, the cicada did not agree.

The Christmas Bush came out in indifferent small white flowers, but in December the blossoms would turn a dazzling red. "When it's like that," Clancy had once been told, "it's really dead."

The thought of Christmas worried Clancy. For then, she felt, would be the migrants' testing time.

Winter was something they knew, spring, but summer could try them with its strength and length.

Most of all how would they understand a Christmas set in hot weather?

She remembered her own nostalgia, not helped by the Australians' cheerful interchange of cards full of holly and sleighs, for only a few adopted local motifs. They even glued cottonwool to windows for snow, then went nonchalantly down to the beach for Christmas dinner.

How soon would a new chum understand that? And it had to be soon for some of them . . . for the Gillespies.

The Gillespies were no happier . . . at least Mrs. Gillespie was not.

Lyndall was eating again, Mr. Gillespie's complaints had become mild and infrequent, John, Clancy suspected, had really crossed the date line, but the mother, the heart-beat, was still back in England.

Frequently Clancy pointed out to Mrs. Gillespie the importance, the financial importance to ordinary people, of hanging on, but each time Mrs. Gillespie said, "I thought you would understand."

Once in desperation, when she was going through some papers with her employer and he asked idly about her visits to the Hostel, Clancy had burst this out to Guy Osman.

Instantly his brows had met in that straight uncompromising line and his eyes had become glaciers.

"What are you trying to run, Miss Clyde, an expense account against Australia?"

She had felt the dull red creeping up her cheeks. She had not meant it that way . . . she had meant that if the Gillespies lasted out two more years they might last for twenty-two, she had not intended him to conclude that she was only advising them to stick it out so that they did not have to refund their fares.

He was staring at her furiously, and the fury froze any explanations she would have made.

"Upon my soul," he said, "what do you think we're offering out here, a shuttle service for free provided the tripper marks time between trips for a period of twenty-four months?"

"Not free, it's ten pounds," she said thinly.

"*You* should know," he came back. He had closed up the book.

"That's all, Miss Clyde," he had said.

And that's all to my confidences, now and the future, thought Clancy. I was a fool to speak as I did.

She could speak to others, though, not just English Dick and Bron but Australians. And, unlike *him*, they understood and sympathized.

"Time will help," they all advised.

"Yes," said Clancy, "but will Mrs. Gillespie permit time?"

Now that Guy Osman was back at his desk, Dallas Wyse was a frequent visitor. She would swing through the outer office to Guy's office, not bothering to toss even one greeting word.

Only upon the first occasion did she speak to Clancy. She had paused, then come back to stand by Clancy's desk.

"Oh, hullo," she had said.

"Good morning, Miss Wyse."

"I didn't know this was where you worked."

Clancy said nothing.

"I thought you occupied your time sitting on platforms and getting bouquets," said the tall dark young woman.

"I have to earn my living."

"Particularly at Jarrah Publications?"

Clancy had glanced up quickly at that.

"What do you mean, Miss Wyse?"

"Migrants are 'directed' to jobs, aren't they? What strings did you pull to be 'directed' here?"

"I think you're misinformed. British migrants are not directed—they're placed if they can't place themselves, but there's no direction."

Clancy finished, "I happened on this job from a newspaper advertisement."

"Really? Then what do I say, nice for Guy, or nice for you?"

If you copied Mr. Osman, thought Clancy, you certainly would say the latter. She did not answer this time.

Dallas Wyse gave a hard little laugh and went into Guy's office.

"*Yesterday and Tomorrow,*" grimaced Adrienne as the door closed.

Daph's young lips mouthed an unmistakable "Pig."

After that Dallas never loitered by Clancy's desk again.

The Stantons had been called in to be interviewed again by the Housing Commission.

"It means nothing very significant," admitted Dick, "but it gives you a cheerful feeling."

"End of the Lane in view," Clancy had teased Bronwen, and Bron had said wistfully, "I'd so much like to take Baby into a new house I don't care if it's Beginning of the Street."

"Even situated at Simpsonville?"

"Even Smith Town if there is one."

One Saturday Dick, Bron and Clancy had a picnic at

Warragamba, scene of Sydney's new water storage . . . "Fifty times more stored water per head of population than London has," said Dick, "but it's needed because Sydney has an unreliable rainfall, and, of course, it has no snow-fed streams."

Warragamba meant "tea-tree swamp", but there was no swamp now, only a drowned valley, above the valley a giant spillway, a great white wall.

But more interesting to Clancy than the number of kilowatts of hydro-electricity available was the little town.

Not the fact that it had been built for the men who had built the dam and at a cost of several million, but the fact that it had four hundred and sixty-nine cottages, all served with water and electricity, fourteen shops, a town hall, a school, a medical centre, a baby clinic—*and that it was for sale*.

"That's a fact," said Dick. "The Water Board have advertised it throughout the world. FOR SALE, WITH TOWN HALL, ONE WHOLE VILLAGE."

"A town for sale," echoed Clancy dreamily.

Dick looked at her sharply.

"Now, Clan, none of those thoughts."

But she couldn't help thinking them. She thought them as they returned through the rustic countryside of Wallacia and Mulgoa. Warragamba was only forty miles from Sydney. How ideally situated for a—for——

She mulled it over that night. The next day she told the girls. She had come to the stage now at Jarrah of receiving confidences, of confiding in return.

They were having morning cuppas, and as she spilled her dreams Guy Osman came out from his office with his empty tray. He said nothing, just put the tray down and went inside again.

But it didn't stop at that.

When Clancy went in later to take him a typing assignment he drawled, "So now the Boomerang Girl has turned estate agent. She has her eye on a town."

"Not for what it is but for what it could be," Clancy burst out eagerly. "It seems such a good idea, such a heaven-sent idea when there's a serious housing shortage.

75

As many as are being sheltered at the Hostel could be placed there—but in their own homes."

He had taken out his cigarette material. Slowly he rolled and lit one. Then he insinuated deliberately, "British, of course."

The treacherous red rushed into Clancy's cheeks .

"It's not my idea that British migrants are kept separate from European."

"Or that, unlike European, they can enjoy scot free . . . I'm sorry, for *ten pounds* . . . a regular change of heart."

"You told me that you'd put all that behind you," she cried out, not far from tears.

He got up and went to the window and stared down on the little park in Macquarie Place.

What was wrong with him, Guy Osman was thinking, what had got into him that always he had to pick on her, harp back like this?

He had loved Peter like a brother, but never had he really believed that what had happened to Peter's fiancée had sent Peter to his death. Always Peter had been an indifferent driver . . . it was on the cards that it might eventuate. It had.

It was over, it was finished, nothing would bring Peter back. He had accepted it—until he had met this girl. Why could he not accept it now?

Then all at once it came sharply and forcibly to Osman that he couldn't accept it because he didn't want the reminder of it to come through *her*. For some inexplicable reason he wanted perfection with her. He had to have perfection. But why? Why with this girl?

Harshly, unreasonably, he turned from the green shadowy unreality of Macquarie Place to the brown office reality of his room.

"Why in God's name did you write those things?" he flung.

Clancy took up the papers, as steadily as she could.

"I think you're obsessed," she observed at length.

He did not answer for a while, then he said sarcastically, "You're the obsessed one, planning to buy a town."

"You know I planned no such thing. How could I?"

76

"But you have in your dreams, and how dare you, Miss Clyde, how dare you!"

Clancy put the papers down on the desk again.

"I think it's time that article was re-published," she said coolly. "Written in every newspaper in New South Wales. Written, and if my statement beneath it that it was *not* my work is unacceptable, then concluded at least with the declaration that the views expressed are now changed. And then, I think, Mr. Osman, I shall find most Australians are not so thin-skinned as you."

She was right, of course, Guy realized. He *was* being thin-skinned. He had never been before, but he was now.

Why? *Why?*

He could not answer her, so deep was his perplexity. For the first time in his life his quite remarkable self-possession seemed to have deserted him. When he turned back from the window where he had crossed again she had gone.

But the next night there was a mild furore. Clancy had been as good at her word, she had sent her article to press.

It was not her doing that the editors soft-pedalled what she submitted, made much more of her change of mind and her return to Australia, but Clancy knew that *he* would think it was.

Meanwhile she had expected a measure of censure over her disclosures, a few frowns. Instead she received only congratulations and applause.

The girls were excited over her photograph, over the fact that she had gone back to England, returned again.

Acquaintances greeted her cordially with: "So you saw the light, Miss Clyde." . . . "So you gave us a second chance."

She had hoped to slough off a vague unhappiness with that article, clear her conscience. She only achieved the latter. The unhappiness still remained. Not a large unhappiness, perhaps, but a carping perpetual one. She could not have put a finger on it, have expressed it, it simply was there.

She found that her publicity had done nothing to her

77

popularity . . . indeed she was in demand more than before. Not only to British migration now but all migration.

She was invited to the European Migrant Information Service to watch . . . possibly, the director insinuated, to suggest. But there was little to suggest there, it was all so helpful. There was advice about land prices, ways in which money could be borrowed for that purpose, addresses of social clubs, free English lessons, monetary system explanations, wages and taxes. Every European language was represented, as well as Arabic, Afrikaans, the rest.

She went to a naturalization ceremony. She saw each applicant repeat his oath, then put down the Bible. She knew that for most a thousand mental images of years spent in another country were flashing before them . . . childhood years when all was right with the world . . . then war years.

She saw a watchmaker, an artist, a mechanic, a doctor pledge themselves.

Afterwards one shrugged, "For a year, two, three, I would have gone back had there been anything to go to . . . I didn't like it here. Then one day it was like putting on a nice soft shoe."

"It fitted?"

"I did," smiled the mechanic from Yugoslavia.

Yes, he fitted. The others fitted. As far as Clancy could see all the *Loch Maree* passengers had fitted . . . except one —Mrs. Gillespie.

But Clancy had learned her lesson, she must never speak openly, never within certain earshot, on that subject again.

She must never babble about buying a town—as though she could, anyway! Indeed all she could do, she sometimes thought, was say "Good morning" . . . "Good evening" . . . to the man who sat at Guy Osman's desk.

CHAPTER 11

IT was Guy Osman who broke the ice.

One evening just as she was about to leave, Clancy's employer came and stood beside her. He had a springback folder in his hand and he held it out to her.

"Got room for this?" he asked.

"What is it, Mr. Osman?"

"A manuscript. I'd like you to read it."

This was not her usual work, so Clancy said, "You want *me* to read it?"

"If you will."

"I'm not a reader."

"I'm aware of that. My own reader already has reported on it. Now I'd like another opinion."

"Mine?" She could not help sound incredulous.

"Yours," he concurred.

She started to ask more questions . . . what type of manuscript, when he wanted her answer . . . but Guy Osman gave a cool "Good evening, Miss Clyde" and went back to his room.

Clancy put the folder in her string bag along with her purse, compact and a box of strawberries for Bron, and fairly ran up to Wentworth Avenue. The Brown Bombers, as the Sydney traffic parking men were called because of their brown uniforms, frowned on standing cars, especially at this peak hour.

Dick raised his brows at the bulky manuscript.

"Homework?" he grinned. "Looks like there won't be any Scrabble tonight."

"No," said Clancy, "I'm to read instead."

She felt a curiosity about this manuscript that Osman had placed in her hands. Why had he done it? He had never done such a thing before.

After dinner she sat in the reading lamp's rosy pool of light, Dick and Bron playing a two-handed game on the other side of the light, and opened the book.

As yet it had no title, it only bore the author's name. Simon White.

She began reading. It was not a long book, indeed it was a volume you could take at one sitting. But long after she had finished it Clancy just stopped there with it in her hands.

It was not good, not artistically good, never, she thought, a commercial find, but there was something about it that made her want to take it up to find the parts that had leapt out at her again . . . find the flame among the ashes . . . feel the warmth of the flame once more.

Simon White, she thought. I wonder what he's like.

It was several days after Osman had given her the manuscript that Clancy met the author. He came to Jarrah with Dallas Wyse.

Dallas walked carelessly in, looking more like a red poppy than ever in a perfectly cut deep red suit. But behind her this time was a tall, blond-haired young man, very thin, a little stooped, perhaps delicate-looking, with a sensitive mouth and long hands.

Dallas, without a word, went through to Guy's office.

The man just stood there until Janet got up.

"You'll sit down?"

"Thank you."

He did.

Janet should have been a hostess, Clancy often thought, she liked mingling people. She did now.

"We don't know your name," she smiled, "but we're Glyn Heriot, Clancy Clyde, I'm Janet Cooper." The other girls were in the second office.

"I'm Simon White," the man smiled back. He nodded to each of them.

Clancy was remembering the manuscript still in her bag, for she had had no opportunity yet to return it to Guy Osman. She glanced at the man, to find he was looking at her.

"Clancy," he repeated.

"I know," she accepted patiently. " 'I had written him a letter' . . . They all say that."

"Then I won't. I'll say *my* verse."

"Yours?"

He smiled diffidently; it made him look only a boy. Shyly he said:

> " 'And the bush has friends to meet him, and their
>   kindly voices greet him
> In the murmur of the breezes and the river on its
>   bars,
> And he sees the vision splendid of the sunlit plain
>   extended,
> And at night the wondrous glory of the everlasting
>   stars.' "

The everlasting stars . . .

Clancy remembered this part of "The Overflow" . . . his part, too, he had just asserted, this young man's. She remembered something else as well. His book. The manuscript she still held in waiting. Why, that must be its title, of course. "The Everlasting Stars."

Eagerly she said so to him.

Eagerly he said back, "I thought that, too."

"You didn't give it a name?"

"I just wrote it," he admitted shyly.

Dallas came out just then to take him in to Osman. But before she did she stood at Osman's door, staring coldly at Clancy talking to the tall fair young man.

When the two had gone into the inner office, Glyn whistled, "Wow, Clancy, she gave you a dirty look. Hands off if ever I saw the words written in two vindictive black eyes!"

"You're exaggerating," said Clancy, but she had not missed that look either, and it had been exactly as Glyn had said.

"I can't understand Dallas Wyse," frowned Janet. "She probably doesn't want him herself, but she still must keep him. She's entirely possessive, she wants everything around her."

"You mean," said Glyn, "everything male."

"I should think," observed Clancy, "that no male with eyesight would be adverse to that. She's certainly beautiful."

"So is fire," Glyn said, "but it will burn you up. And I think that that's what Dallas will do to him."

Deliberately . . . she did not know why . . . Clancy misunderstood, "To Mr. Osman?"

"Guy? Good heavens, no. No one, not even Dallas, could burn our Guy. No, Clan, the sensitive plant, Mr. Simon White."

Clancy saw more of Simon, for every time Dallas came in, and that was often, Simon trailed behind her.

He had an easy, likeable, relaxed personality, and all the girls approved of him.

"He's nice. Weak, of course, but I like pliable people," Daphne confided.

Simon talked with them all, but mostly he talked with Clancy. How much did she know of Australia? Where had she been?

When she told him Sydney and only Sydney, both this time and last time, he asked, "Then what would you know of everlasting stars?"

"What I read," she answered at once, "in your book."

"My book," he echoed. "Will it ever be that?"

"I think so, Mr. White."

"I call you Clancy," he reproached.

Clancy paused. "I think so—Simon." She glanced up at him. "Does publication matter very much to you?"

"I'd like to see it complete in my hands," he admitted boyishly, "though just now I'd like something even more."

"Yes?"

"I'd like you *really* to see those everlasting stars."

"Where would I, Simon?"

"The inland . . . the centre . . . only there."

"The sunlit plain extended . . ." murmured Clancy.

Simon White said, "Yes"

A few nights afterwards Guy Osman asked for the manuscript. "And your opinion, Miss Clyde."

She gave it eagerly . . . not very comprehensively, she

thought, her enthusiasm was so much that she found her words tumbling out and tangling up.

She stopped suddenly, aware of his cool regard.

"Are you praising the book or the man?" he asked.

"The book, of course. How ridiculous you are."

"Not at all. You've had the manuscript a week, yet not until now, now *after* you've met the author . . . and may I suggest been attracted to him . . ."

"You may suggest no such thing," Clancy interrupted furiously.

"No?" Guy Osman drawled, "but it looked remarkably like that."

"Mr. Osman, do you want my opinion of the book or not?"

"You've just given it to me, I don't want a repeat."

"Then what *do* you want?"

"I want an explanation as to why you carry the book around all this time without reporting to me, then suddenly after you meet—and like?—its author, decide to enthuse."

"That's unfair!" she retorted.

"To you?"

"*I* don't matter. You've always been at pains to tell me that ever since we met. No, it's unfair to Simon."

"To *Simon*." Guy Osman said it significantly.

A little silence fell between them.

Clancy broke it.

"Did *you* read the manuscript?"

"I did."

"May I ask your reaction?"

"I," reminded Osman hatefully, "am male."

She had not thought he could be so petty, so small-minded. She said so aloud. He just sat looking at her, that thin scornful smile on his lips.

"I'm no artist, I'm a hardheaded business man, and I'm extremely puzzled that my official reader puts in a very contra report, yet you put in a very enthusiastic pro." Guy waited.

She should have left it at that—after all, reading was not her job—but she could not believe how anyone whose job it *was* could not see the pearl that was in the oyster. Because of the pearl she had recognized she tried once more.

"Really, such enthusiasm," Guy Osman shrugged, and the sneer in his voice made Clancy turn away.

On her next visit out to the British Hostel Clancy found that now she *really* had a problem. Mrs. Gillespie had gone further than being merely unhappy. She had acted; she had put down a deposit on four return fares.

"Oh, Mrs. Gillespie, you didn't!"

Mrs. Gillespie said stubbornly, "The booking is heavy what with all these Australians taking their holidays abroad, so I had to get in while I could."

"You'll lose a percentage if you cancel."

Mrs. Gillespie had looked directly at Clancy.

"You mean *when* I cancel."

"Oh, Mrs. Gillespie," was all Clancy said.

It saddened her even more because she sensed intrinsically now that the Gillespies could have settled in.

She saw it in the fact that Mr. Gillespie's complaints, that had grown milder, had now entirely stopped. He was quite excited that the grandfather of one of his workmates had come from the same town in Sussex. He went over often to share a pipe and a talk with the old man. And when he came away it was not with nostalgia but with satisfaction at being able to enlighten Mr. Jessop.

"Old chap was surprised when I told him how the town was still the same," he grinned. "Springley, I said, now that's a different story, gone ahead t' at place."

"Has Mr. Jessop settled?" asked Clancy innocently.

Mr. Gillespie looked surprised.

"Of course."

Clancy wanted to tell him that he could, too, if he only tried . . . tried more with his wife. But Mr. Gillespie was an easy-going man, and she knew that he would abide by his Peg.

Young John meanwhile was entirely happy.

"Took the History prize," said Mrs. Gillespie, for a moment forgetting what sat upon her heart and permitting maternal pride. "He was the only one who knew the Wars of the Roses."

"And Lyndall," pointed out Clancy, seeing Lyndall's vivid red tongue, "has been eating *Australian* rock."

"Apple on a stick," corrected Lyndall. "It's better than rock 'cos you get apple besides."

Mrs. Gillespie tightened her lips again.

Clancy told the girls the next day. She had to open the floodgates somewhere, for Bron, getting very anxious about Our House now that her time was shortening, had her own cares and worries.

"Well, Clan, she won't lose all that much if she cancels the fares," they tried to cheer her.

"It's not if I'm worrying about—it's when, and she'll lose much more than they can afford, the payment back of their passages out here as well as their return trip.

"Besides"—Clancy's face was sad—"she'll miss something else as well."

They all looked at her, and she said a little humbly, "This land."

"And that," commented a voice at Guy Osman's door, "is very sweetly spoken. Shall we afford our very charming agent some well-earned applause?"

They all clapped, clapped sincerely . . . but Clancy knew there was no sincerity in the man who stood and led it all.

"And now, Miss Clyde, can I see you?" he said when the acclamation died.

He was back in his chair when she came in. He waved her to the other chair.

"So the faint-hearted Mrs. G. has booked a home passage," he drawled.

"Did you call me in to discuss that?" she asked coldly.

"No . . . to discuss another home matter. Mine."

"Greenmarley?"

"You remember the name." He was looking at her through narrowed eyes.

"Yes, I remember." As though she could forget anything about it . . . the carved columns, the flagged verandah, the century-old trees . . . the curious sense of regret. She became aware that he was looking at her sharply now, and she flushed.

"I want you to be my guest tonight," he said.

This time she looked at him sharply. He met the glance.

"I'm having a small dinner . . . only four of us . . . you, Dallas, young Simon White, myself."

"But—but why me?"

"Why not? Simon will be there."

"But——"

"Look, Miss Clyde, I don't know the ritual in England, but here when we receive an invitation we don't question, we accept or decline."

She would decline, of course. She even opened her mouth to do so.

But, the words on her lips, she thought of Greenmarley again, and how instinctively, intrinsically, she loved it . . . how irresistibly she wanted to be there again.

"Yes or no, Miss Clyde?"

Feebly Clancy said, "Yes."

CHAPTER 12

BRON and Dick were going out for dinner.

When she had left for work that morning Clan had been directed where to find what, assured that all she had to do was put a match to the range.

As soon as she arrived home . . . later than usual as she had had to travel by train . . . Clancy put away Bronwen's preparations, wrote a quick note so that the Stantons would know where she was when they came in, then ran the bath.

She had planned to wear a cool tussore silk she had bought coming out, but on sudden impulse she pushed it back and took out instead a dark gold moiré.

She had just finished combing her hair when she heard the car pull up. She had rather expected transport. Everything Guy Osman did would always be impeccably correct. But it was not Guy she opened the door to, it was Simon.

"I'm instructed to come and deliver you," he smiled. He looked down at her. "Clancy, tonight you *are* my everlasting star."

"Stars are silver," she reminded him.

"Not in the Centre. They're big and they're gold."

"I think, Simon, you're getting confused with the moon."

"Not as far as you're concerned, Clancy. The moon is cold, but you are never that."

"Not the cool, reserved Englishwoman," she teased. She took up a light stole, closed the house and followed him out.

When she got to Greenmarley she felt inordinately pleased over her impulse to wear something more dramatic than a tussore suit.

Dallas was tall and poised and very striking in décolleté black. The table setting, too, called for dressing up. It was lit with slender candles, it was set with gleaming linen and shining silver, and the two men wore their dinner suits.

She wondered if it was an occasion . . . perhaps Guy had decided to publish Simon's book, perhaps this was in its way a book dinner.

But no. "The house was becoming dull," explained Guy Osman carelessly. "Old houses like Greenmarely have a tendency like old pots to stew over their old tea-leaves, to keep their windows shut to keep out new ideas."

"You're so right, Guy," agreed Dallas vivaciously. She was looking eagerly around her. But from where Clancy sat she saw a different expression from eagerness, she saw acquisition.

Well, why not? she thought. It's certainly a glorious house.

But somehow she was saddened. Somehow she knew that Dallas would change it all.

New cunning lights instead of the old-fashioned and not very efficient chandeliers; nothing revolutionary, Dallas would be too intelligent for that, but little touches here and there, "improvements", and when it all was done it would emerge as Dallas's house, not Greenmarley any more.

"Was there a history to this house?" Clancy asked, shrinking from her thoughts.

Guy nodded.

"It was built in 1847, which no doubt makes it a newcomer to you." He nodded coolly at Clancy.

"Well," she said, "we all have to be new chums some time."

"You've done it twice, haven't you?" Dallas remarked with quite unconcealed spite. Her eyes were on Clancy now, on her ash hair, the moiré dress that matched her pale gold colouring so perfectly that it might have sprung there just for that purpose.

There was the slightest frown on Guy Osman's brow. Somehow he seemed displeased. For a moment Clancy thought, "He doesn't like her speaking like that." Then she thought acidly, "He likes to do it only himself."

To do him justice, though, she knew that Guy Osman would strongly disapprove any stricture of one guest by another.

"Its first owner was a woman who was transported here at the age of fourteen for the heinous sin of catching and riding a neighbour's pony," said Guy.

Clancy waited for more stricture on his part now, some comment on English justice, but Guy just went on. She had the feeling, too, that although he had not said anything he had sent Dallas a silent warning, for the woman did not comment either.

"She fell in love during transportation with the mate of the ship, who in return fell in love with her. He asked her to wait till his next voyage. She waited longer than that, of course, she had been transported for seven years, but eventually she married her sailor lover, and they carried on a successful shipping business, and built this house."

"And where does your family come in, Guy?" asked Dallas.

"I've told you," smiled Guy crookedly.

He looked directly at Clancy.

"Convict stuff," he said.

After dinner Guy escorted them round. Clancy had seen the old kitchen, but that was all. Now she was shown the stone wall built from convict-chiselled rock, the high-pillared back verandah where two stairways curved to meet each other in a complicated and delicate design.

Simon had taken Dallas across to the ancient stone trough in which now spilled flowers instead of water.

"There is a bell-tower," Guy said to Clancy, and the next moment she was being impelled along a dim corridor and up a flight of dark steps.

She could scarcely see a hand in front of her . . . she could not see, only sense, the man. His hand was on her arm, though, lightly, inconsequentially, for no other purpose than to guide her up. But she felt the weight of every finger, felt it distinctly . . . and warmly. It was a cool night for November, his hand was cool, but where his fingers touched she burned.

"Why a bell-tower?" she asked, for something to say.

"To announce the arrival of the ferry boats that used to travel here."

"The Osmans did themselves proud," she said flippantly.

They had reached the top of the steps. For a while they both breathed hard; it had been a steep ascent.

"Yes, we've always done ourselves proud," Guy said.

As he said it he kept on looking at her. Curious to know that in a dark room, so dark you could scarcely see more than a few inches in front of you, someone's eyes did not move away from you.

She heard Guy take a box of matches from his pocket, open it and strike one. The scratch of the ignition made a sound like a little mouse. The first match flickered and died, the second lived and for a few moments soaked up the dark.

It showed the dusty old bell, the narrow turret . . . it showed a lean dark face with bright blue eyes that looked across into Clancy's own gold-green.

"It's a far cry from a transported convict to a house with your own bell-tower, isn't it?" he said coolly.

The eyes held something sharp and quiescent, but she could not read it.

Irritably she said back, "Why do you keep harping on that?"

"On what?"

"On your convict origin."

"You might have observed," he pointed out, "that I have a penchant for harping."

"Yes," she said, "I have noticed that."

"But this time I have a purpose."

He was lighting a cigarette now. It glowed in the dark room. When she did not comment he prompted, "Well, aren't you going to ask?"

"No."

"No?" The black brows had raised steeply at her. Only his face was lit up by the glow of the cigarette. It could have been just a face there, nothing else, narrowed eyes in the face, lifted brows.

"I'm sorry, I'm not the perfect guest, am I?" she said. "I don't ask the required questions."

"I had no intention of making you the perfect guest."

"Then to spite you I will be one. What is your purpose of harping on your convict forebears?"

He looked closely at her.

"Would you care to try an answer yourself?"

"It wouldn't be a try," she said coldly. "I already know the trend."

"You do?"

"Certainly. It's the old, old story, isn't it?" She said it a little wearily. "It's the old down-with-England theme that seems to run through your every song. Now it's down again, but not because of a carping female who dared criticize your country, or so you insist upon believing, but down because a great-great somebody or other was transported here when every place in the world was transporting, or victimizing, because they were primitive in those days, because they knew no better.

"But that doesn't matter to you. The other countries, I mean, the primitive era. To you all of it happened in only one corner of the world."

He could not have finished his cigarette, but he was grinding it under his heel. When he spoke his voice was very cold.

"So that's why I brought you up to a bell-tower," he said, "to point out to you that the country you've just come from sent my great-great-grandmother out here in the nineteenth century for borrowing a neighbour's horse."

"I didn't say that."

"No, and I didn't . . . nor did I intend to, either."

"What did you intend, then?" she stammered.

"I intended to cover you with cobwebs," he said furiously. "I intended to make Dallas really jealous. What do you think?" He began the descent.

"I think that last," she snapped, coming down the stairs behind him.

And when she got to the bottom she thought it again.

Simon was sitting on the edge of the stone trough, but Dallas was walking up and down the flagged verandah.

She stopped pacing as they appeared and went across to Guy.

"Darling, coffee's served." She took his arm.

Only once did she glance at Clancy, and then it was a deep, thoughtful, intent, wholly vindictive look.

* * *

It was after that dinner at Greenmarley that Clancy found a difference in two of the three who had eaten with her there.

Not Dallas. Right from their first meeting Dallas had not bothered to hide her claws, and she did not now.

No, the difference was in Guy . . . and Simon.

Guy's change was the more subtle. Somewhere or other, somehow or other, he seemed intangibly to have withdrawn. That was the only way Clancy could describe it. Withdrawal.

But how, she often asked herself, how when he had never stepped forward anyway as far as she was concerned, *could* there be withdrawal?

With Simon there was nothing subtle, only an acceleration. A surprising acceleration, for although Simon had always sought her out he had never sought her out as he did now. He met her when she emerged from the office, he called often at the Stantons', he booked her up for shows, dinners, the rest.

She knew that she was being coupled with him, but it puzzled more than worried her. Deep down she could not help feeling that Simon's sudden acceleration of attention was not so much inspired as contrived.

Because she liked Simon, liked him simply and instinctively, she did not break up their partnership. Although she guessed at what other people must be thinking she knew what *she* was thinking. There was nothing really between them, and the two concerned, she honestly believed, were fully aware of that.

So they went out together, and people drew conclusions.

Clancy was assured of this one night when Dick said rather apologetically, "You know, Clan, I've been hoping you'd settle, but I didn't think it would be quite as soon as it is."

He had gone on thoughtfully.

"And I had someone different in mind for you, Clan. Not"—hastily—"that he isn't a nice boy, but—well, he's just that, isn't he?"

"Isn't who?"

"Oh, Clan, don't be evasive. Simon, of course."

"And Simon is what?"

"Nice. But, Clan, he's a leaner. You'll have to be strong, my dear." Dick had looked a little worried as well as apologetic as he said this.

Bronwen, seeing an expression in Clancy's eyes, had assured hurriedly, "She is strong . . . and, Dick, you should mind your tongue."

"It's only because she's our girl now," defended Dick. "Clancy knows that."

"For how long?" Clancy had laughed, deciding to break up the discussion now that it was becoming so personal. "Until you get a girl of your own?"

"Our girl is a boy," promised Bronwen, "and his name is Noel."

"Why Noel? Is it a preference or a family name?"

"It's a Christmas name," smiled Bronwen.

"But"—this was Dick and Clancy together—"you're not due until———"

"Noel," said Bron in a secret way.

And Christmas did bring the Stantons their firstborn, only it was a girl, and they called her Holly.

"Totally unsuitable," admitted Dick proudly, "but after all, isn't the entire Australian Christmas that?"

It was . . . but who cared? thought Clancy.

The Christmas cards kept coming in full of sleighs and snowmen, the houses kept up their garnishes of cotton wool on window panes, and all the time the sun blazed down and the mercury soared to the nineties.

Clancy went with the girls to their long-planned Christmas "do", and as she gazed around the hotel trappings, the glitter of tinsel on fir-trees, a decorator's cunning suggestion of blazing Yule logs and silver filigree of snow, she suddenly knew that the arrow line of the composite fir was pointing just as surely as any real one could have to Heaven.

It was just as symbolic . . . and how desperately she wanted Mrs. Gillespie to understand this.

She wanted her to realize, as she herself did in this minute, that a *southern* Christmas with its golden grain pouring into wheat silos, its campfire-red Christmas bells, its eucalyptus tang, could catch the gleam of the Star just as surely, that a paper candle with a paper flame could leap just as high with hope.

But it was no use. She realized it at the British Hostel.

She had gone there for another purpose besides pre-Christmas. She had gone to ask if she could be allotted a room.

Dick had stormed at that. "When do you think we're living, Clan, in the eighteenth century? All that chaperone stuff went out with button boots. Bron will be home in a week."

"Look, Dick, you've been terribly kind, but I never intended stopping—anyway, not when you go into Our House, which should be quite soon." She had smiled fondly at him. "It will be your first house, you'll have to carry Bronwen over the threshold."

"As she'll be carrying Holly I may as well make it three and carry you, too."

"Not on your life! I'm going back to Lucas."

"Lucas?"

"He's the general factotum out there, he always was. I don't know how it is, he doesn't appear to be official, but he's the little king."

Lucas had been characteristically unenthusiastic.

"I suppose we could fit you in, but I don't like singles, I've said that before."

"But why, Luke?" protested Clancy.

"Hangers-on," said Lucas gloomily.

"I never worried you that way last time."

"You're prettier than you were last time," Lucas grunted ungraciously. "Well, I suppose if you've nowhere else . . ."

Prettier than she was last time. Clancy was unconvinced

about that. I'm just older, she thought. When she came out of the Gillespies' flat she decided it was people like Mrs. Gillespie who accelerated the ageing process. Amidst the Dreams Come True and the Make-Believe of Christmas Eve, Mrs. Gillespie had sat with a set face.

Clancy came out with her bag on Christmas Day, having first visited the little mother who was so pleased and proud to have had allotted to her almost the same time as had that other Mother with the Christ Child.

The inmates were taking Christmas seriously, Clancy was pleased to find. Mr. Piper was dressed in all the Santa trappings and doing the rounds. Only, alas, something happened. Mr. Piper fainted. Mr. Brown who ran the St. John's at the Hostel came forward at once and loosened the beard and tunic.

"Heat prostration," he diagnosed.

Mr. Piper recovered miraculously after a long and pertinent drink and insisted on finishing the festive business.

That he did it in shorts and sandals and carrying his beard in his hand apparently did not seem amiss to anyone, unless it was Mrs. Gillespie, and looking around Clancy saw that she had gone indoors.

"What's it matter, anyway?" pointed out Mr. Piper wisely. "Everyone knows it isn't the thought, it's the gift that counts."

Clancy laughed with the rest . . . and then her laughter left her.

Coming across the strip of green outside the Hostel was Guy Osman . . . and he was crossing to her.

CHAPTER 13

HE sat beside her on one of the benches. He began talking pleasantly to those around him . . . the Tauntons, Bert Smith, Jack Gillespie. He talked for quite a while with Mr. Gillespie.

Clancy, who soon moved away to join the children in a game of Botany Bay, saw Guy take out a notebook and pencil.

Always writing memos, she thought angrily. People mean nothing to him except data.

" 'Here comes an old woman from Botany Bay,' " chanted Clancy's side.

" 'What have you got to do today?' " chanted the rival team.

" 'Anything to please you.' "

" 'Set to work and do it.' "

Clancy set to work with the rest . . . it was Dressing a Christmas Tree and it looked like a winner at first, for no one seemed to be able to guess.

Then Guy was calling out the answer and racing after the old women . . . after *one* old woman, not so old . . . name of Clancy.

He caught her just before Base. She was laughing hilariously, straining to escape him, then suddenly she felt his fingers tightening so that she could not move, and then she stopped fighting.

Standing there in the midst of the children racing to Base pursued by their own screaming, she seemed all at once to be standing in silence.

And in the middle of that silence Clancy heard something, she heard a kind of secret personal alarm going off. The alarm was the fact that unwilled, unasked, unwanted, she was coming to care for this tall, cold, enlightened Australian who held her in those tight arms.

The shock of her discovery struck inwards. She stood there trembling in the surprise of the disclosure. He's unsympathetic, misunderstanding, overbearing, dominating, he—he's frozen, but I'm getting to *care* about him, she thought.

He still kept tight hold of her, so tight that she could not even quiver.

It mustn't be that, protested her shocked heart, it *mustn't* be. Love is a warmth, a reaching out between people, and there could never be that—from him.

I don't love this man. I *can't*.

She withdrew. It was difficult because the fingers kept holding her. At last she pulled almost violently away and jumped to the other side of Base.

"You cheated, Clancy," called a child voice. "You were caught, I saw you!"

"Yes," said Guy Osman, "she is a cheat."

They started another round of Botany Bay, but this time children only. Clancy would have joined in if only to get away from him, but he had hold of her again, under the elbow this time, quite lightly yet nonetheless definitely, and he was taking her to his car.

As she went to get in something attracted her. It was her bag on the back seat.

"Yes," he answered her unasked question. "I put it there. You're not stopping at the Hostel, Miss Clyde."

"Who packed my things back again?"

"Mrs. Gillespie did. You might have noticed she was not present. I came here earlier and told her what I proposed. Being Mrs. Gillespie she was very approving."

"Of what?"

"Of not having you . . . having anyone . . . stay at the Hostel."

"I'm stopping."

"You are not."

She had got into the car . . . after all, it was no use protesting when her possessions were already there and not back in her room . . . and coming round to the driver's seat he got in, too.

"It's not your right place," he said coolly. "You were

97

only being 'fitted in.' Also as far as I can see of the *Loch Maree* batch there now remains only a handful to whom to play the little mother."

"I had no intention of playing that," she said sullenly, but she was thinking unwillingly that the other thing he had said was true. Of all batches of immigrants perhaps this batch had been the most fortunate. Right and left they had snared houses, flats, rooms. There only remained a handful, as he had observed. The rest of the hostellers were now strangers to her.

"I don't believe you're aware why I came here," she said stiffly as the car moved away from the kerb.

"Perfectly aware. Mrs. Stanton is in hospital with her baby."

"I suppose that makes no sense to you," she blurted.

"On the contrary," he baited, "I'm a firm believer in family life. I intend one day to have a family of my own."

"Not that. I meant my stopping on in the cottage."

"On the contrary again, I'm a firm believer in propriety. That's why I'm removing you from the Hostel now."

"What?"

"Removing you. Hence the bag. There are few single rooms at Bunnerong, it's mostly family accommodation. The authorities are agreeable but not burningly enthusiastic over young women being housed there. It could encourage hangers-on."

"You," accused Clancy in a rage, "have been talking to old Lucas."

"Yes, I have been talking to old Lucas. He said girls bring trouble, pretty girls big trouble. Then he paid you a compliment, Miss Clyde. He said yours would be the big sort because you were a pretty girl."

"Lucas dodders," cried Clancy angrily.

"Perhaps," shrugged Guy, "but I, too, have the evidence of my eyes."

"If that's meant as another compliment——"

"It was a statement." Guy shrugged again. "I'm not acutely aware of looks."

"Yet you told me once it must be satisfactory to the

98

Immigration to have a young and attractive female boomerang," Clancy flashed.

"I see," he flashed back, "that you keep my words in mind."

"Does that please you?"

"Yes . . . as a matter of fact."

"You like your sarcasm to be recalled."

"I like to know you remember," he said quite simply.

She noticed that they were travelling east . . . to the coast.

"Where are you going?"

"I want to talk with you. I couldn't back there."

"No, I noticed that. I noticed that you were concentrating on Mr. Gillespie."

"Anything wrong in such concentration?"

"Nothing, but nothing right either."

"What do you mean?"

"You were not doing it in a helpful spirit," she said. "You were using Mr. Gillespie merely as material."

"I've told you many times that I'm a business man, not an author."

"Yet you're writing a book on local publications."

"I'm editing it," he said. He negotiated a bend.

"We will discuss what is to be discussed out at La Perouse."

"There again?"

"I'm sorry, some other place, then. I'd forgotten how soon you tire of a scene."

She did not answer, and he did not change their venue.

They came suddenly on the blue shout of Pacific Ocean, the green hill with the little plot of French soil, the shell-selling lubra, the boomerang man.

They did not get out of the car. They just sat there watching the little launch crossing to Kurnell, a white snake of foam in its wake.

"Well?" Clancy asked.

He did not speak for a while.

When he did it seemed he had to rouse himself to do it. He seemed quite content just to sit there and look out. But what he had to say he said directly.

"I'm taking you to Greenmarley, Miss Clyde."

"To where?"

"It's a century-old house on the Lane Cove, you might remember, and it has a bell-tower."

"You're being ridiculous!" she protested.

"In what way?"

"Thinking I shall go there when—when——"

"When?" he asked, brows raised.

"When I'm moving out of the cottage for that reason," she flung at him, and she knew her cheeks were scarlet.

"You mean avoid one act of impropriety to adopt another. But, my dear virtuous child, I have a housekeeper, you may recall."

If she could have got out of the car she would. But the same thought must have occurred to him. The lazy arm at the back of the seat now had hold of the door handle.

"Calm down," he advised. "Besides the housekeeper, Dallas will be there."

"Dallas?"

"As a matter of fact it's as much because of her that I want you to come. Whatever you might gather to the contrary, I'm a very discreet man."

"Why will Dallas be there?"

"Her apartment is being reorganized. An author is susceptible to these things."

"Does Dallas know you've asked me?"

"Yes."

A dozen questions rushed to Clancy's lips. How does she like another woman there? . . . What did she say? . . . In what way did she react?

"She doesn't like it," said Guy Osman, reading the unspoken words, "but she was happier when I extended the invitation to Simon."

"Simon?"

"Yes."

"Is Simon's apartment also being reorganized?"

"Simon," said Guy Osman drily, "flutters from hotel to hotel, he has no fixed abode. I'd keep that in mind if I were you."

"Why?" she asked directly.

Again his brows raised, but this time in undisguised incredulity. He did not answer her question, he just let that incredulous look be his own hateful reply.

"What are you staging," asked Clancy, deciding to be silent on the subject, too, "a house party?"

"I could say I was inviting Mr. White for you," Osman drawled, "but I'd rather hoped the two of you would get in some work."

"What sort of work?"

"With Mrs. Frank attending to the domestic side, certainly not the housekeeping," he said shortly. "I thought the two of you could get on to White's book."

"You are publishing it?"

"Not in its present state. Perhaps not at all. Remember I employ a reader and that that reader has given a contra report."

"If my opinion was not worth consideration then surely my co-operation will be worth as much."

"I'll tell you that when I see the reconstructed book."

"*If* I help to reconstruct it."

"I think you will. I think you've become too fond of White to refuse."

She was suddenly aware that his eyes were on her, probing, searching, delving for something. She turned her glance away.

"I can help him without living in the same house as Mr. White," she pointed out.

"You mean the same house as Mr. *Osman.* All right, Miss Clyde, give me an alternative. You have a flat in view? A room? One of the girls at the office has invited you to share an apartment?"

"No, I have only the Hostel until Bronwen returns."

"A hostel would not be conducive to work. Remember old Lucas and his hangers-on. He wouldn't countenance White within half a mile of your dormitory. All your work would have to be done in the common-room, Miss Clyde."

As she still sat silent he said briskly, "Come, be sensible. Until Mrs. Stanton comes out of hospital Greenmarley is the *only* place."

The launch was plodding back from Kurnell, the next

crossers had gathered on the jetty. Some fishing boats were coming in, too, and a crowd was collecting to help with the beaching and to buy the wares.

"Make up your mind, Miss Clyde, before I go down to select our fish. An extra mouth to feed, you know."

"Hasn't my mind been made up for me?" she said bitterly. Then she said pettishly, "And fish on Christmas Day is outlandish."

"This whole land is outlandish," he reminded her remorselessly, "or so an ex-migrant once said. But all that is over now. The burning question concerns the migrant, ex no longer, and whether she takes fish."

"Yes, I take it," climbed down Clancy.

She walked to the beach with him, saw him choose big silver bream.

They came back to the car, then abandoned the blue coast for a green river. For Greenmarley.

Even before they swept through the big old gates Clancy felt the charm of the place upon her again. She turned her head away because she had a curious feeling that, although his eyes were strictly on the road, really he was looking at her.

And she did not want Guy Osman to know that in this minute in the drive-sweeping car that she felt an odd sense of coming home.

CHAPTER 14

GREENMARLEY could have housed fourteen as comfortably as four. But housing only four rendered it possible for that four to go days without seeing each other . . . made it simple, for Clancy anyway, to slip into an empty room if she glimpsed someone she did not want to meet coming down one of the long flagged halls.

She did this frequently—with Dallas and Guy. She did not do it with Simon. She liked being with Simon; anyway she did not have a chance to avoid him, for Simon practically never left her side. From morning to night, whether working on the book, or resting, Simon was there.

They were well into *The Everlasting Stars* by this. Not having to attend the office had given Clancy the opportunity to keep Simon regularly at work. He needed supervision. Without it he would have turned in little better than the rather slipshod manuscript that Guy first had handed Clancy to read and assess. She had assessed it with enthusiasm, but she had not been blind to its inadequacies. Now, between them, perhaps these inadequacies could be overcome.

So word by word, chapter by chapter, Simon's book began emerging purely, rather—or so Clancy often thought —like a gem emerging purely from encasing stone.

Now she could see why Guy had hesitated. The manuscript had not been ready, as he had said.

But as the beauty of Simon's words unfolded and became more beautiful after deeper consideration and more searching care, Clancy kept wondering how any reader could have failed to recognize its intrinsic worth.

It reached all lofty heights, she thought, it plumbed deep depths. She believed in this book.

She found it easy to avoid the other two in the house,

for Mrs. Frank, on her request, had waived set meals and provided instead an open kitchen. By choosing hours when she knew Guy would be away from Greenmarley Clancy managed very well.

But one afternoon she was caught. She had sent Simon up to revise a passage, then decided to spend the time till he returned in brewing a pot of tea.

Mrs. Frank was out, but that made no difference. She was on good terms with Mrs. Frank, who had told her to come and help herself whenever she wished.

"A woman's kitchen is very close to a woman's heart, but I don't mind *you* coming in, dear, you're not"—Mrs. Frank had sniffed—"like some people." Clancy knew that Dallas and Mrs. Frank did not get on at all well. Dallas had done the unpardonabe . . . intruded without first being asked. The pair had warred silently since that first trespass.

Clancy pottered around the big old kitchen now, finding untold pleasure in having the room all to herself. As she boiled the electric kettle she laughed softly. This old galley was made for big black pots, for shining copper pans, not the electric mod cons with which Mrs. Frank had been provided.

She dragged over a stool to reach the cookie jar, chuckling to herself again. You would have thought this was a house of children and cookies to be stacked out of reach. But then, she recalled, Mrs. Frank was a substantial person and probably did not have to drag across a stool. She decided that, as regards cookies and processions, under-averages like herself were at a definite disadvantage.

It was not until she was aloft the stool that Guy came up behind her. He had been there a while watching her. The kitchen was not the modern bright type, it had dim concealing corners. When he put up his arms and swung her down again Clancy gave a little scream.

"Sorry," he said, "I didn't mean to startle you."

"It's such a stupid thing to do," she cried. "I could have hurt myself."

"What, in my arms? Though perhaps being in such a position automatically would inflict a hurt on you." He waited for an answer.

104

She was quite shaken. It was a huge old house and she had believed that there was only Porter in the garden and Simon in his room.

"It could have been a stranger," she defended.

"Wasn't it, Miss Clyde?" he suggested.

When she did not respond he said. "Why have you been avoiding me? Have I the plague or something?"

"Don't be absurd!"

"Then don't *you*. Jumping into empty rooms whenever you hear my footsteps. Hiding behind doors. Did you think I didn't know?"

She had thought that; she did not know now how he had been aware that she was hiding. Perhaps a shadow had showed. perhaps——

"No," he said, reading her thoughts in that uncanny way of his, "I believe I could sense you wherever you hid, Clancy Clyde."

She felt very childish standing there at the foot of the steps and still in the lazy circle of his arms.

"Well, I'm down now," she remarked.

"Yes," he agreed, but he still did not remove the arms.

Aggravated, she ducked down and escaped under them. She made for the door, but with surprising agility for such a tall man he was there before her.

"Far be it from me to spoil a cosy cuppa," he drawled. "Go ahead, Miss Clyde, but make it for two now. Or"— glancing past the door—"should it be for three?"

"Four," she said shortly. "Porter besides Simon takes a cup."

"We'll need the big pot, then," he said, and he reached up.

He took over the tea-making, so Clancy merely set out the cups and piled a plate with cookies. Like most men he was very careful with his tea-making. He warmed the pot first, he carried the pot to the kettle, he instantly encased the brew in Mrs. Frank's large red cosy.

When he poured it he took up the outside tray before she could.

"I'll deliver it to White and Porter," he told her. "Frankly I don't trust you. You'd not come back."

"I mightn't be back when you return, anyway," she pointed out.

She said it impulsively, not meaning anything so infantile as running away from him, so was considerably annoyed when he said, "In that case——" then when he went out turning to secure the door.

She sat down at the table, fuming at the man. She had not started on her tea when the key turned in the lock and he came back into the room once more.

"Oh, you waited for me. Nice of you, Miss Clyde."

"I didn't want anything."

"And why the change of mind? You must have wanted something before—or was the brew only to revive our author?"

When she did not reply he taunted, "Don't tell me that besides all your other failings you also sulk?"

"I resent being treated as a child," she burst out.

"I resent being treated as an ogre," he came back. "What am I, to be avoided as you've been avoiding me ever since you came?"

"I'm not here socially. I'm here to work."

"Is every minute you spend with Simon White work?"

"I think so. Would you like to see how far we've progressed?"

He put two lumps into his cup, then stirred it rather absently.

"Later," he said, also rather absently. "Just now——"

"Yes, Mr. Osman?"

But it seemed after all that he had nothing to say to her. He just sat there looking through the narrow window . . . all the windows at Greenmarley were narrow and mullioned . . . but Clancy had the feeling that he was not looking out, as she was, on Porter sitting on his upturned barrow and dipping his cookie into his cup of tea, that he was looking in his mind's eye at something else.

Presently Guy Osman rose . . . and instead of being relieved Clancy knew a stab of disappointment.

"You haven't finished your cup," she pointed out.

"It doesn't matter," he said, and he went out without another word.

106

After that Clancy did not hide in empty rooms when she heard steps other than Simon's in the corridor. It meant that she ran into Dallas, and this proved anything but pleasant, but at least Guy Osman could not accuse her of regarding him as an ogre.

Not that Guy ever had anything to say to her. He simply nodded briefly and went on his way.

Dallas, however, always had something to say. On the first occasion it had been:

"Ah, Miss Clyde, so you've had yourself directed to Greenmarley this time."

"No, Miss Wyse."

"But you're here, aren't you?"

"It was not direction."

"No? Then perhaps something more subtle than that? However, as I said once before, nice for you."

Another time it was:

"Still here, Miss Clyde? Convenient of Si to write a muddle, wasn't it?"

"It was not a muddle."

"What, then?" The bold black eyes fairly snapped into Clancy's.

"It always was fine material. When Mr. White has finished I believe it will be a fine piece of work."

"*You* believe—— And how, pray, can *you* tell? Are you experienced in these things?"

"No, but——"

Dallas had lit a cigarette and she had narrowed her eyes as she inhaled.

"Then I would gather it's Mr. White who is the fine material?" she had baited.

"No."

"Then perhaps"—the eyes were narrower still—"Mr. Osman, Miss Clyde?"

Clancy hadn't answered that. She had slipped past Dallas down the hall . . . but when she had reached the end of the hall she had wanted to go back and tell Dallas the truth in case she gleaned some wrong ideas.

But what is the truth? asked something deep inside of Clancy. *Could* you go back now and say honestly to Dallas

Wyse that Guy Osman means nothing to you, nothing at all?

She knew that she could not.

She knew that that secret alarm that she had heard that day when she had played Botany Bay with the Hostel children, that alarm that had warned her that right now, unwilled, unasked, unwanted, she was coming to care for the tall Australian, had not rung without reason. She knew that overbearance, domination, coldness, all that admitted, she still felt something for this man that she would not refuse to herself, could not turn aside.

So, resigning herself to Dallas' undoubted speculation, Clancy had gone on.

But as she had walked down to the garden where Simon was working, she had thought about Dallas.

Why did the woman want both Simon and Guy? Guy, undoubtedly, was her first bid, but Simon, Clancy still felt, Dallas Wyse always kept carefully under her eye. Without question she was fond of him . . . but it was a controlled fondness, it was a disciplined affection. Or was *possession* the right word?

Yes, possession, decided Clancy . . . possession is what Dallas feels about Simon, she thinks of him as her possession. And perhaps he is that, too, but would one speak derogatively of a possession as Dallas just spoke of Simon and his work?

What had she called his work? A muddle.

But it was never that . . . and Dallas, an intelligent woman, must know it.

Was Dallas the reader who had told Guy it was not a good work? And why would Dallas say that?

But when Clancy joined Simon she put all such thoughts behind her. She left the world of reality and entered Simon's world . . . that world of beauty, of flowing words —of everlasting stars.

She noticed that Simon looked tired. He never did appear robust. But now his eyes had dark rings of fatigue.

"You must rest tomorrow, Simon," she said.

"Yes, I thought that." Simon ran his fingers through his thick fair hair.

"Where will we go, Clancy?" he asked.

"I was speaking of *you*."

"Yes, but we must be together." All at once Simon must have become aware of what he had said, for he flushed.

"Why must we be together, Simon?" asked Clancy quietly. She felt there was something here to be understood. But Simon was more alert now.

"Yes, I'll put the book away tomorrow and rest," he agreed.

It was just as well he did. They were now into January and the "dog days" had begun.

Mostly it was shimmery summer weather, but occasionally a hundred degrees and over would slip in, and then all you wanted to do was lie around and sip long cool drinks.

This day proved a "dog day." At dawn it was well over ninety.

Guy, in the Australian's summer "uniform" of white shirt and grey slacks, warned his house guests that it would reach a hundred and ten by noon.

"Don't go out in it . . . sit on the verandah. With luc! we'll have a southerly buster in the afternoon."

Clancy obeyed in the morning. She sat on the ston flags, usually chilled flags but today clammy and warm.

Mrs. Frank disappeared to her room after lunch. "I'm all done up," she confessed.

Clancy came out to the flags again, but did not sit down. The sun had slipped round the house and the big slabs of stone were red-hot. She certainly couldn't stop here. Suddenly she thought of the river, the green tranquil Lane Cove. She put on a sun-hat and wandered down.

Even the cicadas were silenced today, there was no bird-song, the usual jocky lizards that scuttled away as you approached must have been prostrated as well.

Down by the river it was cooler, though . . . as cool as any place bar a refrigerator could have been on a day like today.

Clancy had never been down to the river since that afternoon she had wandered along the bank and met the *Loch Maree* purser. And come up to Greenmarley to find Guy Osman there.

Now that she looked at it she was surpised to see that the old house had its own baths.

It was a wonder that Guy had not mentioned this before, it would have been fun to have had an early morning swim. Had it not meant a climb back in the broiling sun she would have swum now.

But why not now? She was wearing only a brief sunsuit that could easily improvise.

Barely had the thought struck her than Clancy was tossing down her hat, kicking off her shoes and wading in. The water was not exhilarating, but it was distinctly pleasant. She did not dive or do anything strenuous, she simply floated on her back and gazed up at the overhanging trees. Seen through the green leaves the sky did not look so brazen blue. A delicious torpor took possession of Clancy. I believe I could go to sleep here, she said drowsily, just float and dream . . .

She was awakened rudely.

Guy Osman did not wait to call to her, to throw a branch or a pebble to arouse her, he simply raced in just as he was, immaculate grey slacks, white shirt.

"You little fool!" he called, and he half dragged, half impelled her up on the bank.

"What are you doing?" she started to say, but she did not get it out.

For the Australian was shaking her . . . shaking her with the unleashed fury of a man who has just seen a close brush with death. He shook and shook. He shook Clancy until her ash hair hung in wisps over her eyes, till her teeth literally chattered, till she gasped between breaths for him to stop.

He did stop, and she saw as she pushed back her hair that his brow was wet with the violence he had put into the shaking of her.

I only hope he collapses from it, she told herself with hate.

"You fool," he repeated thickly. "What made you do such a foolish thing as that?"

"As what?"

Exhausted though he was, though she was, for a moment Clancy believed he was going to repeat the performance.

She half stepped back.

"As going in there," he snapped, and he pointed to the river.

"Why not? This is quite as good as a suit." She looked down at her sun-rompers already drying in the hot air.

"The water," he said hoarsely. "This is not the protected end of the Lane Cove above the weir, this is a river that runs into the harbour."

"Well?" she asked.

Now he fairly shouted at her. "Hasn't anything occurred to you even yet? Hasn't—*danger?*"

"The baths——" she volunteered.

"—Are not in use. They haven't been for years, not since there was a child at Greenmarley, and that was when I was a boy. Look at the gaps in the wire, look at the tumbled piers."

She looked, but was still unperturbed.

"Well?" she asked again.

He stared at her incredulously.

Then he said, "Sharks."

"Sharks? But sharks are on beaches."

"You stupid child, you half-wit, they're *more* in the rivers, in the quiet waters, they abound in the secluded reaches of the Lane Cove and the Parramatta."

"Then," said Clancy, more lightly than she felt, "I've been fortunate indeed."

"More fortunate than you will ever realize," he said soberly. "Porter sets a bait every night in these old baths. It's been his burning ambition for months to catch the monster that took Bellboy last year."

"Bellboy?"

"Porter's retriever Bellboy used to swim in the baths."

Clancy could not hide her dismay now. For all the heat of the day she began to shiver.

"Has the bait ever been taken?" she whispered.

"Frequently. It's a continual fight between man and fish, and so far fish has won. If Porter had known you were

111

coming down here he would have stopped you in your tracks."

"Why did you come down?" she asked.

"To tell you that Bronwen Stanton has gone on to a mothercraft home for a week or two, in which case you will have to content yourself at Greenmarley for another spell."

"You sound ungracious about it."

He did not speak for a while, but looking at him she saw that that was not because he had nothing to say but because he had first to control himself.

"Do you think I can be gracious at the prospect of housing someone who should by rights now be mangled and torn and dragged away to some dark river bend?"

"You're exaggerating."

"Am I? Then look for yourself." He had impelled her round.

"That's what I saw when I came down to the bank," he said, "only it was closer then than it is now."

Clancy stared horrified . . . saw the long ominous form cruising just outside the hole in the wire . . . saw it inch past the tumbled pier . . . saw the grim sweep of its dorsal fin cut the surface with only the slightest of ripples to stir the fallen floating leaves. It looked twice the length of this man.

"It would touch thirteen feet," he said.

She sank down, sick with horror, and he did nothing at all to help her. He did not assist her in any way.

He simply said, "When you've recovered you'd better make your way back to the house. I'm going up now."

And he went.

CHAPTER 15

CLANCY had longer than the "week or two" more at Green-marley. She had a month.

If she had known in advance she certainly would have searched very thoroughly for other accommodation, but as it was each succeeding day brought the hope that this was the last day, and so the days of January grew into February, and the year got into its stride.

Bronwen had not picked up as she should have; Holly was still a much-too-tiny babe.

It was mostly the weather. It was a bad time for any new mother, let alone a not quite acclimatized one. It was proving an exceptionally hot summer, and because Bron was inexperienced with both heat and babies it was thought best to keep her at the mothercraft home.

"She'll be all right," Dick told Clancy. "These people know their mothers and infants. They should, you know. The Tresillian method was born only across the way, in New Zealand, Clan."

Clancy smiled at his "across the way." It was remarkable how soon, even in an Australian city, you began to toss distances around as though they were a section in a bus.

She went out to see Bron, and was relieved to find a little colour coming back to her cheeks, to be reassured that Holly was getting as big as a house. The extra weeks were doing a lot of good.

But they were not doing someone else good, Clancy thought, coming back to Greenmarley. They were not doing *her* good. Although she loved the old house, although she knew she always would, she did not like it under these conditions . . . Simon always beside her in that persistent, almost *contrived* way, Dallas sending her deliberate barbs,

113

Guy . . . most of all Guy. Guy might have been a stranger, for sometimes he did not even nod, at the most he would only pass a curt time of day.

Simon's book was through its first revision now. The subsequent revisions were not so important. It was no longer necessary for the pair of them, Simon and Clancy, to hurry over breakfast each morning and settle down to a long day's work. Indeed Clancy felt that she could return to the office and spend only the evenings on Simon.

Gathering her courage one day, for it took courage to corner that tall, unsmiling man, Clancy suggested this to Guy.

"Return to the office? What's wrong with Greenmarley?"

"I feel I'm poaching on you. I feel I should be back at work."

"You are working now. Why don't you answer a question when it's asked, Miss Clyde, not bypass it?"

"Did I?"

"I asked you what was wrong with Greenmarley."

"Nothing is wrong."

"But you find the entire day here boring?"

"I didn't say so, Mr. Osman. I said I thought I should be back to work."

"But by that you meant the office?"

He should have been a prosecutor, his questions, his assessments, his denunciations came so thick and fast.

Defeated by the quickfire cross-examination, Clancy said wearily, "Yes, I meant the office, and I want to go back there."

"Because you're tired of it here?"

"Why ask when you've already decided the answers?"

He ignored that.

"Because you're tired of Greenmarley?" he persisted.

"Yes, yes, yes!"

He took out a cigarette and lit it. Maddeningly he said, "Why didn't you admit to that in the first place?"

When she did not speak . . . *could* not, in fact . . . he went on.

"All right, start back at Jarrah . . . then if you think you can fit in White's stuff after office hours, go ahead. I'm

114

sorry that's all I can do for you." The blue eyes, icy even on this hot February day, looked unemotionally into Clan's.

"What else is there to do?" she ventured.

"Get you away altogether, for that's what you want, isn't it? I'm sorry that Mrs. Stanton has been so misguided as not to recover at once, if only on *your* behalf; I'm sorry that in this bursting city I'm unable to find you a room."

"Thank you," said Clancy. "I'm sure if you could you would."

"Rest assured of that," he said.

The next visit to the mothercraft home found Bron with cheeks like pink carnations because the doctor had said by the end of the week she could go home.

"Holly is ready, too," Bron beamed.

That night Dick telephoned Clancy. She was going over Simon's work that he had completed that day when Guy Osman came to tell her there was a call, and that she could take it from the office. The old house, because of its size, had been well supplied with plugs.

Clancy accepted the phone from Guy and went into the den.

"Yes?" she asked.

"Clan, it's Dick."

"Yes, Dick?"

"One guess, Clan my darling."

"I don't even need that," laughed Clancy. "Only one thing could cause such rejoicing in your voice. It's Our House."

"You Sibyl, how did you know?"

"Don't waste time on me, tell me about It. Has Bron been told? Where is the house? When will you move?"

"It's lovely . . . it really is, Clancy. No, I'm telling Bron at visiting time tonight. It's in quite a handy area for such a latecomer as I am . . . only a few miles out from Ryde. There's a view of the Parramatta, of the Blue Mountains, and with binoculars you can follow the drive-in movies."

"That will save you a television," laughed Clan.

"The last question of When . . . straight away. I'll move Bronwen directly there."

"Oh, Dick, how splendid," enthused Clancy with him.

She was still enthusiastic for quite some time after she had replaced the phone. Then suddenly she was remembering something . . . remembering *somebody* . . .

Herself.

Where do I go now? she thought.

She always had intended leaving when the Stantons left, but she had not expected it quite this soon. She realized now that as well as pore over Simon's work she should have pored over the newspaper advertisements, she should have interviewed agents, knocked on landladies' doors. Of course there was always the Hostel, but having booked in and then not taken residence after all . . . blame Guy Osman for that . . . made her feel that the Hostel, with its censorious Lucas, must be the last on the list.

No, not the last. Greenmarley must be that.

She did not tell anyone her dismay, not even the girls at the office. She knew they would have fitted her in immediately, but she knew also that already their accommodation was sadly taxed.

"We have to get up singly," Daph once had wailed, "and that time Janet started physical jerks we all had to get out of the room. I tell you, Clancy, there isn't space for even a thought."

She wondered who would go into the Stantons' emergency cottage . . . then she hoped they would enjoy the daffodils. She guessed, what with packing, moving *and* a new baby, that the lifting of the bulbs would not get done after all.

Thinking of the bulbs made her think of the Gillespies. It was not a surprising trend of thought, for after all who was nearer to daffodils than someone from England? Daffodils, narcissi, bluebells *were* England. Oh, how lovely if the Gillespies could get the unit.

Away from the community life Mrs. Gillespie might alter her opinions . . . undoubtedly room could be found, for a while, anyway, for an old friend.

Clancy ran to the hallway and took up the phone. She told Dick what had occurred to her . . . not helped at all by Guy Osman's abrupt halt as he went down the hall.

"Sorry, old girl, that would be out of my province," said

116

Dick. Then he said, "Clancy, we're in a hole. Can you come over to the home tonight and talk it out with us?"

"Why, Dick," said Clancy a little puzzled, instantly forgetting her disappointment for the Gillespies, "of course."

When she put down the phone at length she saw that Guy Osman was now waiting for her.

But *his* wait, he promptly and baldly told her, was nothing to the wait some *Australians* had suffered.

"Years," he expostulated angrily, "of making do in inadequate rooms, yet *you* plan to fit in a family who haven't been here half a year."

"I didn't plan it, I just suggested it, and it was not because of what you think, I mean not entirely, it was also——"

"Yes?" he asked.

But she could not tell him, of course, she could not tell him that once she left his roof she had nowhere else to go, that her scheme for the Gillespies had included that as well.

"Seeing you're so concerned over your fellow Australians," she said cuttingly instead, "why don't you open up your own house?"

"That's quite an idea," he agreed, "except that I've had my final notice that it's to come down."

"What?"

"Greenmarley is to come down."

"Come down?" She stared at him dully, not properly comprehending.

"There's to be a high-speed road through here, an express way. Oh, I'm not belly-aching. This country is new and modern. It's not old enough in civilization years to hang on to old ideas."

"But—but——" She looked out of the narrow window, seeing the flagged verandah, the fluted pillars . . . Then she recalled the air of regret she first had felt with the house and understood why she had sensed its sadness. It was because the house knew what was to happen, and was sad. She was saddened herself.

Osman shrugged. "It will be a pang . . . I have to admit that . . . but a lot of the building could be transferred, if I

117

wished. These present pillars were, as a matter of fact, originally from Macquarie Street's old Burdekin House."

She nodded, seeing his point, admiring him—unwillingly—for his acceptance. The next moment the admiration was gone, for again he was criticizing her, taunting, baiting.

She refused to listen, she said, "Excuse me, please," and went past him. None of the Greenmarley halls was wide, this one was so narrow that when she brushed by him he was only a breath away. She was annoyed, when she reached her room, to find how badly shaken she was by that quick brush.

Dick met her at the hospital gates.

He did not say anything until after they had greeted Bron and peeped at Holly, and then he found three chairs—for of course Bron was up and about now—and they formed a little group.

"It's like this, Clancy," said Dick.

"Yes," appealed Bron, "it's like this."

Out it poured.

They knew how anxious Clancy was to be on her own . . . who could blame her, who wanted her to share a house with a very new young Australian who, Matron had warned, was an excellent night-crier, but——

"But, Clan, if you could only put it off, even just for a while," appealed Dick.

"Clan, if you'd only come to Our House with us and help me get on my feet," begged Bron.

Clancy just sat there and stared, and taking her silence as reluctance they begged stronger and louder.

"If you want to know how helpless I am, ask Sister who consistently wins the all-thumbs contest at nappy time," wailed Bron.

"Clan, the yard is a mess—lime, bricks and mortar, it'll take me weeks of unremitting effort just to clear it. If you could just be keeping the eye that I should be keeping on Bron I'd be eternally thankful."

All at once Clancy's laughter bubbled through . . . laughter with tears not far behind.

It was so lovely, so—so *blessed* to be wanted, as she felt she genuinely was wanted now by these two dear friends.

They were looking at her eagerly, and when she assured them she would come they flashed relieved smiles.

She was smiling herself as she left them, she was smiling as she came back to Greenmarley. But for a while she stood at the head of the drive looking down at the gracious old house, wondering how Guy could face up to progress like he did. But in a way that, too, was tradition. To look forward, not backward, could be this young land's first tradition.

She wondered if Dallas knew yet about the fate of Greenmarley. She did not think so. Dallas still wore that acquisitive expression whenever she looked round the old place.

She walked slowly along the drive, and halfway down Guy Osman stepped out from the hedge of rhododendrons and walked with her.

Presently he halted her with a touch of his hand. "Just where you stand will run the express way," he said. "It will verge here, then cut down the house."

"Will you do anything before that happens?"

"Appeal, you mean? No. The Historical Trust have done that already, but to no avail. Frankly I'm not so whole-hearted over it, either. It's a pity, but to my way of thinking inevitable. Progress is inevitable." He glanced at her. "You wouldn't understand that, of course."

She said, "I might."

"You surprise me—the steeped-in-history English girl?"

"Don't forget I boomeranged," she said.

Before he could make another comment she asked, "Will you build Greenmarley again? Take along what you can of it . . . the flags, the pillars, the same as was done from old Burdekin House?"

He shrugged carelessly. "What would be the use? I'm not a family man."

"And yet you told me you were a firm believer in family life, that you intended one day to have a family of your own."

As he had said once before he said again, "I see that you keep my words in mind."

They were nearly on the stone court now, so there was

119

no time to answer. Clancy was glad of that, for she had no answer. She could not reply, "No, I don't keep them in mind" when by her own evidence she did.

And what could she say if he asked *why* she remembered all he said?

How could she answer to this man what she knew now herself?

CHAPTER 16

THE Stantons . . . and Clancy . . . were moved by the end of the week.

When Clancy had announced her new plans over supper that night Guy Osman had drawled, "But of course we must have a farewell party for Miss Clyde."

"That's not necessary," Clancy had said.

"A lot of things are unnecessary," he had pointed out. For no reason, it seemed, he had added, "In the beginning."

Dallas had agreed about a farewell party. Undoubtedly she would be pleased to see the end of a second female in the house. Mrs. Frank, of course, did not count with Dallas.

So again there was the candlelit table, the gleaming linen and shining silver . . . Dallas this time in luxurious flame silk, Clancy, to be perverse, in the very simple tussore she had planned to wear but not worn on the first occasion.

At this dinner there was no Greenmarley history told . . . and Clancy wondered what Dallas's reactions would have been if suddenly Guy Osman had leaned forward and said that quite soon there would be no future history to be recorded by the old house.

"I don't expect, Miss Clyde," said Guy after dinner, "that you'd care once more to inspect the bell-tower?"

"What is there to see," she answered, "that I haven't seen before?"

"You mean only shadows and cobwebs?"

"Yes."

He was lighting a cigarette.

"Nothing, as you say." He shrugged.

That great day of leaving hospital with your first child

came round for Bronwen. She wore a new blue frock that Clancy had bought for her, feeling that a mother should be dressed up as well as a baby, but Bronwen was still uneasy as a star on a first night.

"The ward was never like this," she confided, gingerly picking up her young daughter. "You felt you weren't the only one to grab your infant the wrong way."

"That's the right way, Bronnie."

"Well, I feel awkward. I feel everyone is laughing."

Bron looked unhappily at Clancy.

"I never told you before, but I was a teacher in England. I never taught here because straightway I started with Baby . . . but I've graduated, Clancy. In Greek! Yet I don't know how to pick up my child. I'm scared to death."

"Pooh," said Clancy, picking Holly out of Bron's arms, "I wouldn't let you carry her out, anyway, not while Aunt Clan is about."

"You're a darling. I'm so glad you're helping us in this muddle."

Dick applauded that.

Clancy was glad, too, not just because of herself but because Matron had had a word in Clancy's ear.

"Her unsureness is because she's still not quite up to par. It's a big relief to me to know that you'll be going to the new home with her. There's always such a lot to do in a brand-new house."

There certainly was.

When Clancy saw the yard she could have cried. Bronwen did.

"We'll never get it clear," she wailed, and Dick's and Clancy's rather dubious "Of course we will" rang very hollow.

But they did . . . and in the first week-end.

On Saturday morning there was a knock at the door.

"We're here to help you, mate, only remember next week you join the navvies, too," twenty males voices chorused.

"Will I!" concurred Dick gratefully.

Bron and Clan spent the morning brewing tea and baking scones for the workers, standing at the window and marvelling just how much can be done when twenty men bend determined backs.

By five o'clock every broken brick had been removed, every hardened pile of old cement, all scraps of timber and asbestos, the yard was bare and clean.

Dick shook his head at the fresh teapot Clan held aloft, and went up the road for a different brand of refreshment with the "mates" instead.

"I can't believe it," Bronwen said for the hundredth time. "It's just too wonderful."

In her delight she swung up Holly and handled her like any mother of a large brood. Then she caught Clancy's amused glance and laughed.

"I believe we're settling in, Clan."

"I believe you are," Clancy beamed.

By some happy fortune the Stantons' house was the last cottage of a little blind street that had been fitted in to use every inch of a large, rather irregular estate. It could be End of the Lane just as Bron had yearned. When it was called that there would be complete representation, Clancy decided, for the first house was named—probably nostalgically—Naples, and the others had followed suit with their own native cities. The Australian owners, of course, had borrowed aboriginal names, sweet, sound-spilling names that captured in a few syllables a wealth of information. Quite seriously one of only four letters was interpreted to Clancy as "peaceful home on forehead of hill with view of river and mountain and courting the north wind."

After that Clancy felt that the Stantons would be very redundant with their End of the Lane.

A housing settlement, Clancy found, was almost as much community-living as a hostel. But she liked it, and she saw that Dick and Bron did, too.

All these people were on the same footing as each other, they had the same limited means, the same bright ambitions . . . mostly they had the same small beginning of a family.

"Clancy," announced Bronwen one evening, "there are

forty-nine houses in this settlement and forty-eight babies under six months."

She was no longer apprehensive as to her management of Holly. She slung her nonchalantly into her arms just as the new Hungarian mother did . . . the Italian . . . the Australian girl who had had twins.

Clancy loved to see the prams go by . . . brown eyes, black eyes, blue eyes . . . all being gooed at in different languages, but when these babies grew up they would be the same, speak the same language. They would be Australians.

This country that had opened its brown and weathered arms had done a good thing, Clancy thought.

She said so to Dick that night, and he agreed.

"But don't forget Australia's necessity for population for the sake of sheer existence," he reminded. "That's why the absorption of a second million is now on the way.

"Don't forget, too, that Australia gains too . . . gains new cultural vitality."

"I have wondered that," Clancy admitted.

"It's true. After the real problem is solved, the only problem actually, that problem of overcoming loneliness, homesickness, language difficulties and strange customs, then there is the benefit, Clan. Allow a period for adjustment . . . assimilation if you like . . ."

Clancy suggested, "Belonging?"

"Yes, belonging is the word, and then everything will be right."

Clancy believed this when she talked to some of the European mothers. Their husbands had come out first, worked willingly in their directed jobs for the stipulated two years, saved hard for a house, then sent for their wives.

"But how do you talk so well in so short a time?" Clancy asked incredulously.

"There are English teachers on each migrant ship. Also we still take class. Our instructor said over four hundred thousand now are taking English class."

It was good to see no huddling together amongst this little portion of a million post-war adventurers from the Old World.

"Old World," echoed Dick when Clancy said it that evening. "Clan, you're so wrong, my child. That world's as young as my Holly. And on that subject I have something to announce, my dear."

"Nice?"

"Very nice. For you."

"What do you mean?"

"Well, we don't come into it, Bron and I."

"Come into what?"

"The old world."

"Dick, if you keep baiting me . . ."

"I'm not, I'm telling you, or trying to."

"All you're babbling about is age."

"That's my subject. So you think Europe is old. It's young, Clan. It's Australia that is hoary with years."

"Oh, I know all that. I mean I've read it, but——"

"But now you'll be seeing it to prove it to yourself," Dick smiled.

"Seeing what?"

"The Centre. The Centre of this oldest country on earth."

"I . . . what . . . I mean . . . why, Dick!" Clancy stared at him.

"I don't suppose I should have mentioned it before you get the official invitation," Dick beamed, "but one's coming, Clan, and it'll be the experience of your life."

"Tell me," she urged.

"It's to mark the centenary of exploration in the Northern Territory. Only a hundred years," Dick mused, "yet this country's years are estimated in many millions."

"But why *me?*" said Clancy, puzzled. "Why not someone else?"

"There'll be lots else . . . V.I.P.s, visitors, others . . . but someone in the Department has had the happy idea of including the Boomerang Girl. It will be great publicity overseas."

Clancy said unenthusiastically, "More photos, I expect."

"Look here, my child, most Australians haven't penetrated to the Centre, yet you're complaining that you might have to put up with a few shots."

"I'm not complaining, Dick, but on the other hand I'll

admit I can't share your burning enthusiasm. All I can imagine of the Centre is desert. Desert and emptiness, nothing else."

"All the same you won't refuse to go?" asked Dick anxiously.

"No, I would like to go, I suppose, I would like to see all Australia. But I still don't know how I can."

"You're to be a guest . . . I told you that."

"I'm also a working girl. I mean I may go there at no expense, but what about my job?"

"Clancy, this is a centenary. Centenaries only happen in a hundred years."

"I'm aware of that, but is my boss?"

"I've no doubt your boss will be there at the Centre as well. It would be a writers' and artists' feast."

"Because he is there it would be no reason for him to allow *me* there," said Clancy, discouraged.

All the same, she mulled to herself, if it happened it could be a temporary solution to what I now have on my mind.

For during these last few days of this initial month with the Stantons in their new home Clancy had been aware of a change. The young householders were becoming established. They were finding their feet. She was not necessary here any more.

Bron had found a niche for herself, she was on good terms with her neighbours, the baby no longer presented any qualms. It was time, Clancy had thought, that she moved out of End of the Lane . . . and now, if this trip materialized, she could do this gracefully as she would wish.

She could do what the Migration people wanted her to do, that was go out to the Centre's celebrations, then when they were finished with her she would return and find her own place.

It was a nice smooth ending to a very happy sojourn. She determined tomorrow to put her name down on every agent's list. Surely by four weeks *someone* could fit her in?

Dick saw her smile and said to his wife, "It's slowly

126

dawning on the child that she'll be leaving this household of dull domesticity and following the steps of John Stuart."

"Who was he?"

"He discovered and named the Alice . . . Alice Springs on the map. Clancy, you certainly must look that up."

As well as look it up she brought it home with her the next day in a big volume, to be re-absorbed while Dick and Bron took turns at the binoculars directed on the Drive-In.

She had not been successful in getting any promise of a room yet, but a lot could happen in a month, she was assured.

And that was how long she should be away from New South Wales. The invitation said so. It had arrived by the afternoon mail, and it invited Miss Clancy Clyde to Alice Springs' Bangtail Muster. What on earth, thought Clancy, ˙˜ a Bangtail Muster?

Holding the invitation in her hands, seeing the aboriginal motifs, for the first time for other than personal reasons Clancy knew a vast satisfaction at being asked. More than that, she knew an unexpected thrill.

The allure of the inland . . . the inland of this oldest place on earth.

CHAPTER 17

CLANCY found it hard to gather information as to what to take and what to wear to the Centre. Dick had been right when he said that few Australians penetrated that deep.

The girls plied her with advice . . . unfortunately all different.

"It's terribly hot."

"It's not. My cousin was stationed there, it's terribly cold."

"It's a bit of both."

"In April," placated Janet, "I think it should be just right."

"Thank you," smiled Clancy ruefully, "but what is just right? I mean is it sun-frocks or woollies?"

"Both."

"Oh, dear." Clancy felt she was not getting very far.

At length they all decided she should take slacks, skirts, casuals, one dress-up dress, one formal evening.

"For the Ball," Daphne gloated.

"Rubbers if you climb Ayers Rock," put in Steph.

Their voices soared so high in their earnest instructions that Guy Osman had to wait for the noise to die down before he could speak. He had come out from his office, and while he stood there with a sheaf of papers to be attended to, he perforce had to listen to what they had to advise.

"It certainly won't be any of your faults if Miss Clyde forgets to pack something essential," he stated drily when they were depleted. But the look he flashed at Clancy made her remember with a sinking feeling that *she* had forgotten something essential.

She had forgotten to ask permission first from this man, or if not to ask permission at least to do him the courtesy of telling him what was proposed. She saw now by his expression that he was aware of this, and was displeased.

When he had gone back, and after the girls had returned to work, she went across, knocked and entered his room.

"Mr. Osman——"

"Oh, it's you. Yes?"—No name, not even a Miss Clyde from him; Clancy felt herself going red.

"I didn't intend to be rude."

He turned a page of his work.

"At least you realize you have been," he remarked.

She bit her lip. Trust Guy Osman not to take an apology graciously. She was sorry for her omission, but it had not been a *sin*.

"I intended to tell you," she said more crisply.

"That's quite considerate of you."

He paused a moment, then resumed, "I gather you were not worrying over the money."

"Money?"

"Usually if notice is not given, then a week's salary is forfeited to compensate the employer for being left, as it were, out on a branch."

Clancy looked at him uncomfortably.

"I . . . that is . . ." she stammered.

"On the other hand," said Osman, "if the employer is decently warned, then the employee is paid her right dues. That, of course, is not a rule, but it is something that is tacitly understood between employer and employee. And rightly, don't you think?"

"I . . . well . . ."

"Yes?"

There was no other way to say it, so Clancy simply blurted, "I hadn't considered *leaving*, sir."

He put the book down now, swung the chair round so that he could regard her from a better angle.

"You mean you were intending taking a month off, then calmly returning here?"

"Well, yes."

"No doubt," he said, "you even envisaged a nice swollen pay packet upon your return. Tell me, did you envisage that?"

"No, I didn't. I'm not that foolish!"

"Foolish or optimistic?" The eyes were narrowed on her now.

She murmured, "Foolish, Mr. Osman."

"I see. Now let me tell you that I'm no fool either. For only a fool would countenance his staff taking French leave whenever they pleased and then coming blithely back."

"I said I was sorry, Mr. Osman, it was only a slip. Why do you have to make such a big thing of it?"

"Why do you have to make all your arrangements but leave out the key one? Employer-employee relations are very important to me."

"I'm sure," agreed Clancy coolly, "that they would be the most important in the world."

"No," he said abruptly. "As it happens they are *not*. But they *are* the only relations I appear to possess."

She could not follow him . . . she really wasn't attempting to. She was weighing up the considerable dismay she felt at the prospect of leaving Jarrah. She loved the work, she loved the girls, she loved——

No, no, I *don't,* she hastened to tell her heart. He's everything I dislike . . . despise. It's simply that I—that I——

To her surprise his next remark was in an entirely different strain.

"I trust you're taking a supply of colour films. That is the chief attraction of the Inland—the bold exotic hues, the clear air that enables you to record them so faithfully."

"You've been there," she said eagerly.

"Yes, but I'm always happy to go back again."

This time she did not say anything, but he answered her unasked question with a casual, "Oh, yes, I certainly will be going along to the Muster."

For something to say she murmured, "Dick . . . Mr. Stanton said most writers and artists would."

"Quite right. Dallas—and White—are going."

"Simon?"

"You seem surprised. Isn't the Centre the place you would expect to find the everlasting stars?"

She did not answer him, so he went on.

"We, of course, will not be in the official party, or should I say in the presence of the V.I.P.s."

"Neither shall I."

"Oh, come, Miss Boomerang, most certainly you will. They'll photograph you sitting in the Simpson Desert, all those magnificent reds, purples, yellows and blues to contrast with your English pale hair." He gave a short laugh.

There was nothing to be gained by standing here, only his taunts, so Clancy turned to go.

But his voice stopped her, crisp, authoritative.

"You still haven't said when you leave."

She had not studied her itinerary yet, so she murmured, "The opening ceremony is at the end of April."

"I know." His voice was characteristically impatient. "But how do you arrive there? If you go overland it will take considerably longer than flying."

"I fly." She remembered part of the programme and added, "Through Broken Hill."

"I see. Then we still can expect your services till the end of the week."

Courage came back to Clancy. "And after I come back?" she enquired.

"I'd gathered that you had already settled that."

"I had, but I'm not the boss, am I?"

Suddenly, quite unexpectedly, he grinned. It made a completely different person of him. He seemed almost boyish.

"No, you're not. All right, Miss Boomerang, direct yourself back to Jarrah, only next time this sort of thing happens see to it you tell your employer first."

She said quickly. "To stabilize employer-employee relations?"

He said quickly back, "You catch on very fast. Yes."

Before she went out she asked, "Are you and Miss Wyse and Si—Mr. White going the same way as I am?"

"Probably, but probably we will take less time, so will be able to leave later. *Our* journey will not be slowed up en route by whirring cameras. What it is to be famous, Miss Boomerang!"

She did not reply to that, so he assured her, "But you'll be seeing Simon at the Alice, have no qualms."

"I wasn't thinking of Simon."

"No? Then of whom? Don't tell me the employee was still mulling over employer-employee relations?" Again the blue ice eyes were narrowed on her.

Inadequately Clancy murmured, "I was just asking for politeness' sake, that's all."

"Of course . . . you have some politeness to make up, haven't you? Also"—looking at his watch—"about ten minutes' work."

"Rest assured you will have that ten minutes, Mr. Osman," Clancy snapped.

"I intend to." His voice, just to spite her, was deceptively mild.

Clancy went back to her desk.

The "Centre" books she had borrowed from the library, the girls' good-natured envious chatter, just the very name Alice Springs in the middle of the map of Australia now began to whet Clancy's appetite.

Only one thing made her reluctant. It was leaving the Gillespies behind. She felt she could not trust Mrs. Gillespie. Given the chance of an earlier return booking than the one on which she had put a deposit she would rush it on the spot.

But an earlier booking was extremely unlikely. The ships were packed; Glyn had assured her of that. "When I walk down the Mall I'll run into half of Sydney," she had complained.

All the same Clancy took a run out to the Hostel.

Lyndall was practising somersaults on the grass, but when she saw Clancy she raced across. The impact nearly pushed Clancy off her feet. Lyndall certainly had grown these last few months. Also, and Clancy saw it with dismay knowing how Mrs. Gillespie would make it another point on the debit side of Australia, she had grown five freckles. On the end of her nose.

They didn't worry Lyndall, though. She gave Clancy a bear hug, accepted a bar of chocolate, then returned to the somersaults.

Clancy went into the flat. She had a cup of tea with Mrs. Gillespie, then told her she was going away for a while.

"The Centre?" echoed Mrs. Gillespie in a voice that doubted Clancy's sanity. "Aren't the edges of this country bad enough?"

"Oh, Mrs. Gillespie——" half laughed, half cried Clancy.

Then she said seriously, "You won't do anything silly like running off while I'm away?"

"That I wouldn't promise you, Clancy. Given the chance I'm afraid I'd leave even my husband and children to go."

"Now you're exaggerating."

"I suppose I am, but oh, Clancy . . ." The woman burst into tears.

"Is it still your mother, Mrs. Gillespie?"

Mrs. Gillespie blew her nose. "It shouldn't be, goodness knows, I get no encouragement from her at all. All she writes in her letters are questions. How hot? How cold? Are people friendly? Have we a nice vicar? Can we buy a decent kipper? Anyone would think *she* was coming here instead of *us* going back there."

Hopelessly, she knew, Clancy said, "And couldn't it be that way?"

"All that time to wait for a passage!" Mrs. Gillespie shook her head.

Clancy did not murmur the alternative, pay her own passage, because she guessed that Mrs. Gillespie's mother would be as restricted financially as Mrs. Gillespie herself.

"Well, seeing you won't promise not to disappear while I'm gone, I'll leave now . . . and keep my fingers crossed," she laughed.

At the door she added, "I'll send you a card from Alice Springs."

Mrs. Gillespie looked pityingly upon such a low fund of good sense.

The rest of the week went quickly. Clancy packed. She went into the Migration to learn what would be expected of her in the Inland. She took instruction from Dick as to how to take a good colour shot.

133

Dallas and Simon came into the office one afternoon. Dallas nodded coolly and went on into Guy's domain. Simon came and sat on Clancy's desk.

He looked thinner, Clancy thought, but his eyes were brighter.

They fairly sparkled at Clancy as he said, "Well, you'll be seeing them, Clan."

She knew what he meant . . . the Stars.

"Yes," she nodded, "I'm looking forward to that. You love your Inland, don't you, Simon?"

"Very much. I was born there, you know. That surprises you, doesn't it? I don't look the type. But I suppose weaklings are born everywhere."

"Oh, Simon dear!" Clancy said it fondly.

"It's true," he said, "I've always been weak. Not just in physique, Clan, in—other ways. Well, I suppose it's too late to mend." He half glanced to the door that Dallas had closed behind her when she went into Guy.

"How is the book?" she asked.

He shrugged.

"Simon, you're still working?"

He shrugged again.

"You must bring it to Alice Springs with you. Together we'll find time to go over it."

"Clancy, it's not worth that."

"But it is, you know it is. Simon, you *feel* it is."

"Put it this way—I *felt* it was."

"Who's been——" But Clancy stopped herself. She did not need to ask, and anyway, Simon never would have told her. But she *knew*. She knew that Simon's new apathy was Dallas's work. No one else but Dallas could have destroyed his enthusiasm like this. Why? Why did Dallas do these things?

She wondered fleetingly how Simon was paying for his trip. She had often wondered about such things where Simon was concerned. He never worked, that was; he never worked like other men did, like Dick, like Guy Osman; he appeared to have no income. But still he had money. Not a lot of money, but for Simon's needs enough.

It must be enough, anyway, for money did not seem to worry him.

And just now, Clancy smiled, nothing was worrying him.

"Yes, you'll see it all," he told Clancy again, and his eyes shone once more. "You'll see 'the vision splendid of the sunlit plains extended.' "

"Is it, Simon?" she asked him. "Are they sunlit plains extended?"

She was to remember that question later on.

Remember with tears.

CHAPTER 18

CLANCY left early on Friday morning.

At the end of the day, sitting in a comfortable hotel at the Alice, Clancy knew that the allure of this Centralia would be difficult to analyse.

She had flown from Sydney over mountains, table lands and plains to Broken Hill, but once they had left the great black scar of the lead and zinc city behind them the scene had begun to change.

First there had been the harsh yellows of the grim arid region . . . a man-made desert, her travelling companion had told her, because mulga and eucalypts had been eroded through overstocking . . . then hundreds of miles further on had begun the great salt pans, Lake Eyre and Lake Frome, then after them the unbelievably strong colours of the Simpson Desert, the almost Arabian Nights richness of reds, purples and blues.

And then came the Alice . . . The Alice or just Alice, Clancy discovered, seldom Alice Springs.

She had stared down on the Alice in fascination, this centre of the earth's oldest country, nestling in an oasis through a gap of ranges.

"The gap is Heavitree and the range is the McDonnell," said her companion. He added, "The oasis is because of assured supplies of bore water which gives the Alice her gardens and citrus trees as well as mulga and spinifex."

She had not found any opportunity to explore the town, but her first passing impression had been one of leisurely tempo, everyone knowing everyone . . . everyone just now showing signs of excitement because of the occasion, because it was the Bangtail Muster.

And at last she knew all about the Bangtail Muster.

The Bangtail Muster was a cavalcade depicting Alice

Springs from past to present. A bangtail muster on a cattle station was a sort of stocktaking. When a new owner bought a property and wanted to know what stock was on it, instead of throwing the beasts the stockmen simply caught them on the run and cut off a strip of hair—a "bang"—from their tails.

Both parties to the purchase tallied the number of bangtails. "No fear with a bangtail of being counted twice," Clancy's narrator had pointed out.

So, in a sense, the Bangtail Muster was the Alice's stocktaking. It would provide Alice, by decorated floats and exhibitions, with an opportunity to account for herself.

"Though," Clancy's informer had finished, "in my opinion the Alice doesn't need past records. I think of her as the Land of Tomorrow."

"Isn't all this country that?" agreed Clancy, thinking of Guy and Greenmarley and the high speed road that was to be the death of his house. She felt she understood Guy's acceptance much better now.

The Land of Tomorrow . . . Clancy repeated this to herself later as she walked down Todd Street.

She thought how the many people who had warned her that the Centre was a "dead heart" would have been ashamed of their words in this bright, well-kept town.

She turned off the avenue of shaggy dark bull oaks and walked past some of the houses . . . sprinklers playing on fine lawns, everywhere signs of comfortable living.

Because of the Muster even these residential streets now had their flurry of people . . . cattlemen in from stations, drovers, prospectors, mining men from wolfram and mica shows, horse-breakers, geologists. And visitors.

Three of these visitors were approaching Clancy now.

So Dallas, Simon . . . and Guy had arrived.

They greeted her characteristically, Dallas coldly, Simon with pleasure, Guy with that old measuring look.

"So our Boomerang Girl has her Australian education completed," drawled Guy. "She is introduced to nullas, waddies, didgeridoos."

"Not yet," said Clancy politely.

Dallas drew Guy away, reminding him that she wanted

137

to buy an Aranda tribe painting. Simon put Clancy's hand under his arm.

"Well, Clan?"

She knew what he was asking, and she nodded back at him.

"I love it already, Si."

"And you haven't really seen it."

"No, I suppose not, in a way. Then how can I? By returning by train?"

He laughed.

"The Afghan Express, or the Ghan, is certainly a railroad experience in unconventionality, but the mountains are passed at night and only the flat, stony stretches by day."

"Why is it the Ghan?"

"Short for Afghan, it used to carry a cargo as mixed as that of an Afghan hawker. When a modern train began they called it the Flash Ghan, and the Oodnadatta Mixed became the Dirty Ghan.

"No, Clan, you won't see my sunlit plain extended there, and you won't see it on the Bitumen."

"The Bitumen?"

"The road to Darwin, a thousand straight miles, as simple as a suburban delivery run, but you *will* see it the way I can take you back."

"Yes, Simon?"

He recited a string of names that meant nothing to Clancy except that some of them were liquid and singing and some of them could have been towns in England. The list ended with Brisbane, which of course she did know.

"Is this another highway?" she enquired.

Simon laughed. "Call it a way," he said.

"But have you a car?"

He hesitated. "I think I can manage that."

Clancy was excited over the prospect. "It sounds wonderful, Simon."

"It is, *it is*."

They caught up with Dallas and Guy and turned once more into the main street.

The next few days went by like a dream to Clancy.

The Bangtail Muster did not begin until the Ball, but the hours between went on rapid feet. She was taken to the Royal Doctor Service, and as she listened-in to the doctor answering questions she understood why Flynn of the Inland had striven so hard for these people of the outback.

The School of the Air she found infinitely moving. To hear children hundreds of square miles apart learning even a simple poem was a very rich experience. The mistress had sat at her desk . . . there had been a blackboard, a microphone, but no class. Yet there had been a class . . . it was in the immense silence . . . and when the microphone was turned on, children, unseen, filled an empty room.

An English folksong went dancing over five hundred thousand square miles of bare, baked land, and children listened-in in three states and from many homesteads.

"Now we will sing our morning hymn," said the teacher, and the Twenty-third Psalm was broadcast.

"Will someone sing it alone?"

There was a clamour of offers.

"Dorothy."

Dorothy's voice raced in over the desert, over saltbush, spinifex and sand dunes. Clancy found tears in her eyes as the little shrill notes banished the parched spinifex and barren dunes with "He maketh me to lie down in *green pastures*" . . . with "He leadeth me beside *still waters*."

The teacher, just as moved as Clancy, related how Dorothy was shy, how she had listened wordlessly for nearly a year before one day she had overcome her shyness enough to announce her call-sign and become one of the class.

"That was lovely, 8GY Dorothy. Now, 8MN Paul, will you sing a verse?"

When the morning lessons were over Clancy learned that as well as the active class, that was the children whose parents could afford radio transceivers, there were many on short-wave wirelesses who couldn't call back.

But they listened eagerly, and no doubt somewhere up in

Birdsville . . . Cooper's . . . a little girl or boy was seeing green pastures in spinifex, still waters in dry plains.

Clancy came away with a lump in her throat.

The celebrations . . . or stocktaking . . . began with the Grand Ball.

Clancy had wisely not taken the matter of dress lightly. She knew that as well as many expensively gowned visitors there would be locals . . . Territorians . . . in frocks flown from different capitals. One model, so the grapevine was whispering, had been sent from Paris.

She had packed a simple white ballerina dress, plain but beautifully cut. She had planned to add Bron's string of pearls.

But when she put it on she was disappointed. Something seemed missing. It hadn't been missing when she had purchased the gown in Sydney, but it was now.

She was still standing in indecision when Guy Osman knocked on the door. When she opened it to him he simply stood there and looked her up and down.

She felt curiously nervous. She found herself shrinking from his frank gaze.

"If you've come to fetch me I can't come," she blurted. "I mean I'm to be called for by the committee."

When he didn't speak she mistook his silence for the usual censure . . . she expected his taunting "Oh, of course, I forgot, you're a V.I.P., you're the Boomerang Girl."

But it did not come.

Instead he said, "That won't do."

"What won't do?"

"You."

"What do you mean?"

"Your outfit."

He was saying what she had thought, but it didn't prevent her from answering angrily, "I'm sorry I don't suit you, but it happens to be the only dress I brought."

"Not the dress itself but its presentation. Look, wait there. Don't move."

He stepped back and closed the door on her. She could hear him going down the hotel stairs.

She was so surprised she did as he said, she did not move. She did not have to obey very long, for in an astonishingly short time he was back. In his hand he held a white case. He handed it to her.

"What is this?"

"Open it."

She did. Then she stood wordless.

"Don't you like it?"

"Of course I like it. It's glorious. But——"

"Take off those pearls. Put it on."

"This necklace?"

"Yes."

"It's an opal, isn't it?"

"A black opal, though that's only a term, it's more fire and flame and sunrise and sunset than night. Ordinarily I wouldn't advise you to wear a black opal, a white one would be best for your colouring, creamy-white with a pin-fire of rose. But here it's different, it's the Centre. The colours are Arabian Nights colours, they are black opal colours.

"Turn round and I'll put it on."

"I——"

"Turn round."

She turned as in a dream . . . as in a dream she felt his warm, strong fingers unclasping the pearls and sliding them over her shoulders into her cupped hands. Then he was fastening on the opal, securing the catch.

It seemed to take him a long time, but with a necklet like this he would have to be very sure.

Where had he got it?

Not very steadily she said flippantly, "Do you carry opal necklaces in your suitcase?"

His answer could not have been briefer.

"No."

Where *had* he got it, then? All at once she thought of Dallas. Had he gone and borrowed it for the night from Miss Wyse? The thought sent a little squirm of distaste racing down her spine and she half pulled away.

"Stand still," he flashed. And then, in that uncanny way of his, "No, I didn't borrow it from her."

141

"Then——"

"Look, can't you ever accept without carping?"

"I'm afraid not, not a valuable necklet like this."

"Then I'll take it back tomorrow."

"Can you?"

"The Tourist Shop in the vestibule assured me of that."

He was standing back so that she could see herself in the mirror. The reflection that looked back at her was the same girl as before . . . and yet vastly different. The girl had come vitally alive. The fire in the stone had lifted the simple gown from the "plain" class, made it a lovely creation. The pale hair, just pale with the milky pearls, now seemed to have light and shade. Her eyes were bog-shadowed.

"You'll accept it?"

"For tonight—yes."

"In that case," he said lightly, so lightly that she did not take him seriously until it happened, "you'll accept this, too —just for tonight."

Then his arms were around her, but not to secure a necklace this time, for his lips had found her soft hair, and then her soft mouth.

It was a light kiss, almost a casual one, he laughed softly as he released her as though he had found it all amusing and wanted her to be amused, too, but Clancy, pulling on her short coat, following him down the stairs, leaving him to Dallas and Simon while she joined the official party, was aware of something very different from amusement.

Aware of a thrill . . . and then a gladness . . . and then, because he had given the kiss so lightly because obviously he intended it to be regarded lightly, she was aware of a little ache.

CHAPTER 19

THE Ball was a glittering affair . . . though Clancy found herself more interested in a group in one of the corners than in the rotating figures.

One was a Territorian of fifty years' standing, and she described her first dance at the Alice . . . the sign "Welcome" over the door and only two women for the men to dance with. "Light came from slush lamps . . . tins filled with sand and fat, and when the gramophone ran down that was the end of the hop."

The festivities went on into the small hours of the next morning, but this would not prevent that day's activities.

Indeed, it was regarded as a short ball by the locals. "Hardly warmed up," grumbled one reveller to Clancy. "When the war was on," related another, "all the send-offs lasted days. One"—he chuckled reminiscently—"went on for two weeks."

The ceremony on Mount Stuart with old scenes re-enacted was formal, but after that everyone relaxed and had fun. There were sporting carnivals, race meetings, Clancy saw her first corroboree, there were native arts and crafts exhibitions.

What she enjoyed most, she thought afterwards, was the Baby Show.

The winner was a little dusky girl with eyes like shining pansies. There were many dark competitors, but this one had white foster-parents, and their pride in her success knew no bounds.

When Clancy saw the procession she really understood why it was called a Bangtail Muster. It actually was a stocktaking of this Alice, she thought.

Floats, horse and camel teams, wagons, then lines of modern machinery stretched for more than a mile. The century since John Stuart had passed this way was reviewed historically. Aborigines, clad only in brief nagas and looking

143

much as they must have looked to Stuart, went ferociously by, armed with long killing spears and clutching boomerangs, their bodies daubed with ochre and oil.

The floats represented the pioneer settlers, the cattlemen, miners, missionaries and mounted police, all of whom had played their part in shaping the Alice and the Northern Territory . . . Land of Tomorrow.

In between all these festivities Clancy had many impressive tours.

That there was always a photographer to record the Boomerang Girl at Bitter Springs Gorge . . . at Little Flower Mission . . . did not dismay her for long. There was something about the Centre, about its clear light air that sometimes seemed golden and sometimes blue-mauve, that made her forget she was a "free passenger," as Guy Osman would undoubtedly have reminded her, for so long as she smiled obligingly back for the clicking cameras.

She had not seen Guy much since the Ball. The committee had claimed her, and any spare moments had been eagerly filled in by Simon.

Knowing the Alice, Simon knew the corners that would delight Clancy. At Jessie Gap he told her that he believed they could be fixed up with a conveyance to take them back the "vision splendid" way.

"A car?" she asked, not sure of that "conveyance."

"No, Clan, a vehicle with a four-wheel drive. Essential where we'll be going."

She felt no qualms about it. It did not occur to her to reason that a track that required a four-wheel drive must be a very demanding track.

She just nodded happily. The Alice was like that.

"Look," said Simon, "perhaps you'd better not mention all this to Guy."

She had had no intention of mentioning it, but she asked, "Why?"

"Well, he mightn't approve."

"Of the two of us?" She laughed.

Simon hesitated perceptibly. Then he said a little hurriedly, "Yes, that's it . . . of the two of us."

Because Clancy had absolutely no idea of the immensity

144

of the journey that Simon was contemplating, she accepted his word that Guy's concern would be solely because of the social aspect. Indeed, anything other than that did not enter her mind.

"How long will it take, Simon?" she asked, shrugging off Guy's probable disapproval.

"Not so long. I've been poring over maps and I believe we can make a station each night." He smiled across at her. "It will be all right, you know."

"Oh, Simon," she said fondly, "of course I know."

She was a little puzzled over the vehicle, though. Four-wheel drives sounded expensive affairs. She felt sure that Simon had little, even no money, so how could he hope to obtain a Land Rover or whatever it was he intended to drive?

She asked him, and he smiled and patted her hand.

"Leave it to Simon, Clancy of the Overflow."

That evening Clancy took the opal necklet along to Guy Osman. There would be no more official evenings so she would need it no longer. She tapped on his door and when he opened it she handed him the white box.

"What's this?" he asked, looking down at her extended hand.

"The necklace."

"Oh, for heaven's sake," he said irritably, "can't you accept graciously, woman?"

Woman now . . . not the Boomerang Girl. Although it was said in unconcealed irritation somehow it gave Clancy a queer little thrill.

"I only borrowed it."

"Well, keep it, I don't want it back. I don't go round handing out opal necklets, whatever else you may think."

"I didn't think that at all. I only believed what you told me, that you had got it from the Tourist Shop and that they would take it back."

When he did not comment she offered politely, "Would you like me to take it back for you?"

"No!" He said it so forcefully she was startled.

He saw her surprise and added hastily, "It's quite value-less, really. I'd look a fool."

145

"I would look the fool," she corrected.

"I tell you," he said furiously, "it's *not* to be taken back."

In a mood like this there was no arguing with him. Later, she thought, when he's not here, I'll take it down myself. Docilely she put the case back in her pocket.

He changed the subject abruptly.

"You've been seeing quite a bit of the Alice."

"Yes."

"With White."

She paused, then said, "Yes."

"Tomorrow," he stated . . . he neither proposed it nor did he invite her . . . "we'll do Palm Springs."

"You mean—the four of us?"

"I mean you and I."

"But——"

"If it's good enough to go with Simon White it's good enough to go with me."

"But—but why would you want to go with me?"

"What if I answer 'For the same reason as Simon'?"

"Then," she said steadily, "that would be to see the Alice."

He looked at her directly, it was a probing look. *"Would* it?" he asked.

She felt disconcerted. She said evasively, "I don't know if I can come tomorrow."

"May I remind you that you have never severed your connection with Jarrah Publications?"

"In other words," she interpreted coldly, recovered from her embarrassment now, *"you* call the tune."

"A prerogative," he agreed drily, "usually reserved for a boss."

He bowed derogatively.

"We take off at sun-up. It's only eighty miles west, but roads round here are not like the Bitumen, they require——"

"A four-wheel drive."

He narrowed his eyes at her at that.

"What do you know of four-wheel drives? Not contemplating a trip of your own, are you?"

146

"Of course not."

"Not contemplating one with White?"

She did not reply.

"Answer me!"

Really, he was impossible, this pigheaded, authoritative Australian.

"I'm contemplating nothing," she said. In a way it was not a lie, it was Simon who was doing the contemplating.

He looked at her a long moment as though doubting her.

Then he shrugged and repeated, "Tomorrow . . . dawn. I'll knock on your door. Don't dress up."

Clancy said, "No, sir."

When she obeyed his knock in the morning and hastily pulled on shirt and slacks and came down into the court-yard she found him waiting beside a Land Rover.

"Had something to eat?" he asked.

"No."

"We'll boil a billy by the Mission, then."

They crossed the Hermannsburg territory, the long flat "mummy-like" Mount Sonder in the distance in the eternal blue-mauve of these Centralian hills.

When they spanned the Finke River, Guy told Clancy it was a thousand miles long and that in the "wet," which was December to April, the waters poured down from the ranges and swirled in huge torrents until the valley was impassable.

Clancy could not have said what time it was they came to Palm Valley, for here, she realized at once, time did not exist any more. This was not the Land of Tomorrow, nor of Today, it was thousands of years ago, untouched by civilization, silently revealing its age in huge red sandstone rocks, proud soaring beautiful palms.

"It belonged to the Aruntas . . . the great painter Namatijira was one. Also the Arandas were once here."

Clancy nodded dumbly. She had never seen a place just like this.

It was almost like being in another world . . . the cloud-less sky, the warm air, the red sandstone changing from red ochre to vermilion even as you looked at it.

There was not a whisper in the vast stillness, and Guy let the velvet silence sink into Clancy before he spoke.

Then—"What is there about it?" he asked softly. "No gentle green grass, only rich red sand; no trickling waterfall because six or nine months of the year there's no water, the creeks dry, the rock pools empty . . . and yet it's paradise.

"Or"—fumbling in his pocket for his cigarettes—"do English eyes see differently, Clancy Clyde?"

He had never called her by her first name, and though now he added the Clyde it still gave Clancy a curious feeling.

Quietly she said, *"These* English eyes see the same, Guy."

She realized what she had answered and corrected hurriedly, "Mr. Osman."

"The first will do."

She did not know what to say back to that, so she said nothing. She began walking between the palm trees and on the soft red sand beside her she heard his quietened steps.

What palms they were! Some must have reached a hundred feet.

"They're five thousand years old," said Guy in a low voice . . . like Clancy he seemed reluctant to break the vast stillness . . . "and those toddlers there would be about two hundred winters and summers."

The palms grew out of rocks, from the ground, in ledges, and they spread out their soft fan-like fronds in unbelievable delicacy.

Clancy had not realized that Guy had left her until he returned from the Land Rover with the food hamper.

He snapped his fingers and said, "Come out of your dream."

"I was enchanted."

"This Glen of Palms *is* enchanted; there is no today, no tomorrow, only yesterday. Yesterday I met you here, Clancy Clyde, you were five thousand years younger." He laughed as he spread out the lunch.

"Then I was an Arunta," she told him.

"Could have been an Aranda," he smiled.

"And John McDouall Stuart wasn't even thought of."

He was slicing a long loaf, spreading it deftly with cheese and onion. She had noticed before how deft Australians were with picnics.

"May I congratulate you on your colonial history, Boomerang Girl," he praised.

Whether he was taunting her or not she suddenly did not care. She was all at once too hungry to bother.

"Can an Arunta begin eating?"

"Certainly. A piece of snake or a witchetty grub?"

As they replenished together he pointed out the different trees between the palms . . . bloodwood, beefwood, corkwood, mulga with its bride-like blossom.

"Have you enjoyed the Bangtail?" he asked.

"I wouldn't have missed it," she assured him sincerely.

"And tomorrow it's all over . . . for me, anyway."

"You're going back?"

"I'm a business man, remember."

"I'm a business girl."

"It's different for you. You'll feel obliged to return with the party."

When she did not comment he said sharply, "You do intend returning with the official party?"

The old authoritative note in his voice grated on her.

"I presume it's the employer speaking now," she said irritably.

He peeled a banana. "I can assure you it's not the person you knew five thousand years ago, Miss Clyde."

Something of the beauty had gone out of this Glen of Palms for Clancy.

"I would never have known you, Mr. Osman," she stated clearly. "We were worlds as well as centuries apart."

"All this is not answering my question as to whether you're returning next Wednesday."

She remembered that Wednesday was the day that Simon had mentioned to start their overland trip back.

"I'm leaving on Wednesday," she said glibly. She could not help adding, "Satisfied?"

"I don't know," he said, pulling on his cigarette. "Something inside me feels curiously *un*satisfied."

"What do you want me to do—write and sign a declaration?"

"Would you?"

She felt the colour rising in her cheeks. She hoped he would take it for anger and not guilt, for guilt was what she was feeling. It was absurd, really. He was not her keeper, why should she react like this?

Before she could give herself away he said, "All right, don't explode, Miss Clyde. I won't ask for that declaration, just see that you're back at Jarrah the following Monday, that's all."

She began packing up the picnic things.

"Is Miss Wyse returning with you?" she asked.

"Yes."

He looked at her steadily.

"Is Mr. White returning with you?"

"I was not aware he was in the official party."

"I was not aware of it, either."

"Then—then why do you speak like that?"

He shrugged carelessly.

"I think," he said presently, "that when we were here five thousand years ago we probably threw woomeras at each other. Let's ask the hills, shall we? They are the only ones who could tell."

She laughed unwillingly. He really was absurd . . . yet it was a relief not to be cross-examined any more. Also for all his foolishness the immense silence had encompassed her again. Have I been here before? she wondered dreamily.

Has Guy?

They came back through the blue, the mauve, the ochre, the vermilion, past rocks lit by the sunset as though lit within by a million fires, past ghost gums with slender white arms.

At the Alice he said almost abruptly, "We leave early in the morning, Miss Clyde. I'll say goodbye now."

"Goodbye, Mr. Osman, and thank you for a lovely day."

For a moment longer he lingered as though still unsatisfied, then shrugging once more he bowed to her, and went up to his room.

CHAPTER 20

THERE were two more days before Wednesday.

Clancy found the time dragging. She put it down to the anti-climax of the celebration, to the fact that she had very comprehensively "done" the Alice, to Simon being busy with the preparations for their trip home. She never put it down to the absence of Guy.

She would not even admit that she missed his measuring looks, his taunting words, but several times she took out the opal necklet and fingered it. Once she took it downstairs to the Tourist Shop.

But when she got there she did not have the courage to return it. Anyway, Guy had said she was not to. For want of a better excuse for standing at the counter with the box in her hand she murmured something about the necklet's clasp.

The attendant was very concerned. "One must be careful with a precious thing like this."

"Precious?"

"Why, yes, Miss Clyde, this was the stone that caused such a sensation last year at Lightning Ridge . . . it's the Crimson Prince."

"Oh," was all Clancy could say.

Now she could not keep it. On the other hand she could not hand it back to the girl. She would have to wait and give it to Guy. She took it upstairs and locked it in her case.

On Simon's suggestion she had said goodbye to the committee, but had not told them how she was returning home.

"But why?" she had asked, a little uneasy.

"You know what committees are like, they would fuss and insist upon returning the goods." He had smiled affectionately. "*You* are their goods."

"I suppose so," Clancy had agreed, wishing the little uneasy feeling would go.

So, the next morning, not farewelled by anyone, the four-wheel drive with its two passengers left the Alice, skimmed for a short stretch along the Bitumen, and then turned due east.

Right from the first mile the track shocked Clancy, for it was scarcely even that. Sometimes it was only an old wheel pattern, sometimes it was merely an indentation, and always there was nothing at all significant around them, nothing pinpointing, only the same stony stretches, spinifex, distant copper hills.

At lunch she asked Simon if anything had changed since his last crossing.

"I've never crossed, Clan, I've always wanted to, but never done it till now."

"Never crossed?" She did not know why she should feel so dismayed. Simon was Territorian stock, this was the twentieth century and pioneering days were over, they were safe as the hills. But even as she thought that the copper-coloured hills changed their hues, turned to vermilion, and again Clancy experienced the little unease.

According to Simon's estimation they should make Jeffery's that night.

A month ago Clancy would have asked, "But can we call unannounced on people like that?" Now she didn't. She knew that in this Centralia all houses were open houses. All hearts as well.

At six o'clock it was apparent they would not make Jeffery's. It was useless to think of trying to cover any ground in the dark, so they ate, and settled in for the night.

It was far colder than Clancy had thought it would be, but the sky was superb.

Simon, who was sleeping under the jeep, kept on rolling out to call up to Clancy, "Look at those everlasting stars, Clan. Now do you see what I meant?"

"Lovely," she called back, more at peace than she had been all day.

He told her about his youth . . . he had not been on a station, but his father had been an agent and sometimes he had taken young Simon with him.

He spoke about the natives. "Contented ones are a big asset, Clan, but they're never with you every day in the year. All at once they come and say, 'Want to go walk-about, boss,' and away they go for weeks—for months. Then back they come, empty-handed and hungry, and begin again where they left off." He paused reminiscently. "It's a strange old land," he said with love.

They started early in the morning but made bad time. A flooded creek held them up.

"I thought this was the dry, Simon."

"It is. They must have had a freak fall somewhere up in the Downs, it's certainly swollen this waterway. We'll have to skirt round."

She did not like that. She had the feeling that once they lost that indentation they might never find it again.

They did, though . . . at last they skirted the lignum growing like giant clumps of cane grass and clustering round the watercourse and struck the track. Or was that supposed track only a whim of the wind? Clancy asked herself. The wind blew strongly across these plains.

One thing, they were relieved they did not meet the creek again. But they met mirages instead. Silver ones, some-times . . . sometimes larkspur blue . . . sometimes green with mirrored green trees.

Simon consulted his compass frequently, he said they were still on the right course. "But I can't understand it," he complained. "I expected Jeffery's before this, and though I certainly didn't anticipate traffic I did expect someone on the track."

Clancy forbore to ask, *"Is* this a track?"

That afternoon, Jeffery's still not reached, Clancy no-ticed the first difference in Simon. It was not so much his manner which was not as sure as before, it was the white-ness around his lips.

"Simon, are you all right?"

"I'm desolated," he admitted with a rather wan smile. "I'd planned to be at Abel's by this, yet here I am, not even to Jeffery's, to first base."

"I meant do you feel all right?"

153

"Of course." He smiled again.

Later that afternoon it seemed to Clancy that there was a faint blueness as well as the whiteness around the mouth.

He pulled up the jeep quite suddenly and turned and looked at Clancy.

"Ever driven?" he asked her.

"Yes."

"In England, I suppose, nice respectable roads, nice respectable cars?"

"Yes. Why, Simon?"

"How," he asked quite lightly, "would you like to try a four-wheel drive?"

"I don't think that's necessary, is it?"

"Of course not." He spoke hastily. "I just thought it would be a handy thing to have up your sleeve.

"There are two gear controls," he went on, "you must understand, one for the front wheels, one for the back."

He showed her carefully, explained how and when to engage both controls. Then he suggested that she try for herself.

"But this seems so time-wasting, Simon. Why don't we drive ordinarily while we can, push on? Jeffery's can't be far off now."

"I'd like you to try," he persisted, and to satisfy him Clancy did.

It was growing dusk by the time they had finished, so again they bunked down.

The two days had not been pleasant, but they had not given any warning of the nightmare that lay ahead.

The next morning Simon was still under the jeep when Clancy got up. She got the breakfast ready, then called him.

He came out slowly, and now there was no white around the lips at all, there was a grey-blue.

"Simon!" she gasped.

"A cup of tea, Clan, it will do me good."

"What's wrong?" she asked, handing it to him. She added firmly, "You'd better tell me, Simon."

He drank, then said, "I suppose I'd better."

He looked away from her and mumbled, "I have a heart thing, Clan."

"A——"

"I'm sorry, Clancy, I've always had it . . . right from a boy. It's been better lately . . . better for a year."

"And now——?"

He did not answer. He put the tea down unsteadily. It spilled a little amber pool on the ground that sank in at once.

As calmly as she could Clancy said, "What do you think we must do, Simon?"

Miserably he said, "I think we should go back. I've been considering it all night and it's our only course. Oh, I hate doing this to you, Clan, I know how you feel."

"How could I feel, my dear, but sorry for you?" she asked gently, infinitely moved by his utter wretchedness.

"You could feel contemptuous, you could be amused at this strong tough Centre with its weak son. For that's what I am, Clancy, what I've always been—the weak son."

She decided not to argue that. Arguing could sap strength, and just now it appeared they needed all the strength they could muster.

"How do you feel now, Simon?" she asked.

"I feel a little better after that tea," he admitted, "I believe I can drive. But that's why I instructed you on the four-wheel drive yesterday. Just in case, Clancy. We'll have to go through the lignum if we meet it this time, not around . . . probably we'll encounter some of the rubble hills." He frowned and ran a thin hand through his blond hair.

"Oh, Simon," she said thinking of what he must have been going through in his mind and not telling her, "oh, Simon dear."

They packed up at once and got going.

The compass now was set for south-west. Again, Clancy worried about the track. Was it a track or a wind whim? How could anyone know out here?

Afterwards Clancy could not remember much about that day. All she knew was spinfex, some ringneck parrots

155

above, a wedge-tail eagle higher up still, the eternal copper hills with no filter of shade, the mirages, the hours that must have gone by because of the changing position of the sun. She knew the blueness around Simon's mouth.

At dusk they pulled up and made a pretence of eating. Then they bunked down again. Clancy did not sleep, but she kept very quiet in the hope that Simon might.

The stars had been up a long time when he spoke to her and she knew that he had not slept either.

"Clan——".

"Yes, Simon?"

"I'm sorry about all this."

"It's all right, dear."

"Guy will be furious."

"Does that matter?"

"I don't know if it does to *you*," he said simply back.

She did not answer him, and presently he spoke again.

"I want to tell you something . . . I want to tell it now in case——"

"Yes?"

"In case I can't—later on."

"Oh, Simon!"

"No, let me, Clan. Did you ever wonder why I was so persistent in Sydney, why I shadowed you like I did?"

"Yes," she admitted. "I did wonder sometimes."

"That will prove to you my utter weakness . . . the weak son, the weak stock. I did it for Dal."

"Dallas?"

"Yes. She *paid* me, Clan."

"Paid you!"

"She gave me money. She's always given me money for so long as I've known her. She's kept me, you could say. And I, because of what I am, have accepted it, Clancy."

"But—but why would she give you money to—to——"

"To hang around you. Isn't it obvious? She wanted to keep you from Guy, she wanted Guy to believe that there was something between us, Clan."

"Dallas wanted that? I can't believe you. Dallas would never be concerned about *me*."

156

'There you're wrong. She recognized Guy's interest in you right from the start."

"Simon, you're mad, she's mad. Guy has never been interested in me."

"Clancy, my heart is weak, my morale is weak, but my eyes have still been seeing for me. How blind can *you* be?"

"I don't believe you," Clancy cried.

"Well, that doesn't matter," Simon said presently. "The thing that does matter is this: Once I fell in love with Dallas; I believed that in her possessive, entirely selfish way she even cared a little for me.

"If I'd been half a man I wouldn't have stood around while she played her cards for Osman . . . I wouldn't have agreed to have put myself out after you simply for Osman to see and draw his own conclusion."

"It's a fantastic story," interrupted Clancy breathlessly.

"It's a true one," he said. "But, Clancy, it has a different ending from what Dal planned. She paid me to appear fond of you, but I don't think for one minute she ever believed I would be . . . in the end.

"Clan, I've learned a lot these last few days, I've learned that what I thought I felt for Dal doesn't exist. It exists only for you.

"I love you, Clancy. You're sweet and kind and you have pity, and you don't despise weakness. More that that, you would never have kept me weak like she did.

"I was convenient, Clan, a convenient second-string to have around. And that's why Dallas kept me around."

"You could be wrong," said Clancy. "She could have loved you."

"And still made a play for Osman? Not just played for Osman but paid me to take you out of the picture? Oh, no, my dear. Dallas only loves possession, possession is the only thing that matters to her. I like to believe that that's why she spoke against my book. It *was* Dallas, I know. I like to think it was not any lack in the book but a lack in Dallas. If my book had been successful I would have been independent of her, and independence was something she didn't want in me." He paused. "In *anyone*."

157

"Simon," said Clancy carefully, "you mustn't talk any more. You're exhausting yourself."

"Yes, I mustn't talk," he agreed. "There's tomorrow to face . . . but when I thought of tomorrow, Clan, I knew you must know tonight."

"Why, Simon?"

"Because I don't know about tomorrow," he said helplessly. "I just don't know, Clan dear. But I do know I love you . . . you and my everlasting stars."

Blessedly at last his voice trailed off.

Clancy dozed, too, at length, but when she woke in the morning it was with a cold dead feeling. She leapt out of the jeep and went down on her knees.

He was all right. In fact he looked a lot better. He was actually smiling at her.

They breakfasted and started off again.

Simon drove really well that morning. Around noon he suggested that she take over. She looked quickly at him but saw nothing to worry about. He was just a little tired, but that seemed all.

She drove for several hours, she estimated, another hour or so and she would brew tea. She wished she could lose that eternal copper hill that seemed to travel with them however far they went.

They came to a difficult patch and she engaged the four-wheel drive successfully and he commended her new skill.

About half an hour later she first felt Simon's weight on her shoulder. She smiled a little, happy for him that he could sleep.

Some time later again the smile left her. It was such a complete weight . . . such an inert weight. Oh, God, she thought, not—that.

She went on. She dared not stop. She dared not look.

She did not know how long she travelled like this. Then all at once the copper hill began to leave them, all at once they seemed to be coming somewhere. The horizon had opened out, that horizon that Simon loved so much with its sunlit plain extended.

"Look, Simon," she said. "The vision splendid, dear."

But he did not speak.

There was something in the distance . . . it was something she had never seen before. For a while she believed she was going mad.

It began with a large oblong bulk that appeared black against the sky. Something moved behind it like a big black snake.

Afterwards Clancy was to be told it was a road-train . . . the oblong bulk the Diesel engine, the snake the trailers . . . she was to be told that a hundred bullocks were being moved south.

As she came nearer she still did not understand it, but she understood that there was a road beneath the thing, not a track, not a whim of the wind.

She was almost on top of the column of dust now, dust that rose high, she could hear the growl of the Diesel engines, but she still could not comprehend.

She did not try; she only tried to call out. It was ridiculous calling out in this vast emptiness, but she remembered opening her dry mouth.

"Lucky we saw you, miss," the driver told her afterwards. "It's so empty you miss things—that sounds crazy, but you do . . . Bill here said, 'That looks like a jeep, and by heaven it looks like a girl driving it.' I thought it was a girl mirage he was seeing . . . days on the road and you get like that.

"I said 'No track there, where would she come from?'

"'Don't know,' said Bill, "but I'm going to stop.'

"So we did—I'm sorry it was too late, miss."

For it had been that—for Simon. Clancy knew it would have been too late an hour before they met the road-train. She believed death had come when she first had felt that weight upon her and thought Simon had fallen asleep.

Had that been before or after the vision splendid of the sunlit plain extended? she wondered.

She did not know. She could not remember. But she was glad that anyway Simon had looked up the night before to his everlasting stars.

CHAPTER 21

THOUGH Clancy insisted that there was nothing wrong with her she was kept at the Alice until the end of the week.

In the hospital where they had insisted she rest, she was watched for prostration, for shock, for any of the things that could have followed exposure to the elements, have followed the sudden blow of an unexpected death.

Simon, too, had not left the Alice. It had not helped Clancy that *she* had been asked to decide on that.

It appeared that there was no one left who had belonged to Simon. In which case they had come to Clancy and asked for her to say.

She had sat very still, clasping and then unclasping her hands. She knew where she believed Simon would have wished to lie, but who was she to decide? Why not Dallas who had known him first?

"There is a Miss Wyse in Sydney. I think she should be asked . . ." she suggested.

"Mr. Osman said you, Miss Clyde."

"Mr. Osman? You've been in touch with him?"

"No. He's here, at the Alice. He flew back at once."

Guy . . . in the Alice.

I can't meet him, Clancy thought, but she knew she must —in time.

She did that afternoon.

He was shown in just after the doctor had gone. The doctor had been pleased with her.

"You came out of it well, Miss Clyde, no repercussions."

Of the body, no, thought Clancy drearily, but what of the mind?

As though he had read her thoughts the doctor had said,

"It has been very unfortunate, but try to look at it in this way—for that poor fellow it was inevitable anyhow very soon."

Clancy wished she could . . . wished she could find a little ease in the realization. But it was no use.

She was sitting desolate like this when Guy came in. Her bed was in a corner of the wide verandah. He leaned back on the balcony post. His opening words were deceptively casual.

He said, "Doc Fuller says you can get back to the Big Smoke."

She tried to be casual, too.

"Yes, I don't believe there's anything to keep me here."

At once the storm broke.

"No," he agreed in a low, taut voice, "not even him—along there."

He nodded indicatively as he said it, but she did not see the nod because her eyes were filled with incredulity, incredulity that he could speak so brutally as this.

"I didn't do it," she cried passionately. "You have no right to accuse me like that!"

"Did I accuse you? All I said was that there was nothing to keep you here."

"You said no *one*."

"Correction, please, my exact words were 'not even him.' "

"You meant that he died because of me, and it's untrue . . . untrue!"

"You're very imaginative, Miss Clyde."

"But I didn't imagine that."

There was a silence between the two of them, then Guy Osman agreed coolly, "No, I suppose you didn't entirely imagine that."

She stared at him aghast, and he went on.

"I didn't intend all this to come out . . . but when I saw you sitting here so prettied-up and comfortable"—he flung a violent arm towards her pink negligee, the cushions the Sister had put at her back—"I thought of young Simon White, only comfortable in death."

"Don't! Please don't."

161

"Why not? He's dead, isn't he, he's dead because of a damn trip he never should have undertaken but which he did undertake . . . because of a girl."

"That's untrue."

"Everything appears to be untruths to you. But who are you to judge veracity, Miss Clyde, you who told me at Palm Valley you were returning with the official party."

"I didn't say that. I said I was leaving on Wednesday."

"Which, no doubt, you classified as a subtlety on your part, not, as it's turned out, a hellish evasion."

"Mr. Osman, what business is any of this of yours?"

"The same business as death is to all of us."

"Don't speak to me like that!"

"Good gracious, woman, how otherwise can I speak?"

"Si—Simon would have gone back that way whether I'd gone with him or not. He loved the Centre, he had always planned to take that track."

Brutally Guy Osman said, "On what?"

"I don't understand you."

"Then understand this: Simon White didn't have a penny. Vehicles don't spring out of the ground like daisies, he must have had money to get that jeep. *Where*, Miss Clyde?"

She looked at him in helpless disbelief. "You don't think that I——"

"What else is there to think? You've been living cheaply at Greenmarley, haven't you?" She winced at that, but he went on. "You've been paid a very good wage. The money must have piled up."

In a reluctant voice she whispered, "Dallas . . . Miss Wyse . . ."

"Oh, it's Dal now, is it? I rather expected that. In fact I even questioned Dallas. She admitted she had slipped Simon a note now and then, Dallas had always been generous, but never would she have been so cruelly misguided as to have done what *you* did."

"What did I do?"

"Either paid for, or contracted for, a vehicle to take you over to Queensland so that you could see even more of this land that you've already seen at no cost."

162

"You're wrong," Clancy cried.

"I'm right, there has been no cost to you." He paused a significant moment, then said, "Only a cost to White."

"He loved this country, he urged me to go," she persisted.

"Think back, Miss Clyde. Could it not have been *you* who urged *him* to go?"

"No, no, you're wrong."

"I'd like to think so. I'd like to believe Doctor Fuller that Simon White was not intended for a long life, anyway, but it's hard, Miss Clyde, it's hard."

Guy took out his cigarettes and lit one.

"I find it too hard," he said.

Clancy took a deep breath, but it did not steady her.

"Why don't you say straight out what you think of me?"

"Haven't I said it?"

"You've said I'm a liar, but you haven't yet said a murderess."

"Oh, come," he chaffed. "Cut the dramatics. I'm not going that far."

"Not in words, but in your heart."

"Since when," he flung, "have you been able to read my heart?"

He paused, and then:

"Look, we'll leave it at that, leave it at your unfortunate incentive to Simon, or agreement with him, call it what you will, for him to have done what he did, for you to reap what you're reaping."

"What am I reaping?"

"Tears," he said readily, "hot and blinding. Cry yourself out, Miss Clyde, it will do you good."

But no tears came to relieve Clancy, she just sat dry and despairing.

He rose from the balcony rail.

"All right," he said, no tears. But one thing you must have is a decision."

"A decision?"

"About White. It's only up to you."

"Why should it be me?"

"Good lord, woman, you went into the desert with him. Who else?"

"Dallas," she whispered. "Once he loved Dallas."

Her words were unfortunate.

Guy Osman looked coldly at her and echoed. *"Once* he loved her. Before you came along?"

She could not reach this man to tell him, explain to him. That barrier of ice was too hard.

"Why should it be my word?" she cried again.

"It *is* your word," he said implacably, "so stop the heroics. Where is White to be buried, Miss Clyde?"

Miserably she whispered, "This was his love. The sun-lit plains . . . the vision splendid . . . the everlasting stars."

"Did you find them like that, too," asked Guy, "before he died?"

She did not answer, she just rocked herself in her misery.

Suddenly angry beyond measure, he came across and took her shoulders.

"You were three nights out there . . . Was it only stars?"

"Guy, you're hurting me!"

"Answer me, then."

"You're speaking of a dead man."

He said with brutal significance, "He wasn't dead then."

With a very great dignity Clancy said, "Simon was my good *friend.*"

Tightening his fingers, Osman probed savagely, "Were you his?"

"Of course . . . at least . . ." She found herself turning away from the searching blue eyes, found herself remembering that last night and Simon whispering, "But I do know I love you . . . you and my everlasting stars."

"You see," Guy Osman snapped.

A silence fell between them. In the hospital kitchen someone clattered a pan. A little black girl wandered past the verandah and stared up at them as she went with her solemn velvet-soft eyes.

"I'll tell who has to be told, then," said Guy Osman formally. "I'll tell them that Simon White shoud be buried here. Or"——he paused——"would you prefer to do that yourself?"

"You do it, please."

He nodded expressionlessly.

"You'd better wait until it's all over . . . it will look better."

"I'd want to," she mumbled indistinctly.

"That's nice of you," he said insincerely.

He was lighting another cigarette.

"I'll stay and help you through. Not because of you entirely, but because as his publisher I feel that I should."

"You are publishing it, then?"

"Yes."

"Why didn't you tell him so?" she whispered. It seemed inordinately sad to her that Simon should die before the knowledge of the culmination of his book.

"I had had professional advice against the manuscript," he reminded shortly.

"You haven't now," she murmured. She was remembering Simon's "If my book had been successful I would have been independent of her, and independence was something she didn't want in me."

But there was nothing to be gained by Dallas in refusing the book now.

Simon was independent of her. He was independent in death.

She became aware that Guy was looking at her sharply, searchingly, and she turned her glance away from his. For a moment she believed he would pursue the matter, but with a slight shrug he got to his feet.

"Well, we'll leave it at that."

She had risen, too.

"I don't want you to feel you have to see me home," she murmured.

"I don't feel that at all, but I expect we shall be travelling together all the same. You're quite fit, or so I've been assured, and you have to report back to work, remember."

"You're not serious, of course."

"I am serious. You'll finish off this manuscript of White's if it's the last thing you do."

"You can't want me back?"

"I want the book."

165

"I see," she nodded. "Business, that's the only *real* thing to you."

"Business," he agreed, "first, last and always.

"I'll see you then tomorrow . . . if our bookings coincide on the plane I'll see you the day after that . . . most certainly I'll see you on Monday at Jarrah. Agreed?"

"Yes," Clancy said.

* * *

The air was golden when Simon was laid to rest. The colours on the rocks beyond the Mission were glowing as though lit within again by the million fires.

The plain extended around him. At night the stars would look down.

"Goodbye, Simon," Clancy whispered . . . and she remembered a boy's smiling face, a boy's fair hair, a boy's laughter as he had called her "Clancy of the Overflow."

"Come along, Miss Clyde," Guy Osman said.

CHAPTER 22

CLANCY had dreaded her return to Jarrah, but she need not have worried. She took up the threads just as if she had never put them down. The girls questioned her with inter-about the Alice, but their questions were put tactfully. On the other hand they did not make things worse by avoiding any mention of Simon.

"We'll miss him," Glyn had said for them all. "He was a nice boy."

With that their chapter on Simon was closed.

Clancy wished she could have closed hers as simply. She knew she would always remember Simon, she wanted to remember him, but she wanted to recall him through his book, through her affectionate memory of him, not as she *was* recalling, through Guy's harsh words.

Guy she seldom saw at all. Dallas did not come in. It was as if with the passing of Simon a chain had been snapped.

The final revision of the book was nearly complete. After that, what? Guy Osman had never mentioned any other assignment, all he had spoken of was Simon's manu-script. "You'll finish it off," he had said, "if it's the last thing you do."

Well, it was nearly finished now.

She discussed the position one night with Dick and Bron.

Holly was thriving; her cheeks now made her name quite suitable. Bron remarked this with vast satisfaction.

"I hated saying Holly before when so obviously it should have been Lily," she confessed.

Clancy asked Dick if there was a vacancy in the Im-migration Department.

"No doubt we could place you, Clan, but I think the Department would perfer not to. It might make those spontaneous appearances they call on you to make from time to time seem staff duties."

Dick had looked at her closely.

"I'd rather thought you'd found your niche."

"I like Jarrah," Clancy confessed, "but by the end of the month I'll have run out of work."

"White's book?"

"Yes."

"I've never said anything before, Clan, but I was terribly sorry. Simon White, I mean."

Again Clancy said, "Yes."

"Did you . . . I mean, was it——"

"Dick means," interrupted Bron—then found she could produce no words, either.

But Clancy understood what they meant.

"There was nothing between us but friendship, but it was a very dear friendship," she said quietly. "That," she added, "is why I'm looking for a post."

"But why?"

"My employer has a different slant on it . . . It just makes it impossible, that's all. Sometimes," frowned Clancy, "his attitude makes *everything* impossible. Dick, I've wondered a lot lately if I should go back."

"Go back? Where?"

"Where I came from."

"Greenmarley," said Bron a little too brightly.

"England," Clan said.

Dick poked at his pipe.

"You couldn't, you know."

"Oh, yes, I could."

"You would have to forfeit your passage out here."

"I could do that." I'm well-off, she thought, a little weari-ly, I lived cheaply at Greenmarley, I've been paid a good wage, the money has piled up. Or so *he* pointed out.

"Clan," said Dick soberly, "I don't like hearing you talk like that, not even in a joke."

"It's no joke. I like it here . . . most times I love it . . . but I just don't think Australia was meant for me. Or

168

perhaps"—Clancy smiled wistfully—"I wasn't meant for Australia. We just don't rub."

"You mean," said Dick perspicaciously, "you and Osman don't."

"Well, isn't he Australia?"

"Part only. Big enough in his sphere but small in an entirety. The obvious solution, Clan, is to get away from Osman. I'm sorry about that. I would have sworn you were right together, but a man can be wrong."

"Dick, you're very wrong," Clancy agreed.

Dick still frowned.

"You realize, Clancy, that besides your forfeiture of money there would be something else?"

Clancy looked enquiring.

"The boomerang," Dick reminded her. "It only returns the once. I mean you can't keep on coming back and back."

"I didn't intend that," said Clancy. She looked at Dick regretfully. "I'm sorry about all this, but I just think your department chose the wrong girl."

"I don't think so." Dick looked back at her urgently. "And don't you go thinking so, either, not to the degree, anyway, of doing anything rash."

"Like giving Jarrah my notice?"

"Like booking up on a ship."

"That's not so easy," said Clancy, remembering Mrs. Gillespie. She felt a little guilty. She had been home two weeks but had not found time to go out to the Hostel.

Bronwen said a little defensively, "It's a good place, Clan, even if Holly took a long time to live up to her name. After all you can't expect red cheeks in a temperature of a hundred degrees."

"I'm not saying it isn't a good place," said Clancy miserably. "I'm just saying it wasn't written on the stars for me."

"The stars are everlasting," reminded Dick. "You mustn't make a rush decision on what's not written on them. There may be something on the next of the galaxy. You may be looking at the wrong one."

"And Australia's all right," urged Bron. "You ask Mrs. Jovanovitch."

169

Clancy laughed a little unsteadily.

"What has Mrs. Jovanovitch to say?"

"Ask her tomorrow."

So Clancy asked.

The young Polish woman's eyes filled with tears.

"They are coming here . . . my sister and her husband and her family."

"That's lovely."

"It is more than lovely, it is very wonderful, and you know why it is, it is because Antonio, my sister's man, has heart defect." Carefully Mrs. Jovanovitch said, "It is con-gen-it-al heart."

"Yes, Mrs. Jovanovitch?"

"This country says yes, bring him in, bring in the handicapped. Five hundred a year they will accept, they say, soon many more, they hope.

"It was so sad to see how people were picked over before a country would accept them, Clancy. Hopeless these people felt when countries said no . . . not wanted, they felt. My sister felt that because of her man.

"But what happens? Come, they say, and when you are here a specialist will see your husband and he can be helped."

Mrs. Jovanovitch beamed.

"And something else."

"Yes?"

"Already around good friends are giving me linen and blankets for them, even a box of groceries. It is like this, they all tell: you talk of a million people and you think how can I help a million, but you hear of one family, my sister's famiy, and you know things you can do.

"They do it," Mrs. Jovanovitch said with bright tears in her eyes. "It is a good land."

Clancy made time to go out to the Hostel the next Saturday.

Only Mrs. Gillespie represented the Gillespie family.

"Lyndall has gone to a party," she told Clancy, "and young John and his father have gone to a football match." She looked a little bewildered. "It's not Soccer either," she

170

worried. "At home Dad would never see anything but Soccer. It's so strange for him."

"He's settling in."

"He can't do that, we're going home."

"Lyndall and Dick have settled, too."

"Children root shallow," said Mrs. Gillespie. "You can pull them up and put them in, they have no loyalties."

"But, Mrs. Gillespie, what have they to be loyal to? *This* is England, too."

"Winter coming on when it should be summer," scorned Mrs. Gillespie.

"Now you're being difficult. It *is* England, just as your husband is a Gillespie the same as his father, as you are your mother's daughter."

Alas, Clancy could not have said anything worse.

"Mother!" burst out Mrs. Gillespie. "No word for six mails. She's growing away from me, we're growing away from each other."

"Nonsense!"

"Either that," added Mrs. Gillespie, "or she's very ill. Nothing else would keep Mother from writing."

She put the pink sweater down that she was knitting for Lyndall and rose and walked up and down the flat.

"It's the distance," she cried. "I keep on thinking of Mother over there . . . probably sick . . . all by herself."

"She would have good friends . . . good neighbours."

"But no one of her own. I'm the only one she's got. And why doesn't she write? Why doesn't she answer? I thought of something the other night——"

"Yes, Mrs. Gillespie?"

"I thought perhaps she's very ill, so ill she'll—die, and then Jack will say, 'Now, Mother, we may as well stop here.' He would, you know, Clancy, I can feel how it's becoming with him. But I would never stop here, not even if there was *nothing* to go back to." Mrs. Gillespie bit her lip. "Why doesn't Mother write?" she sighed.

Clancy would ordinarily have tried a dozen reasons, but with Mrs. Gillespie she knew it would be no use.

The next day at Jarrah she confided the story to the girls. They already knew how concerned she was about the

171

Gillespies, they had discussed the family many times. As she related despairingly how only Mrs. Gillespie now remained unsettled she felt glad that Dick was not around to hear.

He would have raised his brows at such talk. Hadn't she said in all seriousness that *she* might forfeit and go home herself?

"Mrs. Gillespie's mother hasn't written," said Clancy.

"Oh?" said Janet. Neither she nor the rest of the girls showed their usual warm interest. Clancy was momentarily disappointed. Yet after all, she thought, to them it was only a story, a rather foolish story of a rather foolish woman who has never grown to real maturity as she should. Why should they be as concerned as I am?

She had told Bron and Dick that she would be late that evening. She had thought it was the night of the month that the girls had dinner in town. Either she was wrong, for it had not been mentioned, or she was not included this time.

How foolish she was becoming, she thought, almost as foolish and touchy as Mrs. Gillespie. Nonetheless she could not help noticing that the girls often seemed to have their heads together . . . that they were a little evasive . . . that when they left the building that evening they said a hurried goodbye to her and went off in a little bunch.

Something *is* wrong, she thought. What is it? They were all right when I came back from Alice Springs, so it can't be anything to do with that.

She felt she did not want to return to Our House, not now that she had said she would be late. She had no doubt that there would be a welcome for her there, there always was, but she had no doubt, too, that Bron and Dick would appreciate a dinner alone. So she wandered down to the Quay, skirted the wharves round to the old tram terminal where the Opera House would soon rise, and stood beyond Fort Denison looking out at the harbour.

It was half dusk, but the lights had been lit and they sent opalescent colours into the wine-dark waters.

Opalescent . . . Clancy clapped her hand over her mouth. She had not yet returned the opal necklace to Guy. But

172

then since her return she had not seen Guy very much, and never alone.

A liner was going out. She watched its great bulk go slowly past Farm Cove.

Janet had once told her about Mrs. Macquarie. Mrs. Macquarie had been the wife of an early governor and she had come down to the Cove every day to watch any ships that might be going home. She had sat on a rock and it had been called Mrs. Macquarie's Chair.

Clancy closed her eyes a moment to shut out the rainbow lights of the ferry boats, the candy glitter of the fun park on the northern side.

When Mrs. Macquarie was here, she thought, there would be none of this . . . no tall buildings, no electric lights to send yellow, green and crimson snakes into the harbour water. There would only be a few modest shops, a handful of settlers, convicts among that handful no doubt. I wonder, she thought, if Guy Osman's great-great-grandmother who was transported for catching and riding a neighbour's pony used to walk round here to meet her sailor lover.

She wondered what that pair had been like . . . she tried to trace them back through Guy. High cheekbones, she decided, a proud straight nose, length and leanness—and eyes of blue ice.

She laughed a little . . . but not so much in amusement as in defence. For suddenly she was finding that even this casual thought of Guy made her want to cry. So she laughed instead.

She turned back to the city to find a place for tea. As she stepped out of the shadows someone stepped out of a black car parked at the kerb.

"Miss Clyde?"

Clancy came closer because it was still rather dim here, then she said in surprise, "It's you, Miss Wyse."

"Yes. Dallas. I—I want to talk to you. Would you get in the car with me? Perhaps you haven't had dinner, then would you have it with me at my flat?"

For a moment Clancy hesitated . . . and in that moment she saw the girl's white face, the lines around her mouth.

173

At once enmity flowed away from her and she knew only a very deep pity.

"Yes," she accepted, getting into the car, "that would be kind."

CHAPTER 23

WHILE Dallas weaved her way out of the city her attention was taken up by the early evening traffic. Clancy had the impression that the girl was grateful for this, grateful for the snarl of cars, for she saw by the gleam of teeth holding the trembling bottom lip that Dallas was under considerable strain.

Even in strain, though, she was an excellent driver. Unbidden came the thought to Clancy: But can she manage a four-wheel drive over a rubble hill?

She noticed that Dallas was not turning to cross the bridge as she would be to go to Greenmarley. But of course not. Had she not just now invited Clancy to her flat?

Aloud Clancy murmured, "Your apartment is finished." To herself she thought with ridiculous happiness, she has left there, Dallas has left as well.

"Yes," Dallas said, skimming expertly past another car and beginning to climb William Street, "I think you'll like the scheme."

They manoeuvred through teeming King's Cross and ran along Macleary Street.

"Here we are," Dallas announced.

It was a quiet block in a leafy setting. Clancy followed the tall poppy of a girl into a carpeted vestibule and up a flight of stairs. Dallas opened the door and they went in.

It was all much as Clancy had imagined . . . modern, uncluttered, good lines, cool colours.

"It's charming," Clancy commended.

"Thank you," Dallas acknowledged.

She poured a long drink for her guest, excused herself and went out to the kitchen.

Clancy sat with the frosty glass in her hand and looked around. She wondered what all this was about. As she glanced over the room she tried to find signs of Simon here . . . of Guy.

Somehow she could find nothing of Osman in this airy space, somehow it did not seem his place, though not for a moment could she think he had not been here, and often. Then Simon, she thought with that little tug that always came to her when she thought of Simon now, would not have been in this room since its re-decoration. He had died before that . . .

She put down the glass. Abruptly she became aware that Dallas was standing in the doorway looking at her. Not speaking, just looking, looking with dulled eyes.

"I know what you're thinking," she said. "You're thinking that Simon, too, knew this place. Yes, he did. But it was different then."

The girl came right into the room. For a while she did not speak. The moments grew into minutes, and Clancy grew uneasy.

She watched Dallas bestir herself with difficulty, cross to a low table to take up an ornament, then put it nervously back.

Then:

"Tell me about him," she whispered in a broken voice.

Clancy could have said "Whom?" but suddenly and intrinsically she sensed something that amazed her.

"Simon?" she whispered, and Dallas inclined her head.

"You were with him when he———"

"Yes, Dallas."

"Tell me," Dallas said again.

So Clancy told it—at least, all that she could.

The girl nodded from time to time, her eyes bright with unshed tears. At other times she interrupted with eager questions that Clancy tried her best to answer. But she did not entirely answer them for her. She could see that.

Dallas stood restless and unsatisfied, then she turned and said too brightly. "I'm a poor hostess. What must you think of me? It won't be long now." She went out.

Clancy sat on for a while, then on an impulse rose and crossed to the kitchen.

Dallas was not there. The grill was done, but Dallas had

not even turned it low. Clancy did this, lowered some other flames, then went softly up the hall. As she had expected, she found Dallas in the bedroom.

She had not thought to find her as she did, though, face down on the bed, great rending sobs shuddering through her slender body.

Clancy went quickly to the girl's side.

"Dallas!" she whispered.

Dallas sat up, tried to scrub at her eyes.

"I'm sorry, I should never have followed you to ask you to come. What must you think of me? I'll get up now, fix things . . ."

"No," Clancy said, "not yet."

She sat down on the bed and put a restraining hand on Dallas.

"Let's talk first."

"That's what I wanted to do, why I brought you here . . . but now I can't, Clancy, I can't!"

"Then perhaps I can," said Clancy gently.

She talked quietly about that ill-fated journey, not the unanswering things she had said before but the answering ones.

How Simon had rolled from under the jeep that first night to call out, "Look at those stars, Clan, now do you see what I meant?"

His desolation at not making Jeffery's, not even first base, as he had put it. The first time she had noticed the strain around his lips. His determination that she learn to manage the four-wheel drive.

"Yes?" nodded Dallas hungrily, and Clancy went on.

As she did she found it becoming harder . . . harder to talk about Simon in those last rending hours . . . hard to skirt around what she had sensed some time ago must not be said.

For she was quite convinced that Simon had been right when he had told her that once he had believed that Dallas had cared for him. She had cared for him. She cared now. Cared into eternity. Oh, Dallas, why did you leave it so late?

Dallas was telling her why in that dulled voice.

"I've always been spoiled, Clancy . . . indulgent parents, too much money, everything too easy—including love."

"Simon's love?"

"Yes."

Dallas paused.

"It was a boy's first warm love, and if I had been a real woman I could have made it a man's love . . . I could have made Simon a man. But I didn't want that, not equality, not give and take. I wanted possession, I wanted ascendancy.

"I wanted Guy Osman's status and prestige but Simon still answering to my whistle. And I knew I could have Simon's compliance because Simon was always weak. But what I didn't recognize was *my* need of Simon."

Dallas put her head in her hands and again she cried.

"I knew Simon's book was good, but I wouldn't say so. I didn't want him to be independent of me. And because things had always come easy I thought I didn't want a man as easy as Simon, I thought I wanted Guy."—*Thought*, repeated Clancy in her mind.

"Not that I ever could have had Guy," Dallas went on in self-absorption, "but I liked to think I could. I liked to think I could have him and have Simon as well. I was so sure of myself that I flung Simon at you. Did you know I did that?"

"Yes," Clancy said.

"Did Simon tell you?"

"Yes," Clancy said again.

"Did he tell you why I did it?"

"Yes," a third time. "But it made no sense," Clancy added. "Guy Osman has never been remotely interested in me."

Dallas was still only absorbed in herself.

"I paid Simon to dance attendance on you." Her face crumpled piteously. "Clancy, I *paid* him to take that trip. I *paid* him to die."

"Oh, no, Dallas." Clancy put her arms around the girl.

"I did, I did . . . I knew Guy would never forgive you for going off like that. He's very circumspect, Clancy, he doesn't seem so, but he is.

178

"So I bought the jeep . . . had it set up ready. When you have too much money you can do these things. And you can do something else. You can kill. I killed the man I know now I loved."

Clancy's arms tightened.

"You didn't kill him. Simon would have died, anyway. Didn't you know he had that sort of heart?"

Dallas stirred out of her arms to look up at Clancy with wide dark eyes.

"Simon did?"

"Yes, he had it from childhood. Always it was threatening him, Dallas, always it was inevitable. You must believe that."

Dallas said harshly, "Cold comfort words from a doctor, I expect, after he was gone."

"Yes, the doctor did tell me he would not have lived long —but Simon told me before that."

"*Simon* told you?"

"Yes." Clancy waited a moment. "So you see, Dallas, it's no use you blaming yourself, it just was to be."

"You're not just saying this?"

"I've told you, Dallas, *Simon* said it."

Now came the question that Clancy had dreaded . . . wondered how she could meet.

Dallas said quietly but demandingly, "What else did Simon say?"

There was no mistaking that question, no mistaking the need of a simple direct answer, no evading it with a subtlety or a half truth.

It had to be the truth—or a lie.

Unfalteringly Clancy chose the lie.

"On the night before Simon died," she related gently but clearly, her arm around the girl, "he looked up to the sky and said, 'I don't know about tomorrow, I just don't know . . . but I do know I love Dallas . . . Dallas and my everlasting stars.' "

For a long while Dallas rested in the circle of Clancy's arms. Then she said in a quiet, comforted voice, "Thank you, Clan."

She was almost calm while Clancy told her about

179

Simon's resting place . . . the golden air, the colours on the rocks glowing as though lit within. The extended plain.

"I'm going to write," she said later, "*really* write, Clancy. Not the sort of stuff I've written before, but something for Simon. For Simon's stars."

It was quite late when Clancy left the apartment. It would be midnight before she reached Our House. But the prospect of the long journey did not dismay her. She found herself walking on lighter feet than she had for many days.

She knew that whatever she might come to regret in her life something never would be regretted.

That—"He looked up to the sky and said, 'I love *Dallas* . . . and the stars.' "

CHAPTER 24

SEVERAL things happened that week. One was distasteful. One Clancy met with mixed feelings. One brought her unexpected joy.

The distasteful episode happened a few mornings after her evening with Dallas.

Dallas came into Jarrah, flashed Clancy a quick smile, then went in to Guy.

She left not long afterwards . . . once more that smile . . . and not long afterwards Osman sent for Clancy.

"Sit down, Miss Clyde." Clancy sat. "You saw Miss Wyse?"

"Yes."

"You know what she came about?"

"I think I do. She's planning a new book."

"That," said Guy Osman lighting a cigarette, "was incidental." He looked at Clancy through narrowed eyes.

Then—"Nice of you to have been so generous," he drawled. He paused deliberately, then suggested, "Or was it the generosity of giving away something you could no longer use?"

Clancy looked back at him in bewilderment. "I don't understand you."

"I think you will. Three names should prompt you. Dallas's. Simon's. *Clyde's*."

"I still don't understand."

He sat back, regarding her through the spirals of cigarette smoke. "Oh, come now," he smiled. It was a thin, edged smile.

Clancy clenched her hands in her lap.

"I would be obliged, Mr. Osman, if you would say what you're thinking."

"But I've already said it. I commended you on your generosity . . . then asked if it was the generosity of giving away what you could not use any more."

"That was what I heard but couldn't understand. Please explain yourself."

There was a tight sort of silence, then briefly and brutally Guy Osman said, "White."

"Simon?"

"Simon White. Nice of you to give him to Dallas . . . now that he's dead."

"Did Dallas say that?"

"Dallas did not say that. Dallas is in an aura . . . she's all lit up. Apparently you told her some sweet lie about White whispering her name with his last breath."

"Well, what did you want me to do," flashed Clancy, "destroy that girl?"

"So," Guy drawled, "it *was* as I said—a lie."

"I don't think so. I don't think Simon was responsible at the time. I think he was wandering. I think——"

"*I* think you lie." Guy looked at the tip of his cigarette. "I think its all dead sea fruit now for you, I think its ashes in your mouth. I think if White had survived it would be a totally different story for Dallas. After all, how can you use someone who is no longer here?"

"You're unspeakable!" she flashed.

Clancy got up.

He had risen too. His eyes flicked out at her. His voice was a whiplash.

"I may be unspeakable, but I can speak, Miss Clyde, I can speak my mind, something Miss Wyse probably doesn't wish to do. No doubt it's a greater balm to her to have things as they are."

"Then why don't you leave them like that?"

"I shall . . . for Dallas. It was just for my own curiosity that I probed."

Clancy said coldly, "I trust you were rewarded for your trouble."

"I wouldn't term it reward," was his dry reply.

They stood facing each other across the room.

"What do you want me to do," Clancy said furiously,

"go to that heartbroken girl and tell her what Simon really said?"

"No, I would not want that. I'm quite fond of Dallas."

Fond . . . *fond!* Clancy thought.

"But I want to know why it had to happen, why you had to go with him. Was it to see some more of this free land or was it because you couldn't resist the tenderness of his eyes?" Guy gave a brief laugh.

Angered beyond measure, Clancy said, "You may take your pick, Mr. Osman."

"Then I'll take the tenderness," he came back, but his voice was not tender, never had she heard anything so flint-hard.

"I don't know how much Dallas told you," Clancy proffered in a low reluctant tone, "but—but she financed Simon."

"She told me," he shrugged.

"Then—then why are you victimizing *me* like this?"

He had finished his cigarette. He stubbed it out before he answered.

"There was a pop song some years ago that the young-sters used to whistle," he said hatefully. "It was called 'It takes two to tango'. Does that answer you, Miss Clyde?"

"No."

"It doesn't answer that if you'd not gone with White there would not have been any need for a lie?"

Clancy clasped and unclasped her hands.

"I went in good faith," she proffered at last. "I was a new chum here, I had no idea of the immensity out there. I had no idea that Simon would—would——"

"Die, Miss Clyde, die with *your* name, not Dallas's, on his lips."

Clancy looked piteously at him. "Why don't you stop? What is it to you? Why do you have to have perfection in everybody all the time?"

For the first time since she had come in here it seemed she really reached him. He gave her a surprised . . . almost startled . . . look.

"Perfection?" he echoed blankly, as though he had never heard the word before. He repeated it. "Perfection."

Clancy spun round and ran out of the room.

The second thing to happen also happened in Osman's office.

When Clancy came back from lunch several days later Janet announced, "There's someone here who knows you. He's talking now with Guy. You're to go right in."

When Clancy went she stood at the door and gasped. Of all people perhaps the last she could have anticipated was Terry Kent.

Terry got to his feet and came forward with his hand outstretched, the same rakish, unreliable, uncaring, irresponsible Terry, the Terry who had wasted his years bringing out with regular irregularity a newspaper that no one read, anyway . . . only a man thousands of miles away . . . the man who stood beside him now.

"Clan, you're blooming, you're a peach," Terry boomed. "No wonder you hot-footed it back again. You look prettier out here."

"What are you doing in Australia?" Clancy asked, still incredulous.

"I saw a poster with the Boomerang Girl on it," laughed Terry, "and suddenly I was sick of Dray Hill."

He nodded towards Guy.

"Your boss is giving me a trial. I like the sun on my back, I like the beer. I think I'll be stopping, Clan." He winked. "Not like someone else we know."

Though Guy was the last person Clancy wanted to speak with, as soon as Terry had left she turned and faced her employer across the desk.

"Why did you say you would give him a trial?" she demanded.

"Because I *am* giving him one, Miss Clyde."

"But why?"

"I think I gave you this reason before: because I like the best my money can buy, and that man can write, there's no doubt on that score."

"Write lies?"

"Look," said Guy Osman, "if Kent wrote a true report on you it was good accounting, if he fabricated it was good imagination. But in either case it was *good*."

"You mean you didn't ask him—ask him——"

"Ask him whether you said those things or he made them up, you mean? No, I never asked. This is business, Miss Clyde."

"And business," she concurred, "comes first and last."

Again she spun out of the room as she had before.

The next occasion there was no need to escape him, for when she looked round he was not there. He was there when she went in . . . and when it all happened . . . but after it had happened Guy Osman, it seemed, had slipped away.

For weeks now the secrecy of the girls that she had felt after her return from Alice Springs had worried Clancy.

The girls were nice, they were polite . . . but they were not as they had been before. She could not have put a finger on it, explained it, but something was not there.

This morning it had seemed stronger . . . she could almost have said they were avoiding her.

When she went out for lunch she went in low spirits. It was no good saying it did not matter, because it did. She liked her fellow workers at Jarrah. In these nine months they had become part of her life.

She came back to the office on laggard feet . . . back, she thought, to those secretive looks, that air of something being kept away from her.

When she turned the handle of the Jarrah door and pushed the door open, it was to see the girls—and Guy—in a circle around someone . . . round an old lady. As Clancy was drawn into the circle Guy went quietly out.

"Introducing one of your own, name of Mrs. Parsons," beamed Janet, "and presenting Clancy Clyde." Then she said, "Clancy, guess who this is."

"Mrs. Parsons," said Clancy promptly. "You just said so."

She smiled at the smiling old lady.

"Yes," prompted Janet, "but *who?*"

"Why why, Mrs. Parsons, who else?" Clancy looked round helplessly. "Am I supposed to know?"

"Not really supposed to, I expect, but we thought you might. Look again."

Clancy looked . . . looked closer . . . saw a set of mouth she had seen before, a little quirk of raising the brow over the left eye.

"Mrs. Gillespie's mother!" she gasped.

"Yes, Mrs. Parsons," Janet beamed again.

All the group began to talk at once, Mrs. Parsons as well.

"You might have noticed we curtailed our monthly splurges," laughed Janet.

Clancy said in confusion, "Oh, you curtailed them for yourselves as well."

"Clan," they said in a chorus, "would we have left you out?"

She knew now they wouldn't, and for the times she believed they had she bowed her head in shame. But not for long. There was too much to be found out.

"How? Why? Where?" she began.

"By air . . . more convenient for Mrs. Parsons," answered Daphne.

"Because we could see how important it had become to you," answered someone else of the second question.

"If that 'Where' means where did we get the money . . . well, Mrs. Parsons had a little sock put away, our social fund was in good shape, and as for the rest . . ."

"Yes," said Clancy, "the rest." For *she,* thought Clancy, knew exactly to the penny the price of a London to Sydney air-fare. How many times had she checked for herself and then despaired?

"Guy," said the girls.

"Guy? Guy Osman? But why?"

"Why not? Some people like to give to one thing, others like to give to another."

"I," beamed Mrs. Parsons, "was just happy to come."

"So that's why you haven't written lately," said Clancy.

Mrs. Parsons, unlike her daughter of very stalwart stuff, said stoutly, "A waste of money writing when you'll be there soon."

"But, Mrs. Parsons," cried Clancy, "Mrs. Gillespie is very difficult over Australia."

"Stuff and nonsense. A place is what you make it. I'll

186

tell that girl a thing or two." Mrs. Parsons nodded her head.

"But—but *you* mightn't like it."

"I like it," said Mrs. Parsons. Nothing else. Just "I like it."

"And now," she said briskly, "when can I get out to Mary? Not"—hastily—"that I want to leave you, but I do want to have a few words with that foolish girl of mine."

Clancy was pushed off with the old lady. She wanted to stop to thank the girls, but that could be done later. She wanted to learn how they had managed this miracle, but that could come later as well.

The thing now was to settle Mary Gillespie for all time.

And Mary was settled . . . there was not the least doubt about that.

When Clancy knocked on her flat door she opened that door and said "Oh!" and rushed into her mother's arms.

But then a strange thing happened. Instead of Mary Gillespie pouring out a tale of woe, many tales of many woes, she became quite proprietorial about the place.

"It's a bit hot in summer, but at night it's pleasant-like, you'll stand it all right, Mum. The autumn is beautiful, and this weather that we have now is early *winter*, can you credit that? The children like the school and Lyndall is brown as a berry."

"She has freckles," reminded Clancy.

Mrs. Gillespie shrugged. "What's a freckle or two?"

There was so much to be said between them that Clancy decided to slip away. Later on, she thought, I can visit them and rejoice with them, though if I know anything it won't be here, in the Hostel. Mrs. Parsons is just the type to walk into a house agency and say "A house, please," and *get* it . . . just like some cheese or a loaf of bread. She laughed at her thought.

But Mrs. Gillespie did not laugh as she saw Clancy off, as she kissed her.

"I'll never forget this . . . I'll never forget those kind-hearted girls, that wonderful Mr. Osman. To think when he sat talking to Dad on Christmas Day and writing in his

187

book that he had *this* in mind. I'm so happy I could cry. I *am* crying. But, Clancy dear, they're tears of joy."

And in tears Clancy left her. Next time it would be laughter. All was well from now on with Mrs. Gillespie's world.

She waited for the bus, but it was a long time coming. If it didn't arrive soon, she thought, she would not be back in time to see the girls . . . to see Guy.

It was after five when at last she reached the city. The office would be closed. A pity. She wanted to thank them all while her heart was full like this, she wanted them to realize the fullness and be a little repaid.

Well, it would have to wait till tomorrow. Even if she went round to their flat she could not thank them all, for half of them were home-girls. Better to leave it, then, and make it one entire load of thanks.

But, she thought, I could thank the big benefactor, I could thank Guy.

Nervously, unwillingly, but bound by what was right, Clancy hailed a cab.

CHAPTER 25

A CAB was something Clancy seldom allowed herself, but
suddenly it was vital that she see Guy Osman just as soon
as she could.

The taxi-driver talked companionably as they slid out of
the city.

"You won't know this Sydney in a few years. Bursting its
seams, it is . . . That suburb you've given me, did you
know there's to be a new high-speed road?"

"Yes, I knew," said Clancy. She added, "It's going right
through the house where I want to go now."

"If it's the house I'm thinking of it's *gone*," said the
driver. "A pity, but that's the way it happens out here."

"Yes, *he* said that . . ." murmured Clancy, then she
asked urgently, "Gone? You mean Greenmarley has been
dismantled?"

"The bulldozer began this week. I had a fare out to
Figtree and I sat and watched for a while. A shame, but as
I said we need that road." The driver glanced in his mirror
at Clancy. "If that's the place you wanted will you still
want it?"

Clancy considered a moment. Then she said, "Yes."

When they arrived at the old gates Clancy paid off the
cab, got out, and then she stood dismayed. The entrance
was still there, but that seemed all. The rest was a pile of
rubble. The old house lay in ruins. There seemed nothing
left.

But there was.

The bell-tower.

Tomorrow undoubtedly the bell-tower would be crushed,
too, crushed under that bulldozer, but just now it still remained.

Mechanically Clancy walked down where the drive had
been, climbed over the rubble, came to the spiral stairs.

She could not have said afterwards *why* she climbed the stairs. What was there there for her, only dust and shadows and cobwebs? She could not have said afterwards how she knew that he would be there when she reached the top.

Guy was standing by the window looking out, and as she came into the room he whirled round.

"Miss Clyde!" He couldn't have seen her come down from the road.

"Yes, Mr. Osman."

"I didn't expect you." In the semi-darkness his face looked brightly eager, but shadows, she knew, were deceiving things.

"It was the only place to come," she pointed out banally.

"That's true" . . . now the eagerness seemed gone . . . "The rest is ruins." He shrugged.

Pityingly she asked, "Are you very hurt over it?"

"The house? Not really, I told you my views before."

"Progress . . ." she murmured.

"Always progress," he agreed. "Always look ahead, never look back."

He turned from the window and regarded her. "Always look ahead," he said again.

"That's all right," she argued, "if you have things that you don't want to look back on, but Greenmarley is different, I think. You would want to remember."

"It's bricks and mortar," he dismissed. "It's nothing I can get over it."

"And the things you don't want to look back on? The things from which you're resolved to go forward?"

"That is harder," he nodded.

She must not pursue this, she thought. Hurriedly she babbled, "I came to thank you. I can't imagine why you did it—Mrs. Parsons, I mean."

"A whim," he shrugged. "Every man gets numerous moments like these, charity occasionally springs into most breasts."

"But this was such a *personal* charity, I mean it can't be deducted from your income tax, I mean——"

"You mean my principle of business first, last and always has suffered a defeat. It's only temporary, I assure you."

He was lighting his cigarette, for a brief moment the little flame soaking up the shadows, illumining his strong lean face, his tall lean figure. For Osman there was the slender, ash-haired, golden-eyed girl.

Hurriedly, as though afraid of the light, of what it showed her, Clancy said, "Mrs. Gillespie will want to thank you, too."

"Good. I like being thanked." He laughed.

"Will—will the tower come down tomorrow?" she asked.

"I expect so. It can hardly stay here in the middle of an express-way, can it? Besides, what is its use now? There are no ferries for it to ring for any more."

"The great-great-grandmother who borrowed and rode a neighbour's pony will be sad," observed Clancy, a little sad herself.

"I don't think so. Like this country I think she was of more progressive stuff. You can't sit and moan and at the same time marry and raise a sturdy family and build and run a house and build and run a ship chandlery as she— as they did. No, I believe they were of different bone."

"I think," persisted Clancy, "she would be a little wistful, though. I think when the mate of the ship married her and they built this house and fixed this bell they would both have bells ringing in their hearts."

"What is this?" said Guy Osman shortly. "An application to write for the romantic fiction department? Miss Quilter is doing very satisfactorily, thank you, Miss Clyde."

"It was just a regret for a house," Clancy proffered.

"Then put that regret aside. The house is being moved."

"Being moved?"

"All that can be moved—which, as it happens, is quite a lot. The flags, the ancient kitchen surround, the trough, the stairs."

"To where?" Clancy asked.

"Down by the river. You may remember there's a sufficiency of space. That great-great of mine must have foreseen a difficulty like this and snared a big lump of land." He glanced sharply at Clancy. "Probably, being of convict stock, she had no intention of living 'fenced in.' "

"Why must you bring that up again?"

"To observe your reaction."

"Why should you observe that?"

He shrugged.

"Anyway, spare your tears," he advised. "Greenmarley will rise once more."

"By the river . . ." she said, seeing the gracious house looking out on the cool, satin-watered Lane Cove.

"You like the idea?"

"Oh, very much."

"The bell-tower can come, too . . . the gates . . ." For a moment his voice sounded boyishly enthusiastic.

"You're not so much the progressive type now," she pointed out. "You're leaning backwards."

"That's just what I'm *not* doing, Miss Clyde, I'm progressing. Isn't to build a family house out of a bachelor one progress? You of all people should see that."

"Why?"

"You emigrated to help swell our numbers here, remember."

"Remember," she prompted back, "I went home."

"Then came back again," he reminded.

She crossed to the window he had stepped away from. She looked out at the ruins that last week had been a lawn and flowers.

She had said what she had come to say, she had thanked him, so why was she lingering like this? Was it to hear *whose* family house?

"You'll never forget that, will you?" she remarked of his last observation. "You'll never forget that article. I'm sorry, Mr. Osman, that I'm so imperfect, but you seem to demand far too high a degree of perfection, I think."

"Because," he said suddenly, very soberly, "I'm perfect myself."

She stared at him in incredulity and he went quickly on.

"A *perfect* fool . . . a *perfect* example of blind, pigheaded jealousy."

"Jealousy?" she echoed. *"You* jealous?"

Still in that very sober voice he said, "Over you."

"Over me?" All she could do was echo him, it seemed. It was silly, but she could find no words of her own.

"Over you, Clancy. I was jealous of White. I didn't see light until you first flung up at me my standard of perfection. I *did* want perfection in you, I'll admit that. Anyone would want perfection in such a perfectly beautiful girl. I was angered that very first minute I saw you in Tim's office, that the only woman I knew I would or could ever desire had chosen to be so imperfect as to have said the things she did."

"I didn't say them."

"I know."

"Then you did ask Terry."

He made an impatient gesture. "I knew long before that. Anyway, it was of no consequence at all."

"Of no consequence? Yet you brought it up time after time."

"I had to. When a man is so stirred that it's either a declaration or an accusation, he has to choose the accusation. That is," said Guy, "if that's the only right he has."

"What other right is there?"

"The right," he said, "of a lover . . . but I knew you would never give me that. Because for all the imperfection I tried to see in that report of yours I still really believed you perfect, and how could I face up to that?"

"Then you said what you did that day in the office, you jibed at my standard of perfection, and I saw you for what you are."

"What am I?" she breathed.

He looked directly at her. "A woman with all the failings of any woman, a woman who might"—the look was eager now—"meet the failings of a man."

"What are they, Guy?"

"Oh, Clancy; as though you don't know! Imperiousness, dominance, quick anger, a hatred of criticism, intolerance, jealousy most of all."

"You said jealousy before, but I couldn't believe you."

"Can you believe me now?"

"No, Guy, how could I? How could I believe you were ever jealous of Simon when I never even mattered anything to you at all?"

That was what she tried to say, but did not finish. The

rest of the words after the first few were drowned in the tweed of his coat.

For his arms were around her, roughly, urgently, his lips were searching hers. He was kissing her, kissing her many times, and in each kiss she sensed the aching hunger, the months of needing her, that had kept him persistently that initial cold, considering man.

But consideration was not there now, only love, love pure and simple, love warm and rushing at first, then love with a complete belief, a quiet trust, the love of being loved. For although she had not responded yet she had not moved away from him, and she knew he was realizing that.

For a long moment he kept her there, then with a little laugh he pushed her off. At arm's length he held her and looked down at her with eyes that were strong and warm.

"You went away, you came back . . . Do you want to go away again, Clancy Clyde?"

"Oh, no, Guy, not ever, not ever!"

"Then you must make the full cycle, you must entirely return."

She stood back a stilly moment, feeling a sweet flood of decision drowning any doubt she ever might have had.

Then she knew she could extend this moment no longer, so she stepped back into that circle of arms, she completed the cycle, the homeward flight.

Guy said, "As a boomerang should."

SEPTEMBER STREET

September Street

"All women are in love with Rico," his cousin, Rosita, knowingly warned Clair. And the young Australian girl conceded that the lordly Portuguese marqués had a devastating charm.

But she must not forget he was now her employer, or that he had rescued her from being a drudge to the egocentric Mrs. Henry.

He had engaged Clair to look after his young nieces. If only he wouldn't treat her like a little child, too!

CHAPTER ONE

This ship is about to sail.

The announcement came through the loudspeaker first in Italian for Italian ears, then in English for Australian, for the luxury liner *Firenzo* plied between Sydney and Genoa via the South African sea route, and was carrying as many colonials travelling to England but seeing the continent first as it carried its own native sons.

Clair, standing at the rail amid a tangle of streamers, was watching a long scarlet ribbon to which someone had attached at intervals a bright line of balloons. The balloons bobbed precariously a few feet above the slowly widening water between the great ship and the teeming dock. Two hands held the ribbon aloft from each end. The young girl standing beside Clair lifted the hand not clutching the scarlet ribbon to throw a kiss. Clair saw the boy on the wharf throw one back.

A little abruptly, Clair turned away from the rail. Ever since the *Firenzo* had left Sydney Terminal, where, because of Mrs. Henry, she had been prevented from joining in the exciting farewell, she had determined to watch at least one departure.

Now, three departures later here at Fremantle, she had at last succeeded in escaping, temporarily, Mrs. Henry's heavy demands, but found little of what she had warmly anticipated when none of the waving hands were for her.

A sudden loneliness encompassed Clair, a loneliness magnified by the sight of all these people so unmistakably belonging to someone. I, she remembered, belong to no one at all.

She wondered for the first soul-searching time since she had accepted Mrs. Henry's offer if she had been wise to have agreed to it so eagerly. When the chance had come, it had seemed like a life-saving raft in an empty ocean, and from that moment on she had had no time to examine her feelings, to question her decision, but now, with time to do so, and with the sight of those hands reaching out to other hands and knowing she had none to reach out to, unless they were Mrs. Henry's plump white ones extended to have the long nails re-painted, Clair was uncertain.

Better, perhaps, she thought wretchedly, to have stayed on in Sydney, to have taken on any job, however humble, that she could snare, and with her lack of training it would have had to be humble, than to have accepted this. In Sydney at least the background had grown familiar, some of the faces, but here there was only a sea beneath her and a sea of faces around her, of which the only face she really knew was Mrs. Henry's.

Mrs. Henry. Clair tried to convince herself that the little shiver that involuntarily encompassed her was because of the sharp, wet-knife air that was blowing, or so someone at the rail had remarked feelingly, right from the South Pole. She tried not to think that it was the plump, effusive, easy-going woman, who, almost as soon as Clair had promised to accompany her, had changed to a complaining, shrewish, demanding employer.

It was not as if Clair had not expected demands, she knew as an employee that demands must be made of her. But Mrs. Henry's demands had been too hard and too long. Often they had been belittling.

Instead of the few hours' attendance on her that Mrs. Henry had generously dangled as bait, there were few hours left to her own device, instead of the slightly less accommodation that she had been assured would be her lot as a travelling companion, Mrs. Henry had refused even to allow Clair to sleep in the annexe of her luxury suite, had booked for her instead a passage in the Classe Turistica, even then a minimum berth in a dormitory type cabin.

Not that Clair minded that, indeed, for company, she would have welcomed it, if only she had had the opportunity to get beyond a quick, all-embracing smile each day, then a hasty 'Good morning' to the two of her Australian sleeping companions, a rueful *Buon giorno* to the three others.

'I'm convinced you don't like us,' one of the Australian girls on a working holiday had laughed.

'Always as soon as you come, you go,' Gina, the pretty Italian, had reproached.

Clair, hurrying off because Mrs. Henry wanted her hair set, had had no time to explain.

It was really because of her adroitness with hair, she thought a little regretfully now, that she was here on this luxury ship.

Mrs. Henry, in need of an immediate appendectomy, had been hurried into the same hospital at which Clair's mother had been dying. Clair had known her mother was leaving her, and she had known her mother had known, but between the two of them had persisted bravely that same brightness and companionship that had made them more contemporaries than mother and daughter.

Mrs. Wardle had accepted Clair's dainty bedjackets and pretty nightgowns as though she was living for ever instead of only a month. Perhaps, because she was living so briefly, it had to be for ever, Clair often had thought.

The hospital had been very busy, it had been necessary for a short period for Mrs. Henry to 'share'. She had been outraged, and had had no qualms in voicing her outrage, but slowly the calmness of Mrs. Wardle had doused her fires.

She had watched astounded while Mrs. Wardle and her daughter played their game of 'For ever' . . . a Sister had whispered to Mrs. Henry that her companion's time was running out . . . she had marvelled at Mrs. Wardle's almost girlish delight in the pretty things that Clair sewed for her, at the charming way her daughter's fingers set the now silver hair into waves and curls.

'You mean you weren't trained?' she had said once to Clair.

'Not trained for anything, I fear,' Clair had said ruefully. The Wardles had been Island people; when Mr. Wardle, a planter, had died several years ago they had not thought of leaving Daybell Island, Daybell Island where, apart from the pineapple plantations where the men superintended the crops, no one worked, and certainly never its women. The island provided amply for their simple needs.

But the island had not been able to provide the medical attention that Mrs. Wardle had required, so, selling the last interest they had in Daybell, mother and daughter had flown to Sydney.

Mrs. Wardle had entered hospital immediately, and, in a bed-sitter as close as she could get to the Southern Cross Clinic, Clair had spent what little was left – after the hospital fees for her own rent and food had been paid – and had waited for the end.

After that, she did not know what lay ahead. She would have to find some sort of work, she would not have enough money to return or to live again in Daybell, but for as long as her money lasted, and her only prayer then had been that it would last long enough, she was determined to spend as much time as she was permitted with her mother. Spend it 'living for ever'.

When the end had come, Mrs. Henry's operation had been over, and Mrs. Henry had been recuperating in a luxury hospital suite; Mrs. Henry always insisted on luxury suites. She had sent for Clair, and the sympathy and commiseration she had poured forth had warmed the girl, cold and bewildered in her new aloneness.

'I am going abroad,' she said. 'I dislike air travel, but I find sea travel difficult without a helping hand. Since Mr. Henry died I have had several companions, but none to my satisfaction.' That should have alerted Clair, but, abstractedly, she had barely heard it.

She had heard the next statement, though.

Mrs. Henry had said, 'Will you come?'

'With you?'

'Yes, dear.'

'To Italy? You said you had decided on an Italian ship.'

'I thought it would be a change. Yes, to Italy first. After that, who knows? Particularly' – coyly – 'if you are a good girl.'

Again Clair had not been alerted. All she had been aware of was a raft in an empty ocean, a saving hand.

'What – what would you want of me? I'm untrained, I

202

mean I have no typing, shorthand, nothing like that.'

'Silly child, I would only want you. Also you do marvellous things with hair.'

Clair had thought briefly that her mother had had the hair to do marvellous things with, but the thought had been very brief. *Then.*

'Also you are clever with your needle.'

'I can't make dresses, Mrs. Henry,' Clair had pointed out.

'Alter, adjust, little bits and pieces, dear. Then there's my nails ... oh, a dozen things. All' – hurriedly – 'very small and very undemanding.'

'And for that you – you would—'

'Pay your passage and add a little spending money, yes, dear.'

'Mrs. Henry, you're too good,' faltered Clair.

Mrs. Henry had put her plump white hand on Clair's thin brown one, brown from island suns. 'Then it is yes?'

'Oh, yes, yes! Thank you, Mrs. Henry.'

How soon after that had the flow of sweet effusion turned sour?

As soon as she had embarked at Sydney, Clair had been aware of a change. The cabin had been a surprise, but not an entirely unpleasant one. The five young women she had been placed with had been much her same age group, and that, Clair had thought sensibly, after tending Mrs. Henry would be a diversion. But before she had been able to orientate herself, look out on the fabulous farewell that Sydney gives all its departing ships, she had been paged by the First Class Purser. 'Wanted in the Rose Suite by Mrs. Henry!'

Wanted in the Rose Suite by Mrs. Henry.

How often had that resounded since, from Sydney to Melbourne, from Melbourne to Adelaide, across the Great Australian Bight with its mercury-grey waters to here at Fremantle.

Wanted in the Rose Suite by Mrs. Henry.

It had even echoed down to the lower level of the Fremantle Terminal, where, freed awhile, Clair had snatched a quick glance of the lovely western state, the only glance, she had

203

known ruefully, she would be permitted to take. She had looked longingly out on Fremantle's darkening streets . . . the *Firenzo* did not sail till eleven . . . then had wandered resignedly instead to the Terminal's window displays.

A very tall, very dark man with a somehow ducal manner had been standing at the wool demonstration looking at the Elizabeth Durack pictures of the red heart of Australia and at the wool samples beneath it. He had glanced at Clair, and, glancing back, she had wondered if he was a *Firenzo* passenger. If he was, it would be in the Classe Prima, she mused, for she could not picture those haughty brows, that olive skin, those high planes of cheekbones in the Turistica section. However, he could be seeing someone off, and she rather thought this might be, for in spite of similar colouring there was something quite un-Italian in his dark looks.

Dismissing the subject, she had stood beside him and had followed with deep interest the text of the display. The patterns of wool were labelled: Super Fine Merino, Fine Merino, Medium Merino, Strong Merino, Comeback. Beneath them were inscribed 80s, 70s, 64s, 60s, 58s.

She had said, meaning to say it to herself, 'Eighty shillings, seventy, sixty – is that what it means?'

At once she had heard his low amused laugh, and immediately after the laugh his apology.

'Pardon, *senhorita*, that was unforgivable of me, but I did not think to hear such an interpretation from an Australian. You are Australian?'

'Yes. But I lived on an island.' Clair had added heavily, remembering the days that were gone for ever, 'Daybell. It was almost tropical.'

'So,' he had smiled. He had added graciously, 'Then you are forgiven. Please' – at once – 'do not interpret that wrongly, it is just that I would not like to think that a mainland Australian did not know that that s, of course, means the count of wool.'

'Count?' she queried.

'The strands, *senhorita*.' *Senhorita*, Clari noted, not *signorina*, as an Italian would have said. Then he is not a native son, but Spanish.

'Portuguese, *senhorita*.' He must have read her thoughts.

'I didn't think you were Australian,' she submitted, a little embarrassed. As though, she knew, I could have mistaken him for an Australian! Those dark eyes, that olive skin, those high planes of cheekbones.

'For a non-Australian,' she ventured, 'you seem to know much about wool.'

'Very much. It is my – job, you call it?'

'Job,' Clair nodded.

'I am a buyer,' he explained. 'One might almost say for the world market. I cover, anyway, *senhorita*, many, many countries.' He had taken out a silver case and he flicked it open and offered the cigarettes to Clair. 'Australian wool is the world's best. Since you do not know wool, *senhorita*, let me go further. Super Fine would be for delicate materials, fine furnishings, the Fine would be a count of wool not quite so sensitive. And so it goes down, through knitting wool and blankets to wool for carpets, then rougher floor coverings, the rest.'

'I see,' Clair had said.

'Now perhaps,' he had asked politely, 'you will tell me about your island. Did you export copra, or trochus shell, or was it fruit?'

'Pineapples. My father had a plantation.'

'He has it no longer?'

'He died.' A little abruptly Clair had added, 'And my mother.' To her annoyance, for the last thing she had wanted was to let go of her still straining emotions, tears had sprung to her eyes.

Quickly he had placed himself between Clair and the people, who, attracted, too, by the display, were now milling round the window. Gently he had placed a hand under her arm and led her away, gently – but with a certain air of innate authority.

'*Senhorita*, we do not sail for five more hours. Yes. I am a passenger also on the *Firenzo*. Perhaps you would do me the honour of travelling into Perth, seeing, with me, that city

205

in its beauty of lights. You have seen Perth at night?'

'No.'

'It is beautiful.' He had stood waiting for Clair to reply.

For a moment she had stood silent, wondering eagerly if she could go. There was a faint ghost of a chance. Mrs. Henry had lost her temper with her this afternoon, sent her away and told her not to come back. The last time she had said that she had had her paged within an hour. Now it was several hours, and there was a possibility that Mrs. Henry was really piqued. She thought of the little bit of the westland of Australia she had seen, the freshness of it, the smiling openness, the white sands, the trees. She thought of Perth that the returning passengers had praised among themselves as perhaps the loveliest of the Australian capitals, thought of it from the heights of Kings Park and Mount Eliza, wearing its dress of glittering lights.

'I would love to come. Thank you.'

That was what she had started to say, but had not finished it. For to even as far as the lower level of the Terminal the voice had found her.

'Wanted at once in the Rose Suite by Mrs. Henry . . .'

At once this time! What had she done? That tiny scorch mark on Mrs. Henry's blouse, so tiny that even Clair's young sight had been unable to mark it clearly, had she found that? Or had she not screwed the top on the nail polish and some of the enamel leaked out?

Or – Or—

Those preliminary pre-announcement crackles were coming over the loudspeaker a second time, reaching, like unseen tentacles, down to grab her up. The voice began again.

Suddenly unable to wait till the message was repeated, Clair had turned and fled. Only when she was half way up the escalator had she remembered that she had left him without an explanatory word, that tall, dark man with the curiously ducal manner. The *senhor*.

She had half turned, vexed with herself and her bad manners, seeing the rising stairs behind her and knowing she could not return to apologize to him until she reached the top and descended again.

He still stood near the wool display, but when she looked back he bowed formally. Then, as if to reassure her, he had raised his arm.

Reassured, though what could it matter when most certainly attending Mrs. Henry, she would not encounter him again, especially on a large liner like the *Firenzo* where no one ever seemed to see the same person twice, Clair had boarded the ship at the Classe Prima end. She had hurried to the Rose Suite to find Mrs. Henry churlishly forgiving.

'You did my nails abominably, you couldn't have been attending, and the collar you altered is not sitting correctly. Also my hair, Clair, I've decided to change the style. However, I don't wish to be hard, especially as this is the final port in Australia. After you do these things you can go for the night.'

After?

After had been now, a full five hours later, the hours in which she had been invited to see a beautiful city don its dress of lights and instead had re-painted nails, re-painted them again and again until they finally satisfied, pressed, sewed, set hair.

It had been now, with 'This ship is about to sail' echoing first in Italian for its native sons and then in English for its Australian tourists. What, Clair had mused, had been provided for a Portuguese *senhor*?

She had stared down at the widening water, at the red ribbon with the balloons breaking at last and the girl giving a little cry of distress.

But at least the girl was saying good-bye to someone, and even if he was to be far away from her, he was still nearer than – well, than a *senhor* she probably would never see again. It was not the difference of Classe Prima to Turistica, not the unlikelihood of encountering the man on such a large ship, it was Mrs. Henry. Always, Clair knew drearily, there would be Mrs. Henry, and with no money at all in her pocket unless it came from Mrs. Henry, how could there be any other ending for her but, like that girl, a broken ribbon of balloons?

'Wanted in the Rose Suite . . .' Once again the voice summoned her.

With a glance back at the fading Terminal, the blurring lights, Clair obeyed the call.

But this time her call was to be quite different, and Clair sensed it at once, sensed it with a hollowness that bordered on foreboding. Instead of a fussing Mrs. Henry there was a furious one, instead of mere irritation there was ire. Anger against someone as yet unestablished. It did not take long for Clair to establish for herself that that was why Mrs. Henry's spacious cabin was so full of people. Besides the room steward, the bath steward and the maid there was a number of other people, including no less a figure than the Classe Prima purser. Clair had had dealings with the Classe Prima purser, so recognized him at once. He had made the arrangements that rendered her daily transits between Turistica and Prima more simple than the arduous climbing over the barrier on which the other venturesome Turistica passengers, mostly the young ones, had to depend.

He was, when Clair entered, talking with careful patience to Mrs. Henry.

'But, *signora,* could there not be an error, an unintentional error?'

'Thieving is never an "error".'

'I mean, *signora,* could you have *thought* you put the necklet there?'

'I am not in the habit of *thinking* where I put a six-thousand-dollar diamond pendant,' Mrs. Henry snapped. It was typical of Mrs. Henry that she had to state the price, though six thousand, if they were speaking, as Clair thought they spoke, of the diamond piece that had been Clair's job to bed after every wear in its black velvet box, then it was no over-statement. It was a beautiful piece, and probably worth every cent of six thousand.

The suggestion that she had only thought it had disappeared had brought a fire to Mrs. Henry's rather dull little eyes. Even the purser, trained, as all pursers are trained, to face wrath, indignation and often sheer unreasonable fury, withdrew a step.

'Of course I don't think it, I know. My diamond necklet simply isn't there.'

'Have you looked carefully?'

'What sort of fool do you think I am? Certainly I've looked. While you're wasting time asking these ridiculous questions the thief could be on his way. Not' – heavily – 'that I believe he is anywhere but in this room. There is never smoke without fire. Whoever stole my diamond necklet—'

'*Signora!*'

'I repeat, *stole* my necklet, must have been someone in daily contact with me.' Her little eyes raked the group that were gathered in the suite.

Someone must have murmured defensively aloud that anyone, anyone at all, who had seen the necklet on the *signora* could also be included in the list. Such a magnificent necklet as the *signora* described . . . so many lire . . . why, anyone, the defensive voice went on.

'Pha!' said Mrs. Henry. 'The fools aboard this ship' – she glared at the purser – 'would think it was only paste. Only those who have been around me, seen the care I have taken of it—'

The purser was saying that the *signora* should have deposited her necklet in safe custody along with her visa.

'I do not wear my visa,' she said haughtily, 'and anyway on such a ship would it even then have been safe? Even in your office?'

The purser, very red, was reaching for the right words, as a purser must. Mrs. Henry went wildly on.

'Only those in contact with me, who saw the care I took of it, instructed my companion to take of it—'

Abruptly Mrs. Henry stopped. She had turned her gaze on Clair. As if by a magnet all the other eyes turned.

'My companion—' Mrs. Henry repeated in a low revealing voice. 'You,' she said at last in a long hissing breath, '*you* put away the pendant.'

The others in the suite were looking at Clair with unconcealed relief in their eyes. They were sorry for her but more glad for themselves, glad to be free to get out of this unpleasant room and away from this unpleasant woman. They were pleased to see someone else made the scapegoat.

'Yes,' Clair said as evenly as she could, 'I put it in the velvet box as usual and in your drawer.'

'Here is the box,' said Mrs. Henry, 'but nothing in it. Explain that, you – you—'

'*Signora!*' appealed the purser.

Mrs. Henry whirled on him.

'You may have another name for it in your country, but in my country we call it stealing. I demand that you force this wretched girl to tell us what she has done with my pendant. Search her cabin. If it's not found there, cable back to Australia; she went ashore at Fremantle.'

'Only briefly. Only as far as the Terminal.' Clair marvelled that her voice remained so steady.

'So you say,' flashed Mrs. Henry. 'I know you were not with me. Whom you were with is another question.' She looked demandingly at the purser. 'Your question, my man.'

The purser began to murmur something again about the *signora* making sure, very sure. It was so hard to take back a harsh word if one was wrong.

His soothing words only seemed to incite Mrs. Henry. 'I insist you have her cabin searched!' she almost screamed.

Clair, seeing the distaste on the purser's face, said at once, 'I would be pleased if you would.'

The purser, obviously reluctant, nodded to the steward.

'The key, *signorina*?' the steward asked politely.

'I have none. I mean we share a key.'

'You and another *signorina*?'

'Five others,' Clair explained.

'But this is the Classe Prima.' The steward was obviously puzzled.

'I am in the Turistica.'

'But the *signora* whose necklet—'

'She is not with me, of course.' It was Mrs. Henry. 'She is where she should be, as befits her position. At least' – icily –

210

'that's what I thought. Now I can think of another place.'

Clair looked levelly at the steward. 'The number is 573.'

'*Grazie, signorina.*' He went out.

Mrs. Henry was still unsatisfied. 'Are you going to stand and wait until he returns? What of that statement of hers that she went no further in Fremantle than the Terminal, don't you intend questioning it?'

'*Signorina?*' the purser asked Clair almost wretchedly.

'I went no further,' Clair confirmed.

'Ask her whom she met, then!' shrilled Mrs. Henry.

'*Signorina?*' he muttered again.

'The usual travel information people, the banks changing Australian currency into lire.'

The purser smiled faintly at Clair. 'And you spoke to no one?' He glanced at Mrs. Henry almost triumphantly.

'I – yes, I did,' Clair said with difficulty. 'I spoke – with a man.'

'His name, *signorina?*'

'I don't know.'

'More lies!' said Mrs. Henry. 'Undoubtedly the pendant was passed over then.'

'He was a passenger,' Clair volunteered, 'from this ship.' She hated involving the man she had met on the wharf, but now the situation was becoming more than a farce, it was becoming serious.

'And you do not know his name?'

'That, I can believe,' interrupted Mrs. Henry spitefully. 'It would be natural for this young woman to speak to a man and not know his name. I only wish I had not been so impulsive and generous in the first place. I saw this person and I was hoodwinked by the innocent act she put on. Again my generous heart has betrayed me. I always have trouble through my impulsiveness and kindness. My dear late husband always warned me. "Normelda," he said, "you'll have trouble".'

Clair, who had helped Mrs. Henry with her visas, was a little surprised at that 'Normelda'. On the official forms only Norma had been inscribed.

'So you cannot tell us the name,' the purser said regretfully.

On an inspiration, and undoubtedly goaded by a steely look in Mrs. Henry's eyes, 'You can describe him, perhaps? Tell us something about him?'

'Ridiculous!' snapped Mrs. Henry. 'This is a very large ship, there are some hundreds of Firsts and many more hundreds of Seconds.'

'Turistica,' corrected the purser. 'Can you, *signorina*?' he repeated.

'He was tall and dark.' How foolish that sounded! Ninety per cent of the men aboard were dark. 'Very tall,' added Clair weakly. She added, not very hopefully, 'We talked about wool.'

'Wool!' sneered Mrs. Henry, but the purser did not sneer.

'Wool, *signorina*? The gentleman appeared interested in wool?'

'Yes. Very interested.'

'Then that would undoubtedly be the Marq— Senhor Montales. He is the only wool man aboard. He was Portuguese, *signorina*?'

Clair nodded. 'He buys,' she recalled, 'for a world market, or for many countries at least.' She added hastily, remembering the tall, aloof yet strangely kind and considerate figure, 'But I would not want the *senhor* to be troubled.'

'To the Marq— to Senhor Montales such things would not be trouble. We must request him to come at once.'

Mrs. Henry was looking a little less sure of herself. 'As though it would mean anything!' she interrupted. 'This man could be as much a liar as this wretched girl. They could have put their heads together.'

'You are speaking, *signora*, of the Senhor Enrico Montales.' The purser nodded peremptorily to the steward still remaining in the suite, and the man obeyed.

A rather uncomfortable silence fell on the group in the Rose Suite. Clair was uncomfortable because of the embarrassing position in which she had placed the man she had briefly met on the Terminal. Mrs. Henry was uncomfortable because in some dim manner she could see that things weren't going quite so much her way. The rest were uncomfortable because occurrences like this were always uncomfortable, and into the

212

atmosphere of unease stepped the tall, dark wool man Clair had met in Fremantle.

At once everything seemed to change.

Clair, though in her embarrassment she did not look up at him, relaxed instantly. Mrs. Henry, her interest piqued, began to fluff up her hair, straighten the collar of her blouse. Her little eyes summed the wool man up. His impeccable clothing did not escape her, his haughty carriage, his ducal air.

'Of course,' she began at once, 'mistakes are made. When one has so much one can be a teeny-weeny bit careless. My late husband often reprimanded me.' She looked coyly at the newcomer. 'It was just,' she smiled, 'that this was such a favourite trinket.'

'Trinket, *senhora*? At that high price?' Evidently Enrico Montales had been acquainted of the facts. 'So many dollars!' he pointed out. 'So many lire!' he shrugged. 'So many escudos!'

'I don't understand money matters,' pouted Mrs. Henry, coy again. 'I leave it to my little help.' She nodded to Clair.

Clair stared back at her. How could she speak like this, how *could* she, when only five minutes ago she had said the things she had, when even at this moment the steward was searching Clair's cabin?

'I have been given to understand,' the *senhor* said in correct, clipped English, 'that you have accused this girl of theft.'

'Oh, no. It could have been a mistake. We all make mistakes.'

'Not mistakes like that,' Enrico Montales replied.

'You're made of steel,' pouted Mrs. Henry coquettishly. 'Yet I like a man of steel. You must find sympathy, though, *signore, senhor*' – she made the correction cosily – 'for a poor, bewildered little woman. You see, I looked for my pendant and found an empty box.'

'I suggest you look again. Now.'

'Of course. Clair dear—'

'No, not the *senhorita*. *You*.'

'But—'

There was no evading the man, no turning away from the

213

polite but emphatic order, and making a show of coy submission, Mrs. Henry began to go through the drawers.

At the third she stopped.

'*No!*' she disbelieved. 'How could it have got there?' She took out and held aloft the glittering piece. Then she put it against her throat, looking up at the *senhor* for approval.

He did not appear to notice the display. 'How has this come about?' he asked instead.

'I put it away last night,' submitted Clair.

The man took no notice of her; she might as well not have been there.

'Well, *senhora*?' he asked Mrs. Henry.

Mrs. Henry was crumpling her plump face into what she possibly thought was feminine confusion.

'I remember. I tried on my pink frock after Clair had left. She had altered it for me and I wanted to make sure of the alteration. She's not always thorough, the naughty girl.' She looked fondly at Clair.

'And you took out the pendant?'

'Yes.'

'And when you had finished with it you did not replace it?'

'I thought I did.'

'But you didn't?'

'I couldn't have, could I?' Mrs. Henry gave him a sweet smile.

The *senhor* did not smile in answer. Instead, of all things, he said clearly, 'I suggest then that you apologize to the young *senhorita.*'

'Clair understands me,' pouted Mrs. Henry. 'She knows the serious operation I have undergone, how delicate I am.'

'The apology, please.'

'But – but good heavens, I'm paying the girl's passage!'

'Turistica. A six-berth.'

'Well, what do you expect? She is after all only my servant.' Now there was no coyness in Mrs. Henry. Even the dark good looks of Senhor Montales, his undoubted air of wealth and importance, could not stop her indignation.

'She was, madam.' No more Portuguese '*senhora*' or even

214

Italian 'signora', only the clipped, unsentimental 'madam'.

'She is. The girl can't leave me. She has no money, nowhere to go.'

'You are in error. I have a post awaiting her, I have for her a destination.'

Mrs. Henry stared incredulously from the senhor to Clair, then back to the senhor again. At last she turned to Clair.

'You sly little piece!' she fumed. 'You let me put out my cash for your passage, you accepted my wages—'

'The monies, have no fear, will be attended to, madam, you will be amply repaid. And now, unless the senhorita wishes to wait for the apology that seems so long in coming, I suggest that we break up this distasteful gathering, remove ourselves to the open air. There is freshness there.'

Clair was only half conscious of fingers under her elbow, of being impelled out of the Rose Suite.

Behind her she heard Mrs. Henry storming at the maid. Poor girl, she would take the brunt now. Who would press Mrs. Henry's frocks, sew their collars, do Mrs. Henry's hair?

But much more disturbing than that was: Who would look after Clair? If – no, when – Mrs. Henry demanded repayment of Clair's passage, withdrew the small salary she had given at the end of each week, what then?

While she mulled it over she had been impelled out to the Lido, or boat, deck. She had never seen this lavish deck before, her visits to the Classe Prima had only consisted of going straight to the Rose Suite, coming straight back.

Though they were only a few hours from Fremantle, the weather was already growing silky, the ocean losing its Australian Bight swell for the placidity of the Indian Ocean. A big gold moon was coming up.

The senhor was leading Clair to a chaise-longue, he was plumping luxurious cushions, putting her gently down.

'Yes, I insist,' he said with a gentle firmness, and he nodded into the darkness, though it could not have been entirely darkness, for presently a long-stemmed glass was put by a quiet steward into Clair's hand.

'Drink first, senhorita,' the senhor said, more firm now than gentle, 'and then, I think, we talk.'

His white teeth flashed in the smooth olive of his skin. A. he bent over to shield a little breeze from the cigarette he had taken from his gold case, he looked up, and his black eyes, remote and aloof yet at the same time kind and encouraging, most of all indisputably authoritative, met Clair's.

'You are pale, *senhorita*. That is understandable. It has been for you a very unhappy scene.'

'It has been the same for you—' Clair hesitated a moment, then finished, '*senhor*.' She found she could not adopt her own tongue, as he had done for her, to this olive-skinned, flashing-eyed man.

The little hesitation and then the shy address must have amused him, for a small smile flickered briefly at the corners of his long, sensuous mouth.

Almost at once, though, it was gone.

'What I cannot understand, however,' Enrico Montales resumed, 'is that you ever allowed yourself to be in the employ of such a person.' He permitted a slight moue of distaste. 'Surely your pride, *senhorita*—'

'When one has nothing at all—' Clair defended herself weakly.

'Then one is even prouder. My servants—' He stopped abruptly.

'Who, *senhor*?'

'Men I have known who serve menially and possess very little still possess their pride.'

'Men you have known,' pointed out Clair, 'but not you yourself?'

'No, *senhorita*.' The answer came after a slight pause.

'Then it's quite different,' Clair said a little angrily. How dared this obviously affluent person criticize her for something he would not remotely understand?

His dark brows were raised at her. It occurred to Clair that quite feasibly in all his life he had never been spoken to like this. She had read in books that in Portugal—

'In Portugal,' the *senhor* remarked, reading her mind, as

he had on the Fremantle Terminal, 'the women do not argue with men in such a manner, *senhorita*. But do not be embarrassed' – a quick charming smile – 'I have travelled far. I have perceived – and often approved – the Australian way of life.'

'That is most kind of you, *senhor*.' Clair could not help her voice emerging stiff and aloof. Although she knew she should make allowances to his nationality, as a Colonial herself, bred to emancipation and independence, she could not help squirming under his gracious patronage.

'Now you show resentment, a trait I was pleased *not* to observe in your countrymen, *senhorita*.'

The gentleness of the reproach – or was it the quiet compliment? – undid Clair where a continuance of the arrogance would have stiffened her.

'I'm sorry,' she smiled at him. 'I shouldn't have said what I did.'

'Your generous submission disarms me. I should not have said what I did.'

'Submission?' Clair could not help echoing that.

When she looked at him she saw that his eyes were laughing at her.

'You question that word? But why? Isn't to submit to yield, and to yield to pay or repay? At the same time as you, in an apology, submit to me do not I, in my apology, submit to you?'

She thought that over, and agreed. 'But,' she added doggedly, 'please don't add "In Portugal –", *senhor*.'

'In Portugal,' he persisted, 'the woman would not speak in your Australian way, but' – a twinkle – 'the woman would think it, and I believe I prefer the open method, *senhorita*.'

'Thank you, *senhor*.'

He had snapped his fingers for more drinks. There was an autocratic crispness in the gesture, and yet he spoke kindly to the steward and must have rewarded him generously, for Clair heard the ring of approval in the waiter's thanks.

When he had gone, the *senhor* resumed the conversation.

'You are sorry for what you said to me, and I am sorry for what I said to you. We have understood each other and craved each other's pardon, so all that now is over. Then will you proceed, please?'

'Proceed?' she queried.

'I cannot believe that straitened circumstances alone made you concede to that person. Tell me, *senhorita*.'

'It's of no importance,' she refused.

'It is of vast importance. If you accepted Senhora Henry simply because you had no money, you would accept me in the same manner. That would not be sufficient to me. Now do you understand?'

'Not really. I mean so long as I do my job—'

His brows had met in one dark, arrogant line.

'It would not be enough. So tell me, please.'

It was futile to try to stave off this man. A little wearily Clair said, 'It was not only the money, she was kind – at first.' Briefly she told her little story.

When she had finished, he sat tapping the tips of his fingers together. A glance at his serious face told Clair that for all the gravity there, her explanation had satisfied him.

'So,' he said, 'it was not just your circumstances, *senhorita*, it was your hope in this person as well.'

'Yes.'

'That is good. It is not good that she failed you, but it is good that you embarked on something with more than reward in mind. I am happy, *senhorita*.'

'Now, *I* shall talk.' He moved his chair a little closer.

He did not begin at once, though. First he opened the gold cigarette case again, and offered it to Clair. When she shook her head, he ashed his own cigarette, replaced the case and took out, instead, a cheroot. From somewhere in the soft darkness a steward appeared to light it. Clair noted that Enrico Montales accepted the service graciously but without surprise. He gestured for their glasses to be refilled, then gestured again that they were to be left alone.

Clair took a sip of the cool lime punch he had ordered for her and the *senhor* drank a mouthful of the red wine.

'Undoubtedly you are wondering, *senhorita*, a number of things. Why I supported you just now beyond stating that I was with you on the Terminal? Why I have said I have ready for you a post? What is this post?'

'Yes, I do wonder,' confessed Clair. She paused, then went off on a tangent. 'I also wonder why a wool buyer would be taking such a long route to his market. Australian business men fly.'

'I, too, fly, *senhorita*, but not on this occasion. That, I do believe, is my good fortune.' He inclined his dark head almost regally to Clair.

She flushed with pleasure at the gallant compliment and was glad it was night-time and he could not see her pink cheeks. For a moment she wondered what it would be like to be a Portuguese lady, born to such noble attention. On the other hand, she mused, a Portuguese lady did not answer back.

She became aware of the dark glitter of his eyes; they shone even through the deepness of the night. Had they seen her heightened colour after all, so that he, smilingly, had put her down as an inexperienced child?

She stammered something about her good fortune, too, but he waived her words aside.

'I did not fly on this occasion, *senhorita*, because I was accompanying my cousin home.'

'He is on this ship as well?'

'She, *senhorita*, and her two children. Now' – a little laugh – 'you are wondering why a Portuguese chooses an Italian line.'

'Is there a Portuguese line to Australia?'

'No, there are only English, Greek and Italian lines.'

'In that case,' proffered Clair, 'perhaps it's that you prefer Italian cuisine.'

'I like Italian food, yes, but I also like English food.' He gave a little gesture of unimportance. 'So long as it is good food it does not matter. No, *senhorita*, I chose the *Firenzo* because of Signora Dal Rosa.'

'And she is—?'

'My cousin.'

'But *signora* – that's Italian.'

'You learn, little one.' He gave a low laugh. 'Seeing that this post I have in view for you includes my cousin, I think I should explain.' He sat back and smoked a moment, the blue spiral from the cigar misting around him, its aromatic scent merging with the faint spiciness now creeping into the sea breeze.

'A Portuguese lady invariably weds a Portuguese gentleman, though a Portuguese gentleman sometimes looks further afield.' He shot her a quick, enigmatical look. 'Invariably to Britain, *senhorita*. Between our two countries there has always been a close bond.' Again she was aware through the night of the dark glitter of eyes. 'You are British,' he stated. 'Australia is British.'

'Yes, *senhor*,' she said, her own glance averted, for some reason absurdly shy.

'My cousin Rosita met her husband while on vacation at Cannes. These things happen,' he shrugged.

'You were displeased?' Clair could not help that, nor the tone in which she said it; she had noticed the dispassionate lift of his broad shoulders and had reached a conclusion.

'Because he was Italian? By no means. But because she acted impulsively and with undue haste. Rosita was not being Portuguese in that. But then' – another shrug – 'she was playing what you British call tat for tit. Correct?'

'Tit for tat,' said Clair. 'You mean—'

'I mean she was piqued over a love affair that did not run to her wish, so promptly made a new love affair of her own. Luckily for her, Umberto Dal Rosa, was a fine man, even though he was many years her senior.'

'Was, *senhor*?'

'Sadly the *signore* died recently in Queensland, Australia.'

Clair nodded, 'There's a large Italian community there. They produce most of the sugar.'

'Umberto Dal Rosa had several mills,' Enrico Montales said. He smoked a moment. 'Fortunately I was in Melbourne on business at the time. I flew up and saw to Rosita's affairs. Then I agreed to accompany Rosita and the children home. We decided that a sea trip would be to their benefit.'

'Home to Portugal or Italy, *senhor*?'

He gave a helpless gesture. 'You tell me, little one, and I

will tell you. In Portugal, it is expected that a wife will never cleave from her husband, in which case Rosita would remain the *signora*, not the *senhora*. But Rosita—' He gave a rather fond little laugh, followed by a slight sigh.

Clair was plainly puzzled and to hide it asked, 'What about the children?'

'Two girls, aged nine and ten.'

Now Clair felt she had a clearer picture of Rosita Dal Rosa. She would be in her thirties . . . a motherly soul.

'Where,' she inquired, feeling more at home with the maternal, thirtyish Rosita she had in her mind than the impulsive Rosita that the *senhor* had painted, 'do I come in?'

'You are needed for Juanita and Amalia.'

'The children? The girls?'

'Yes.'

'But they're not Italian names.'

'Rosita, of course, would have what *she* wishes. She has always been, as I said, an un-Portuguese woman in that.'

'Un-Portuguese? Yet she called her daughters by Portuguese names?'

'A true Portuguese woman, whatever her own whim, would comply with the man.'

'You think that is good?'

He shrugged in the darkness. 'I am not a true example, *senhorita*. I have left the walls of the *palacio*.'

'What is that, *senhor*?'

The man flicked away an ash almost sharply, as though he was annoyed with himself.

'A term,' he said shortly, 'meaning—'

'Yes?'

He did not reply.

'I think you mean you have found wider fields,' Clair suggested, and he agreed at once. Agreed too quickly?

'Yes, *senhorita*, I have found wider fields.' He put the cigar in his mouth again.

What, wondered Clair, as the smoke wreathed aromatically around her, was a *palacio*, whose walls he had left?

'So,' shrugged the *senhor*, 'it is not for me to say. Besides, *senhorita,* we are speaking of my cousin Rosita, not of myself.'

Chastened, Clair was silent.

'Rosita, of course,' he resumed, 'is still in a period of mourning, something' – he looked at her through the darkness – 'which you have discarded.'

'By no means, *senhor,* we still mourn as we ever mourned, but it's here, in our hearts, and not in custom and dress. I' – her voice was low – 'still mourn my mother.'

'I am convinced of that,' he said gently. After a moment he added, 'I would ask you, *senhorita,* to be as convinced of the seriousness of *our* period of mourning, that is, if you could so bring yourself.'

'But of course, *senhor,* to question your beliefs would be intrusion on my part. I would never dream of showing such disrespect.'

'I am assured of that,' he nodded gravely. 'Rosita,' he continued, 'in accordance to our custom will mourn Umberto Dal Rosa for the space of yet another few weeks.'

'She will wear black, you mean?'

'Most certainly, but I did not refer to that. She will keep to her suite, *senhorita.*'

'Not come out on deck?' Clair could not understand this. 'I mean,' she stammered, 'I would sympathize with her wish not to join in any functions, but surely—'

'Already,' he reproved quietly, 'you are not "convinced" as you claimed you were.'

'I'm sorry,' Clair said instantly. 'It's simply that – well, I'm a believer in fresh air. I mean, *senhor,* perhaps your cousin would be in better health if— But there, I intrude, and I said I wouldn't.'

'You are excused,' he proclaimed graciously. 'And have no fear for Rosita's health. Rosita' – there was a tinge of amusement in his voice – 'thrives.'

She digested this for a few moments, then asked, 'And the children? Juanita? Amalia? Do they mourn as well?'

'No. Rosita is Australian when it comes to her Australian-born daughters. The children are not confined to the suite.' The *senhor* took a sip from his glass. 'That is where you come in.'

'I, *senhor*? But I'm no governess, no nurse.'

'You are an adult young woman who is not obliged to remain in a cabin. That is all that is asked.'

Clair, recalling what this man had already done for her, stammered, 'It's little, surely.'

'It is what I need.'

'You, *senhor*?'

'Rosita'– his brows had met in a frown – 'is uncaring about such things.' At her look of puzzlement, he explained, 'About the needs of children. I do not mean the physical needs, the meat, the bread, the time for bed, for the daily bath, the *Firenzo* most surely satisfies these, but the need of an adult hand to take at times, a woman's hand, not a man's, and not the hand of a governess or a nurse, but the hand of a friend. A friend to take them to the innumerable children's teas and fancy dress frolics that these Italian ships delight in. The *bambini*, it has become apparent to me, is the *Firenzo*'s most precious cargo.' He gave a low laugh.

Clair joined in. 'Not just the *bambini* but the older children as well. They even have their Orario Sala Ragazzi, or Teenagers' Room, *senhor*.'

'Juanita and Amalia will come somewhere between that and the nursery,' he nodded, 'and, being 'twixt and 'tween – is that right, *senhorita*?'

'Yes, *senhor*.'

'Will be more than ever in need of that hand of which I spoke. There will be many times a day you will be needed, have no fear. The before-breakfast romp round the deck, the need to chatter and stretch young limbs after the hours of lessons.'

'Is there a governess?' she asked.

'It was not considered necessary for only a month. I am instructing them myself, *senhorita*, though briefly, each morning. Then there is the initial shy hanging back at the children's teas when most little ones need kindly encouragement to join in, encouragement from an adult hand, but, mind you' – he smiled slightly – 'a woman's hand. You agree?' He raised his brows in question.

'Of course,' nodded Clair, unable to picture this proud, remote man with a child's hand in each of his hands and giving each child a kindly forward prod. No, that would not be the *senhor*.

'In short,' he finished, 'you would be their mother in all but the domestic side, you would be there to share their pleasure at their first flying fish, their dolphins, a ship passing by. These things are important, I do believe. I do not like when other small ones call, "See, Mama—" ... "Look, Mama—" ... that Juanita and Amalia have no one to call. You understand?'

'Yes.' Clair did. For a period she had been at boarding school and she had not forgotten the feeling when other parents had visited on visiting day and her own parents, because of distance, had been unable to be there. Anyone would have done, she remembered acutely, even the most distant aunt or casual friend.

But how, she thought, would Rosita consider all this? She murmured her thoughts aloud.

'My cousin has implicit belief in my judgment,' the *senhor* said formally. 'She has already agreed.'

'Already?' Clair looked incredulously at him. How could he have spoken already when only less than an hour ago the unpleasant business had taken place?

'We met on the Terminal, remember,' he said gravely. 'I then made up my mind.'

'But I – but you—' Clair's voice trailed off. This man, she accepted, would be quite capable of making a decision like that. He would decide what he wanted and see to it that he got it. Even had she been happy in her service to Mrs. Henry, in some way he still would have filled his own requirements. Politely, graciously, but none the less definitely, authoritatively. Clair looked at him a little nervously, then her tension left her. Through the darkness he was smiling at her, the teeth white in the olive skin, the eyes kind for all their proudness.

'I am no ogre, little one.'

'I know, it was just—'

'You question my quick decision? But it was a good decision, as one day you will see. I have always made such decisions, *senhorita*, it was expected of me.' His voice was not boastful, it was even a little bored.

'And now I think your room would be prepared. After that unhappy episode you will be ready to retire.'

'My cabin has been ready all the time,' she said, puzzled.

'I did not say cabin, *senhorita*, I said room. My only regret is that I have been unable to procure for you a full suite. Perhaps after Durban—' He flashed her another smile.

'But – but—' she stammered.

'You surely did not think I would leave you where you were, *senhorita*?'

'It was adequate.'

'Perhaps, but it still would be unthinkable to me. This will be much more suitable.'

'What' – Clair squirmed visibly – 'if I meet Mrs. Henry?'

'What, indeed!' The proud brows rose haughtily and Clair knew she had said a redundant thing.

'I must say good-bye to my cabin mates,' she stammered.

'Not tonight.' His voice was firm.

'But—'

'I would not forbid that courtesy, *senhorita*, I have perceived how important friendship among all walks of life is to the Australian, and I have approved of it, but still not tonight. You have suffered an emotional storm, and I insist now upon rest. There are still many things to be discussed, but they, too, must wait.'

'My clothes, my belongings—' began Clair.

'Would already have been removed and placed in your new quarters. Oh, yes, I have instructed these things to be done and my instructions would be obeyed.' He had got to his feet and now extended his hand. 'Your room would be ready, and to that room you must now let me conduct you.'

It was no use to protest, and Clair, indeed, was past protesting. The *senhor* was right, she had suffered an emotional storm. She allowed herself to be led gently but firmly from the Lido through the First Class vestibule to a room on the A Deck.

The *senhor* opened the door, gave the interior a quick probing look, barely nodded, then bowed Clair in.

The bed, not berth, had a pink quilted coverlet turned invitingly down. On the table by the bed a hot drink steamed faintly from a pretty pink stein. On the bedside table as well as the warm milk were flowers, books and a pink telephone. Clair, in her sweeping examination, saw that a bath had already been drawn in the private annexe.

'*Senhor—*' She turned impulsively to him, tears blurring her eyes so that she could not see him.

But when the tears cleared away she still could not see him.

Quietly Senhor Montales had closed the door and gone.

CHAPTER TWO

CLAIR was so tired she did not bother to check whether her belongings had been transferred from her dormitory cabin as the *senhor* had assured her. If they were not, then she would simply have to wear tomorrow what she wore now. She folded the garments and stepped into the compact but ample bath, for all her utter weariness still able to appreciate not having to wait first in a queue. As she lay back luxuriously she sniffed a fresh uncluttered fragrance. Cupping the water to her nose, she knew that bath essence had been added.

This was living as she had never known it. For a moment she closed her eyes and asked, 'Why? Why me?' She did not ponder long, though . . . she would have fallen asleep in the relaxing waters. She got out, reached for one of the pink towels on the heated rail and saw, at the same time, that her night-gown had been placed ready on another heated rail.

It was all too miraculous. She must snap out of this cloud cuckoo land and wash her things for tomorrow.

But she didn't. She tumbled into bed, instead. Drank hot, spiked milk. Thought drowsily of olive skin and dark, flashing eyes. Slept.

Slept until morning.

The stewardess putting a tray beside her bed awakened Clair.

'*Buon giorno, signorina,*' the Italian woman smiled. As she busied herself with napkin and plates she explained, 'The Portuguese gentleman ordered your breakfast. He trusts it is to your taste. There is also a note.'

She finished the arranging and crossed to the bath annexe and took up Clair's discarded clothes. At Clair's inquiring look at this she said, 'They will be laundered, *signorina.*'

'But I can do them myself.'

'The Portuguese gentleman instructed me,' the Italian

227

smiled again. She put out more pink towels, said, '*Buon giorno*' once more, and left the room.

Clair took the pink cover from the tray. Chilled orange juice, a sliver of green melon, a rasher of bacon to go with an egg with a frill of brown lace round it, thin toast, a large pot of tantalizing coffee.

'Why, I'm starving!' Clair laughed softly to herself.

She ate eagerly, remembering ruefully that yesterday she had barely eaten at all. As a matter of fact she had not eaten much since she had left Sydney. Either her appetite had deserted her or every time she had decided on a decent meal that voice over the ship loudspeaker, that 'Wanted in the Rose Suit by Mrs. Henry' had intervened.

Now Clair ate and felt stronger for it.

She got up, took a quick shower, then opened the wardrobe. Her clothes had been placed for her, and where, in Cabin 573, because of lack of space she had been glad of their meagreness, now she felt embarrassed. All those waiting hangers and only four occupied!

She went to the window . . . in her dormitory cabin she had not even had a porthole . . . and peeped out. It was a lovely, sunny day, and seeing they must now be approaching warmer waters, the temperature rising with every knot, she decided to wear the cool simple linen in pale green. She was fastening the narrow belt when she remembered the note. She crossed to the bedside table and took it up.

It was written on the *Firenzo* stationery and was from Enrico Montales.

'*Bom dias*. I trust you had a restful night. Keeping in mind your wish to pay your respects to your cabin friends, I have arranged for eleven o'clock coffee in the Florentine Lounge. I would like to see you there previously. *Graças*. Enrico M.'

Clair put the letter down and glanced at her watch. If the *senhor* wanted to see her before she met her friends, she had better go now. As she ran a comb through her fair hair, she thought how kind it had been of him to take the trouble to arrange the small party. She smiled at the thought of Cabin 573's excitement. Coming into the Classe Prima from the

228

Turistica was something all the passengers loved to do. Thank you, *senhor,* she thought, *grazie* . . . no, that was wrong for a Portuguese. She looked at the note and changed *grazie* to *graças.* She was humming to herself as she went down the passage.

It was not until she was almost on the Rose Suite that Clair realized that, from habit, she had taken the left turn from the vestibule instead of the right.

She wheeled back quickly, but as she did so the door opened, and Mrs. Henry, Mrs. Henry who never emerged before noon . . . was it because she had no Clair now to run to her beck and call that her ex-employer was several hours earlier? . . . came out of the Rose Suite.

'Good morning, Mrs. Henry,' Clair murmured uncertainly. She felt she must say something to the woman.

Mrs. Henry completely ignored her . . . that is, she ignored her by her lack of response. The look she gave Clair was not ignoring, though. It was openly venomous.

Considerably shaken, Clair retraced her steps. She took a quick turn round the deck to calm herself before she went to the Florentine Lounge to meet the *senhor.* How lovely, she thought, standing at the prow, to plough bravely through waters instead of leave them behind as one had to when one was a passenger in the Turistica. Whether it was the more favourable position or just a lovelier day now that the Bight was far behind them, to Clair every white cap on the blue sea shouted glory. She thought of little Juanita and Amalia, and knew that when they cried out their joy at their first flying fish, first dolphins, her heart would be crying out, too. How wise of their uncle to arrange a hand for them to clasp in their pleasure! Right now she could have done with a hand to clasp herself because of that blue sea that shouted glory. Unconsciously her fingers must have reached out, for the next moment they were clasped, clasped and encased in a large, olive-skinned hand, a hand with beautifully manicured nails, fastidious and sensitive for all its size and strength. The *senhor*'s, of course.

She turned from the rail and looked up at Enrico Montales.

'I'm sorry,' she murmured, 'I mean I was coming, *senhor*, it was just that the sea—'

'The sea, the sea, the open sea,' he quoted with a flash of white teeth. 'Yes, *senhorita*, I went for a period to an English school. But apart from that poem, I am one of a seafaring people, remember, even though I myself am many miles from the coast.'

'Then I'm forgiven?'

'Certainly.' He bowed slightly. He consulted his watch and told Clair, 'You still have half an hour before you meet your friends. Instead of discussing what must be discussed in the Florentine Lounge as I said, we shall do it here.'

'It was most kind of you, *senhor*, to invite my friends for coffee.'

He shrugged her thanks aside and snapped open his cigarette case. In the darkness last night she had admired the gold trinket but had not noticed the handsome embossing, an embossing that looked almost like a coat-of-arms. Some insignia, she thought, probably some wool buyers' association emblem. She was not to find out. The lean thumb of the lean brown hand covered the embossment.

'*Senhorita?*' he invited.

'No, thank you.'

'You smoke little.'

'Is that approved?'

He lifted his shoulder to indicate lack of interest.

Feeling chastened, Clair said, 'Yes, I smoke little . . . perhaps a cigarette to relax.'

'Now you do not need to be relaxed?'

She had had need a few minutes ago in the passage outside the Rose Suite, but the need no longer existed. His sea, the sea, the open sea, her sea shouting glory, had taken the tension out of her.

'No, I have no need, *senhor*.'

'Good.' He smoked a moment. 'But there is need for other things. You calling me *senhor*, to begin with. It will not do to be so formal before Juanita and Amalia.'

'Shall I address you as Mr. Montales?'

230

'No. The children, of course, call me Zio.'

'Zio?' she questioned.

'It is Italian for Uncle. They speak more Italian than Portuguese, *senhorita*, and more English . . . or Australian? . . . than both Italian and Portuguese together.'

'Then I shall call you—?'

'I think Rico would be admirable.'

'But is that Portuguese?' Clair doubted.

'I assure you that Rico, short for Enrico, is very Portuguese.'

'I really meant would my addressing you by your Christian name be approved in Portugal?'

'I have told you,' he reminded her, 'I have long left the walls of my *pal* – that I have embraced wider fields, *senhorita*. I think Rico would be acceptable, for you are, after all, not in the usual category of employment.'

'No, *sen*— No, Rico.' She gulped over the name.

He smiled slightly. 'Is it that hard for an Australian tongue? Come, tell me your name, *senhorita,* and I will see if it is as hard for Portuguese lips.'

'You know, of course, that my name is Wardle.'

'That is a strange name.'

'Not so strange. There are many families of that name.'

'Families?' His brows had met together in that now familiar straight line. 'I do not speak of family names, *senhorita*. For a woman, they do not matter.' He waved his hands in dismissal.

'But—'

'I did not know you were Miss Wardle, and I am not very interested now. Your first name, please. Your Christian name.'

'Clair.'

'That is light,' he said, and his black eyes were on Clair's fair hair.

When she did not comment, he made a comment of his own. 'Undoubtedly,' he disapproved, 'the name has been tampered with, as the British . . . and the Australian? . . . do. You are Clare. Or Claire. Or—'

'I am C-l-a-i-r.'

'So.' His eyes were again on the silver-pale hair. 'You are indeed Light,' he proclaimed, and he smiled.

Clair smiled, a little uncertainly, back.

'Last night I gave you a general idea of your duties. You are to be a mother without a mother's responsibility to my two nieces. For this I will pay you—' He gave her a sum in Portuguese escudos that sounded quite generous to Clair, but when they were interpreted in money she understood left her wordless.

'It is not enough, Clair?'

'It's too much. That – and my passage – and the money returned to Mrs. Henry – No, no, *senhor*, no, Rico, I can't accept it.'

'I thought you were complaining it was insufficient,' he shrugged. 'If the complaint is the opposite to what I thought, then fuff!' He gave a sweep of his arm as he said it, and Clair saw that the matter of her salary had been closed.

'Today,' resumed Senhor Montales, 'my steward tells me there is a rehearsal for the small people for their celebration of the Little Princess of the Indian Ocean to be held in a few days time. My cousin Rosita, of course, is apathetic, she does not care if the girls do not participate. But I sincerely believe that ones so young as they are should not be deprived of fun. Since she will not be bothered I am turning to you, Clair. I want you to take them to the Orario Sala Bambini, or the Babies' Room, where, my steward tells me, the rehearsal is to take place while the rightful occupants, the infants, have their usual mothering hour with their mamas. I suggest, Clair, you meet Juanita and Amalia some fifteen minutes before the rehearsal and become acquainted.'

'When is this rehearsal?'

'At four this afternoon.'

'But four is hours away, *sen*— Rico. I must begin to earn my salary before that.'

'It would have been better for you to say I must get to know my children before that,' he reproved gently.

Clair hung her head.

'But I believe it was meant, Clair, I think perhaps you are

232

a little too conscientious, you are so anxious to repay that you would put duty first. Am I right?'

'Yes,' she admitted uncomfortably, 'you see, you've been so good to me—'

Once again the dark brows met in that high straight line. 'Gratefulness I do not want. Please to remember that, *senhorita*. You understand?'

'Not really. I mean when you've been so kind—'

'Your heart must go out then, not your sense of duty. Now do you understand?'

'Not really. I mean when you've been so – so—' Her voice trailed off at the haughty look on his face.

He was waving an imperious arm. 'We will not discuss it at the moment. Sufficient for you to know you are not expected to work' – he looked inquiringly at her at that word – 'until sixteen hours, which is four o'clock. I am sure that settling yourself in your new quarters, finding your way around your new part of the ship, will not let time hang heavy. And now' – looking at his watch – 'the hour approaches for your meeting with your friends. May I conduct you to the Florentine Lounge?' He bowed, and led the way.

Clair had never been in the Florentine Lounge ... her journeys to the Classe Prima had been strictly on business, she had gone straight to the Rose Suite to attend Mrs. Henry, and when she had been released she had been too tired to explore on her own accord, and now the lavish furnishings delighted her – delighted her all the more because she knew the pleasure her friends would derive from it.

She was not disappointed. The two Australian girls were in raptures over the luxury, impressed with the *senhor* who remained with Clair to entertain, and the three Italians smiled with their dark eyes at eyes even darker and kept murmuring as Rico pressed more *torta* on them, more *pasta*, 'Mille grazie, many thanks.'

But when they all had gone Clair adopted the Portuguese version for Senhor Montales. She said, '*Graças*.'

He raised his brows at that, but he seemed pleased.

It had been a very successful gathering. The visitors had

233

struck a pleasant note and kept to it. But then, thought Clair, they were pleasant people.

Enrico Montales said almost the same thing as he and Clair returned from accompanying Cabin 573 back to the Turistica *ristorante* for their luncheon. – 'But after all that pasta I don't want a bite,' Belinda had stated.

'I see, Clair, why you wished to speak with your friends,' Rico said thoughtfully. He added, still thoughtful, 'I need not have remained with you after all.'

'It made it much nicer,' Clair said gratefully. 'They loved it. You talk so well, *sen*— Rico. You've travelled so widely. And then your account of Oporto.' She was pink with pleasure. 'I really can't think why you took so much trouble with us. It must have been boring for you speaking with six women.' It suddenly came to her that he had said a curious thing. He had remarked, 'I need not have remained with you after all.'

'Senhor—' she began.

'Senhorita?' He emphasized that in reproach.

'Rico,' she corrected, 'you said just now after you spoke so well of my friends that you need not have remained with me after all.'

'I did say that, Clair.'

'But – but why?' She looked at him with puzzled eyes.

'Is it not apparent?'

'No, it is not.'

'Then perhaps,' he said quietly, 'we will leave it at that.'

'At what?'

He did not answer her question directly. He was looking musingly out on the sea, and he smiled rather than said, 'A child to look after children. And that is right. Three children together.'

'What do you mean, Rico?'

'You are very unworldly, little one, it would be a pity for me to explain.'

'Please explain.'

He sighed slightly, but complied.

'The world . . . and the *Firenzo* . . . is not made up entirely of Cabin 573. There are also, unhappily, Mrs. Henrys.'

'I still don't understand.'

'I remained with you to protect you, *senhorita*. Some tongues can be very unkind. But, as I said, I need not have remained at all.'

'You mean – what do you mean?'

'Because you do not know I am reluctant to tell you, but as you insist—' He gave his characteristic shrug. 'Your position is an unusual one – to some eyes. Not all accept innocently and without jealousy, my child, as your friends have accepted.'

'Accept what?'

He turned his dark eyes from the sea and gave her a long, steady look.

'You are a remarkably lovely young woman,' he stated. 'Surely you are not unaware of that?'

'No, *senhor* – I mean Rico, no, no, I'm unaware.'

'In anyone less lucid and direct I might suspect coquetry, but not with you, Clair. I do believe in all truth you do not consider yourself a beautiful girl.'

'Why, no!' Clair looked a little startled. She had always been somewhat dissatisfied with her looks, especially when she compared her fairness to the bronze of the average Australian. Pallid, she had judged herself, understated.

'What,' she murmured, 'has appearance to do with all this?'

'The Portuguese gentleman,' he reported detachedly as though speaking for someone else, 'removes the beautiful young Australian from her Turistica dormitory to a single room in the Classe Prima. There' – in annoyance – 'now the flower in you droops, *senhorita,* your eyes are opened and you see the twisted ways some people see. It makes me sad.'

'It makes me furious,' Clair fumed. She thought a moment, 'I also don't believe you,' she ventured boldly.

'I am glad to hear such trust and innocence,' he commended. 'Let us hope you are right, Clair. And now we will discuss this distasteful subject no more. I have business to attend to, I still have my work to do even on the *Firenzo*, so I will leave you to your own resources. Remember your assignment at four o'clock with the children, but much more than that you must remember to come to me if anything of what I have just spoken happens to arise. You understand, Clair?'

'It will not arise. People are different now, they—'

'*You understand?*' His voice, proud and authoritative, broke through her conjectures. It demanded to be answered.

'I understand, *senhor*.'

By the time Clair had amended '*senhor*' to 'Rico', Senhor Montales was halfway down the deck.

The *senhor*'s warning, for all Clair's insistence that it had no grounds, nagged at Clair as she exercised round the ship before lunch. Naturally shy, now she found herself growing apprehensive each time she passed a group of fellow travellers. Were heads turned to watch her? What were they thinking? What did those lips say of the new passenger?

Eventually she had to admit she had exercised enough, and found a deck chair and sat down.

'I was wondering when you'd stop,' said the smiling voice of an elderly woman passenger. 'You must have walked a mile. I'm lazy, I'm afraid. But then I've been under the weather.'

Clair murmured her sympathy, but the passenger shrugged. 'Seasickness, once it's over, is quite a distant memory. Besides, I was in good company. More than half the ship suffered. That Australian Bight certainly bites. The next time I'll do as most of the wise ones did, I'll fly to Western Australia and embark there. I suppose, dear, you being a hardy soul have been at this exercise every day.'

Clair, relieved, happy to know that to most of the ship, anyway, hers should be a new face among many new faces, said she had. In a way it was the truth. There had been numerous errands for Mrs. Henry. Along to the ship shop, back from the ship shop, up to see if Mrs. Henry's lost scarf had been given in at the office, up to see if it was too hot or too cold or too windy for Mrs. Henry to venture on deck.

More people joined the elderly passenger, who was a Mrs. Jamieson, and Clair was included in the group. They were pleasant people, like the Cabin 573 people. Definitely, Clair thought, the *senhor* had been wrong.

She sat enjoying the conversation, enjoying the silkiness of the breeze now that the weather had grown kinder. When her group rose and said they must wash before lunch, Clair rose with them, feeling she had no cares in the world.

The daintiness of her room struck her afresh. She combed her hair, put on fresh lipstick and even found herself anticipating the midday meal. Perhaps it was that the Classe Prima ate later than the Turistica, or perhaps it was her contented state of mind, but, unlike Belinda, she found she could comfortably forget the eleven o'clock feast of *torta, pasta* and *caffe* topped with *crema,* and think in terms of salads.

At the door of the dining-room, though, she stopped. At the centre table of the beautifully appointed Classe Prima *ristorante* sat Mrs. Henry. It was a large table, and Mrs. Henry was holding forth in her strident voice. Because of the location of the table it would be impossible not to be seen by Mrs. Henry as she was conducted to her own position. What if that position was at the same table? But no, a quick look satisfied Clair that at least she would not be eating with Mrs. Henry. The table was complete.

'The *signorina* is thinking perhaps she would sooner eat at the buffet on the deck,' the head steward was suggesting, 'for it is, indeed, a lovely day.'

Clair could have embraced him. 'Thank you, yes.'

But how foolish she was, she thought as she followed the man to the verandah café; she had to go into the *ristorante* some time.

It was very pleasant on the *terrazza*, though. Clair went over to the buffet and selected a cold cut and salad. She came back to the rattan table and chair that the steward had put by the window for her and sat down. Scarcely had she begun the meal than Enrico Montales came across, behind him a steward with a second rattan chair.

'I see you, too, like to eat informally, Clair,' said the *senhor* when the steward had gone. He excused himself and went across to the buffet to return with a dish of olives. He glanced at Clair's plate and raised his black brows. 'Such

237

British food!'

'But I am British.'

He shrugged in the same way as he had shrugged when she had given him her family name, as though, Clair thought, annoyed, family names and nationality were of little import — *to a woman*.

He must have read her resentment, for he smiled faintly.

'I am fond of British food, Clair,' he placated lazily.

Still annoyed, she reached for the mayonnaise, only to have her hand caught by his lean fingers.

'The Indian Ocean has accelerated the British temper, *senhorita*.'

'I don't like being laughed at, *senhor*.'

'I was not laughing. I do like British food. But not to preface it with Italian olives!' He raised his brows in horror.

'Italian and not Portuguese?' she came back.

'On the *Firenzo*,' he said equably, 'the Portuguese olives are not available. A shame, for irresistible as are the Italian olives, the Portuguese are—' He gave an exquisite gesture. In his deep, fine voice he began to describe the olive groves where he lived. 'Around the *pal*—In Elmoda they make a green world, Clair. We are very fortunate in Portugal. We can grow cold country firs and yet dates also can thrive. From oaks down through chestnuts, corks, limes, the whole scale of tree stature, nature smiles, but most of all, I think, does she smile on our olive groves.'

As he spoke he was pushing the plate to Clair, and, listening enchanted to his green world of birches, carobs, lemons, almonds, and greenest of all the olives, Clair nibbled at one, reached for more.

'You see, little one,' he smiled, 'you can like English food and also like Portuguese. Would it not follow that you could also be both of these fine places?'

'How do you mean, *senhor*?'

'Rico.'

'Rico. What do you mean?'

He rose, crossed to the buffet and came back with a plate of collation.

'Portugal is Britain's oldest ally,' he stated, beginning his meal. 'We are almost one, you might say.'

Clair could not see how this answered her question.

'I am pleased to see you on the *terrazza*,' Rico said presently. 'I always take my luncheon here. The *ristorante* is beautifully appointed, but beautiful appointments, the same as beautiful adornments for a woman, should be kept for candlelight. You agree – but then you do, of course, for are you not here?'

Had she not paused before answering, Eenrico Montales might not have pursued the subject. But the hesitation, infinitesimal though it was, alerted him.

'You did not come here on your own accord?' he said sharply.

'Oh, I did.'

'Then it was not your original intention, Clair?'

'I – well, you see—' It was no use, he would find out, he always found out. 'Mrs. Henry was already seated,' she blurted. 'She – she was in a very seeing position.' Clair bent over her salad.

The *senhor's* angry voice sent her glance flying upward again. His brows were the old, by now familiar straight high line, his lips were thinned.

'I am displeased with you, Clair. You show neither British courage nor Australian independence.'

'What,' asked Clair, near tears, 'do I also not show in Portuguese pride?'

'At this stage, that is not required.'

'What stage, *senhor*?

'Where you are now,' he snapped. 'The other will come later.'

'The Portuguese pride? How could I ever have that?'

'I could tell you, but it is not a subject for a lunch table, it needs—'

'An olive grove?' Her voice was bantering, but she sobered at the cool, aloof look he flashed her. Could anyone, she thought, look so remote and aloof when it suited him than Enrico Montales?

They did not speak for the rest of the meal.

239

The *senhor* asked briefly, 'Cheese? Fruit?' and when she shook her head called for two coffees.

'Please,' he said after they had come, 'to understand, Clair, that tonight and other nights you dine at my table with me.'

'But, *senhor* – Rico, that's wrong. I mean, as your employee—'

'I have spoken,' he said finally. 'Also you enter the *ristorante* with me, we enter at a time when others are seated, and we enter proudly. You understand?'

'I—'

'You understand, Clair?'

'Yes, Rico.'

'Now if you are finished I advise you to go and rest. Even to the young, the very young can be tiring. You can meet your charges at half past three on the boat deck. We have established the habit of walking together at that time each afternoon in the hope of seeing either an iceberg, a whale or Sinbad himself.' He smiled – and Clair, still rankling a little from his authority, managed a weak smile back.

She went down to her room, as he had advised, to rest. Relaxation would not come, though. She kept on hearing the *senhor's* voice. 'You enter the *ristorante* with me. Enter proudly.'

She jumped up from the bed and crossed to the wardrobe. How proud could you be in either a pink or a blue or a yellow cotton dress? The fourth piece of apparel, the green linen, she had worn all day.

She tried out different belts, different accessories. It was no use. They still remained simple, uncluttered, fresh, quite pretty – and totally unsuitable.

Restless, she put on the green linen again and went up on deck. She was early, she knew, but she could not relax.

The sound of laughter attracted her to the swimming pool. It was the children's hour and the level of the water had been lowered. She wondered if the nieces of Enrico Montales were among the dark-eyed little girls shouting and splashing there, and decided if not, that in the future they must be. She was a firm believer in children being taught to swim.

She stood watching the fun on the slippery dip for a while, then strolled to the port side. Further along the deck she saw a tall man with two children clasping each of his hands. It was the *senhor,* and the children, girls, would be her future charges. For a moment, unseen, Clair regarded the little girls. They were not alike. One, even at this tender age, was a beauty, the other – well, the other was just a little girl.

Juanita? Amalia? Amalia? Juanita? Which child was which? Already to herself Clair had decided that the homelier little girl took after Rosita, the motherly Rosita she had established in her mind, while the handsome child resembled her father. What had been his name? Umberto Dal Rosa. It was a handsome-sounding name.

At that moment Enrico Montales turned and saw her. He beckoned her across.

'You are early, Clair? You did rest, I trust?'

'Yes, Rico.' She pretended interest in the small girls so as not to meet those probing black eyes.

'These are the *tirannos,*' he introduced.

'That is Italian for tyrants,' explained the prettier of the little girls. She had a cool, disdainful voice. 'You understand Italian?'

'No, dear.'

'Portuguese?'

'No, dear.'

The child said deliberately, 'Oh, dear,' and her uncle gave her a quick, sobering look.

'We can do without your wit, Amalia.'

So this one was Amalia, Clair thought.

'Juanita, as the elder, must be presented first,' said Enrico Montales. He gave a gentle little push to the plainer child. Not only plainer but smaller, Clair judged.

'Say how do you do to Clair, Juanita.'

'*Comé sta?*' the child said shyly.

Amalia did not wait to be introduced. She said good afternoon in English, Italian and Portuguese.

'Now that you have established how clever you are, you will keep a quiet tongue for ten minutes, Amalia,' Rico decreed, and though Amalia looked displeased, she still, Clair noted, obeyed. But, thought Clair, it would have taken a very brave person to disobey the *senhor*.

'We have been looking for icebergs, whales and Sinbad the Sailor,' said Rico.

Amalia looked more disdainful than ever but, forbidden speech, did not voice her contempt.

Juanita, though, was starry-eyed. 'I look for a mermaid. Have you ever seen a mermaid, *signorina*? Or' – doubtfully to her uncle – 'should it be *senhorita*?'

'It is to be Clair,' Clair invited.

'Clair? I like Clair. Have you seen a mermaid, Clair?' With her eyes starry like that the child was as pretty – prettier – than her sister.

'I always hope to,' Clair said, and Amalia gave a snort, adding defensively, 'I never spoke, Zio Rico.'

'Zio is Uncle, Clair,' Juanita explained.

Evidently Zio had full control of his more headstrong niece, for until he left the three of them, exactly ten minutes later, Amalia did not again break her imposed silence.

Then she said to his retreating back, 'Pig!'

Clair, unsure whether it was too soon for her to voice a reprimand, was glad she had not done so when Amalia added almost at once, 'But a lovely pig. I admire him very much. All the ladies are in love with Zio Rico. Are you?'

'I scarcely know him, Amalia.'

The little girl turned her attention from her uncle to Clair.

'I do not think you will do,' she said doubtfully. 'I do not think you will do at all.'

A little dismayed, Clair said, 'I'm sorry about that. I like you very much.'

'Oh, I think I like you, too, but Mama—' A long, estimating look at Clair. 'No, I would say you would not do.'

Clair had taken Juanita's hand and begun to walk. Amalia, on her own accord, took the other hand.

'You are pretty, you see. But' – triumphantly – 'very pale, very washed-out, so perhaps you may do after all.'

'Thank you, Amalia. And now shall we go to the rehearsal?'

'It is all very silly,' complained Amalia. 'A rehearsal, I mean. Since there is no need really for all to rehearse, only one. I, of course, will be that one. I will be chosen for the Little Princess.'

Juanita simply smiled and agreed.

'Because we are children,' resumed Amalia loftily, 'we have this silly play. I would sooner adult games like they had that time we crossed the Equator. Do you remember, Ju?'

'It might not be such fun,' warned Clair. 'You could be thrown in the swimming pool. On that subject, girls, do you bathe in the pool?'

'Sophia says she has no time and Zio insists we are accompanied.'

'Who is Sophia?' asked Clair.

'Our maid. Mama's maid, but she attends us as well. She is cross.' Amalia tilted her chin.

Juanita said eagerly, 'Could you take us to the pool, Clair?'

'I think so. Would you like that?'

'I would like to swim like a mermaid.'

'I would love a bikini,' said Amalia. 'Could I wear a bikini?' She explained, 'That is the Italian in me. I like high fashion.'

'I think we could find a very nice suit, but most of the children don't wear bikinis.'

'Let us go to the ship shop and see now.'

'Not now, it is time for rehearsal.'

'Oh, that rehearsal!'

But when Amalia got there and got the applause she knew she would, she dropped her disdain. She had said she would be the Little Princess, and she was.

Looking around the assembly of dark-eyed children, lovely, luscious children, for, thought Clair, were there any children more beautiful or luscious than Italian *bambini*, Clair still knew that Amalia stood out. Her eyes were darker, her carriage prouder, her smile ... put on for a purpose ... flashed.

'Princess Amalia,' the children's officer announced, and no one was surprised, least of all Amalia herself.

But someone was surprised at Clair. She was a tall, patronizing young woman who had brought along a small son, Nino. She was very elegant, very sophisticated, and she looked at

Clair and drawled, 'So you are the person who will look after Rosita's daughters! But this is amusing! This is fun!' She laughed.

'I don't understand,' said Clair.

'Of course not, and I do apologize, but it's still funny, frightfully funny. I mean, if Rosita *knew*.'

'The children's mother is aware that I'm standing in for her, I'm sure of that.'

'Yes, but she doesn't know all. Oh, dear, you must excuse my mirth, but really—' The woman took the little boy's hand and ran off, still laughing.

It was not the end of personal comments for the afternoon, first Amalia's comment, then Nino's mother's. There was another yet to come. Sophia's, Rosita's maid's.

'Oh, you are the girls' companion,' said the black-eyed woman. '*Si, signorina?*'

'Yes.'

'I am Sophia, the *signora's domestica,* and I have come to take the children to have their baths.'

'Of course.'

'I notice,' said Sophia, whom Clair, though she would not have agreed openly with Amalia, could quite imagine could be cross, 'you do not wear a uniform. The *signora* would not like that.'

'I do not think you will do.' That had been Amalia.

'If Rosita knew—' That had been Nino's sophisticated young mama.

And now: 'The *signora* would not like that,' from Sophia. *What was the cousin of Enrico Montales really like?*

But rather than dismay Clair, Sophia's comment gave her an idea. Ever since she had seen her few frocks hanging forlornly in a wardrobe made to hang many, she had been at a loss as to what to do. Obviously she needed more clothes, but she had not the means to buy the right clothes – unless the right clothes were the simple clothes that Sophia had just mentioned. Uniforms. Not exactly uniforms, perhaps, but plain little frocks of service. Any of the four she possessed, buttoned high, belted, denuded of ornament, could fit the bill, and slender though her purse was she could afford more of that calibre.

'I intend wearing a uniform,' she told the Italian woman.

'Black?'

'I have no black.'

'Well, I suppose a plain colour will have to do, though the *signora* will not like it.'

The *signora* would have to like it, Clair decided; she would have to like whatever else she was able to buy. Until then she would wear the frock that she had on now, its companion frocks, wear them primly and plainly to proclaim her position, and so settle the matter of dress – and of what the *signora* liked – for all time.

Clair turned the children over to Sophia, and went along to her room to look over her apparel, make suitable adjustments – then count her money to see what extra purchases she could afford from the ship shop.

CHAPTER THREE

As clothes to wear in the Classe Prima *ristorante* of the luxury liner *Firenzo*, Clair's wardrobe did not amount to much, but as uniforms, she decided, holding each garment out at arm's length, adding in her mind a demure bow, a prim belt, they were neat and suitable. She tried the bow and belt on the dress she wore, and nodded her satisfaction.

So now the problem of what to wear tonight in the dining room when she entered beside Enrico Montales full of British courage, Australian independence and Portuguese pride – though she still was at a loss as to where Portugal came in – was solved. She would not enter at all. She would dine quietly – and suitably, suitable for her rank – here in her room. She was quite sure that her obliging stewardess would have no objection to bringing her meal to her on a tray, just as she brought breakfast. Lunch entailed no worry. Never, she thought, would Mrs. Henry, or Mrs. Henry's kind, eat on the *terrazza*.

The relief of sparing the *senhor* embarrassment by her appearing, as he would evidently *not* expect, from that remark of his, that 'beautiful adornments for a woman should be kept for candlelight', in a humble frock, was almost as great as the relief to herself. Happily, Clair slipped into the self-imposed role if not exactly of *domestica,* then something very near.

She knew, though, that she should tell Enrico Montales that she would not be dining with him as arranged ... arranged or decreed? Not knowing the location of his cabin, though, and for that matter not, in her heart, particularly relishing the job of telling him, she took up the telephone instead and asked to be put through to the *senhor's* suite.

As she waited for him to respond she realized that her heart was beating unevenly. How absurd to be nervous like this, he was, after all, only an employer.

None the less she was vastly relieved when the Italian

steward answered and told her that the Portuguese *senhor* was at a business conference with some representatives on board and would not be returning to his suite until it was time to dress. Could the *signorina*, or *senhorita* . . . Clair told him, it was miss . . . trust him with a message? The miss could. Clair told the man to give the *senhor* her compliments and tell him she would not be dining in the *ristorante* tonight.

Vastly relieved, she replaced the phone, took up her purse, and went along to the ship shop, or the boutique as it was called in the Classe Prima.

There was the same brisk business that Clair had noticed in the Turistica on the few occasions she had gone there for toothpaste or pins. People, it seemed, loved to shop on the high seas; even those who declared for budget or carrying reasons that they would not succumb to the duty-free goods at some time during each day found themselves buying from the fascinating store.

There were little groups now exclaiming over cultured pearls from Japan or hand-painted brooches from Limoges. Clair edged by them to the row of frocks.

Mainly they were shift types, of beautifully flowered materials inspired in Hawaii. Clair fingered them wistfully but passed resolutely on to some well-cut shirt-waists that should fit her bill not only for simplicity and neatness but – looking at the price tag – availability.

She selected a pearl grey and a brown check and was about to edge around the shoppers to ask the assistant if she could try them on when a woman in a group exclaiming loudly over some exquisite Venetian glass saw her and came across.

It was Mrs. Henry.

Clair's uncertain, 'It appears the sea makes no difference, doesn't it, we all love a bargain' trailed off at the venomous light in Mrs. Henry's small eyes.

Catching up the hems of the dresses that Clair held, she said in her penetrating voice, 'So it doesn't stop at a de-luxe passage, there is also a free wardrobe. How fortunate for you!'

'It isn't . . . I mean if you look at them . . . I mean . . .'

What was the use? Mrs Henry was smiling that smile of hers

247

that never reached her eyes, she was including others who were standing around in her private joke.

'Certainly a modest beginning.' She was examining the shirt-waists. 'But quite good strategy, my dear. Oaks, after all, from little acorns grow.'

'Excuse me, please.' Clair did not wait to take the dresses back from Mrs. Henry and hang them up again, she just bundled them on her and ran blindly out of the boutique.

She did not know where she went, where she turned, she just sped down corridor after corridor, her cheeks burning, her eyes blurred with shamed tears. She ran on and on, till, rounding a corner, she ran into a tall, well-remembered man. She should remember him, she thought, choking, wasn't he the one who, according to Mrs. Henry, besides paying for her passage was paying for her—

'Oh, no, no!' she cried aloud.

Enrico Montales did not waste time in asking questions, he simply rotated Clair and impelled her down another corridor, through a door into a room. No, not a room, a suite, a much vaster suite than Mrs. Henry's, and instead of pastel colours and frills, mannish tans and straight, unadorned lines. Not waiting for her to explain, not even waiting to ask her to sit down, to calm down, he flashed, 'What is this, Clair?'

'I – I—' How could she tell him? It was embarrassing enough as it was, if he learned it as well she felt she could never raise her head again.

'I was running,' she said inadequately.

'I am aware of that.' His voice was ice. 'I am also aware that running into me was something so distasteful that you even cried out your dismay.'

'You're wrong, *senhor*.'

'Did you not just now see me and call "Oh, no, no!"'

'I did, but it was not that.'

'What then?'

'I can't tell you,' Clair replied.

'There is no need,' he said frigidly. 'My man was waiting for me with the news that you would not dine with me to-night. I went out at once to learn what absurd reason was making you so childish, *senhorita* – and I do learn – in three short words. Oh, no, no.'

'It's not that at all,' Clair cried in distress.

He was looking at her closely now, estimating her nervous state. With sudden unexpected kindness he put her into the easy chair, then crossed to a little table and rang a bell. When the steward came in he said, 'Bring two brandies.'

'*Si, signore.*'

'Not for me—' protested Clair.

'Two brandies.' The *senhor's* face was stern. The steward did not wait for confirmation or otherwise from Clair, he obeyed at once.

There was silence after he had gone, a silence that continued until he returned with a decanter and two Napoleon glasses. The silence was not broken until Enrico Montales bade Clair gently but firmly to drink. In spite of the authoritative note in the deep voice Clair still sat cupping the bowl of the glass with her shaking hands.

Rico rose and came across.

'Drink, little one.'

'I—'

'Drink, Clair.' He took the glass from her trembling fingers and held it to her lips. For all his solicitude Clair had the impression that if she did not drink on her own accord, he would force her to do it. Too tired for a scene, she complied – and felt better for the stimulant.

'Now,' said the *senhor*, satisfied, 'we talk, *senhorita*.'

'There's nothing to say.' So anxious was she not to let him know the reason for her distress she even spoke lightly. It would have taken better histrionics than Clair's, though, to have deceived Enrico Montales. She might not have made the bright response at all for all the notice he took. He withdrew his cigarettes, offered her the case – still with that thumb over the emblem – and, as before, when she refused, put back the case and lit himself a cigar.

'I am to understand,' he said coolly, aloofly, 'that your exclamation of distress just now was not, as I thought, because of your misfortune in encountering me.'

249

'No, *senhor*.'

'Then—?'

'I told you before Rico, that I cannot—'

'Yes, you told me.' He gave an impatient gesture. 'But I still must learn, of course. We will start from where I left you, standing on the deck with my two nieces. Was the trouble there, Clair? Do not be afraid to tell me. I have no illusions over the young. Juanita may be a flower, but her sister Amalia, for all her looks, is a thorn.'

'I got on well with the children.'

'Then there was an upset at the rehearsal?'

'No upset.'

He thought a moment.

'Someone else at the rehearsal, perhaps?'

'No. I mean—' Clair was thinking of the sophisticated young matron.

'Yes, Clair?'

'It was nothing.'

'Everything is nothing to you.'

'Well, there was a mother of a little boy who was interested in me and kept repeating how amusing it was that I was looking after Rosita's daughters.'

The brows were in their high straight line again. 'That upset you?'

'Of course not.'

'Who else was there? Who else did you encounter?' When she did not answer, he said triumphantly, 'Sophia, Rosita's *domestica,* would come to fetch the children for their baths. What did she have to say?'

'Very little.'

'You need not protect her, she can protect herself.'

'She said very little, *senhor*,' repeated Clair, 'just that the *signora,* your cousin Rosita, would prefer me in a black uniform. I have nothing black, and I have no uniform, but Sophia gave me an idea.' Had she glanced up, Clair would have seen the thunderous look on the *senhor's* face, but her eyes were on the Napoleon glass of brandy.

'It solved a problem for me,' she said frankly. 'I had been

worrying how I could go with you into the Classe Prima *ristorante* tonight. You see' – apologetically – 'my clothes barely pass for the Turistica.'

'Pray proceed.' His voice was ice, but in her absorption Clair did not notice.

'I decided then to take up my correct role of – well, if not exactly of *domestica,* then—' Clair stopped abruptly. She had raised her glance from the glass and the impact of that furious countenance, those flashing dark eyes silenced her.

'How dared you disobey me,' said the *senhor* in a soft, almost hissing tone, 'how dared you, Clair?'

'I don't understand.'

'You are an intelligent person,' he said impatiently. 'You must have gathered right from the beginning that I, not my cousin, am the one who gives the orders. You answer to me, and to me alone. I thought you knew that.'

'The children are Rosita's,' Clair murmured in self-defence.

'I employed you. Remember? You were dubious at the time, so I assured you that my cousin has implicit belief in my judgment.'

'But Sophia—'

'Sophia is a *domestica,*' he said aloofly.

'So am I, *senhor.*'

'You are what I say you are, *senhorita,* and that is not what Sophia thinks.'

'Rosita—'

'Rosita, too, will do what I say.'

'Everyone,' dared Clair, 'will do what you say.'

'One at least will,' he returned levelly. 'You, *senhorita.* You will go to your room now and dress for dinner.'

'No.'

'I am serious, Clair.'

'So am I, Rico. Can't you see' – she gulped – 'can't you see I'm already dressed for dinner? That's the whole trouble. I don't wish to embarrass you, and I have very few clothes.'

'What you have,' he said icily, 'you have buttoned up and belted in, made to appear a uniform. For such impertinence, Clair, I could even shake you!' For a moment his black eyes

251

held hers across the room, and Clair knew, a little nervously, that he would be capable of just that.

'Worn lower, looser, a string of pearls, perhaps—' he shrugged. 'I am no expert on haute couture, but I am certain you would pass.'

'You said adornments for the woman should be kept for candlelight,' despaired Clair. 'I have only working dresses, so must not expect candlelight.'

'At least,' he awarded, obviously pleased, 'you listen to what I say. Listen further, little one.' He leaned forward in his chair and looked across the room at Clair. 'With the male of the species,' he stated clearly, 'the instinct is to strut. I, true to my sex, would wish to flaunt you, *senhorita,* show you off. But clothes are a very small bagatelle – is that correct?'

'Yes, *senhor.*'

'They play a small part. I could be equally proud entering a room with a woman in cotton as a woman in silk. You have been making a mountain out of an anthill.'

'Molehill,' Clair barely murmured.

'So,' he said finally and grandly, 'the small storm is over. You go and unbutton that high neck and we dine as arranged.'

He got up – but Clair sat on. Aware of his burning gaze but unable to meet it, she mumbled, 'I can't, *senhor.*'

'What is this?' He had strode to her side. 'I have asked you, *senhorita,* but that was a courtesy only. I really order you, Clair.'

'I can't, I—'

'There is more to this than feminine vanity, more than just disobedience,' Enrico Montales declared. 'You have not told me all, *senhorita.* After Sophia spoke of uniforms, and after you had decided upon the role you would take on yourself, what then?'

'I went through my dresses and decided they would do admirably, and, seeing the part I would want them for I – I realized I could afford several more.' She closed her lips, hoping he would leave it at that.

But not the *senhor.* The dark eyes had narrowed. The mouth had thinned.

'I believe I begin to understand. You went to the ship shop, to the boutique?'

'Yes.'

'And there you bought something?'

'No. I mean I intended to, but—'

'Yes, Clair?'

'I – I – it was very unimportant – what happened, I mean.'

'It was so unimportant that you run down corridors with wet eyes and a trembling mouth.'

'I was foolish, Rico.'

'You were, little one. Women like her are not worth worrying about.'

Her glance shot up at him and met such kindness in the return glance that her tears began to fall again.

He had taken out a snow-white handkerchief, a man's big handkerchief, and he put it in her trembling hands.

'It was Mrs. Henry, wasn't it?'

'Yes.'

'She said something to you?'

'Yes.'

'It caused you to run out of the shop, run blindly anywhere at all so long as it was away?'

'Yes.'

The inevitable question came, the question that Clair knew must come, but still cut her to the raw.

'What did the woman say?'

'I—'

'The words, *senhorita*!' There was no evading the dominant note in that sharp, imperative voice.

'She said—'

'Yes?'

'It's – cheap, Rico.'

'Tell me, please.'

'She said "It doesn't stop at a de-luxe passage, there is also—" ' Clair could go no further, she began to cry.

He left her to cry, and she was grateful for that. Had she looked up Clair would have seen that Enrico Montales was undergoing a storm of his own.

He had himself in control, though, by the time she had recovered, no sign of the fury that had taken possession of him. In fact his voice was deceptively lazy.

'I see your point, Clair. I see why dining in the *ristorante* would be distasteful to you. It would be distasteful also for me to dine anywhere near that person. So' – he was crossing to the bell on the table – 'until we reach our first port, which is Durban, we dine in this room.'

'Until we reach Durban?' puzzled Clair. 'But I don't understand, Rico. Mrs. Henry is going right through to Italy.'

He was ringing the bell now, waiting carelessly for the excellent service he always received. In an almost uninterested voice he said, 'No, *senhorita*, she is not.'

'But I attended to the tickets, and they were to Naples.'

'Durban is very interesting, Clair, quite an intriguing city. You will like it, I think. So' – he took the menu and wine list that the steward, evidently anticipating such a request, had brought along with him – 'will Mrs. Henry. She will disembark there and proceed by air.'

'But—'

'Minestrone,' the *senhor* was ordering, '*bistecca, gelati.*' He took the wine list. 'Rosato Collameno.' Then he, turned and smiled charmingly at Clair. 'It will only be a matter of several days, my child, and then' – a gleam of coal black eyes, a flash of white teeth – 'candlelight.'

Deftly the steward had carried the small table to the window, covered it with a gleaming cloth, drawn up two chairs.

Rico tasted the wine, nodded his approval – but as an afterthought gave a further order. Champagne. Scintillating. Bubbling.

'After all,' he said to Clair, 'this is an occasion. Have we not vanquished an enemy?'

'Have we?' Clair was not certain.

Rico gave a low, confident laugh.

It was very pleasant sitting in the well-appointed room, the waiter soft-footed and efficient, the food excellent, Enrico Montales at his most charming, the music from the Flora

Salon where the strings played every evening stealing in sweetly and faintly. It was, decided Clair, much nicer than it could be out in the lavish *ristorante,* even with candlelight.

He must have read her thoughts, for, the meal over and waiting for coffee, he said, 'This is the best of all, I think. This is the home touch.'

Home touch! Clair glanced at all the luxury and smiled faintly. 'You must have a very expensive home, *senhor.*'

He looked annoyed with himself, even a little with Clair, and amended stiffly, 'I meant, of course, the quietude, the privacy. Naturally I do not dine like this myself.'

'Naturally,' accepted Clair. 'Who but a duke would?'

He looked at her sharply but did not comment.

A little disconcerted, Clair began describing the meeting in the Orario Sala Bambini, or Babies' Room, for the choosing of the Little Princess of the Indian Ocean.

'Undeniably my niece Amalia,' frowned Rico. 'For some reason she is always chosen.'

'She is very pretty.'

'Fuff,' dismissed Enrico Montales. 'Tomorrow,' he informed Clair, 'we circle an island.'

'An island? But I thought on this route—'

'It is out of our way, but when I suggested it to the Captain—'

'*You* suggested it?'

Loftily, 'Yes.'

'What is its name?'

'A Portuguese one that would be unfamiliar to you and difficult to the tongue. It is very small and very unimportant, for which reason I am most grateful to the Captain for conceding to my request. Though, of course, as he said, it will create a diversion for the passengers. Especially I hope will my nieces be entertained and instructed.'

Clair looked thoughtfully at him. He is a fine uncle, she decided, and he would make a wonderful parent.

'I doubt,' Rico resumed, 'if Amalia will be very interested in the island, but nevertheless I wish her to be instructed about it. Juanita, of course, is thirsty for all knowledge and will lis-

255

ten gravely to what I have to tell.'

'You know it, Rico?'

'I have been on it. A friend of mine works for the Phosphate Company there. The Phosphate Commissioner's steamer calls once every three months, and on one occasion I went with him. We should circle this isle around noon, so if the girls are wearing you down I shall give you respite and take them off your hands.'

'Thank you, but I, too, would like to learn about this remote island. Don't forget I was an islander myself.'

He said warmly, 'By all means, Clair. I wanted to include you, but I believed you might have other plans.'

'No plans, except—'

'Yes?'

'The swimming pool. I rather gather the children don't swim.'

'Possibly. Swimming would be as unimportant to Rosita as it is important to you.'

'And you, *senhor*?'

'I would be as concerned as you, Clair. I *order* them to learn to swim.' He said it quite naturally, and now that she knew the man so much more, Clair took it not as an arrogance but a way of life.

'What about togs?' she asked.

'Togs?'

'We call swimsuits that. I don't believe the children have any.'

'Charge them to me at the boutique,' he shrugged.

'What variety, Rico?'

He frowned. 'I told you, I am no authority on haute couture.'

'These are not haute couture, they're simply swimsuits for two little girls.'

'Then buy just that.'

'It's a little difficult. Amalia wants—'

'Something very adult, very sophisticated,' he laughed.

'A bikini.'

Now he didn't laugh. 'Amalia will be permitted only plain

– what do you call it? – togs. You must see to that, Clair.'

After that, conversation lapsed, but lapsed naturally, easily, there was no trying to think of something to say to break the silence, because the silence was too pleasant to want to break.

Clair relaxed and stared out at the darkling waters of the Indian Ocean. The air through the window was as soft as silk and the sea was almost slumbrously still. There was no sharpness in the small breeze, and a moon almost beyond belief was rising. Clair murmured aloud that it was like a sovereign.

'No,' smiled Rico, 'on an Italian liner it is like a twenty-lire piece.'

Quite soon after that Clair felt her eyes growing heavy and was glad when the *senhor* suggested that she went early to bed.

When she came out of the little bathroom she saw that her stewardess had brought in a parcel as well as a nightcap of milk. She opened the parcel to find the pearl grey shirt-waist she had chosen this afternoon and the small brown check. There was a note enclosed.

'You forgot to take these purchases from the boutique when you fled. Please shed no tears, they have been written against your salary and will be duly paid by you. But one order: Do not buy for candlelight. *Arrivederci*. E.M.'

She put down the note with a smile. *Arrivederci*. That was Italian, not Portuguese. But after all, as he had said of the olives on the *terrazza* buffet, as he had said tonight of the moon when he called it a twenty-lire piece this was an Italian ship. Besides, was there a Portuguese word as music-making as *arrivederci*?

She wondered about the frocks. How had he known which ones she had chosen? The only way would have been to go to the boutique, inquire whether anyone had noted her choice, and circulating among passengers like that would have been the last thing she could have imagined in the *senhor*.

There was an alternative; he had seen Mrs. Henry. But that Clair could not credit, even though he had confidently stated that in Durban the woman would disembark and proceed by air, and to secure such a happening, which he had seemed so calmly positive that he could, he at least would have to interview Clair's ex-employer.

She tried the dresses on and they were a good fit. She would wear the pearl grey tomorrow; she did not mind wearing it when she knew that it would be deducted from her salary.

It was only when she was in bed that she remembered his order. 'Do not buy for candlelight.' What did he mean? Why had he given such a strange instruction?

Her last thought, though, was *arrivederci*. Till tomorrow. She was smiling as she slipped into sleep.

She wore the pearl grey dress the next morning. The *senhor*, when he saw her, said it could have been a continuation of her almost silver-pale hair. 'The head in the sunlight,' he said, 'the dress in the shadow.'

A little embarrassed, Clair said, 'I like it very much. Thank you, Rico.'

He raised his black brows. 'For what? You are paying for it.'

'Thank you for going to the trouble of getting the frocks for me.'

'It was no trouble.'

'No trouble for a remote Portuguese *senhor* to go to some woman and ask, "Which were the dresses chosen by Senhorita Wardle?" '

'Is that what I appear to you, Clair, remote?'

'Not so remote perhaps so much as – as—'

'Yes?'

'Withdrawn. Sufficient.'

'Withdrawn, yes. Sufficient, no. Not sufficient by any means, Clair.' His dark grey eyes on hers had a curious probing look.

Rather hurriedly Clair asked, 'How did you discover which frocks? How distasteful was it?'

'I asked. It was not distasteful. Are your questions answered?'

'No. You see I simply can't imagine you circulating—'

'Circulating?'

'Going chattily around like – like an Australian would, and saying, "Look here, last night Miss Wardle chose a frock.

258

Which was it?" '

'You are right. I did not.'

'Then—?'

'I requested the madam to come to my suite.'

'The madam?' she queried.

'Senhora Henry.'

'She came?' Clair was incredulous. Mrs. Henry did not come. Like the *senhor,* she summoned. But then perhaps Mrs. Henry had come in a coquettish mood, perhaps the *senhor* had purposely not stated his requirements.

'Oh, no.' His smile had an edge as once again he read Clair. 'I did not send an inviting note, I did not inveigle her along, I simply ordered her to attend. As you have remarked, *senhorita,* I am used to ordering.'

'I should not have thought Mrs. Henry would have been used to obeying.'

'She obeyed me. She told me which frocks. Then, after an appropriate talk, she also told me she would disembark at Durban.'

'But – but Mrs. Henry is rich.'

'What is that to do with it?'

'You would not be able to "buy" her off the ship, Rico.'

'I did not need to resort to bribery. Even had she not been wealthy I would not have used such a method. I simply and briefly told her to pack.'

'What?' Clair stared. After a few moments she murmured wonderingly, 'You can do this? You have shares in the *Firenzo*?'

'Perhaps. But it does not matter. I do what is right. Right is always easy. It is the wrong that is difficult.'

'But how?' again she asked.

'I simply pointed out how uncomfortable she was going to be after I had spread around the ship her abominable behaviour.'

'She believed you?'

'Certainly.'

'But you wouldn't have done it?'

'Yes, *senhorita,*' said Enrico Montales, 'I would. But now

259

she is going, and her poor associates without their champion will soon fade into obscurity. Have fears no more, little Clair. Gather your small ones and walk round the deck, perhaps see your first flying fish. Afterwards select the togs – right? – then have your swim. Afterwards again it will be the remote Portuguese island. Let us anticipate it. Let us enjoy it.' Suddenly a boy and not a withdrawn, remote, almost regal man, he laughed and left Clair.

Clair rather had dreaded the buying of the swimsuits, but to her gratification there was no trouble. Juanita, amiable, agreeable, was easy to please, but Amalia, with whom she had expected tantrums, took a liking to a plain deep blue which undoubtedly her uncle would approve.

'These girls with their frou-frous,' she sniffed, 'I like the simple line. As for decolleté' – she pronounced it perfectly – 'this season the trend is for cover-up. Did you know that, Clair?' She was sophisticated beyond belief; she was also very clothes-wise. When Clair, unable to resist making the comment, reminded Amalia that yesterday she had spoken of a bikini, the child tossed, 'Ah, but I only jested. I know how clever it is to be different from others. When I am a young lady I will be very different, Clair.' She gave a little satisfied smile.

Her satisfaction was wiped off in the pool, however. Better than her older sister in most things, she demonstrated almost at once that even if she learned to swim she would only be an indifferent performer. Juanita, on the other hand, was a 'natural', and within half an hour could dog-paddle several strokes.

'It is silly, anyhow,' pouted Amalia, 'it is much nicer to lounge back on a li-lo and be brought a cola.'

'Your uncle wishes you to learn to swim.'

'Oh, fuff!' pouted Amalia.

Clair was adamant, though. She took a serious view of swimming, and she towed Amalia to the centre again and demonstrated the elementary stroke. Amalia, only half attending, the other half of her attention on some teenage boys waiting for the pool to deepen again and spending that time watching the little ones – though Amalia preferred to think they were watching her not as a little one but a young adult – shot back her arm without looking where she swung and caught Clair a hard blow. Although the water was barely chest-high, Clair went down like a stone. After that, she knew nothing, though at rhythmical periods through the nothingness came a tide resembling awareness, an awareness that ebbed, returned, ebbed, but that eventually won. It was then that the resuscitation that had been given was stopped and restorative administered instead. Clair opened her eyes to Enrico Montales and the pool attendant; everyone else had been pushed back.

Amalia, however, very distressed for such a self-sufficient little female, broke through and knelt by Clair's side. 'I did not mean to drown you, Clair.'

'Was I drowning?' Clair managed a weak smile.

'Zio Rico jumped in the water as soon as you went under. If you were drowning, it wasn't for long,' Amalia said anxiously, glancing at her uncle in the hope of measuring his displeasure.

He said with neither censure nor forgiveness, 'No, you were not drowning long, as Amalia points out, but it is not to her credit. She did not strike you intentionally, but on the other hand she did not attend to you as she should. However, only a short resuscitation was required.'

'Geniale' – Geniale was the *Firenzo* swimming attendant – 'considered none was required at all,' reported Amalia. 'Zio Rico, though, was in a terrible flap.'

Rico said sternly, 'Go to Sophia and stop in your room for the next hour.'

'But Zio—'

'You did not intend harm, as I said, but on the other hand you were not strictly obedient to Miss Wardle, and obedience, as you know, Amalia, I must have. Obey me now and go down to Sophia at once.'

'But the remote island—'

'Only when it means being sent to your cabin are you interested, Amalia. Now obey!'

Pushing out her bottom lip, Amalia went. Juanita, always soft, always sympathetic, hurried after her.

261

'It is true,' admitted Enrico Montales after the children had gone, 'that you were not in dire straits, Clair.'

'Is it true also,' asked Clair, trying to imbue a light touch, 'that you were in a terrible flap?'

For a moment he looked quite furious, then a slow smile turned up the corners of his long firm mouth. 'And what if I was? What if I considered you sufficient cause to "flap", as Amalia says? What if I still insisted, even though Geniale protested it was not necessary, that you have resuscitation, restoratives? What then?'

Clair was at a loss for an answer and would have let the question pass had he not repeated insistently, 'What then?'

'I don't know, *senhor*.'

'You don't know?'

'I mean – well, I mean thank you for being so careful of my health.'

He looked at her oddly, looked a long time. Then he said a curious thing. He said, 'No, you don't know, do you, *senhorita*?' But his tone did not demand a reply this time.

The crowd had drifted away. The young lady was perfectly all right. The anxious passenger had been taking unnecessary precautions it seemed, it had all petered out – and besides, the Portuguese island was rising out of the turquoise Indian Ocean.

Clair, in a deck chair now, and sipping the brandy that Rico had insisted upon, said she was feeling fine and would like to find a spot at the rail to see her first landfall in days.

'But we shall observe. of course.' said Rico proudly, 'from the bridge.'

'The bridge?'

'I will speak to our captain.'

'But—'. Clair did not like to tell Rico that even Classe Prima passengers of the luxury suite category were not free at will to invade a ship's holy of holies, the bridge.

But—

'If you are recovered, Clair, we will go up now.'

Weakly, though not physically weakly, Clair obeyed.

She need not have worried for the *senhor,* though. He received no polite refusal, no tactful rebuff. Instead he was literally bowed in.

Clair sank into a chair put at a vantage point for her, accepted binoculars focussed in readiness, nodded thanks for a drink at her elbow. What couldn't this Enrico Montales summon up?

There was more he could summon, she soon found.

Gazing at the fairy-like island as it rose verdantly from the blue sea, its coast silver with columns of spray that Rico told her were caused by caves ending in vents, Clair murmured – more to herself – how she would love to set foot on the pretty place.

He got up abruptly, leaving Clair still gazing and dreaming, and in a few minutes was back again.

'I am Aladdin with the wonderful lamp,' he smiled. 'Oh, yes, even in Portugal we know Aladdin. I have rubbed the lamp and lo, there will come a little launch and take us ashore.'

'I – you – you're joking,' she began.

'No, Clair.'

'You actually mean we can walk on that lovely island?'

'Run, if we please, though as it is so small we could not run very far. Rather we shall stroll, Clair, stroll through coffee, cocoa and pepper plantations. Yes, that is so, it is very temperate here. I would also like to show you the small phosphate works, but by the time the *Firenzo* circles the island there will not be sufficient time for that. Look, Clair, already my message has been transmitted. There is the result.'

The result was a trim little inboard pushing out from a jetty and leaving a smooth ribbon of water behind it as it dipped rhythmically in the direction of the liner.

Enrico Montales was pulling Clair to her feet, warning her that the *Firenzo* could not stop, only go at a reduced speed, that she must be prepared to jump, did she think after her ordeal in the pool she was equal to that?

'Oh, *senhor!*' Clair's voice was breathless with joy.

He smiled back at her. 'Such a child! Such a happy child!'

They went down in the lift, and were waiting at the appointed place as the little launch drew alongside, matching its speed as well as it was able to the *Firenzo*'s.

Arms were held out to Clair, Rico gave her a gentle push, and the next moment the small boat with its two visitors was speeding to shore.

'The captain will circle the island for the passengers, then pick us up again around this spot. It is, in fact, the island's only access. The rest of its coast is undermined by those caves and vents that give it its silver setting.'

'I'm rather amazed at this boat,' admitted Clair with fantasy. 'It seemed such a faerie island I expected something more gossamer. And certainly an elf or sprite to meet us, not a human being.'

He smiled at that. 'The population is mostly Chinese.' He was waving now to someone on the jetty.

'Your friend?' asked Clair.

'Yes. Alvarez. But he is so long away now he is only distantly Portuguese and more Islander. I see he has brought his jeep.' Rico looked pleased. 'We will be able to see some of the surroundings.'

They wasted no time in climbing on to the jetty, exchanging happy but hurried greetings, getting into the jeep and beginning their quick tour.

'What,' said Enrico Montales suddenly in Clair's ear, 'if that big white ship did not circle, as the captain promised, proceeded onward instead – what of that, my child?'

Clair laughed. 'I would live on this silver island, that's what,' she said.

'I too, would live on this silver island,' Rico reminded her.

'You would have a friend in readiness.' Clair nodded to Alvarez who was speeding the powerful little jeep up a soaring road wooded each side with coconut palms.

'Oh, yes, my friend,' Rico nodded. He did not speak again until they reached the plateau.

It had to be a hurried tour. From the pinnacle of the highest hill where Alvarez took them they could see the *Firenzo* circling the island. It looked a child's plaything from this great height, a small white boat that a boy might sail in a pond.

They went quickly through a coffee plantation, the evergreen shrubs with their shiny leaves and beautiful flowers enchanting Clair with their sweet scent. Alvarez badly wanted Clair to sample coffee he himself had ground, but there was no time, Rico refused, if the cocoa and pepper also were to be viewed. Already – looking down on the toy ship – the *Firenzo* was rounding another bluff.

The pods of the cocoa bushes were crimson and ready to be cropped. Alvarez grieved that he could not give Clair a cup of chocolate.

'Perhaps,' suggested Rico with a twinkle, 'Clair will agree to sampling the island's third crop. Would you like a spoonful of local pepper, child?'

Clair refused, but was still very interested in the pepper shrub with its articulated stems and flowers with no petals. She was sorry when Rico said definitely they could tarry no longer but must get back to the tender.

On the jetty Alvarez kissed her hand, Rico lifted her into the inboard, they both waved goodbye to the ex-Portuguese and to the phosphate island, and were borne over a placid blue sea to the *Firenzo* again.

A little rope ladder was waiting for them, and barely had Clair put her foot on a rung than Rico was beside her and guiding her up. It was not until she had climbed to the last rung that she glanced up and saw the onlookers clustered round the rail. A little embarrassed, she turned her attention to getting safely into the ship.

'Well, child?' They were in the lift now, just the two of them.

'It was a wonderful experience.' Clair hoped her voice did not lack lustre, but somehow some of the lustre had been dulled by those steady stares.

A futile hope. The *senhor,* of course, caught the dulled note. '*Senhorita?*'

'It was wonderful,' she repeated.

'Only your lips say it.'

'But it was. It's – it's just—'

'Yes?'

'Do you think, *senhor* – oh, don't misunderstand me, don't think I didn't appreciate every minute, but—'

'Yes?'

'All those people.' Clair's voice was troubled.

'Yes?' he demanded a third time.

'It was such a *special* trip,' she said wretchedly. 'I mean their eyes said so, their eyes said "Why you?" to me, I mean – well, I mean—'

'I know what you mean, *senhorita*.' He spoke stiffly. 'You are afraid that without words they are saying what Mrs. Henry did?'

'Well, if I am afraid, it's for you.' Clair's voice was sober. 'You're an important person.'

'Who told you this?' The interruption was rapier-sharp.

'Of course you are. You are an international wool buyer. You travel in a de luxe suite.'

'Oh, that.' Almost visibly he relaxed. He waited a moment. 'You are a sensitive child, but please do not be sensitive for me. If I choose to take you ashore, if I please to do other small things, that is my concern. Only if it displeases you will I desist.'

'Oh, no, *senhor!*'

'Then let us be excited again, let us talk of silver islands, of cocoa pods and pepper bushes.'

'Coffee?' added Clair.

'The flowers of the coffee,' he nodded, 'so like stars. Your eyes had stars when you fingered them, Clair.'

'They were beautiful.'

'Yes. Beautiful.' His own eyes were holding hers.

Only when the bell of the lift shrilled impatiently to remind them that others wished to ascend or descend did they realize that they had reached their deck and not opened the elevator door.

CHAPTER FOUR

THE affair at the ship pool had sobered Amalia somewhat, with the happy consequence that at the children's celebration party for the Little Princess of the Indian Ocean an amiable small Princess sat on the seaweed-festooned throne instead of the scornful little sophisticate that Clair rather had dreaded.

Clair stopped with the girls during their revels, danced with them, played games, feasted on little iced cakes and lemonade, and frankly thoroughly enjoyed herself.

There was also a celebration for the adults: an Indian Ocean Queen instead of a mere Princess ... and when the junior fun was over, Clair took each of the little girls' hands and went to watch the older affair.

Amalia looked enviously at the more sophisticated entertainment, but when the frolic finished up with meringue pie being thrown around, decided fastidiously she was glad she had been Ocean *Princess*.

Clair noted that Zio Rico was absent from the ceremony, noted it but was unsurprised. She smiled at the idea of his being present, not that tall, aloof, haughty man.

Yet hardly had a last reveller been thrown into the pool than he strolled down the deck, the stark white of his suit making the bedraggled participants and crushed onlookers appear rather unkempt. Clair tried to straighten a crumple in her own dress.

'Ah, little ones' – he included Clair – 'you have enjoyed the fun?'

'Si, Zio.'

'Yes, Rico.'

'Also the cassata was enjoyable,' he suggested, laughing, raising his brows at a spot on Amalia's frothy pink dress.

'Oh,' said Amalia in annoyance, for she liked to be immaculate, 'I must change at once.'

'Take Juanita, and when you have done go to the Orario

Sala Ragazzi, to the Junior Room, and read or play a card game, for I wish to speak with Clair. Now go.'

'*Si*, Zio Rico.' Always obedient when it was Rico who gave the orders, the girls went.

The *senhor* put cool fingertips under Clair's elbow and led her to the rail. They stood looking out on the Indian Ocean. The air was warm, the breeze gentle, the sea quite glassy, though the *senhor* remarked that this was more an exception than a rule.

'It can be extremely rough in this southern Indian Ocean.'

He gestured for deck chairs and settled Clair, then settled himself.

'We are getting nearer the second largest continent,' he remarked. 'Soon there should be some sea activity.'

Clair said she was glad of that, they had seen no vessel . . . apart from the inboard that had whisked her and the *senhor* to the dreaming island . . . since they had left Fremantle. She said that she would fetch the children up and tell them to be on the watch.

'There is plenty of time yet,' he detained her. 'When we near Durban we will tell them. That brings me to what I wish to ask, and for which there is *not* plenty of time.' He looked inquiringly at Clair.

She raised her brows faintly in response.

'I have a business conference in Durban, *senhorita*.'

'Wool?' she asked.

'The south of Africa has its own, but my answer is still yes, as it happens. A certain finer standard that only Australia grows.'

'Superfine,' she smiled. 'Eighties.'

'Miss Clair,' he smiled back, 'I believe you pay attention to me.'

'I pay attention, and I'm pleased for you. Pleased about the business conference.'

'Thank you, *senhorita*.' He bowed to her. 'There will also be a dinner in Durban, Clair. Naturally I shall be expected to take with me a lady.'

'You know one there?'

'No.'

'Then you will have to ask one from the *Firenzo*.'

'Yes.'

Clair wondered who it would be; she had not seen him with anyone.

Then the deep, correct voice cut into Clair's conjectures.

'I shall be most honoured, *senhorita*,' the *senhor* said. He had risen and was bowing very formally and deeply now. He couldn't mean – Not her – Not to a social dinner in a big city!

'Most honoured,' Enrico Montales said once more.

Clair was silent.

'Well, *senhorita*?' asked Rico.

'I – you did mean me?' She was still uncertain of that.

'Assuredly.'

'But – but would it be correct?'

'The *senhorita* never need worry about correctness.' The *senhor*'s voice was cold.

'You know I didn't mean that, you know I meant was it correct to – to invite an employee.'

'I have spoken on this subject before.' Now the tone was icy.

'I – I'm sorry, Rico.'

'Then you will accompany me?'

'No.'

The black brows had formed their old straight high line. 'What is this, Clair?'

'It's consideration for you, Rico. I haven't led a social life but I know – well, to be brief I know it's not for pearl grey shirt-waisters, however good the fit.' She looked directly at him and waited.

He had said before that clothes were a very small bagatelle, but he had also said that the instinct of the male of the species was to strut – and flaunt. Which trait, she asked herself, would be salient now?

'Both,' he pronounced in that uncanny way he had of always reading her thoughts. 'I would gladly take you in the little ship dress for the sufficient reason that the dress encased the one I had decided to accompany, but on the other hand I

269

would also take you in a remarkable gown for the same reason that it encased my choice. However, Clair, given a preference, and keeping in mind this particular Durban hotel, the social importance of the occasion, I would prefer the remarkable gown.'

'Which—' began Clair.

'You do not have,' he finished for her. 'So now, *senhorita*, we know where we stand, and we can progress from there.'

'If you mean—' she began to protest, then was silent. Silent and flushed. She had started to say, 'If you mean you had intentions of footing the bill—'

'No, I did not mean that,' he returned gravely, reading her again.

Deliberately, almost punitively, he did not speak for several moments, and then he suggested more than stated, 'I did not mean what that person, Mrs. Henry, insinuated. I also did not mean the arrangement we came to for the articles of wear you are using now, your payment through me.'

'Then—?'

'No, *senhorita*, I meant you could buy this suitable gown yourself.'

'But, *senhor*—'

'Wait!' He held up a big authoritative hand.

When she did wait, he explained.

'You are going to say you have not much money. But you will be surprised when you discover the modest amount you will need. That is' – a smile – 'if what I have just thought of can eventuate.'

Clair thought to herself it would have to be even less than modest. Her mother's illness had depleted her slender means, she had embarked on the *Firenzo* with a very meagre sum, and apart from the first and only hand-out from Mrs. Henry, she had received no money at all. She knew that the *senhor* would not know this, that if he did he would have advanced her a sum before. But pride would not permit her to tell him now.

He was looking at her shrewdly, but respect for that pride prevented him from asking questions that came unerringly to his lips.

'If you accept this assignment, *senhorita*,' he said carefully instead, 'it will, of course, be outside your normal duties. Your remuneration at present – which, incidentally, I have not advanced you—'

'*Senhor*, it is only a few days.'

He ignored her interruption. 'Which I have not advanced you, is for standing-in with the children only, not for accompanying their uncle on a special mission. To be brief, *senhorita*, this is beyond your expected service, and as such will be paid for beyond your usual stipend. Is that the word, Clair?'

'It is, but—'

'But?'

'You're trying to dress it up for me, Rico, and it's very kind of you – but it would still be charity.'

'Dress it up? I do not comprehend. It is you who buys the dress.' He looked bewildered.

'You're trying to make it easy for me to accept your generosity.'

'Fuff!' he dismissed.

They seemed to have arrived at a deadlock. There they might have stopped had Enrico Montales not suddenly changed his tactics. Instead of insisting again that this was in the category of work for which he would pay he turned simply and said, 'Clair, I wish you to come with me, will you do that?'

And instead of protesting, pointing out, arguing, Clair found herself just as simply saying: 'Yes.'

For a moment they just looked at each other, then Clair giggled, giggled helplessly.

'*Senhorita*?'

'It's – it's just that I'm agreeing to something that according to British convention simply isn't done.'

'I can assure you,' said the *senhor* stiffly, 'that in Portugal what you are thinking of also "isn't done." Portugal, *senhorita*, is much more convention-bound than Britain.'

'Then—?'

He had taken out a money wallet, like the cigarette case it bore an insignia, and like when he took out the cigarette case his thumb now obliterated the scroll.

He withdrew a wad of notes. 'For standing-in with the girls,' he allotted first, 'and for depriving yourself of a free night to accompany me,' he allotted next.

'But – but, Rico—'

'If it will make British convention happier I will have you sign along a dotted line.'

'Would that make Portuguese convention happier?' she asked.

'I don't know,' he shrugged. 'I only know you will make a Portuguese *senhor* happier by dropping the post-mortems and being your usual pleasant self.'

'Thank you, Rico, but you're wrong about post-mortems, they come after it is all over, not before.'

'They do? But when it is all over naturally you will be happy, little Clair, you will have had a wonderful time.' He took out a little notebook and wrote something in a swirling hand. 'Dress it up,' he read aloud seriously to her, 'meaning – now how can I say it, *senhorita*?'

'Cajolery,' she suggested.

He inscribed it.

'Post-mortems,' he wrote next, 'come after.' He looked up at her. 'Then how would I term your protest before the occasion, Clair?'

She considered, and suggested, 'Qualms.'

He wrote studiously, 'Qualms.'

'Oh, Rico,' she laughed, 'you're mad!'

He gave her a surprised look. She knew by the look that he never had had such a thing said to him before. For a moment she wondered how he would take it, then he was smiling ... laughing. Clair laughed back. They closed on that note.

Clair had her dinner in her own room that night. The *senhor* sent a message that he would be busy all the evening but for Clair not to go to the *ristorante* alone. To make sure she did not, the letter arrived with the meal.

As well as his apologies for not having her join him, there was the intimation that early tomorrow morning he wished to see her on an important matter.

272

'What important matter? How important?' puzzled Clair – and later slept on that. She might have awakened to it, too, but that Senhor Montales knocked on the door and aroused her first.

'It is I, Clair. I wish you to join me as soon as you can.'

'Is anything wrong, Rico?'

'Must there be?' he reproached.

'No, but—'

'Hurry, little one.' She heard him leave.

She skipped through the coffee and biscuit that was brought and showered hurriedly.

Her quick toilet did not show, but her sparse refreshment must have, for the first thing he did after she had knocked on his door and been bowed in was to ring for a substantial breakfast.

'No, *senhorita*,' he refused when she tried to stop him, 'I can see you have only eaten like a bird.'

There was no more said on the subject, only trivialities, until orange juice, buttered eggs, thin toast and conserve had arrived and been consumed, and then, pouring coffee and handing a cup to Clair, Rico Montales began.

'You were speaking of being unsuitably gowned for a social dinner, *senhorita*,' he said.

'Yes.'

'I have visited the ship boutiques and am in agreement with you that there is nothing there.'

'Then,' she breathed, believing this was why he had summoned her, to withdraw his invitation, 'I can be excused?'

At once he frowned at her; she could see he was genuinely annoyed.

'By no means. You have given me your word and I will keep you to it.'

'But—'

'Yes, Clair?'

'The dress. The dress, *senhor,* that I don't have.'

'That is what I wish to speak about, Clair. I have thought of a solution . . . it came to me yesterday, indeed . . . a quite triumphant idea.'

273

'What, *senhor*?'

'Perhaps, or perhaps not, you have seen me upon occasion in the company of an Indian gentleman?'

'Yes,' said Clair, 'I have.'

'He is a Mr. Prasad, a very successful merchant ... especially successful seeing that he has only himself and his years of ardous work to thank for his present prosperity. May I tell you about this gentleman?'

'Please.'

'He came from a very impoverished family, but he did not let his straitened beginnings tether him to a lifetime of poverty; on the contrary he made hardship a challenge, and finally arrived at what he is now: a man of means and influence.'

'In what particular channel, *senhor*?'

His coffee was finished and he pushed the cup away, and, at an acquiescing nod from Clair, took out his usual cheroot.

'Apparel,' he said. 'I believe, *senorita*, that that is the word.'

'If you mean attire ... clothes ... gowns ...'

'I do.'

'Then yes.'

'Mr. Prasad went through every stage, and even today has not lost his unerring touch. Why, he even told me last night when I spoke on this subject that he still would be capable of outfitting you himself.'

'*Senhor*—' she began.

'But there is no need, of course. Travelling with Mr. Prasad is his small select team of chosen workers. This trip for them is both an education in apparel the world over as well as a reward. A reward for service to an employer who appreciates what they have achieved him and now achieves them something in return.'

'They are – tailors?'

'And modistes, couturiers, makers of dresses ... choose your own word.'

'Men?'

'That doesn't matter, but – yes.'

'But what about materials, *senhor*?'

274

'Ah,' smiled Rico Montales, 'now you begin to understand.'

'But I don't, *senhor*. How can a gown be made without material?'

'There *are* materials. Many, many materials. Mr. Prasad had an eye for new openings and has come prepared.' An exhalation and a wreath of blue smoke. 'I believe when you see them you will be enchanted, Clair. As I was.'

Shyly Clair asked, 'Can I see them?'

'Mr. Prasad is waiting.' Rico Montales had risen and his hand was extended to Clair. 'Come, child,' he said.

Mr. Prasad had a bracket of rooms on Ponte B, and he bowed deferentially to Clair as he invited her and the *senhor* to take seats.

He did not waste time on unproductive talk, and Clair supposed that this trait had helped him become the successful business man he was.

Pulling aside a curtain he displayed a rainbow fall of glittering stuffs, all so breathtakingly beautiful that Clair gave a little cry of delight.

Never had she seen such an array of glorious fabrics. Rich brocades, flowing satins, Thai silks with lights darting out of them, lengths of fine jersey that could have been fitted into a coffee cup. The rainbow colours of them, the patterns ranging from splashy flowers to oriental dragons. It was all the Arabian Nights, Clair thought, gathered in an armful of dreams that frou-froued softly as folds fell gracefully to the floor.

'Madam likes?' The Indian was smiling at her pleasure.

'Oh, yes, yes!'

'Madam will choose?'

'That,' sighed Clair, 'won't be easy.'

She fingered a muted blue Thai silk, but only muted until the light picked up glittering tangents of peacock blue and jacaranda purple. Her eyes fell, too, on a flame-hued brocade with the old willow pattern story but told in glorious crimson instead of blue.

'Take both, Clair,' advised Enrico Montales. 'The reasonable cost will astound you.'

Clair put the fabrics down. '*Senhor*—'

'Yes, that is so.'

Clair turned to Mr. Prasad, and he, too, nodded confirmation.

'Had you ever travelled to the East, Miss Wardle,' he said, 'you would know this already. We sell at a very low price.' Taking out a silver pencil and a memo pad he jotted some figures, then tore out the sheet and handed it to Clair.

She looked at it incredulously, then turned to the *senhor*.

'I don't want to pay Mr. Prasad this and then have you see him privately and give him a supplementary sum.'

'What do you mean, *senhorita*?'

'I want him to write down the full amount now.'

'You doubt Mr. Prasad? You doubt me?'

'I doubt materials like these being so reasonable.'

'It is the margin of profit on which I work,' said the Indian. 'And' – with humility yet pride – 'I am a rich man.'

'Well,' interrupted the *senhor* a little impatiently, 'the blue as well as the crimson, Clair?'

'I fell in love with the crimson, but could I wear it?' When he looked inquiring, she explained, 'My colouring, Rico ... or at least my lack of colouring.'

'Snow White and Rose Red,' he reminded her at once. His eyes were on her flaxen hair. 'I had that in a translated English fairy tale, Clair. Yes, you can wear it.' It seemed an effort for him to take his glance away. Clair wondered uneasily if her hair was immaculate; she had learned how important exquisite tidiness was to this Portuguese gentleman. Her hand wandered up to tuck in a curl. He observed the gesture.

'You must buy a shady hat No' – smiling – 'nothing expensive. Perhaps a cabbage straw, one that flips. Is that correct?'

'Flops, Rico. But why will I need a hat?'

'We will be seeing more of Durban, of course, than a luxury hotel, and Durban can be hot. Also, we will be seeing it today.'

'Today?'

'That is so. Had you been awake last night, little one, instead of dreaming of faerie islands, you would have noted the

276

Firenzo's increased speed. The stabilizers were removed to catch up the time lost on that faerie island of yours, but so clement was the weather that not only was distance regained, but gained. Indeed, we arrive this morning. That is why you must make up your mind about these gowns at once. Even with a team to work on them the time is short.'

'They could never do it.'

Mr. Prasad smiled, 'Had you been to Hong Kong, Miss Wardle, you would not say that.' He turned to business again. 'Madam favours both fabrics?' he asked.

'Yes. But I don't know how I would like them made.'

At once the Indian took the pencil and pad from his pocket again and began to sketch. It was wonderful to watch the deft strokes.

'I think an Empire bodice and then a bell skirt.' – Thank goodness, thought Clair, he has the fashion terms I understand. 'Not full, madam, yet not tight either. I would suggest a gentle flow.' He spread his hands. 'That, for the Thai silk, but, ah, the crimson! I think here, perhaps, a suggestion of the eastern cheongsam, only westernized. It is the right material, madam, for that.'

'Am I the right type, though?' doubted Clair.

'Only a breath of a suggestion, madam.' The Indian blew softly to illustrate. 'A decolleté instead of the usual high neck, perhaps, but the tight sleeves, of course, and – if the *senhor* permits – the split in the skirt.' He looked inquiringly at Enrico Montales. Clair looked, too. To her surprise Rico nodded with enthusiasm.

'Yes, Clair, that would be admirable, it would bring the east and west together most magnificently.' He bowed his head at the Indian, and Mr. Prasad, pleased, rang a bell for his steward to bring his small team of tailors to the room.

They took no time at all; Clair had stood much longer in Australian shops to have a tape measure run over her and her sizes recorded.

In no time she was out of the improvised fitting room, and Rico was sitting waiting with Mr. Prasad and holding a cabbage straw hat that 'flipped', that he informed her he had bought at the ship shop.

The Indian gentleman bowed them out of his rooms, and that – well, that was that.

'I didn't pay,' protested Clair breathlessly ... things, she thought, had happened much too quickly.

'But I did. You will pay me. Have no fear' – at a look on her face – 'you will pay the right amount. I will even tender you the bill.'

'I didn't ask if I would need a second fitting.'

'You will not,' the *senhor* assured her. 'I often order suits myself.'

'I didn't find out whether either of the gowns will be done in time.'

'Both of them will. And now, Clair, before you begin another "I did not" please look around you.'

Clair did ... and gasped.

While she had been draped and moulded and fitted something had happened to the *Firenzo* as well. It had come into port.

'I did not,' disobeyed Clair, 'fetch up the children.'

But there was ample time after all for the children. It was exactly one hour after the *Firenzo* entered the breakwater that she finally berthed. In that period Juanita and Amalia had all the water activity they could have asked for, for there were several ships also nosing into wharves, many little sailing boats dipping by and speed boats dashing past.

When they grew tired of water they could look up to the wooded hill known as the Bluff that protected the harbour from the Indian Ocean.

To the girls' delight ... and Clair's, too, for she found joy in their joy ... the *senhor* announced that he intended to take 'all three little ones' to see the Zulu dancers.

As they were four, he chose a cab in preference to Durban's colourful rickshaws, drawn by Zulus in fanciful costumes decked with beads and feathers. Had he patronized the rickshaw 'boys', he smiled, they would have been assured of a rather startling journey, for the tall, often six-foot men would often stop suddenly out of sheer fun and tilt the rick-shaw, putting the surprised passenger in a rather precarious position, the while the 'boy' leap and danced.

Durban, Clair saw at once, was a beach city ... beaches that brought an exclamation even though she had come from a beach country. The vividness, too, of the city attracted her ... poinsettias, jacarandas, bougainvillea, the scarlet blossoms of the flamboyant tree, the orange bells of the African Flame.

They drove down West Street with its multiple stores past the statue of Botha, the first South African Prime Minister, stopping at the driver's suggestion to look at the Durban race-course which had a golf course in the middle of it.

At Mitchell Park they saw the five-hundred-years-old Thunder Tree, then crossing the river by a viaduct they drove over a bumpy green to where groups of highly decorated Zulus were performing their war dances. Accompanied by tom-toms and shouting, it was a very impressive performance as the dancers swung their assegais and shields made of animal skins high in the air. They seemed to wear a sort of kilt, Clair thought, of many-coloured strands, red feathers in their hair and anklets of sheep's fleece.

The performance finished, Amalia wished to buy some multi-coloured beads, and as she chose them Clair found am-usement in a love potion made from crocodile fat ... so she read ... and presented in a little bead bottle.

'You must have it, Clair.'

'No, Rico.'

'You are afraid of it? Or' – an enigmatical glance – 'you have no need of it?'

All at once embarrassed, unable to meet his black glance, to brush his offer aside in a joke, she said a little agitatedly, 'I – I will have a string of beads, too, if you don't mind.'

'*I* do not mind,' he answered blandly. 'Love potions to me would be re-dun-dant. Is that the word?'

'I think Juanita wants a string of beads, too, *senhor*.'

He looked at her silently a moment, then ordered, 'Three strings of beads.'

Returning to the *Firenzo*, Clair was intrigued by long lines

279

of bright washing belonging to some large edifice, perhaps a hostel, a hotel or college, but looking more like pennants run up to welcome a princess.

'Me,' claimed Amalia.

'It could be your sister or Clair,' reminded Rico.

Clair refused that.

'Then perhaps' – a slight pause – 'a countess appeals?'

Something in his voice took her attention and she glanced at him, but the black eyes that met her inquiring blue were bland and inscrutable.

When they reached the ship, Enrico saw them safely aboard, then said he was returning to the city as he had business to do, but that he would knock on the *senhorita's* door some minutes before eight.

'But – but my dresses?' she queried.

'They will be there, Clair. They will be there now.'

'This soon?'

He inclined his head. 'You will have no need to try them on, either, no dress rehearsal, they will fit you like a gauntlet.' He looked at her uncertainly.

'Like a glove.'

He nodded. He bowed. He took his leave.

Clair went to her room, and the first thing that met her eye were the boxes on her bed. She saw from the labels that they were indeed the dresses. She could not credit that they could be made and delivered in such a short time. She snapped the strings and withdrew the contents. She examined them thoroughly. One thing, the quality of craftsmanship had not suffered by the speed of production; the frocks were perfectly, beautifully made.

In spite of the *senhor's* assurance that she would have no need to try them on, Clair did so, and was delighted at the fit. The flame brocade with the hint of the Orient in its fashioning, its suggestion of the cheongsam, its straight split skirt, was entirely different from anything she had ever had. She was still standing staring at her reflection when there was a knock on the door.

'Are you there, Clair? It is Amalia. I have come to ask you

to show me stem stitch. Zio Rico bought me some embroidery from the ship shop and the instructions say stem stitch. Why—' for by this time Clair had opened the door – 'Why, Clair!'

Juanita, who was with Amalia, but, characteristically, Amalia had only announced herself, stood spellbound.

'You look wonderful, Clair,' she gasped at length.

'Yes.' Amalia circled Clair critically. 'Yes, you do.' Any glow that Clair might have felt were extinguished immediately by Amalia's next words. 'My mama will not care for that.'

Twice . . . in a way thrice . . . before such a thing had been said to her, and it had given Clair the same hollow feeling she experienced again now. When she first had met the children, Amalia had announced, 'I do not think you will do.' She had lifted the load a little when she had added more cheerfully, 'You are very pale, very washed-out, so you may do after all,' but nevertheless an uneasiness had remained. Then later there had been the elegant young mother, Rosita's friend, and she had said, 'But this is funny, terribly funny. I mean if Rosita *knew*.' Finally there had been Sophia, the *domestica*, and Sophia had looked her up and down then said, 'The *signora* would not like that.'

Why wouldn't she do? What was terribly funny? What was it the *signora* would not like?

Not liking the unease she felt herself, Clair suggested to the little girls that they return to the Orario Sala Ragazzi and she would come as soon as she had changed out of her new gown and show Amalia how to do stem stitch.

'I should have liked to see the Thai silk on you,' observed Amalia.

'Another time, dear.'

'Are you going out tonight? Will you wear one of these then?'

'Yes.'

'May I watch you walk down the corridor?' asked Juanita breathlessly.

Always more to the point, Amalia said, 'Which one will you wear?'

281

Which one. Clair did not ponder over it then, she was too concerned with what Amalia had carelessly tossed, that shrewd 'My mama will not care for that.'

As the afternoon wore on, however, and the echo of Amalia's voice died away, she began arguing with herself which would be the better gown for an important social function, a function at Raffles.

At seven o'clock, her bath completed, Clair was still fingering the blue, then the crimson, when, with a knock at the door and the entry of her stewardess, her mind was made up for her. Made up by the exquisite spill of flowers that the stewardess took from a small box. They were red poinciana. So she must wear the red. But would flowers be right with an already embossed dress?

'Ah, but he knows, that Portuguese gentleman,' smiled the stewardess. 'The *signorina* wears the flowers as a *braccialetta. Si?*'

'*Braccialetta?* Oh, a bracelet? A bangle?'

'Yes.' The stewardess put the spill of flowers over Clair's wrist. '*Bella,*' she applauded.

Clair gave an excited little laugh, and allowed the stewardess to help her dress.

She need not have worried over the suitability of such a vibrant hue for such fair colouring as hers. The result was at once both arresting and flattering, the slight suggestion of the oriental cheongsam most charming and unexpected, the split in the narrow skirt so much part of the whole that Clair gave it no more attention.

She had piled her fair hair on top of her head and was looking for an anchoring comb when the stewardess clicked her tongue for Clair to wait a moment and then deftly removed one of the poinciana blooms and attached it to a pin. Folded in the flaxen strands it gave the finishing touch.

'*Bella,*' said the stewardess.

'But could I – I mean—' Clair looked at her reflection, and knew she could.

A few minutes to eight, as he had promised, Enrico Montales tapped on the door. The stewardess had gone, and Clair

282

opened up rather tremblingly. Was the flower too much? Had she overdone it? Could there be Rose Red and Snow White together as he had said?

For several minutes she was not to know. He just stood and looked at her in silence. Then he said a little huskily, 'We must go.'

'But – but Rico—'

'Yes, Clair?'

'Will I – I mean am I all right? Will I do?'

He did not say she looked wonderful as Juanita had, *bella* as the stewardess had, he said simply, 'You are a flower.'

Because the corridor was not wide enough for both of them, he stepped forward protectively and led the way. As they were approaching the gangplank Clair felt more than saw the concentration of eyes on her from above, not the usual attention of the passengers standing at the rail and watching the arrivals and departures, but two eyes that looked only for her and on her. Turning at the bottom, she looked up at a dark young woman, a woman older than herself but only older in the way that a full blossom is older than a flower that has not yet stretched its petals to its extent. The woman was vividly beautiful, dark, flashing-eyed, crimson-mouthed.

'We have taken on a new passenger,' Clair said to Rico, 'a very lovely one, too.'

He turned lazily, followed the direction of Clair's gaze and raised his arm. It was only then that Clair saw that the woman was flanked on either side by the two little girls, by Juanita and Amalia. Could that mean – Oh, no, Rosita was thirtyish and maternal, not – not a raving beauty like that.

But – 'She's not new, she's been on the *Firenzo* as long as you have, Clair. She is Rosita, my cousin, the mother of the children. Taxi! Taxi!'

Without further explanation, Rico put Clair into the car that pulled up, and carelessly directed it to the arranged hotel.

The fact that she was in a new country should have been a triumph for Clair, but the thrill fell flat. She had not expected Rosita to be so breathtaking, but more than that she had not expected such a look on her face. A disliking, resentful, one might almost say baleful look. Even before she meets me she is antagonistic, Clair gloomed.

'What is it, *senhorita*?'

'*Senhor*?'

'It is not a sad moment, it is supposed to be a happy occasion.'

'Of course, Rico. I'm sorry, Rico.' Clair looked out on Durban, like all similar latitudes indigo dark once the day had fled, and stuck now, like a pincushion with glittering pins, with scintillating lights. The lights undid her, they were so beautiful, and she smiled.

'That is better,' Rico said.

They pulled in through a palmy drive to the appointed hotel.

A doorman in a uniform so starkly white that it almost dazzled the eyes stepped forward and opened the door. Rico's firm, cool fingers, cool in spite of the warm evening, propelled her through the lavish doorway into halls of marble. Once inside, the warmth was a forgotten thing.

The *senhor*'s party claimed him at once; be became the centre figure of a group of obviously very important people, all of whom, Clair noted, listened deferentially to every word he said.

An alcove had been reserved for before dinner drinks. Over her cold lime punch, Clair quietly assessed the other members of their group. She had been introduced formally and at length to each in turn, but she had had no time to study them. She noted the lavish dressing of the ladies and understood why Senhor Montales had desired her to wear a 'remarkable' gown. One of the women ... it was an international group ... was Indian, and her amethyst sari a thing of rare beauty. She saw Mrs. Sandhu's pleasure at her obvious admiration and asked her about the sari. It had threads, Clair was told, of pure gold. A sari must be six yards long and two yards wide and should not show the ankles.

Deft waiters, since the party had decided not to leave the alcove to dine but to remain where they were, quietly changed the drinks table to a glittering dining board. The Indian woman reluctantly left Clair to take her position between two gentlemen. A tall, fair young man took Mrs. Sandhu's place. Unmistakably he was English, and Clair smiled back at him.

'I've been watching you, Miss Wardle,' he greeted, 'though I guess you can't address me by name like I can address you by yours.'

Ruefully she admitted that all the names had sounded the same and all the faces had looked alike.

'Yours didn't to me.' His tone was a shade lower.

Dinner was being served and for a while Clair and the young man had no chance to converse.

'Since I didn't register on you, Miss Wardle,' he started again when the waiters had gone, 'I must try a second time. I'm Gordon Sindel. *Gordon*. You are?'

'Clair Wardle.' Clair added, liking the freshness of his good-looking young face, 'Clair.'

'You're Australian, Clair.'

'Yes.'

'One of my top nationalities. I mean that. And I should be able to say because I travel around a lot. I like the forthrightness of the Australian, and when it comes wrapped up in English blonde looks like yours, I'm sunk.'

'I haven't the skin for tanning,' submitted Clair, a little embarrassed.

'Good for you.' A brush of her hand with his.

Another round of drinks, then Gordon Sindel again monopolizing his companion. Not that it mattered, thought Clair, a trifle piqued, for Enrico Montales had not spoken to her since they had sat down.

'Where do you feature in this picture?' asked Gordon. 'You're not a woman executive, by any chance? A career girl?'

'I accompanied Senhor Montales.'

'Oh, our regal Portuguese. Quite a figure, isn't he? Do you curtsey before you greet him, Clair?'

'Of course not,' she laughed.

'Nothing to be flippant about. I'm sure he rates a bow in

285

his *palacio*. Who wouldn't with that bearing?'

'Senhor Montales is very kind and generous,' Clair assured him, waiting her chance to ask what that '*palacio*' was.

'Also very remote,' suggested Gordon Sindel. 'You couldn't get to first base with him. Yet people talk of the English aristocracy, my aunt!' He took a long quaff of his drink.

'The Portuguese—' began Clair.

'Are England's oldest allies.' Gordon openly stifled a yawn. 'But they're still the wrong side of the channel to me.'

'Australians must be the same, then.'

'Never. Australians are improved English.' He grinned boyishly. 'You can't knock that compliment back, can you?'

She laughed at this impudence, and the laugh tinkled into one of those brief silences that inevitably intrude into the busiest conversation. Eyes turned on Clair, smiling, sympathetic eyes: the young Englishman, the young Australian girl it was only natural that they merge. But one pair of eyes did not smile.

'Why are you in Durban?' asked Gordon Sindel.

'I'm only passing through,' answered Clair.

'By air?'

'By sea.'

'Then you must be a passenger on the *Firenzo*, it's the only liner in port.'

'Yes,' nodded Clair.

'Where are you bound?'

That was more difficult. Where was she bound? She did not know. Lately she had been so at peace in her mind she had been content to drift from day to day.

'Where?' persisted Gordon.

'The ship is bound for Genoa.'

'And from there? For you, I mean?'

'The usual places,' she murmured, hoping it would do, and it did.

'It's an excellent way to get to England, by seeing Europe en route. I've half a mind—' His voice trailed off as desserts began to arrive.

The talk became general over coffee and liqueurs, but once

they were finished, Gordon, by putting his elbows on the table, encircled Clair and monopolized her again.

'When do you sail?'

'Not till tomorrow.' Clair added, 'The late afternoon.'

'What are you doing with yourself before Blue Peter?'

'I don't know, I mean – well, you see it depends on the *senhor*.'

'His royal highness?'

'He's not that.'

'Near enough,' Gordon smirked. 'But, seriously, how does it depend on him? Is there an alliance or something? You can tell me, I won't be shocked.'

Clair said with dignity, 'I'm a companion to his nieces.'

Gordon shrugged amiably. 'Undoubtedly there is more staff. I know these royal Portuguese, they take a retinue with them. I'll be out to fetch you in the morning.'

'But Gordon—'

'In the morning.'

'But I don't know if I can— I mean—'

'You'll just have to try. The British must stick together. We're the same sort, Clair, neither of us are outsiders.' Into a second of the silences his voice intruded. Clair tried to assure herself that no one would know what they were talking about. She felt sure by the smiling eyes that they didn't know. Yet, as before, two eyes did not smile.

Not long after, the party broke up. Clair walked along the red carpet out of the marble vestibule into the hot street. A taxi was waiting. She was helped in. The *senhor's* hand under her elbow was not cool now, it was ice.

'You enjoyed yourself, *senhorita*?'

'Thank you, yes.'

'No post-mortems? You see, I use it correctly now.' Although he made the bantering remark, his eyes, as in the hotel, did not smile.

'No post-mortems. And you, *senhor*, did you enjoy yourself?'

'To me it was a business gathering only. All these people were business associates only. The young person who sat by you was a new representative to me, and also' – a pause – 'only a business encounter.' Was there a subtle emphasis somewhere? Was there a slightly patronizing note?

'I found him very charming.' The tinge of patronage ruffled Clair.

'Of course, are you not both British?' The answer was suave.

'*Senhor*—'

'Portugal is England's oldest ally. Here we take time to yawn.' Enrico Montales yawned. 'But it is the wrong side of the channel, which Australia is not, for the colony is an extension of Britain not a separation, so the one blood. Outsiders' – he inclined his head – 'are another breed.'

'*Senhor*—' Her voice was full of distress.

'Forgive me, *senhorita*,' he said at once, 'I spoke in bad taste. Consider that all unsaid.'

'It is difficult,' murmured Clair.

'It was difficult for me to listen to that – to that—' Knuckle bones showed white through the olive brown wrists.

But when Enrico Montales spoke again he was in complete control of himself. He was even uninterested.

'Tomorrow, *senhorita*, I shall not need you. I shall see to it that the girls also have no call on your time.'

'It doesn't matter, *senhor,* I mean—'

'Whatever you protest you will still not be required,' he insisted.

'If you're doing this because of Gordon—'

'Gordon?' The dark brows lifted in the old proud way.

'Mr. Sindel,' Clair flushed, 'if you're doing this—'

'And if I am, *senhorita*, why not? Is it still not youth to youth, the call of the young to the young? Surely I am not too old still to be aware of that.'

'You are quite wrong, *senhor*. You are not old either.'

'Nor young?' There was a sharp interrogation in his voice. She sat by his side, completely at a loss, too wretched to summon up a response. 'It is of little importance, anyhow,' he shrugged carelessly. 'A mere baga— What is the word again?'

'Bagatelle,' she said mechanically. '*Senhor*, I'm sure Gordon

– Mr. Sindel meant nothing when—'

He made an imperious gesture. 'It is over. No post-mortems. A bag-a-telle' – he said carefully – 'is not worth a moment's thought. Tomorrow you are free. Enjoy yourself.'

The taxi had pulled up at the dock. The great white ship ablaze with lights loomed above them. Rico paid off the taxi, helped Clair up the gangway with cool, impersonal fingers barely touching her arm. He conducted her to her room, and at the door he bowed formally, said, 'Many thanks, *senhorita*,' and went.

Clair watched him go, an aloof, proud figure, making the corridor look small as he covered it with long, rapid steps. Not once did he turn.

She let herself in, thinking unhappily of his final words. 'Enjoy yourself.' As though she could – now. As though she would think of going anywhere, of doing anything but remain on board.

But even then she was not finished with upsets. On her dressing table there was a message on the *Firenzo* stationery. A very brief, to-the-point missive, this time a woman's hand.

'I shall expect Miss Wardle in my suite at nine o'clock to-morrow morning.' It was signed: 'R. Dal Rosa.'

'No "please". No "can you?" No "kindly". Also no alternative. Just "I shall expect".'

What did the cousin of Enrico Montales expect?

Clair recalled that unfriendly expression this evening, that baleful look, and added apprehension to the load she already bore.

CHAPTER FIVE

At five to nine the next morning, wearing the grey shirt-waister done right up to her neck, Clair presented herself to the Signora Dal Rosa. It was as hot as yesterday, promising later an even greater heat, and the high buttoning was a torture, but Clair wanted to give a different impression to the children's mother than she had last night.

She tapped on the door, and Sophia, in black, answered it. She did not address Clair, she simply said to the *signora*, 'The *signorina* is here.'

'Come in!' Rosita called in English.

If Clair had not dressed herself for the weather, Rosita Dal Rosa certainly had undressed herself for it. She wore the flimsiest of negligées that succeeded in making Clair, observing the comparison in their garb, all the more unbearably hot.

'Sit down, Miss Wardle,' Rosita yawned.

At closer quarters she was even lovelier than Clair had judged. She was a glowing red ruby, or a striking tourmaline. Now Clair understood Amalia's pitying, 'You are very pale, very washed-out.' Beside this glowing jewel she must seem very insignificant indeed.

The thought must have occurred to Rosita, too. She looked Clair up and down and seemed rather pleased.

'You are a different person from last night, Miss Wardle.'

That brought back the memory of last night, and she bit her lip, not so pleased. The girl had looked really beautiful – if you cared for that soft type, of course.

'Did you ask my cousin to escort you out?' she asked sharply.

'Certainly not, *signora*, he asked me. I mean' – at a look on Rosita's face – 'he asked it of me in the line of duty. He had this business conference, and as it was in a social setting he was expected to bring a lady.'

'Of course,' Rosita smiled. 'Of course it would be only

290

in the line of duty. I do trust, though, *signorina*' – a quick upward glance – 'that you are fully aware of that?'

'I just told you the circumstances, *signora*.'

'You told me, yes, but are you really aware of them?'

'Most assuredly,' Clair said a little testily.

'No need for you to lose your temper, dear. I must ask Rico if he really thinks you have the right nature to act as companion to two little girls. The appropriate type should be amiable and placid. Like my *domestica*.' Rosita darted a quick look to see if Sophia was in earshot.

'Sophia,' intervened a young bored voice, and for the first time Clair noticed that Amalia was in the room, 'is a crosspatch, and you know it. She tugs my hair. Clair' – magnanimously – 'is nice.'

'Be quiet,' said her mother. 'Also leave the room.'

Amalia did so, but slowly, impudently.

'She is a naughty one,' Rosita despaired.

'But a very pretty one.' Clair did not say it to placate, but if it did placate, all the better. She expected a smile from Rosita, most mothers melted with praise of their young, but Rosita only pouted.

'I was far prettier.'

'You are very pretty now.'

This time Rosita did smile.

'You are not,' she said in a more reasonable tone, 'the person I would have employed, Miss Wardle. However, undoubtedly my cousin was desperate, just' – in inspiration – 'as he would have been desperate last night. You realize, of course, that had *I* been available *I* would have accompanied Rico.'

Clair murmured something, she did not know what.

'You are a young girl,' Rosita went on, 'and I would not like you to gather any extravagant ideas. Were I able to join in the ship's activities you must know that Enrico Montales would not spare you a second glance.'

'At no time did I say he would, *signora*. All this is quite ridiculous. I am simply in the employ of Senhor Montales, nothing else.'

'In the employ of the *senhor* but in the service of my chil-

291

dren. Since children, as Rico repeatedly tells me, come first, that makes my word the final word. You understand?'

'Not fully.'

'Then, though Rico may appear to give orders, it is my orders that really matter.'

'The *senhor* said,' put in Clair, suddenly brave, 'that he was the one I had to answer to.'

Rosita laughed, a cool little tinkle of sound. 'These men, ah, these men! I will tell you something, *signorina*.' She leaned forward confidentially. 'Rico is so impatient for me to be out and around that he simply does not know what he says, poor dear. For a man like Enrico Montales it is quite unthinkable that he has not the most outstanding woman on the ship to accompany him.' She looked naively at Clair. 'I, indisputably, am that.'

'Yes, you are, *signora*.'

'But Rico, also, for all his brave new outlook, is still as steeped in formality as is any member of any old European house. That is the only reason' – she pouted – 'that he does not insist I join him at once in spite of my period of mourning. Meanwhile, Miss Wardle, like all men he amuses himself with a pretty face. You are quite pretty, did you know?'

'Pale ... washed-out ...' Clair murmured automatically.

'The British are,' said Rosita equably, 'and you are British, really.' She finished, 'So now you understand?'

'No, *signora*. You see, at no time did the Senhor Montales amuse himself with me.'

Now the black eyes flashed. 'You do not mean to imply that he was serious?'

'Certainly not. He was simply a considerate employer, and that is all.'

Rosita thought this over. 'Well, we will see. My period of withdrawal is concluded this week. I shall have paid my due respects to my dear Umberto. My husband was very kind, Miss Wardle, but oh, so old. It is hard for a young wife.' She gave a pathetic shrug.

'You will join in the ship's activities?' asked Clair a little awkwardly. 'That will be nice for you.'

'And for the *senhor*. Rico will be a different man. These weeks have been hard on him. I have no doubt that the circumstances in which he found himself prompted him to choose you in the first place, a young person instead of the type he would ordinarily have picked for my little ones. After all' – another tinkling laugh – 'men are men, and loneliness is a terrible thing.'

Clair could not imagine the *senhor* lonely, he was too self-sufficient, too strong for that.

'Is this a way of telling me you will not need my services any more?' she asked outright.

'By no means, Rico would not care to discharge you now, it would make it look like a misjudgment on his part in the first place. No, you carry on, Miss Wardle, but strictly in your category of employee. You accompany the children, but that is all. Is that clear?'

'Yes, *signora*.'

'To make it absolutely clear, my dear, I will tell you the terrible strain poor Rico has been under. Rico and I were betrothed before I married Umberto. I was a foolish girl of seventeen, and in a moment of pique I ran away with a man twice my age. It broke Rico's heart, but unlike many men he did not turn to another woman for solace, he remained unwed.' A pause. 'He waited for me.'

Clair was thinking of that day of the *senhor*'s offer to her. She was piecing together a credible story from what the *senhor* had disclosed and adding what Rosita was disclosing now.

They had been in love, Rosita and Rico, but like many young love affairs, for Enrico Montales would be quite youthful then, it had not run smoothly. 'Tit for tat,' she recalled Rico relating, though he had termed it 'tat for tit', which must mean that Rosita must have been piqued because Rico had paid attention to someone else, so promptly had found herself a new interest. Not just an interest, either, a marriage partner. And Rico? Rico, stricken, had waited all these years.

Only one thing did not seem to ring true: it was Enrico Montales paying attention to someone else while he was in love with Rosita. Not just because Rosita was so outstanding but because such a trait seemed foreign in the *senhor*. He was a very formal man, very proper. Clair could not see him in the philanderer's role, and yet – tit for tat.

She became conscious that Rosita was looking at her shrewdly, estimatingly, and to her distress she felt her cheeks begin to burn.

'So,' Rosita said musingly, 'it was not all business on your side, Miss Wardle.'

'I assure you it was.'

'Yet when I tell you that Rico and I were once in love, are still in love, you smoulder. Oh, yes, you do. You are quite pink.'

'I – you—' Clair could find no words.

'Do not give it another thought. All women are in love with Rico; it amuses him immensely. But also' – warningly – 'do not give it another thought as regards any progress you believe you have made or possibly will make. In brief, Miss Wardle, Rico is mine.

'Now, go.'

This dismissal, the curtain to the little scene, came so abruptly, so finally, that Clair was out in the passage before she could realize it.

Sobs were in her throat, disjointed words that could have made no sense had she uttered them on her tongue. Perhaps it was just as well that when she turned the corridor corner she ran right into Gordon Sindel.

He was more discerning than his boyish good looks had promised. In no time he had taken control of things. Quietly he led Clair off the ship and into a car that evidently he drove himself. Even after he had seated her beside him he had the tact only to make a banal remark.

'I hired this jalopy. I thought it would be more fun taking ourselves around, Clair.'

He let out the clutch and put distance between them and the ship.

Until they were out of the city he could not have spoken even if he had wanted to.

The racing taxis, the laden jeeps, the procession of rickshaws and the endless lines of bicycles, between them all the busy people, made driving without full attention an impossibility.

But eventually Gordon weaved through the snarl of traffic and took a coastal road to a pretty, sheltered bay ... one of the bays she had probably seen distantly yesterday when the *senhor* had taken her – because he could not take Rosita.

She had not dreamed that that could hurt so much. At no time had she dared think she could mean anything to him, but the fact that he only had used her for a stand-in until Rosita was available now cut her like a knife. You are a fool, she kept repeating in her heart; Senhor Montales has never given you the slightest indication that he was even remotely interested, and yet you feel desolate, deserted and deflated like this. For it was that upsetting her, and she secretly admitted it. Although Rosita's highhandedness had been hard to take, it was not Rosita, it was Rico. Enrico. Even his name gave her a stab. I have let something happen that I never should have let happen, she thought, appalled. I have let him matter – matter terribly – to me.

Gordon had not gone right to the beach edge, he had taken a side track that climbed a little to afford a better view. When he stopped the car he lit two cigarettes and handed Clair one.

'Nothing's as bad as that,' he said.

'As what?'

'As that face you had when you bumped into me on the *Firenzo*. Boss been bawling you out?'

'In a way,' she admitted.

'It's not worth a tear, Clair. If you must cry, cry over your own sort, not a Portuguese.' He put a friendly hand on her shoulder. 'I'm here.'

With an effort Clair stirred herself.

'Why are you here, Gordon? Why are you in Durban?'

'Business, as I pass through on my way home. Actually I wasn't expecting much, but I've done fairly well, Clair. I can go back with a high head.'

'When do you go?'

He did not answer that at once. He flicked a bush insect that was crawling over his suit out of the window again.

'Oh – soon,' he said. 'Now you, Clair, what are your plans?'

'I told you, I'm companion to the nieces of Senhor Montales.'

'But presumably they're bound for Portugal.'

'Or Italy.' She told him briefly the story of the children's mixed nationality.

'What I meant,' he interrupted, 'was that they would have a one-way ticket, in other words they would not be returning to Australia. But how about you?'

'I shall go back, of course.'

'When?'

'I—'

'When?'

'Well—' she hesitated.

'Admit it, Clair, you've nothing definite.'

'Well – no.'

'Good,' he grinned.

He did not pursue the subject. After they had finished their cigarettes he suggested that instead of touring around they spend the day at a swimming club he had joined.

'I know you can swim on the *Firenzo,* but it can't be fun having to watch two brats. This is a fine pool, and you can enjoy it in an adult way.'

'I didn't bring my suit.'

'Don't worry, I didn't, either. This swimming club will look after that.'

Sitting, an hour later, on a cool chaise-longue by the pool edge, a drink at her elbow, the fluffiest of towels round the shoulders of the becoming suit that the club had been able to provide, Clair began to relax. Gordon was a charming companion, he had a fund of good stories, and he laughed often. Clair found herself laughing frequently back.

Lunch was wheeled out ... pineapple and chicken, then another of the fascinating desserts she had enjoyed last night, something with guava. Afterwards coffee and a drifting off to sleep, then waking up to afternoon tea and little almond cakes, and Clair, seeing the clock on the club tower, saying, alarmed, 'Gordon, the ship sails at five!'

'Of that, my child, I am very much aware.' Had she not become anxious, Clair might have questioned the note in his voice. As it was she hurried over the tea, and went in and dressed.

When she came out Gordon was waiting to drive her to the wharf.

'I don't know what the hurry's about,' he complained good-humouredly as they approached the dock. 'We've an hour yet.'

Clair did not notice that 'we'. She said, glad to see the *Firenzo* still there, 'I can't help it, I'm frightened it will go off and leave me stranded.'

'You wouldn't be stranded long.' His eyes approved her flushed prettiness.

'All the same it's better to be on the safe side. I've had a wonderful day, Gordon, and I can't thank you enough.' As she said it, Clair glanced up and saw that Senhor Montales was standing at the *Firenzo* rail, watching the return of the tourists. She hoped desperately that Gordon would not do anything that would draw attention, like kissing her farewell.

To her gratification he simply got out and formally shook her hand.

'There'll be a surprise for you, Clair.' There was a smile in his voice.

'You shouldn't have,' she protested, thinking in the terms of flowers, or perhaps a souvenir.

He laughed, saluted her, and got back in the car.

Senhor Montales, thought Clair, could not possibly find anything to complain of in that.

When she reached the top of the gangway, he was there to help her over the last steep step. She saw that he was pleased about the young Englishman's leavetaking, though she knew that that approval indicated nothing except a Portuguese gentleman's idea of what was right and what should be done.

'Ah, Clair. You had a pleasant day?'

'Most pleasant, Rico.'

'Your escort treated you well?'

'Very well.'

'And now you have said good-bye?'

'I have.'

Expressionless as he always was, still a satisfaction was there in the bland mask, and Clair could not help recognize it.

'That is very good, *senhorita*. But not so good, I fear, the promise of our forthcoming weather.'

'Is it unfavourable?'

'We will run into Cape winds. A good gale at this time of year is to be expected, but the seas on this occasion are reported to be quite high. Are you a good sailor, Clair?'

'I enjoyed the Bight.'

'According to the glass this will make the Bight a storm in a coffee cup. Right?' He smiled inquiringly.

'We say tea-cup.'

'But then you are British.' A little frown creased his smooth olive brow. 'And so is your young friend.' He was silent a moment. 'However, we will meet that trouble when it comes.'

'The weather, *senhor*?'

He looked quickly, shrewdly back at her. 'What else, *senhorita*? What other trouble?'

'Why – nothing, of course.' She pretended to take deep interest in some agile small boys turning handsprings on the wharf for sweets and applause.

But when she went to her room it was to a trouble of her own. Actually, she thought, she should not call it a trouble, no one should make a trouble of a charming companion for the rest of the trip. But, she added indignantly, Gordon might have told her.

'I did,' he grinned, sitting back in her easy chair, obviously delighted at her widened eyes when she had found him there. 'I told you there would be a surprise.'

'I thought of flowers, or – or a statuette.'

'Admit I last longer than flowers, and that a statuette can't dance at nights with you, Clair.'

'Oh, I know you're entitled to sail in the *Firenzo*, too, and I know I can't object, but—'

'It's not His Excellency worrying you, is it?'

'No, of course not, though I did tell him I had bidden you good-bye.'

'Well, you hadn't, had you? Clair, you might show some spontaneity. This late berth cost me a packet. I also had to forfeit a seat in the plane.'

'I'm sorry, Gordon.' She was contrite at once.

It would be fun to have someone your own age, she tried, though a little weakly, to enthuse, someone you could talk freely to, not choose the right words, someone you could be irreverent with, for certainly you could not be irreverent with the *senhor*, but all the same – all the same—

'Smile, honey, you and I are going to make this ship sit up.'

Alas for fine words! Within an hour of the *Firenzo*'s sailing, they had run into that bad weather, and Gordon was not sitting, he was prone, as were four-fifths of the entire complement of the great Italian liner. The passage round the Cape was to be a nightmare to these sufferers, but to the sea-lovers it was to be sheer delight.

And among those few were Enrico Montales – and Clair.

Suddenly the huge ship seemed as flimsy as a child's toy. It lifted as steeply, when the great waves began their ominous rushes, as if in the claws of a gigantic bird, then it dropped immediately into foaming troughs, great fathomless troughs with dark-green walls like the impenetrable walls of a prison cell. Sometimes the bow thrust so deep down that it seemed it would never return. The decks were awash with angry swirling waters that never entirely cleared away, but licked greedily with every throb of the engines and thrust, shudder and dip of the ship. The rain when it fell between the storms was lashed by the wind until every drop came javelin-sharp.

All social activities stopped on the *Firenzo*. There were no concerts, no dances, no sports, the library and the ship shop were closed. Meals were informal. The hardy ones staggered to the servery between the *ristorante* and the kitchen and staggered back with a plate of whatever the cooks could manage to produce. There was no choice of viands, just sustenance. The windows of the dining-room, through which it had been pleasant to look at sea and sky, had had their curtains drawn. The *terrazza* buffet, of course, was closed.

Gordon had gone down under the weather immediately. So had Rosita, with the consequence that her withdrawal from society that was to have come to a triumphant end after Singapore was extended to another week, perhaps more. 'For,' reported Sophia, 'she is very *malata,* very ill.' The next day Sophia was *malata,* so that Clair had to look after the little girls. She had been told that the young tolerated the sea very well, and looked forward to getting to know Juanita and Amalia much better, but the day after the children were ill, too.

'Just as well,' Senhor Montales remarked on one of their encounters in the corridor or over a meal, 'that Mrs. Henry departed at Durban. At least she is one less for the Medical Officer to worry about.'

'Did she go?' In the excitement of everything that had happened, Clair had completely forgotten about Mrs. Henry.

'I told you, *senhorita,* that I had arranged for her to fly.'

'Yes, but I found it hard to believe.'

'You disbelieve me?' The brows soared on Clair.

'No, but I had got to know Mrs. Henry, and she wasn't the type to be arranged; she arranged others.'

He took out one of his cheroots and proceeded to light it. 'We all of us at some time meet our – our—' He furrowed his olive blow. 'You must help me here, Clair.'

'Fate?'

'No, no, an English battle.'

'Waterloo,' said Clair in triumph. She looked contemplatively at Enrico Montales. That Portuguese *senhor,* she felt sure, had never met his Waterloo.

'Ah, but I have.' Once again he read Clair. 'Yet it did not bring defeat, as did Mrs. Henry's battle to Mrs. Henry, it opened a door. At least, I am hoping it has opened it.' As he spoke his eyes never left Clair's.

A little disconcerted, she said, 'You are enjoying this crossing, *senhor*?'

'As I told you, *senhorita,* the Portuguese are lovers of the

300

sea. Though, strangely, it is for a different reason that I love this sea. At her questioning look he said, 'Come, Clair, I shall show you.'

As she followed him down to the lower deck where the promenade was now strictly forbidden, Clair, in reply to his question as to how she was faring, reminded him in her turn that she, too, was a lover of the sea. 'Often the crossing between Daybell Island and Queensland would whip up almost as fierce as this.'

'But surely, *senhorita,* you would have been in the protected waters of the Barrier Reef?'

'Yes, but the unexpected happens, *senhor,*' she reminded him, and he nodded gravely.

'Yes, the unexpected,' he concurred, 'yet not always the – unwelcome?'

'Most of the crossers did not welcome Harriet.'

'Harriet?'

'The cyclone that hits the Queensland coast upon occasion.'

He nodded again. 'Just as most of the *Firenzo* has an unwelcoming word for our present weather. And yet, Clair—' He gave a rather disarming gesture.

They had reached the Milano Lounge, a favourite hideaway for the more discerning passengers, quiet as it was and rather remotely situated.

A deck beneath the other public amenities, the Milano Lounge was now well below water, and undoubtedly because of this its dark velvet drapes had been drawn over its entirety, since the sight of so much sea, deep down sea, would have depressed anyone resting in the lounge. Not that there was anyone, or likely to be, with only a fifth of the entire ship's complement still on their feet.

Rico crossed to one of the portholes and drew back the drape. A green of such intensity that it caught the breath met Clair's gaze. Down here, seen through the porthole, the sea seemed not fierce any more, it just seemed part of a green, green world.

'I said to you just now, Clair, that for a different reason from the Portuguese reason in me I love this sea, and this is it:

301

I love this aspect of the sea' – he waved his hand to the green – 'because to me it is dry land. That is odd?'

'Very odd, Rico.'

'Then I explain. This is the only green, apart perhaps from the avenue to my *pal*—apart from a drive in my town, that I can liken to September Street.'

'September Street?'

'It is in Rome, Clair, and some of it is so lovely I always want to go back.'

'It has trees?'

'So many that it is like the view through that porthole, a world of green. You can turn from it, as many do, and go down a narrow alley to the Trevi Fountain, and there, of course, if you throw in a coin, it is said you will come back.'

'Have you thrown one, Rico?' she asked.

'Oh, yes, one does the accepted things, but to me the going back would not be to Trevi, it would be to September Street.'

'You love it,' she acclaimed.

'Yes, I love it. It is not part of my own country, but it makes no difference.' He began drawing back the drape again.

'September Street,' mused Clair. 'September in our land means spring.'

'And spring is the beginning, the new hope, the first dew,' he concurred. For a moment, a sensitive moment, he paused. 'The initial time that I saw September Street I felt strangely that this was so, that it held spring, even though September means fall in Rome, and even though the season at the time was winter, the trees bare, their green leaves a memory, I still felt one day that there in September Street I would find spring.' He paused sensitively again. 'My spring.'

'You were walking along September Street, Rico?' she asked gently.

'Yes.' His expression firmed a little. 'With Rosita.'

Clair did not see the firming of his lips, she only heard 'With Rosita.' That was why September Street had been the beginning, the hope, the dew, she thought bitterly. She had no reason to be bitter, she had no reason to expect anything from this man except the usual employer-employee courtesy, but still bitterness encompassed her until it hurt, a bitterness that in its unreasonable immensity blotted out what Enrico Montales actually had said, he had said 'I felt *one day* there I would find spring.' But Clair missed that.

'It is depressing down here.' She spoke almost abruptly. 'I'll go up, if you don't mind.'

'By all means.' He bowed formally. But his eyes, as he leaned forward, leaned in formal salute, were deeply hurt.

The next day they lost the bad weather.

The ship that had seemed a child's flimsy toy grew up to the large efficient liner it really was. It no longer lifted steeply and fell back into deep troughs, it rolled pleasantly for several hours of the morning but by the afternoon was sailing through seas of glass.

From behind closed doors the passengers emerged. The *Firenzo* came alive again.

Sophia, wan but now recovered, reported that the *signora* was still *malata* and would keep to her room for a few more days. Clair was aware of a lifting of spirits, and told herself it was because she would have the children to herself for a little time at least, but secretly knew it was not this at all, it was the fact that her next encounter with Rosita had been delayed. She knew she was no match for the sharp young mother of Juanita and Amalia. She dreaded a repeat performance of their last painful encounter, painful – to Clair – whenever Rosita had spoken proprietorially of Rico, which had been nearly all the time. She had no right to react like this, and she tried to shake off the illicit resentment, but it was no use, the hurt, and the dread of further hurt, remained.

She had fun with the children on deck, played quoits with them, supervised a short, not-too-energetic swim, for they were still a little groggy after their sickness, then, as the *terrazza* buffet was still closed and having never yet been to the *ristorante* and feeling shy at beginning yet not fancying a meal in her room on such a sparkling day, she went with Juanita, and Amalia to the children's *sala*. There were several supervising parents present and they smiled pleasantly at

303

Clair. This was better, she thought, than standing uncertainly at the door of the dining room while the head steward found her a position, for she supposed, now that Mrs. Henry was gone, that there was no excuse for her not to dine as presumably a Classe Prima passenger should dine, and that was formally, and at a table, not from a tray. Though, she reminded herself with a quickening of her heart, the meals in the suite of Senhor Montales had been even more lavishly presented than the *ristorante* would have presented them. Would she dine like that with him again? Would she dine with him at all?

That question was answered as she came out of the *sala da pranzo* with a little girl hanging on each arm. Not only Juanita clung lovingly, but Amalia, who had suffered a worse bout than her sister and was much quieter than usual, clung, too.

'So.' The *senhor* encountered them as they climbed the stairs. 'Three children together,' he smiled.

'Indeed, yes,' Juanita babbled eagerly. 'Clair even ate with us at the children's *sala*.'

Now the lightness left the *senhor*. His mouth pulled down in the old familiar disapproval.

'This is true, *senhorita*?'

'Yes, *senhor*. Why – have I done anything wrong?'

'If you do not think so, no, but to my mind it is not a dignified thing to dine in a room reserved for young children.'

'There were other adults there.'

'That is no excuse. In Portugal, it could not happen. Not at the—' He did not get as far as he usually did before he broke off, he did not say 'at the *pal*—'

'Presumably not in your walk of life, *senhor*,' Clair said quietly but stubbornly, 'but in other Portuguese walks of life perhaps, and undoubtedly in every Australian walk of life.'

'You reprove me.' For a moment the frown went and his teeth flashed against the olive skin in a quick smile.

'I didn't mean to,' she said back, mollified by his surrender.

'And I did not mean to censure you. I was angry, you see, when I could not find you; I was waiting to take you in to the table you will now occupy in the *ristorante*. My table.'

'Your table?' The dismay in Clair's voice was because of

304

Rosita – how would Rosita react to having the companion of her small daughters, a *domestica* you could almost say, sitting at the same dining board?

Rico had caught the dismayed note, seen the unease in her face.

'Clair, you are not happy over the arrangement! But come, child, you could not remain indefinitely in your room, and you had no one else to sit with, had you?'

Scarcely had the question left his lips than those lips tightened to a degree that Clair had never seen before in this Portuguese *senhor*, and certainly this man was in the habit of lip-tightening.

'So.' As before he said it, but this time it came almost in a hiss.

Puzzled, Clair looked up at him, only to find that his eyes were no longer on her. They were following the deliberate progress of a passenger coming slowly along the deck, the slow deliberation of someone looking for someone.

Gordon Sindel looking for Clair.

'So.' Once more the sibilance. 'You did have someone in mind, *senhorita*, you were only filling in time with the children until he could accompany you.'

'No, *senhor*, that's not true.'

'You mean you did not know the English gentleman was aboard the *Firenzo*?'

'I – you see—'

'The truth, *senhorita*.'

'Yes, I knew,' she admitted.

'Yet you deceived me?'

'I did not!'

'You did.' The black eyes were slits now, fierce, gleaming slits. 'After the Englishman brought you back to the ship following your excursion in Durban, I remarked to you: "And now you have said good-bye!"'

'I had.'

'You expect me to believe that when all the time he was a bona fide passenger on this vessel?'

'I didn't know he was a passenger, *senhor*.'

305

'Can I really believe that, Clair? At no time were you aware that Mr. Sindel was aboard the *Firenzo*? It is a big surprise to you now as it is to me?'

She would have liked to have answered 'Yes' if only to escape the angry gleam that she knew once more would leap to his dark eyes.

But besides gleaming angrily, the eyes of Enrico Montales could probe, demand, extract, and they did that now.

'You knew.' His voice was low and accusing.

'When I went to my room,' she admitted.

But rather than help things, the admission worsened them.

'This person was in your room?' The white-hot anger seared Clair.

'He – he had decided not to return by air. He was fortunate enough to obtain a passage.' With desperate lightness she suggested, 'Perhaps even Mrs. Henry's passage?' She forced a smile.

The *senhor* did not smile back.

'And then?' he asked.

'You know what happened then. Mr. Sindel was ill, nearly all the ship was ill.'

'You went and attended him, *senhorita,* smoothed his brow, held his hand?'

'Of course not! I didn't go near him. I – I forgot all about him.'

The *senhor* was snapping open his embossed cigarette case, still with the thumb over the emblem, not offering a cigarette to Clair. 'You certainly had that forgetfulness well in mind as regards informing me of his presence.'

A flash of temper consumed Clair. Really, this man had gone too far!

'Why should I inform you? What business is it of yours?'

'I am your employer.'

'But not my keeper.'

Gordon was coming nearer. His roving eye had caught the corn silk of Clair's hair. He was hurrying now, his face lit up, his eyes smiling, his arm raised.

'No, *senhorita,* I am not your keeper.' On the contrary the

306

senhor's face was bleak, the eyes hooded, the arms stiff by his side. 'Kindly give my excuses to the Englishman, but I have not yet dined.'

Enrico Montales bowed formally, inclined his head the slightest degree to the approaching Gordon, then turned and went.

Gordon's 'What's wrong with His Highness?' came at the same time as Clair's excuses for Enrico Montales.

'Why do you call him that?' asked Clair irritably.

'Then His Excellency, or His Serenity, whatever it is.'

'What do you mean "whatever it is"? You are absurd, Gordon. Rico has gone to dinner; you weren't listening before; he hasn't eaten yet.'

'Neither have I, and I'm starved. I've heard of the ravenous appetites of those recently recovered from mal-de-mer, and now I believe the tales. I could eat you, and' – speculatively – 'a tender dish you would make.'

'Don't look at me with greedy eyes, then. People are staring.'

'Probably could eat you, too. We're all hungry. Come on, before we all tuck in, darling, and you're reduced to bones.' Gordon added, 'Lovely bones.'

'I've already dined,' Clair said reprovingly.

'This early?'

'The children's meals are earlier than the grown-ups.'

'Oh, for goodness' sake, Clair, don't tell me you chose to have soup with animal crackers followed by hundreds and thousands on bread.'

'Quite a few adults ate in the children's *sala,* and the menu the same as for the grown-ups.'

'Oysters? Lobster? Something very bouquet garni as well s ferociously devilled? A *vino* as red as your red lips? I doubt t. Come, my sweet.'

'I've eaten.'

'Then at least drink coffee with me.' Gordon propelled her towards the dining room.

The children had left her when Zio Rico had come along. She had not excuses now not to go. Besides, in spite of his good humour there was a look in Gordon's blue eyes that suggested strongly he would not give in without a struggle, a public struggle, if she did not comply, and Clair, wise now in the curiosity of those who travel by ship, did not want a scene.

Unhappily, she obeyed.

But if she went unhappily towards the *ristorante,* she was unhappier still when the Chief Steward came forward with the smiling information that a corner table for two had been reserved as theirs. 'The Senhor Montales told me to do this thing, *signore* and *signorina.*'

'Jolly nice of him,' approved Gordon.

Clair murmured low thanks.

She wished Gordon could have left it at that, but he repeated how thoughtful it had been of Montales, and swung round in his chair to locate the *senhor's* table and nod his gratefulness. The table was not hard to find, it occupied the best position in the room. The *senhor* was not difficult to pinpoint, as he sat at it alone. He also did not see, or chose not to see, the man he had helped.

'I say, he's by himself,' said Gordon. 'We should have had him with us.'

'If he had wanted us, he would have said so, not reserved us a table as he did.'

'I suppose you're right, but by himself—'

With difficulty Clair said, 'He won't be alone long. There's a lady on board—'

Gordon grinned, 'I see!'

A little defensively Clair said, 'She's his cousin.'

'All the better, Clair, these old European families always intermarry. Must keep to the family name.' Gordon was consulting the menu. 'Sure I can't tempt you, sweet? I'd warrant that oysters kilpatrick sound more interesting than alphabetical soup.'

'It wasn't, it was a very adult consommé, and I couldn't eat a thing.' She couldn't. When her coffee came she could hardly swallow it.

Gordon, however, was in excellent spirits. He began making a timetable of their daily activities, and when Clair questioned this, retaliated, 'But, my sweet, not to participate is simpl. not to be on a ship. That's why you put up with the sea.'

'I don't put up with the sea, I love it.' Someone else had loved it, too, she thought, especially the dark deep waters through the porthole of the deck below, through the Milano Lounge. What had he said? That to him it was the green of September Street.

'Gordon,' she asked abruptly, 'do you know Rome?'

'Rome? Let me think. Yes, I sold fairly well there, old Beresford was particularly pleased, but I did even better in Florence.'

'Do you know – September Street?'

'Via, darling. And September is Settembre.'

'Do you?'

'No.' Gordon finished studying the menu. 'Clair, I think you and I should make a good double for the table tennis.'

'I have the children to watch.'

'Not all the time, even the nannies aren't on duty every hour of the day, and you are much more elevated than a nanny, Clair. Look, my dear, presumably you will only be coming this way once – after all, from Australia to Europe is a long, long hop, so why not enjoy yourself?' His smiling blue eyes held Clair's, and in them she saw her own youth mirrored. Why not, she thought, still feeling reduced in size after the *senhor's* cold words, why not laughter instead of proud aloofness, why not youth instead of maturity? Why not?

Quick to notice the waver in the similar blue eyes, Gordon grinned, 'We'll slay them, Clair!'

As they were leaving the dining room, Senhor Montales came out. Immediately Gordon burst forth his thanks. The *senhor* cut them short by flashing round his cigarette case. He and Gordon spoke for a while about the business potentialities of the different Italian cities, Gordon ending the discussion by comparing Rome to Genoa, to Genoa's advantage.

'And it's there we shall head, Clair,' he pronounced. 'This *Firenzo* goes on to Genoa from Naples, it's only another night.'

Clair became acutely conscious of the stiffening of the

309

senhor's already stiff back.

'Rome, to me,' said Gordon, 'is fusty. I mean, you can take statues or leave them, and I can leave them. From Genoa we could go straight round to Nice, the Riviera. That's the life, Clair.'

The *senhor* had thrown away his cigarette. He could barely have started it, thought Clair, as she heard the little hiss as it reached the water.

'Perhaps, *senhorita*, between your activities this afternoon we could have a few words?' he said coolly.

'I can come now, *senhor*.'

'Yes, you do that, darling,' said Gordon, 'while I go and enter us in the sports.'

Not until they had reached the *senhor*'s suite did Rico speak. Then he said in a curious but quite unemotional voice, 'This "darling" that the English use so carelessly, tell me, *senhorita*, is it an endearment or just a glib address?'

'Just an address.' Clair's own voice was flat.

'It is a peculiarity not used by the Portuguese. Portuguese would not say "darling" unless it came from the heart.'

'An Englishman would often only use it, also, from the heart,' Clair defended.

'You mean you would not know in which way it was said?'

'Well, naturally you would have a fair idea.' She felt very uncomfortable standing like this being put through a third degree, as it were.

'In this instance you knew?'

'Certainly. It was a glib address.' Clair's answer was crisp.

'Thank you, *senhorita*, for enlightening me. I find it hard at times to follow the English mind.'

'Is that what you wanted to discuss with me, *senhor*?'

'It was not. I wished to tell you that you must feel free to join in with whatever shipboard amusement your young friend suggests. I have a suspicion that you have hesitated to do so believing that you have a debt first to pay to me. You have not, Clair, apart from several hours a day with the girls, you are entirely free to do just as you please.'

'Thank you, Rico.'

'Also Clair, now that my cousin is up and about and ready to join in shipboard life – oh, yes, Sophia, the *domestica*, has reported to me that her mistress is no longer *malata* – I am ready to retire from my role of guardian to two motherless girls and allow the mother to step back into her true position again. In which case, of course, you will report to me no longer but to Rosita.' Evidently the deflation in Clair must have been too evident not to arouse a comment.

'You look unhappy, child. My cousin is a charming person, you will see that when you meet her.'

Mechanically Clair said, 'I have met her.'

'You have seen her leaning over the rail,' he said impatiently. 'That is not meeting her. But perhaps' – before Clair could interrupt that she had met Rosita, talked with her, been dismissed by her, 'you are disappointed since you no longer take the orders from a man? Are you one of those women who prefer the company of a man?'

'I have always got on well with my own sex, *senhor*.'

'But preferred the companionship of the other sex, perhaps?' He was blandly insistent.

'If you are making personal comparisons, *senhor*, you should remember that you were not a companion, but a boss.'

'A boss? Boss? Oh, an employer.' His black brows were in the straight line again. 'Yes, I was not a companion but an employer. I am corrected. Thank you, Clair.'

'Thank you, Rico.' She did not know what she was thanking him for, she just said it mechanically.

'There is an exception,' he intoned rather disinterestedly. 'At Cape Town I must attend another dinner – the Mount Nelson Hotel. I would be obliged, and you would be paid, if you would accompany me, Clair.'

'Your cousin—' she began.

'She'll not need you at night, you are not required to put the small girls to bed, that is the *domestica*'s task.'

'It wasn't that—' Clair began

'What, then?'

'Would – would she like it?'

311

'A name, please?'

'Rosita.'

His brows soared. He was deeply displeased. 'That is a very strange question for you to ask. Who suggested such a thing?'

Clair wondered what he would say if she answered, 'She did. Rosita did. She told me everything. She told me how you had waited all these years for her. "In brief", she said, "Rico is mine".' Clair wondered how this proud man, to whom emotion was not a thing to be worn for others to see, would react. But she was not brave enough to discover.

'No one,' she mumbled. 'I just thought—'

'Then pray keep such thoughts to yourself, *senhorita*. I find your words distasteful, indeed. You may go now, but please to keep Cape Town in your mind, in spite of what the Englishman will presumably comment.'

'Not the Englishman, *senhor*, but—' At the dismissive look in the *senhor*'s face, Clair stopped herself. 'I will go, *senhor*.'

'Yes. You might call in and ask my cousin what she has in mind for you for the girls. She will not keep you long, and she will not require from you any more service than you have given me to this date. I have instructed her implicitly about that.'

'Thank you, *senhor*.'

'Thank you, *senhorita*.'

Clair went out quietly. Her feet was leaden as she went down the passage to Rosita's suite. What acid words would come this time from those lovely scarlet lips?

But the scarlet lips smiled sweetly at Clair, she was invited to sit down, have some candy.

'It is wicked of me, I should not eat it, I am not like you, Miss Wardle, a slender reed, I am more the – the fat pouffe, or soon I will be,' Rosita giggled, and selected a Turkish delight.

She seemed very happy with life, pointing out to Clair the beautiful claret satin she intended to wear tonight. 'It has been very dreary, this sea trip, but now the dreariness is over. I do not know whether to have my hair upswept or allow it to flow down. What do you think?'

'It is very beautiful hair.'

'Of course. But whether to upsweep it or loosen it – oh, life is a problem. Tell me, do you find it so?' The eyes still smiled, smiled entirely without malice, and Clair, after her last experience, wondered why, until Rosita, quite delightedly, let her know.

'You are having fun with the young Englishman, you dine at a table for two? Ah, but that is good, I like it very much.' She pressed another candy on Clair.

Clair, a little choked up, asked if she had any directions for her daughters.

'None at all. Do as you wish with them, I'm sure you are most efficient, only, dear Miss Wardle, do not let them interfere with your time with your young man.'

'He is not my young man.'

'No?' A soft laugh. 'But my *domestica* reports otherwise. Such looks as he gives her, she says, and they dine together at a table for two.'

'Your cousin arranged that,' Clair said stolidly.

Rosita was even more delighted. 'He does not want you at our table, then. He did, and I said it was not right, that although you were not like Sophia, it was still not a good thing.' She looked with rather comic dismay at Clair. 'I did not mean that unkindly, Miss Wardle, you must understand that.'

'I understand. You wanted the Senhor Montales to be the only other occupant of your table when at last you dined in public.' It was a daring thing to say, and perhaps a little rude, and Clair drew her breath in apprehension. The words had sprung out. She must remember next time to examine them first.

But Rosita was in an amiable mood. She laughed her applause. 'Yes, you are right, I wanted Rico alone – just as you wanted the young Englishman.'

Clair was about to repeat that she hadn't particularly wanted a table like the one she had been given, but Rosita stemmed the words with another satisfied conclusion.

'Rico, too, wanted you with the Englishman.'

'I'm sure he didn't.'

'Then certainly he didn't want you with us, for heigh-ho, you are at one table and we are at the other. Tell me, Miss Wardle, in what position is this table of ours?'

Mechanically, still hearing Rosita's 'Then certainly he didn't want you', Clair said, 'A centre position, really the pivot of the room.'

'The best table,' beamed Rosita. 'I shall have my hair up-swept. I shall ring for the hairdresser now.' She smiled again at Clair. 'You may go now, dear. What was it you came for again? I quite forget.'

'Your girls.'

'Of course. Do as you wish with them, only don't let them keep you from your young man. You say he is not that – yet. But with African nights with big gold moons—' Rosita rolled her black, black eyes.

'The moon will shine down on you, too, Signora Dal Rosa.'

Rosita now fastened down her scarlet lower lip with even white teeth; it was a moue of triumph. Her eyes sparkled. Unbuttoning the pretty mouth again, she intoned patronizingly, 'But of course, foolish child,' making, thought Clair, the moon sound *her* prerogative, making anything left over after she was done welcome to Clair. For instance, the Englishman for Clair. Clair knew in all fairness to Gordon she should not think of him like that, as a kind of consolation prize, but Rosita had implied it, and the thought brought a deflation.

She was not finished with deflation that day.

When, between rounds of table tennis in the late afternoon, she told Gordon that Señor Montales expected her to accompany him to a business dinner in Cape Town, adding formally that she would be paid for the duty, instead of the pique that she did not want but, being feminine, certainly expected, the pique was Clair's own at Gordon's instant care-free agreement.

'That's all right, old girl, anything for extra cash. These sea trips certainly run away with money. Do you find that?'

This sea trip hadn't run away with Clair's money, she hadn't had any to let run, but the knowledge that Gordon was happy to preserve his, even in a way augment it by having Clair in

314

the position to share the costs by her extra earnings, did not make the moon, that Rosita had anticipated, and which even now was climbing up into a blue plush sky, as romantic as the *signora*, through her pretty unbuttoned mouth, had dreamily promised.

Aloud, Clair agreed with Gordon: 'Yes, the money runs away.'

CHAPTER SIX

CLAIR forgot her pique in the rest of the run to Cape Town. Instead of the Cape rollers she had been warned about the sea became a looking glass, its only ripples those of trade boats dipping by, its changing hues from milky jade to brilliant, almost cornflower, blue holding her in never-waning fascination.

She had succeeded in getting the children interested as well, Juanita in the navigation map that recorded their route and in the thrill of knowing that beneath them lay the wide frozen tracts of the Antarctic; Amalia ... characteristically ... in the clothes of the passengers who had embarked at Durban. She was an extremely clothes-conscious young madam.

To Clair's gratification the children got on well with Gordon. With Junita she had anticipated no trouble, the little girl liked everybody, and even if she didn't they would never know it. Amalia, however, was unpredictable; also she had inherited her mother's acid tongue. But Gordon, gay, carefree, absurdly flattering, had won her at once.

'I am *not* the most beautiful *signorina* in the world,' Amalia trilled. 'I am very pretty, *si*, but the most beautiful?' She considered that, rolling her eyes meanwhile on Gordon, who pretended to swoon.

Juanita did not take to such lavish praise, she withdrew a little, but only a very unobtrusive withdrawal, for Juanita had a soft heart, and Clair's Englishman might be offended.

The weather remained flawless, the children were good, Rosita smiled amiably at Clair, the sheer fun of Gordon and the pleasure of his young companionship made Clair almost as happy as she could have asked. But only almost. Always there was the consciousness of the *senhor* in Clair's mind, and even though she did not see him she was still vividly aware of his appraisal even in his absence, she was conscious of raised brows even when he was not there.

Rosita had made her first appearance at dinner as she had told Clair. Deliberately ... so Clair supposed ... she had arrived late, and on the arm of Rico. She looked wonderful, and Clair could not blame Gordon for putting his knife and fork down with a clatter and saying: 'No! Is she real?'

'She's the children's mother'

'She's the most beautiful thing I've ever seen.'

It was scarcely flattering to sit beside a man whose mouth remained open in sheer admiration, but Clair did not mind. What she did mind was the bland nod that Senhor Montales gave the pair in the corner table, a nod that he would have given to any pair, indifferent, uncaring, just a formal salute.

But if the *senhor* ignored them, apart from that cursory nod, Rosita, in the flush of her successful début, was graciousness itself. The meal over, she glided across to the corner table trilling, 'Miss Wardle, dear!' but her eyes not on Clair but on Gordon.

Gordon had leapt to his feet the moment it had become apparent that the *signora* was coming across to speak to them, and tall, erect, fair-skinned and gay, he certainly seemed a good-looking young man to Signora Dal Rosa.

She looked him up and down, smiling back at his smile, and Clair could imagine what she was thinking. So nice, such fun, she was hearing from Rosita, but young, too young, and probably tiresomely poor. Besides, Rico would be annoyed.

Undoubtedly, Clair mentally agreed, Rico would be very annoyed. He was not smiling now, he was waiting, and waiting impatiently, for his companion to follow him out to the deck.

'This must be Gordon,' acclaimed Rosita before Clair could make the presentations. 'The girls tell me a lot about Gordon.'

Her lashes fanned upward at the tall, fair young man.

'The girls did not tell me near enough about their mama,' Gordon bowed.

'But that bow is very gallant. You have only to learn to kiss the hand and you will be as good as a European.'

'You give lessons, *senhora*?'

'It is *signora*,' interrupted the *senhor* stiffly. 'You must excuse us. Come, Rosita.' He did not even glance at Clair.

Gordon's admiration for Rosita was tempered somewhat with resentment against Rico for the distinctly abrupt treatment that he had handed out.

'That's a brush-off if you like!'

'Oh, I wouldn't say, that, Gordon, you have to keep in mind that he's a Portuguese gentleman, and not accustomed to repartee like that.'

'More like he resented the cat looking at the queen, for she is that, isn't she, though I don't think' – and Gordon grinned – 'Rosita resented this feline.' He indicated himself, not without satisfaction. 'She would be one for fun, that girl, though not with him about. What a beauty, Clair! She's a red, red rose.'

'That's English.'

'Then whatever Portuguese ladies pin in their jet black hair.'

'She's Italian now.'

Gordon looked at Clair with interest. 'Could it be, darling, you're jealous? You're being very perverse.'

'Perhaps.' Clair forced a smile. I am jealous, she knew, but not for you, Gordon, not for you. Oh, how stupid I am, how can I let myself be hurt like this?

Typical of Gordon, he did not sigh over the unattainable but began talking of tomorrow's Fancy Dress Ball.

Clair had not intended to participate, and Gordon was astounded. 'Where's your spirit of co-operation, Clair? Of course we both must join in.'

He had dozens of ideas for partners . . . Daphnis and Chloe, Twin Souls, he even did not reject the idea of nursery Jack and Jill.

Clair acquiesced without enthusiasm, a lukewarmness she had no idea showed so much until Gordon burst out, 'You're as keen as cold porridge, Clair. All right, don't participate, I'll go solo, but don't hang around me when I snare that prize.'

'What is the prize?'

'Cash, I hope. I could do with it with Las Palmas beginning to loom up.'

Sorry she had damned him with her pale interest, Clair said,

'I'll help you out with my Cape Town earnings, Gordon.'

He was repentant at once. 'Sorry, darling, you're a good generous girl. If you don't want to dress up, that's for you to say. As a matter of fact I've been asked by some of the boys to join their group. I won't tell you the masquerade, it would spoil the surprise, but it'll bring the house down.' He grinned at Clair, and she smiled back. He was infectious, this tall, laughing boy, and she liked him very much.

Even though Gordon had upbraided her for not intending to join in the frolic, Clair had still had no thought of changing her mind after all and dressing up – until Rosita stepped in and practically forced it on her.

Of course Rosita did not really force it, no one could make you join in something you did not wish, but the manner in which Signora Dal Rosa suggested the costume, the sulky expression that only lifted when Clair unenthusiastically agreed, seemed to make an issue of the simple thing of participating, or not.

'All right,' Clair had consented a little wearily at last.

She had not wanted to dress. The children's party had taken place in the afternoon, and the effort of getting Juanita and Amalia ready, since Sophia flatly had refused saying it was out of her province and Rosita had been too bored to do her part, had exhausted any enthusiasm Clair might have had for changing herself to someone else.

But Rosita's insistence had decided her, and when she saw Rosita's change of expression at her agreement and compared it to the angry looks the young woman had been darting at her all day, she had thought the effort well worth the result.

She had not known what had upset Rosita, unless it was the kind but final manner in which Rico had told his cousin this morning, when Clair had been in Rosita's suite receiving her daily instruction for the little girls, that he was *not* escorting her ashore at Cape Town as she seemed to think.

'I have only a business dinner, to which I shall conduct Clair.'

'But, Rico, I have not been off the ship.'

'Certainly you have not, Rosita, and for a reason.' He

looked remindingly at Rosita.

'Oh, yes, I know,' she said impatiently, 'and I did what was expected of me, you must admit.'

'You were a good girl,' he allowed.

'But it's all over now, and I want to go ashore.'

'Go by all means, there are many excursions. Take Sophia.'

'A woman?'

He had smiled slightly. 'Perceive, Clair, here is one female who does not get on well with her own sex.'

'Rico, you are unspeakable, of course you shall take me.'

'It is business only, and I am taking Miss Wardle.'

'And will she take pencil and book?' Rosita had asked spitefully. 'I saw her at Durban and she had neither pencil nor book.'

'I will argue no longer,' Rico had flashed, his patience exhausted. 'You are not coming for reasons you well know.'

'My period of mourning—'

'Has nothing to do with it.' He had turned without another word and gone out.

Instantly Rosita's wrath had descended on Clair. 'What a sly one you are, what a schemer, and all the time I innocently thought—' She had bitten her red lips till they were like pouting crimson poppies.

'It's a business appointment,' Clair had echoed Rico.

'Yes, yes, in a fine dress and no pencil, mind you, no pencil at all. Oh, you are sly all right!'

'*Signora*—'

'Why can't it be *senhorita*?' Rosita's face puckered up. 'I am really Portuguese, and as for being a mother, I am far too young, I am little more than a girl.'

'I assure you I don't want to go to this dinner, Signora Dal Rosa.'

'Then be ill,' said Rosita in inspiration.

'I couldn't be that if I'm not.'

'Then do something to make Rico change his mind. But ah' – angrily – 'you will not do that, either. You are sly, Miss Wardle, you want to go though you won't admit it, you won't do anything to prevent it. Oh, I hate Rico for all that

I adore him, he is so mean, so – so proper, for it is only because he is proper that he is taking you instead of me, his soon-to-be-declared fiancée, you realize that, of course?'

'Of course.'

But Clair's docility did not placate Rosita. Angrily she had dismissed her, and had not spoken to her again until the afternoon when she had sent Sophia for her and had suggested a dress for the frolic.

'I, unfortunately, cannot go, it would not be correct.' Rosita had lowered her lovely lashes in a demure manner.

'I would be very glad to sit with you, *signora*,' offered Clair. 'I have no wish to attend, either.'

'But I want you to attend. If I cannot join the festivities, then I wish you to join them. Let at least one of us enjoy ourselves. Please go, Clair.'

It was the first time she had used Clair's name, and Clair had been pleased – yet only partly pleased. Somewhere within her, for all her relief at Rosita's changed attitude, a little doubt had nagged.

Perhaps she was being imaginative, though, perhaps Rosita only wanted her to go to the ball so that she herself could sit at the side and watch what she had inspired, though not much of an inspiration it appeared, that dress that Rosita had thought up, lying rather drably on Rosita's bed.

But in the end the drabness settled the matter for Clair where extravagance and brilliance would have lost the issue. She had no wish to be a bird of paradise, to attract attention, and surely in this dull costume she would be nearly as unobtrusive as not there at all.

So she had agreed.

'What exactly is the dress, *signora*?' she had asked. 'It looks like a sort of peasant apparel, it has a characteristic look as though it belonged to some particular country.'

'You are right,' beamed Rosita, 'and please, Clair dear, to call me by my name. This is what the peasants used to wear in the little village where Rico and I grew up. I know Rico will be most touched if you attend the frolic dressed in this.'

Clair, touched herself, murmured, 'Thank you, Rosita.'

Although the costume was not an attractive one, she felt very grateful to Rosita for having suggested it. In a way, she thought, relieved, it was killing two birds with one stone: placating Rosita by agreeing to her suggestion (and Clair, after the *signora's* spiteful attack, was only too glad to placate) and pleasing Rico by going to the ball in one of his country's national dresses (and Clair, who had felt the *senhor's* disapproval like a whiplash, longed to please.)

'Thank you,' she murmured again.

She fingered the severe grey bodice with its long straight sleeves, the severe black skirt that would reach her shoes and the coils of shawl in dark green olive plaid that would be substantial enough to cover her head, encircle the shoulders and still have folds to spare.

'These are the shoes,' said Rosita, producing a pair of sturdy clogs. 'And black stockings, of course, dear.'

'Would they be seen?' doubted Clair, holding the long skirt against her.

'Above the shoes,' reminded Rosita. 'Oh, you will be very original, Clair, no one else will wear such a costume, and Rico will be enthralled.'

'Yes.' The note of doubt was just a breath outside of Clair's response, she could not imagine anyone being enthralled with the drab garments. However, if Enrico Montales felt sentimentally about it, as Rosita declared, then it was worth getting dressed in an unbecoming costume to please the *senhor*.

Rosita was rolling everything up and putting the bundle into a capacious straw bag. 'Keep the bag,' she said generously. She seemed in high spirits, and that alone decided Clair. The *signora's* good will, she thought, counterbalanced a sombre black skirt.

She took the bag back to her room. The stewardess was there, and she smiled when she saw Clair's burden.

'Ah, the *ballo mascherade*!' She rolled her eyes. 'What is the *signorina* wearing?'

Clair tumbled out the costume and stood waiting for the woman's comment. When none came she said, a little uncomfortably, 'It is a peasant's dress.'

'*Si, signorina.*'

'It is not pretty, but it is authentic.' Why, thought Clair, was she explaining herself like this?

'*Autentico,*' nodded the Italian, but with marked disapproval, '*vero*. But in our country, *signorina*, in Italy, all this' – she gestured to the costume – 'is over, and if not, then nearly so. We are smart, *moderno*.' She tossed her black head. 'No longer *rustico*. Not peasants.'

'But, Maria, isn't it nice to remember your national dress—'

'The pretty parts, *si*, but the others—' She looked again at the drab black and sombre olive green. '*Brutta!*' she declared.

Clair knew the word *brutta*, she knew it meant ugly. 'Really, Maria—' she protested, but Maria had flounced out, obviously not pleased with Clair.

To have a stewardess who looked kindly on you was, as Clair had learned by now, a wonderful asset. Now she had to remember to run the bath, set out her things; then perhaps press the bodice with her travelling iron instead of having an insistent Maria take it away to press it herself. Also, if she wanted afternoon tea she must go out to the *ristorante* and partake of it instead of Maria coming to her room with a silver pot and a thin cup and saucer and insisting that the *signorina* rested while she drank.

Clair decided to forgo the tea and instead hung up tonight's garb. First there was the bodice, needing ironing as she had thought, but she decided to let it remain creased, then the encompassing shawl, the dowdy skirt. On the floor she placed the clumsy shoes and the black stockings.

The bath that she had run was now filled and she went in and bathed, but she did not add the bath essence that she always did; somehow the costume frowned on luxury.

When she came back into her room she stood regarding the clothes another minute. Now they seemed obtrusive through their very unobtrusiveness. She knew she could never pluck up the courage to go into the dining room tonight dressed like that, and yet this, as everybody knew, was the bright spot of the *ballo mascherade*, the colourful – though certainly not

323

colourful from Clair's contribution – primal entry into the *sala da pranzo* before the actual event.

She toyed with the idea of having Maria bring a tray, of dressing after the meal and slipping quietly into the ballroom, where the Grand March was to take place, by herself, but the stewardess's disapproval, which would certainly still be evident by the way she had tossed her head and flounced out this afternoon, made Clair hesitate. The only thing was to forgo a meal, and to hope that Gordon, wondering at her absence, did not knock at the door and become reproachful when he discovered that she had dressed after all.

But it was not Gordon to whom Clair opened the door at a peremptory knock an hour later, the gong for dinner having resounded some time ago, and having been duly ignored by Clair.

It was Enrico Montales, and he stood staring at Clair in her peasant garb and encompassing shawl with an iciness that, even in the coldest, most aloof mood in which she had encountered this proud aloof man, Clair had not encountered before.

'Is this some monstrous joke, Miss Wardle?' Enrico Montales had stepped into the room and closed the door behind him. His arrogant nostrils had flared and there was a white line around his mouth that made the flashing eyes that had previously been Clair's warning of anger in him in comparison seem a mild alarm indeed.

'This is abominable, Miss Wardle!' – No *senhorita* this time, decidedly no Clair. – This is an outrage!'

'But, *senhor*—' she began.

'I have not always approved of you, or of your forthright manner, however I have put it down to the ways of the new world, *your* new world, but up till now I have had no cause to complain of your decorum, your sense of what is fit, your good taste.'

'*Senhor*—'

'But this is different, this is flagrant, this is something I would never have believed of you!'

324

'Senhor Montales,' Clair managed to intervene, 'I don't understand.'

'You mean you do not see anything distasteful in this unkind caricature?'

'No, *senhor,* I do not.'

'Is that because you *are* the new world, Miss Wardle, young, open-minded, uncluttered with tradition, downright, or is it' – a curl of the long lip – 'because you are at what the British call the right end of the stick?'

'The right end of the stick?'

'The scorner and not the scorned.'

'*Senhor, I don't understand.*' Clair's voice had risen.

'Then tell me,' he said, knife-sharp, 'how you would react to a caricature of your people? In leg-irons, would it not be, *senhorita,* for wasn't your country originally a convict state?'

'That is in questionable taste, *senhor.*'

'This' – he waved to Clair's outfit – 'is in questionable taste to me.'

'But this was your national dress, I mean the national dress of your – your—' Clair's voice trailed off.

'And leg-irons was your national dress.' His voice was bland.

'Senhor Montales—' Clair began to protest.

'Miss Wardle,' he cut short, 'by some diabolic means, probably by assiduous study in the ship's library, you have deliberately chosen the most immemorable phase through which our peasantry have evolved. In some parts of Portugal, in some parts of all Europe, in some parts of every country in the world there is a humbleness of which the country is not proud. This' – again he indicated Clair's dress – 'was to my way of thinking a period of abasement, and when it persisted in the simple people in the district in which I lived, I did my best to broaden the outlook and to change such mode of dress.'

'Successfully, *senhor?*' Clair, smarting from his acid abuse, spoke acidly herself.

'Not entirely. To some the uniform had been worn so long it was unthinkable they wear another. But patience and understanding will often win through, *senhorita,* where insult and scorn will break down what little has been achieved. Undoubtedly you think you have been very smart, very original, Miss Wardle. To my mind you have been brash and immature. I say that in preference to the probably truer spiteful and unkind. But it is not my prerogative to prevent you from doing what you started out to do, and that was join a masquerade – or was it a jeering mission? In which case kindly go ahead.' He turned and held open the door for Clair to pass through, bowing in his usual formal manner.

'No!' Clair shrank back. 'No. You don't understand.'

'It was you who did not understand before,' he reminded her. 'I understand perfectly. I will not go so far as to say you were being deliberately destructive but I will repeat my accusation of brashness and immaturity. I am sorry for you, child, for you are still that, aren't you, with your limitations and the small boundaries of your large – in size – world.' He shrugged. 'Since you are not going,' he resumed, 'I shall depart myself.' He half-turned.

From a sudden thought Clair asked, 'Why did you come?'

'Rosita noticed your absence at dinner ... your English friend was not there either ... and suggested I come down to see that all was well.'

'Oh, Rosita—'

Something in Clair's voice must have reached the *senhor.* He gave Clair a swift, searching look, an enigmatical look, then, bowing again, he left without another word.

For a long time after he had gone, Clair just stood there staring at the closed door. A myriad of emotions passed through her, one after the other, in disturbing procession. First anger at what he had accused, resentment, bitterness, futility, and then, slowly but inevitably, the *rightness* of his protestations, the *fitness* of his reproaches. Finally, the deceit of Rosita.

Painfully she remembered the little doubt that had nagged at her during Rosita's animated insistence that she attend the *ballo mascherade* in this outrageous dress, for it was that, and Clair could see it now, it was a caricature, it was an unkindness.

Now she could understand Maria's attitude, understand – and sympathize. 'We are smart, *moderno*,' Maria had said of her own countrywomen, 'No longer *rustico*, not peasants.'

The old world had taken a long time to evolve from its old ways. It had been easier for the new world, they had had everything before them, nothing left behind, history to be made, not looked back on, no shadows from which to emerge. Unless it was the shadows of leg-irons that the *senhor* had coldly tossed.

She could have hated him for that, except that she knew, aware as she had become of the aloof, grave man, that already he would be regretful of his words, sorry that he had allowed, even briefly, a lowering of the very high standards that he set himself.

No, the original fault had been hers, though innocently hers, it was Rosita who had schemed the whole miserable episode. None the less, she, Clair, should have examined that little doubt that had nagged at her, should have refused pointblank to participate in the wretched thing, whatever Rosita's pique.

The obvious thing to do now would be to ask the *senhor's* pardon, but how could she without involving the *senhor's* cousin – no, more than that, and much more, the *senhor's* fiancée? She couldn't do it, and Rosita had known that; she had known she was on safe ground. She knew the Australian girl would not retaliate, so she had gone ahead with confidence, even, when Clair had not appeared at dinner, contrived that the *senhor* came to Clair's room and saw for himself. Saw a caricature and suffered an insult that had not been intended, but how was Rico to know this unless he was told? And who would tell him? Certainly not Rosita. And certainly, and she admitted it as she took off the drab, servile, clothes, not Clair.

When Maria came in some time later to turn down the bed, Clair was sitting on the edge of it, the clothes in a little heap on the floor. The woman looked at Clair and then at the clothes, her face crumpling in concern.

'But, *signorina*, I did not mean to make you *infelice*, unhappy, I did not mean you to be *triste*.' She began taking up the clothes and folding them, putting them back in the basket that Rosita had pressed on Clair.

'You were quite right, Maria, the costume was not suitable, it was unthinkable of me even to consider wearing it.'

Very concerned, Maria began to suggest other masquerades in which the *signorina* could attend, it was still quite early, the Grand March had not commenced, but Clair waved them aside, assuring Maria with a rather shaky smile that she had no wish now to attend, that she was tired and would go early to bed.

'I will bring hot milk, you look worn out,' nodded Maria. She hesitated at the door. 'The *signorina* is not displeased with me?'

'Certainly not.'

'It is just that there is a pride, a pride in everyone.'

'Of course, Maria, I should have known; I do know now,' Clair said wearily, and the stewardess repeated, 'I will bring hot milk, you will have a good rest.'

But when she came, Clair pretended sleep; she did not want kindness from Maria, she felt she did not deserve it. She heard the Italian woman put down the tray, felt her adjust the rugs, then she heard the click of the door again.

Two tears edged down Clair's cheeks.

Since Gordon had joined the *Firenzo,* Clair had got into the habit of breakfasting with the young Englishman on the *terrazza* each morning instead of remaining in her room and eating from a tray. It had been very pleasant sitting by the window, the table spread, as befitted an early meal, with a gaily striped cloth. Gordon, fresh and glowing, would down the orange juice and bacon and eggs with such enthusiasm that Clair soon had caught the habit.

But this morning Gordon was not present, as were many others of the younger set. The waiter told Clair in his broken English that it had been a grand night ... '*Grandioso, signorina*.' He gave her a knowing wink.

Neither Rosita nor Rico were at breakfast, but this was as

usual. Rosita never rose till noon, and Clair had the suspicion that the Spartan Rico skipped the meal altogether and did not eat until luncheon.

She had finished, and was sipping her coffee when she saw the *senhor* returning briskly from the pool. He never swam through the day and she had wondered idly if he had cared much about swimming, but now, from the long, accustomed strides in which he covered the deck, she could tell that he was in the habit of taking early exercise when the crowds were not there.

From her corner table she watched him, his great height and breadth set off by the boxer trunks he wore, his smooth skin positively glowing with health and vitality, the muscles rippling, the firm shoulders carrying proudly the proud, dark head.

She saw the drops of water still glistening on his olive pelt, she saw the firm planting of his thonged feet on the planks of the deck.

Rico. Even his name hurt, and the sight of him striding along the deck hurt more. Oh, Rico! Enrico!

Almost as if he heard the silent name, he wheeled and saw her. For a moment he hesitated as though turning something over in his mind, evidently whether to breakfast or not, and the meal must have won, for he slipped into the towelling robe he carried over one arm, evidently preferring the hot sun on his skin, secured the girdle, and came across.

But it was not to eat after all, it was to—

'Miss Wardle,' he said formally, still standing, 'I had intended to write you a note, but now I can tell you instead. It is this: you will be entirely free in Cape Town after all. I will not require you to come ashore with me.'

'What about the dinner?' Why was she asking him? she thought wretchedly. He had just told her she was not required, did she need him to tell her again?

'I shall attend, of course.' He added, answering her unspoken question, 'I shall take my cousin.'

'Signora Dal Rosa.'

'Yes.'

329

'I hope you enjoy yourselves, *senhor*.' Clair's voice was as formal as his.

'It is, as you may remember, a business engagement.'

'But one may still enjoy oneself?' she dared.

He shrugged as if too uninterested to discuss whether business could be enjoyed or not.

There was a silence between them. Now was Clair's opportunity to say, '*Senhor,* I regret last night. At no time did I wish to hurt or dismay you, you must believe me in that.'

But before she could utter it, though even had Gordon not appeared at that moment looking both a little tousled and a little bleary-eyed she doubted if she still would have uttered it, the *senhor,* first nodding peremptorily to the Englishman, turned and went on his way.

Gordon sat down with an audible sigh, and the steward, with a knowledgeable look, brought quantities of black coffee.

'What a night, Clair my love!' Gordon groaned. 'You did well not to come.'

'But you had a good time?'

'Splendid. But I'm suffering now.' He accepted the black coffee that Clair had poured. 'I expect I look a wreck – I feel one. How can you bear the sight of me after the magnificent specimen who has just left?'

'The *senhor*?'

'His Highness. The sight of his morning magnificence makes me want to crawl into a hole. Only one thing makes me happy.'

'Yes, Gordon?'

'The fact that obviously he has not left you happy. What is it, sweet?'

'Something that will drown your happiness,' she promised Gordon. 'I won't be earning any extra money in Cape Town after all.'

'You're not wanted at the business dinner?'

'No.'

'That's sad news that's not entirely sad. You see, Clair, although I want to share your gleanings – yes, I've no qualms in telling you that, I'm still unmercenary enough not to think of turning handsprings when you say you're not going with him.

I love you to distraction and I hate him enough, because of you, to gnash my teeth.'

'On coffee?' she laughed. Really, Gordon was a tonic!

He shuddered. 'On coffee. My head is the size of a pumpkin. When will man learn!' He propped the pumpkin in his hands. 'Seriously, though, darling, I'm glad. I secretly resented you dressing up and going off with him.'

'Rosita will be dressing up and going off with him now.'

Gordon whistled. 'That way, is it?'

'I told you so before, you said it often happened in old European families.'

'Yes, but I've been watching that pair, and in spite of what I said I didn't think—' Gordon pushed across his cup for more black coffee. 'Cape Town this afternoon and all day tomorrow,' he yawned. 'I've been there before, Clair, but I'm sorry you won't be doing it in style as you did it in style in Durban for all that I'm glad at the same time. But look, darling, you won't be entirely deprived. We'll splurge on Table Mountain at least.'

'Can we, Gordon?'

'Yes, and still keep the Grand Canary in view. You see, while you slept your pretty head off last night, our group in the *ballo mascherade* took off first prize.'

'That's splendid.'

'It was. Each of us received tickets for two for an excursion up in the Las Palmas hills, which means you and I will be setting forth in fine style and at no loss to our restricted pockets.'

'Oh, Gordon, you are kind. Isn't there anyone else you'd sooner take?'

'No one. Not even the beautiful Rosita, who undoubtedly will be going, anyway, with our grandee. No, Clair, you were willing to share your earnings with me, so I'm happy to share this.'

'Then in Cape Town we'll do it cheaply,' agreed Clair. 'We'll take public transport. We'll walk around the city.'

'In which case I'll go back to bed until we get in,' groaned Gordon, 'and try to recover. I'll sleep soundly now that I know you're really mine and not his.'

331

'His?'

'The Grandee's. The Duke's. The Count's.'

'Oh, Gordon!'

He got up, kissed the top of her head and went wearily off.

Clair, watching him go, smiled fondly. She believed she liked him more than any man she knew. And hadn't she read somewhere that liking was more important than love?

She had dreaded going down to the suite of the Signora Dal Rosa for the day's instructions as regarded the girls, but Gordon had done her good, and she found herself walking along the hall leading to the rooms with a firm step.

All the same she could not help wondering how the *signora* would greet her. Would a contemptuous little smile be flickering round the corners of her full poppy mouth? Would the black eyes signal their triumph? Would she question her about the costume she had loaned and which Maria, on Clair's instructions, had returned earlier this morning in the basket that Rosita had given her? Would she insist on Clair keeping the basket, and when Clair refused would she flash into that quick temper of hers? In short, would there be a scene?

Clair need not have worried. Although there was a light of triumph in Rosita, the woman asked no questions, made no demands. Almost she seemed . . . though Clair could not credit it in the Signora Dal Rosa . . . a little uneasy in herself. Clair would not go so far as to say ashamed

But it cheered Clair to know that at least, for all that she knew she had won, Rosita still had the grace not to be flamboyantly the victor. Her soberness gave the impression that she was not entirely proud of her own behaviour, and this helped Clair to stand calmly and attentively to inquire about today's requirements.

'None this morning and afternoon, but tonight I would wish you to look in occasionally on the girls. I know there is Sophia, but—' Rosita shrugged.

'Gladly, *signora*.' Clair recalled ruefully how previously Sophia had been held up as a pattern for the new companion.

'The girls love you,' Rosita said almost kindly, almost as though offering a balm. But she could not erase the triumph as she added, 'I am going out. To dinner. Senhor Montales is escorting me.'

She had won, she was a little ashamed of it, but she still was the victor, and she wanted Clair to know.

'That will be nice, *signora*. I will watch the girls.'

With as much dignity as she could summon, and Clair would have been gratified had she known how Rosita watched that dignity with reluctant admiration, Clair went out.

The *Firenzo* came into Cape Town at noon, a perfect viewing time to see the scenic city with its Table Mountain rising majestically behind it, on either side of the Table the projections of Devil's Peak and Lion's Head.

Gordon, still not very bright, had come on deck and was standing beside Clair.

'We can go to the top of the Table by aerial railway and see both the Atlantic and the Indian Ocean,' he told her. 'Also, the foliage and flowers in the valleys and glens below Table.'

'That should be beautiful besides not being extortionate.' Clair, in spite of herself, was watching Senhor Montales and Signora Dal Rosa, who, with the *senhor's* usual precedence, appeared to be the first passengers off the ship. – So it was not just an evening out, she thought.

Gordon's eyes followed the direction of Clair's glance.

'It's a pity,' he snorted, 'that there's no red carpet.'

Clair did not comment or reprove, her attention was on Rico. For all that Rosita was breathtakingly lovely as usual, Enrico seemed preoccupied. He also, noted Clair, looked very stern. For a brief moment before he stepped after Rosita from the gangplank to the wharf, he glancd up at Clair. It was quite apparent, for even Gordon noticed it, that he became sterner still.

'What did you do to the grandee, darling? Tell him you loved me best?'

'Oh, don't be absurd!' sharply. 'Gordon, what are we going to do? Just watch the others go ashore?' for other passengers now were disembarking.

'Table Mountain—' Gordon began.

333

'Then let's get going,' Clair said impatiently; she felt impatient.

'What's the hurry, Clair?' Gordon was looking at her in surprise. 'We've plenty of time.'

'I'm to look after the girls tonight.'

'Oh, bother the girls. What about Sophia?'

'It appears,' admitted Clair humbly, 'they want me.'

'So do I want you.' He said it ruefully but good-naturedly, for he was quite fond of Juanita and Amalia. 'Very well, sweet, you win. We'll go now, see the Table and the city on the cheap, then get back here for dinner. If you're ready to set off, I'm ready.'

They descended to the wharf, skirting the queues of organized tourists running out to Groot Constantia in Wynberg to see the few remaining Cape houses in colonial-period style, or the Botanical Gardens at Kirstenborsch on the eastern slopes of Table Mountain.

They did not after all take the aerial railway, so popular it was today, but they did drive to the back of the Table to see the Twelve Apostles, twelve gigantic separate granite peaks standing above the Atlantic Ocean.

By now the 'white tablecloth' had settled on the summit, so they came down to wander through the city, a sparkling place of sunshine and flowers . . . pelargoniums and gladioli in profusion, and the national emblem protea, cup of delicate petals in a circle of green leaves.

Clair wanted to buy a trinket each for the girls, left on board under the sharp eye of Sophia. She chose a miniature assegai for Juanita and a shield for Amalia. Gordon, however, was dubious about her gifts. 'Juanita, yes, but a necklace would be more in Amalia's class.'

'I feel they are typical,' insisted Clair, deciding that if Amalia was scornful she would keep the small shield for herself. She looked wistfully at an ebony assegai and a leopard skin shield but decided she could not afford them, and settled for the substitute.

When they got back to the *Firenzo*, Amalia was quite as keen as Juanita on the small trinkets. 'Black and gold,' she praised the substitute skin, 'is quite in fashion this season.'

Pleased that she had done the right thing for the problem girl, Clair put aside her own longing for the ebony and real leopard skin pair— Though she would have loved to have had them.

But when, after bedding the girls, after walking with Gordon round the deck and admiring the shimmer of Cape Town, the golden ladders of light reflected in the port waters, Clair at last came along to her room, on her table stood the set she had admired. Her first thoughts were of Gordon, he had laughed at her delight in the children's trinkets, but as she fingered this set she could see they came from a very different class from her purchases for Juanita and Amalia.

'Ah, such lovely work,' enthused Maria who had come to turn down the bed, 'such *ebano, signorina,* such excellent skin!'

'Yes' agreed Clair. Then she asked, 'How did they get here, Maria?'

'The messenger brought them in with the instruction that I open them up and display them for you.'

'Thank you Maria. But who sent them?'

'I did not know. I thought perhaps you had purchased them yourself when you went ashore. But why worry, *signorina,* they are a very handsome gift.' The stewardess smiled and stroked the shield.

Whether the duo held some magic, or whether the tension of the last day eased, but Clair was smiling, too, as later she put out the light. Relaxing in the rather welcome steadiness of still waters after days of sea rhythm, not unpleasant though the rhythm had been, she found she could think of Rosita and Rico at their dinner tonight without the hurt as before, could remember the stern look the *senhor* had given her as he had left with less misgiving. He could not have thought too badly of her, or of her behaviour, not with her 'twins' on her bedside table. Of course it might not be the gift of the *senhor.* It could be Gordon, spending some of what remained of his money, making a surprise of it in case she objected. It could even be a peace offering from Rosita.

But whoever had sent it, it was a happy thought. Clair

reached out in the dark and took the little shield in her hand. She still held it when she woke the next morning.

The first thing to do, she decided, was to thank the donor of her 'twins', as they were now known to Clair.

That the giver was not Gordon became apparent over breakfast on the *terrazza*, when Gordon began counting his money.

'It looks like it will be an even cheaper day than yesterday, darling,' he sighed. 'Even with free Las Palmas tickets I'm still struggling. Perhaps you shouldn't have bought those things for the kids after all.'

'Are we that poor?'

'Right on the fringe line. No more reckless spending for the next week.'

Clair said carefully, 'Did you spend recklessly yesterday?'

'You saw me.'

'When I didn't see you?'

He guffawed at the idea.

No, it had not been Gordon.

Perhaps, then, it had been Rosita, Rosita, the victor, but still a little ashamed of her victory. Perhaps the ebony assegai and the leopard shield had been her way of asking pardon.

But when Clair went down for her daily instructions she saw at once that no longer was there any asking pardon in Rosita. The young woman was in her angry mood again. She barely spoke to Clair outside of giving a few terse orders regarding her daughters, but she shot her many long, estimating, quite openly disliking looks. Something had happened since the last time Clair had received her orders from the children's mama. There was a defeat in Rosita, but an angry, resentful defeat. It certainly was not the time to inquire, 'Did you send me two charming trinkets?' It would have been redundant, anyway, for most certainly, gathered Clair from that disliking look, Rosita had *not*.

That left only the *senhor*, so she would inquire of him. Someone must have sent the 'twins', and they must be thanked.

But Clair did not ask Rico because she did not see him ... not indeed for days after the *Firenzo* had left Cape Town and was heading up the African coast to the Grand Canary.

Gordon mentioned casually as they stepped out together on the wharf again at Cape Town that before Clair had joined him he had seen the grandee being picked up by an opulent car and whisked away, probably to another of his important dinners.

'So you're out in the cold again, sweetheart,' he grinned.

'Was Rosita with him?'

'Evidently she's being punished as well.' Another grin.

Clair said, 'You're ridiculous,' knowing it was not ridiculous at all, for Rosita had worn a punished, mutinous look. This man, she thought, mutinous herself, is a dealer out of admonishments, and why should he admonish? How is it that he thinks he can judge what is right and what is wrong? Not only think but act on that judgment? What is this Portuguese ogre, this *senhor* dictator, this man Montales, what is this – as Gordon says – grandee? *What is he?*

'He is just Rico,' answered her heart suffocatingly. 'He is Enrico.'

They walked the city again, finding an avenue of brilliant blue hydrangeas, of which Clair asked Gordon had he ever seen such blue.

'Your eyes, Clair.' He was looking at her with an expression she had not met in him before.

'What do you mean, Gordon?'

He did not speak for a while, and then he said quietly: 'Las Palmas next, then Messina, Naples, Genoa. Over the continent to home. My home.'

'Yes?'

'I want you to come with me – as my wife.' When she did not comment he went on: 'Well, perhaps not my wife when you get there, but very soon afterwards. I want to marry you, Clair.'

They had found a bench and sat down. Clair sat staring at the brilliant blue until it misted. She was considerably perturbed at what Gordon had said. At no time had she believed Gordon to be really serious about her the same as at no time had she been really serious about him.

'Gordon,' she said at last, 'I had no idea there was more

337

than friendship.'

'Perhaps I had no idea myself,' he admitted boyishly, 'until yesterday.'

'Yesterday?'

'Yes.'

'What happened then?'

'We bought two trinkets for two small girls, and suddenly, darling, I was a family. Can you understand?'

'I think you had a passing notion of domesticity, that is all, Gordon.'

'It was not that. All at once I saw you in an apron, and Clair, you looked very charming in an apron.'

'Had I become a *domestica,* then?' She crinkled her eyes at him in mirth.

'You had become Mrs. Sindel.'

Clair's laughter stopped.

'Oh, Gordon!'

'Oh, Clair!'

'I like you very much, but I don't love you.'

'I don't like you so particularly, but I love you to distraction, so we should match up. Look, Clair, don't answer me now. I've sprung it on you, it's a surprise, but the fact is the idea was sprung on me, took me by surprise. Out of the blue it came, darling – a house with roses, you in the apron, two little girls.'

'Even an Amalia?'

'Even an Amalia. That surely should prove I'm in love. But don't answer me yet, don't even think about it. But think, Clair, of your immediate future, and by that I mean the next few weeks. Have you made any plans?'

'Plans?'

'We reach Sicily fairly soon, Naples a day after, Genoa a day after that, and Genoa for the *Firenzo* is journey's end. Clair, what has the grandee in mind for you?'

Clair sat silent a moment.

'I don't know, Gordon. He has never said. We have never discussed it. Mrs. Henry had intended to tour Europe, and I was to accompany her.' Clair added uncertainly, 'That is, I think I was.' She was recalling Mrs. Henry's, 'To Italy first,

and after that, who knows? Particularly if you are a good girl.'
But the *senhor* had never offered any such reward, had never
spoken of what would happen when the *Firenzo* reached its
final port.

Gordon was watching Clair keenly. 'You see?' he tri-
umphed.

'But he would never just pay me off,' insisted Clair, 'Leave
me high and dry, not Senhor Montales.'

'I have no doubt it would be a very generous paying off,'
proffered Gordon, 'but if he had any plans for you, had intended to retain you in Rosita's service, don't you think he
would have told you by this? To give the grandee his due,
I've no doubt he'll even produce for you a return ticket to
Australia, but as regards himself and his cousin—' Gordon
shrugged. 'The thing is, Clair,' he asked, 'do you want to go
back to Australia yet?'

'No.' She didn't. The memories were too fresh there, too
hurting. She had left Sydney only a week after her mother
had died. She wanted more time than two months— She also
wanted, but she must not admit it, not with Rosita and Rico
only waiting the accepted period before they married, to be
somewhere nearer than some ten thousand miles away from
the *senhor,* even though, to him, were she right beside him she
would still be that far.

'Then it's time we did something, Clair,' advised Gordon,
'otherwise you'll be disembarking with nothing in view.'

'The *senhor*—'

'He'll shake your hand, or kiss it . . . I don't know what the
grandee does . . . then disappear into the blue. You'll be left at
Genoa, darling, not knowing where to go.'

'No, Naples, Gordon.'

'Genoa.'

'But I'm booked to Naples.'

'It makes no difference if we go on to Genoa, so that, Clair,
would be our best and most economical bet.'

'But I want to see Rome, Gordon—' September Street,
she was thinking, green and cool like the waters through the
porthole of the Milano Lounge . . . Rico saying, 'When I saw

September Street I felt it held spring.'

'We will . . . one day.' Gordon's blue eyes held Clair's blue. He leaned over the bench and took her hand.

'But immediately, sweet, for no extra money we can go on to Genoa, and from there we can get an express train right to London. I'm telling you now because we have to apply for our tickets, the *Firenzo* works in conjunction with the railway, and by selecting our route in advance we can get a considerable cut. I'm sorry, Clair, that I can't forgo cuts, can't come grandly out – as the grandee undoubtedly would – and order a carriage to ourselves, but, darling, the heart if not the money is there.'

'Oh, Gordon, that doesn't matter.' She said it warmly to reassure him, but he took it the wrong way.

'You do feel as I do,' he acclaimed triumphantly.

'No.'

'It's because it's still new, Clair,' he insisted, 'you soon will. Meanwhile, about our applications for tickets from Genoa—'

The *Firenzo* moved out of the quay at sunset, and in a short time the wind had an Antarctic feel and the sea an Atlantic swell.

Contrary to what the passengers had been given to expect, however, in the following days the weather smiled at them, the 'rollers' did not plague them, only the heat as they later crossed the Equator was a trial, and that only on deck during the noisy celebrations, never in the cooled ship.

Now the days drowsed by, the most of the passengers sat indoors. Clair, however, could not take her eyes off the direction of the African coast, a coast with exciting names to think about . . . Gulf of Guinea, Liberia, Sierra Leone.

She had not given her answer regarding the train reservations from Genoa to London to Gordon, and the tickets had to be settled by Las Palmas. It was foolish of her; Gordon's proposition made such economical good sense – but still Clair waited. She could not have said for what.

She still had not seen the *senhor* since Cape Town, days ago. She assumed he must be working on his books and eating in his suite— Or Rosita's suite. Pride prevented her from asking the children, but she often wished their endless chatter would include Zio Rico, but it never did. They were all agog now to meet another Zio . . . 'Not really an uncle,' explained Juanita, 'but our papa's good friend. Zio Rico said it would be nice for us to call the Signor Fuccili Zio Francesco when we visit him in Sicily.'

'He lives there?'

'At Taormina, which is oh, so *bella*.' Juanita added, 'Everyone says.'

'So now you are longing to go?'

'*Si,* Clair, but not Mama, she says this Francesco will be old and dull.'

'Except,' Amalia informed them pertly, 'that Zio Rico said, "You *will* go, Rosita," I believe she would not. Oh, that Rico, was a *direttore!* That means a manager, Clair. I think he is a big boss,' Amalia said quite proudly.

Rosita was still antagonistic with Clair, but self-pity sometimes edged the antagonism aside.

'I am to visit this boring person in Messina just because he was my husband's friend. I hate Rico for the directions he gives. I hate this ship!'

'You are just tired of the sea,' sympathized Clair, 'but perhaps you and the *senhor* will take a trip in Las Palmas and that will be a diversion.'

'Rico has not mentioned it. No doubt he will take *you*.' Rosita looked at Clair with smouldering eyes again.

Hurriedly Clair said, 'No, I'm going with the Englishman,' hoping to appease Rosita.

Rosita, however, only became lacklustre. 'It makes no difference,' she shrugged.

The next day for the first time in over a week Clair saw the *senhor* . . . or at least she saw a corner of his coal-black hair, an inch of his deep olive neck as he bent over to demonstrate some point to a large parcel of children. Evidently the large parcel had begun with a little parcel, his own nieces, for they were in the foreground, and whatever it was he had had to say had attracted the others.

Clair, attracted, too, went and listened.

'Africa,' he was telling them in a low, thrilling voice, 'sparkling veld, crashing waterfalls, lions, leopards, elephants and lemurs.'

'What are lemurs?'

'What is your children's library for, my little noddle heads? Go now and find out for yourselves. For the first to tell me, a rich reward.' He had noticed Clair and was dismissing them.

They ran away and he walked slowly to where Clair stood now at the rail.

'You consider my words too stimulating for children?' He had reached her and put his fingers under her elbow and was propelling her further along the deck.

'On the contrary, I was enchanted. I have been enchanted all this week.' She swept her hand in the direction of the faraway African coast.

'I am glad. The young should be enchanted.'

'And you, too?' she included.

'I have my enchantment, *senhorita*.'

'Your Portugal,' she proffered a little shyly . . . she had been reading up Portugal in the ship books . . . 'wild thyme, cork, ibex and myrtle.'

He inclined his head at her.

'And then,' she said, 'another country. Your September Street. Roma and the Via Settembre.'

'You remember that!' Suddenly his eyes were holding hers, seeking an answer . . . *demanding* it.

What would have happened then, Clair dared not think, for the spell was broken suddenly by the noisy return of the two little girls.

'A lemur is—' they began. And waited for their reward.

After they had received it they remained until shooed away for punishment for grumbling that their mama had said they were not going ashore at the Grand Canary.

'Neither am I, small malcontents, neither am I.'

'But Clair is, she goes with her Englishman, Mama says so.'

There was a silence so sharp it cut like a knife.

342

'No doubt she will write down all about it for you. Now, shoo! Disappear! You have your prize.' He snapped his lean brown fingers and they ran off. He turned to Clair. 'But what reward do we find for a bigger girl who reads assiduously, who listens assiduously . . . the right word, *senhorita*? . . . but who remembers only in her mind? What, indeed?' His voice was low and teasing, but somewhere Clair heard a hard, angry note.

Angry now herself, she retorted, 'How else does one remember?'

He stared at her for such a long time she began to think he did not intend an answer. Then—

'Sometimes there is remembrance in the heart,' he accused. He turned and went away.

CHAPTER SEVEN

A DAY out of Las Palmas ... the sea a softer hue now, occasionally the sight of land birds ... Gordon informed Clair that he must apply for their concession rail tickets by tonight: had she made up her mind?

She had – but it still was with difficulty that she told Gordon that she would remain on the *Firenzo* with him to Genoa as he had suggested and travel on from there – Rome! September Street! There was a hollowness in her as she realized she would not see the eternal city, the city to where all roads lead ... and one road most of all, the Via Settembre.

'Wise girl,' beamed Gordon. 'I'll book at once. We'll take the Riviera route, unless you had set your heart on Switzerland.'

'No.' She had said it dully, then had become aware of a curious look in his eyes, and had forced a quick smile. He had smiled back at her – but a little thoughtfully.

Sea activity began that afternoon, and Clair was glad of the diversion, both for herself and the girls.

The ship shop, as was its custom, was displaying goods typical of the approaching port in its small windows, and having exhausted her young by running them from port to starboard so as not to miss one boat, Clair took them window-shopping.

Juanita admired the exquisite hand-embroidery, the table cloths and napkins. Amalia enthused over the inlaid jewel cases.

Clair moved the flattened noses up another foot or so, and bumped into the *senhor*.

In reply to the girls' curious, 'What are you going to buy, Zio?' he tossed a casual, 'Some gifts for the *pal* – some gifts to take home.'

'Will you choose that red bouncing ball for the gardener's son?'

'Yes, yes,' he answered quite shortly. He seemed a little ex-

344

asperated. 'You may pick yourself a gift, children,' he diverted.

They took a long time over their selection . . . a figure of a lady in Spanish costume for Juanita, a pretty basket for Amalia.

'And Clair?' they both chorused.

The *senhor* looked down in that remote way of his.

'Miss Wardle is not a child and I said children.'

'But when you say little ones, she is always one, too. You know that is so, Zio, for you look at Clair when you say it.'

'Run off now and show your mama your gifts,' was all his reply.

As always with Enrico, they obeyed at once.

'I'm glad I have run into you,' the *senhor* said to Clair as soon as they were out of sight. 'There are several things I wish to say.'

'Yes, *senhor*?'

'They concern your excursion tomorrow. You are still going?'

'I am still going.'

'The first is to remember to take your hat.'

'The one that "flips"?'

He did not smile.

'The second, and more important one, is food and drink. Particularly drink. The food will be the usual Spanish dishes . . . and very delicious and most substantial, too . . . but I would advise you only to eat at the approved stopping places.'

'And the drink?'

'Make it mineral water,' he advised, 'or at least some of the excellent wine.'

'Why, *senhor*?'

'Because the Canaries are undergoing a minor water crisis. There are no rivers in all the islands, and just now the stony ravines known as *"barrancos"* are dry. But there may be a trickle, and in the heat you may be tempted to drink. I would not do this, not, anyway, at present.' He stopped speaking and looked at her in inquiry. 'You are smiling, *senhorita*.'

'Yes, I am smiling.'

'Miss Wardle?'

'I am smiling because although I am too old for a gift, although I am no longer a child, it appears that all this is waived aside once wise advice is the order instead of presents, and then I am considered quite young. Young enough to be told what to do.'

She hadn't meant to be quite so emphatic about it, and glanced . . . not a little dismayed . . . up at him to measure his reaction

He was annoyed at first, but then, quite unexpectedly, a quirk broke through the mask of displeasure on his dark olive face.

'So you wish to be the child, Clair? A Spanish lady, is it? Or some embroidery?'

She nodded, deciding to do her part, to the Spanish figure, and when she received it she said, 'Thank you. She will be beside my twins.'

'Twins?'

'My *ebano* assegai and leopardskin shield. They magically appeared at Cape Town. I don't at all know how, but I do know I like them very much.'

'How nice for you.' He spoke almost, Clair thought, as though he was commenting on the day or a cup of tea.

'I shall leave you now, *senhorita*. Enjoy yourself tomorrow. Remember the heat. The food. The water.' He bowed and left.

Las Palmas, Clair had read, was the most beautiful of all the Canaries, its pear-shaped island remarkable for its magnificent forest, its mountains, its gorges and its green slopes enriched with fruit trees. It was up these slopes by exceedingly twisting roads that their tickets entitled them to travel from Santa Cruz de la Palma to the other towns and villages, stopping to see the bananas . . . no novelty to Clair . . . the raisin, tobacco, and the vineyards at which the island wine, Vino Palmevo, was grown.

Only twenty-eight miles long and seventeen wide, they could almost have encircled Las Palmas, but the twists and the ascent, once they left La Ciudad . . . 'the city' . . . behind them slowed their progress, and anyway, as Gordon shrugged, who, in such a place, wanted to hurry?

They passed quaint villages with narrow cobbled streets and charming houses with overhanging balconies. They stopped at a seventeenth-century church with a fine classical portico with double columns supporting a pediment; within an elaborate fretted ceiling and a carved baptistery.

They ate in another quaint town ... the food was delightful, and so was the island wine.

During the afternoon, though, Clair began to wonder if she had enjoyed the food too well, whether she should have eaten so much of the olive-garnished dishes. One thing, she decided, the wine had not quenched her thirst, a thirst more pronounced than usual because of the hot day and the sharp seasoning of the vegetables and meat. She began to feel a little sick.

She was determined not to spoil Gordon's outing, however. Whenever he enthused she made herself enthuse with him. It was hard, though. Her head had begun to ache, and she pulled off her hat, did not put it back even in the blazing sun as they examined an almond grove. Gordon did not reprove her as the *senhor* would have done, he was enjoying himself too much to notice.

At coffee later she drank quite greedily, ignoring the Spanish pastries. The several cups did not appease her, however, she now had a raging thirst. When they emerged from the wayside café the rather dusty gold of the panorama of Santa Cruz de la Palma far below them seemed to swim before Clair's eyes.

Gordon had taken her to a look-out to admire the view, and had he not heard her little gasp and turned in time, she might have fallen.

'Clair, are you ill?'

'It's this awful heat.'

'But it's not, Clair, not really, darling.'

'Then it's my thirst, Gordon.'

'I'll get you some mineral water.'

He put her down on the grass and turned to go. 'You do seem all out, old thing,' he said, concerned. Looking around him he noticed a small thin stream and went and soaked his handkerchief with the intention of sponging her brow. But as soon as he touched her face she feverishly grabbed the wet handkerchief and squeezed it to her mouth, sucked at it until Gordon pulled it away.

'I didn't mean you to do that, Clair.' He was concerned.

But Clair felt a little better now, and sat up. She pushed back the damp hair from her forehead and took a few steadying breaths. Then she looked around her. 'Where is the coach?' she asked.

'I let it go,' he breezed. 'There'll be another one.'

'So long as there is,' hoped Clair.

For a while Gordon was still cheerfully complacent about the arrival of a second conveyance. 'Quite a few from the *Firenzo* took this excursion, Clair, they can't all have gone ahead, there'll be more buses soon.'

But there was no bus. The owner of the café where they had taken coffee informed them rather uninterestedly that there was no ordinary service along this route, only tourist coaches plied down to Santa Cruz. It was getting late in the afternoon and he began shutting up.

It was almost dark now. Dusk in Las Palmas might come very early, Gordon assured her with forced equanamity, but for all his apparent calm he said it in a faintly uneasy voice.

The stars came out, then a thin sliver of moon. The moon was well up and riding through the night clouds before the car pulled up at the dark café. It came from the Santa Cruz direction, and a tall, broad man got out. It was Senhor Montales. He crossed to where they waited and he addressed Gordon only, he never glanced at Clair.

'This is the third hill café at which I have stopped to inquire. I am glad for my own sake as well as yours I did not have to go any further. Besides being wearying, it would have made my own return to the ship a doubtful journey. Were you not informed of the ship's departure hour, Mr. Sindel?'

'Yes, but we naturally thought there'd be more buses coming along.'

'That was a foolish hazard. You might have been stranded.'

'I realize that now.'

The *senhor* had taken out a cigarette case this time, not his box of cheroots, but he did not offer it around, he simply flipped out a cigarette for his own use. His face was very dark, but it was not the dark of the night, and Clair knew it.

'You realize a little late,' he said sharply. 'What had you intended to do had I not seen your coach arrive at the port and noticed you were not in it? Had you any plans?'

'Only to wait for another bus,' Gordon repeated wretchedly.

'Which obviously you have done. And why did you wait? May I inquire that? It is not all that pleasant here.'

'It was my fault,' Clair intervened weakly. 'I felt unwell.'

At once the *senhor* turned his attention on her. He came across and gave her such a searching, probing look that Clair felt he was peering right through her.

'The heat?'

'Yes.'

'Did you resist the prostration you found you felt and make everything much worse by insisting on seeing what you could, or did you take it sensibly and quietly and give in to it, instead?'

'I rested just now, *senhor*. That's how we missed the coach.'

The *senhor* made a noise in his throat either of irritation or anger.

'I think you carried on in spite of your unmistakable lowness, and that is why the prostration finally caught you up. Well, come now, anyway, both of you, for even with the fast car I have managed to hire we will not have too much time.'

It was not until Clair tried to get to her feet that she realized how ill, how very ill, she still felt.

Gordon had gone ahead to open the door. His back was turned. For a moment Clair swayed, and the *senhor,* moving quickly forward, supported her. Once again he gave that close, probing, searching look. 'It is only prostration?'

'Yes.'

'You have eaten nothing to uspet you? What did you have at the café just now?'

'Nothing, really.'

'And to drink?' Even as he said it, the *senhor's* eyes narrowed almost to pinpoints. *'To drink, senhorita?'* he repeated fiercely.

'Coffee. A lot of coffee.'

'That is all?'

What was the use of trying to evade this man? Clair knew it was useless to lie.

'I collapsed. Gordon went and wetted his handkerchief.'

'The fool!'

'No. Listen, please. He wetted it to cool my brow, but I–I—'

'Yes?'

'I squeezed the water into my mouth.'

'From where did he get the water to moisten the handkerchief?'

'From somewhere there.' She pointed vaguely. Then not vaguely but anxiously: *'Senhor—'*

'Senhorita?'

'It was not his fault, not Gordon's, he particularly only intended to moisten my brow, but I—'

'Yes. You have told me.'

'I was so terribly thirsty, you see, and—'

'You have told me.' Even as he said it a blackness came over Clair again, she had no memory after that moment, not of being carried in Rico's arms to the car, nor of speeding along the road, nor of being borne back to the *Firenzo,* nor of Maria putting her to bed.

She was violently ill. She knew that between the gestures of waking and sleeping. She burned, she froze, terrible pains clamped her stomach, ground into her bones. Sleep was fitful, but to wake up was worse, for then the seething pains set in.

Then, at long last, she came out of the great black tunnel, and things began to take a normal shape again. She saw her 'twins' and her Spanish lady on her bedside table, proper outlines once more, not formidable waving masses ... and she saw, to her surprise, for she was the last person she would have expected to sit beside a sick bed, the *senhor's* future wife, Rosita Dal Rosa. The *signora* wore a mutinous look, which meant, thought Clair weakly, that she had been directed here, had not volunteered.

She did not know what time of the day it was, but, 'Good morning, *signora*,' Clair said.

Rather to Clair's surprise, since all she had expected from Rosita was a sulky acknowledgment, the children's mama beamed warmly on her.

'Ah, Clair dear, you are recovered. Yes, I can tell it from your clear eyes. Poor sweet, how ill you have been. Hour after hour you have been like a dead thing, and then the fever would take you.' Rosita rolled her black eyes in sympathetic distress. 'But now you have come through the worst, and you lie weak and exhausted but your dear, kind self again.' Another beam from Rosita.

Clair felt a little uneasy. The only other time Rosita had been like this had been prior to the *ballo mascherade,* and look what had happened then. What was being planned now in that shiny, jet black head? 'I'm afraid I've been putting you to much trouble, *signora*,' she murmured.

'Rosita, dear Clair, and it has been no trouble to sit by the sick bed of such a sweet friend, by the bed of someone that my children, I do declare, Clair, love even more than their mama.'

'Oh, Rosita!'

'I mean it, and I do not blame them, you are so good and so patient, whereas I—' Rosita sighed. 'Though, of course,' she resumed, 'I have had a lot of sadness. Is that not so, my dear? Do you not agree?'

'Why, yes, Rosita.'

'The sadnesses have made me a little touchy, perhaps. That is why—' Rosita paused. Then unable to keep up the gentle sweetness any longer, she burst out, 'That is why it is so unfair.'

'Unfair?' Clair took it to mean that Rosita resented being by her bedside and hastened to apologize again for causing an upset.

'That is nothing. I told you before. No, it is *him*.'

'Him?'

'Rico. He gives these orders.'

'He ordered you here?'

'No, no, I came on my own accord, I thought it would grat-ify him. Please don't misunderstand, Clair, I would have come even if I had not wanted to look well in the eyes of my cousin.'

'I see.' Clair really thought she did see. Rosita had wanted to impress Enrico, so had sat by her bedside with that goal in view. It was understandable – and rather sweet. To please the man you are going to marry is a worthy thing.

But – 'I don't think you do see,' pouted Rosita. 'How could you know when I did not know myself?'

'Know what, Rosita?'

'This miserable visit that I and the children must make to-morrow.'

'Tomorrow? But whom can you visit on the *Firenzo?*'

'We will be visiting ashore at Messina. In your long illness you have not realized how near we are to the end of our jour-ney. We arrive in Sicily in the morning, Clair.'

'That near?' As she said it, Clair felt a sharp stab. Where had the weeks gone, the weeks since she had known the *sen-hor?* For prior to Enrico Montales, apart from her mother, Clair often felt she had never lived at all.

'Yes, Messina on the island of Sicily, and after that it is only one night and we are at Napoli, at the end of our long trip.'

'This visit, Rosita – you don't want to make it?'

'No. Not at all.'

'Then—?'

'But he, my cousin, insists. He even makes arrangements for Francesco Fuccili to meet us at the wharf.'

'That should be quite nice, Rosita, a change from shipboard acquaintances. Meeting people is fun.'

'An old man like Francesco? Fuff! I tell you, Clair, I will be sadly bored. I wished to go ashore at Messina very much, but to look at the fashions, not visit an old man. Italian styles are very elegant. Many think, and I am one, that they have left the French houses of couture far behind. I would have been very happy to walk the streets, perhaps buy a gown or two, for I am now out of the period of mourning and need new clothes, only for Rico.'

352

'But why should the *senhor* wish you to visit this man?'

'Because Rico is Portuguese and thinks formally, that is why.' Rosita stuck out her lip.

'And you, Rosita?' asked Clair.

A toss of the black head. 'I am no longer Portuguese, I am Italian. Italy is very smart these days. Besides having the leading fashion houses, they make dreamy shoes, remarkable knitted garments, gloves and hats. Also they produce excellent films. Portugal does not do these exciting things, it is conventional and dull and very like England, I think.'

'So you are Italian,' mused Clair. Where did that put the *senhor*? she wondered.

'I told all this to Enrico,' related Rosita furiously, 'yes, indeed I did, Clair, but what answer did I get? "All the more reason," Rico said, "if you are Italian and not Portuguese, dear cousin, for you to visit this Francesco." '

'But why should you?' puzzled Clair.

'That is what I say, even though he was my late husband's dear friend.'

'Oh, that makes it different, then.'

'I cannot see why. You are just like Rico. You are Portuguese, Clair.'

'No.' Clair smiled faintly. 'I am British.'

'The same in character.'

'I don't think so.'

'Well, near enough. Now, the Italians—'

'But, Rosita,' interrupted Clair, 'if you veer to the Italian as you say why are you so reluctant to visit this man?'

'Because I have had many weeks of dullness, so many, Clair, I feel I cannot bear even one more day.'

'He may not be dull.'

'He will be. He will be quite old, Clair, probably also fat. Dear Clair, I do not wish you to misunderstand me, I was very fond of Umberto, my husband, but—' Rosita rolled her eyes – 'I was so young.' Her voice dropped pathetically. 'He was so mature.'

'And this friend—'

'This friend,' resumed Rosita, her voice losing its droop,

'will be mature, too. It will be a day of boredom.'

'It need not be.'

'It will. I shall sit stifling yawns when I could be visiting tl shops, the ever-so-charming boutiques.'

'But, Rosita, you can do all that in Rome.'

'Perhaps. But I do not know for sure. You never know with Rico. I am not informed even yet where I am to be taken. Is it Italy? Is it Portugal? I do not know at all. Oh, it is too bad, and this horrible visit makes it worse still.'

'If you feel that strongly about it, then why go? Stand up to the *senhor*. Say no.'

Rosita's large black eyes grew larger.

'Say no to Enrico? That is an impossibility. What that man wants, he gets. If he says go, people go. If he says come, people come. So he says to me "Visit this Francesco, your husband's friend" so I visit him, I suppose, unless—' She looked sideways at Clair.

Clair wriggled a little uneasily, wondering what came next, wondering what that sly, sidelong glance was for.

'Unless,' said Rosita humbly, 'you will speak for me, Clair. Say to my cousin that it is too soon after my mourning for me to go meeting people, that it would not be nice. Rico would go for that, being Portuguese, like the British, he likes things to be "nice".'

'But Rosita dear, if visiting is not nice so soon after mourning, surely shopping is even less nice.'

'Shopping is a necessity.'

'For some things, but not for pleasant buying sprees in little boutiques.'

'Then tell him something else. That meeting the friend of my husband would cause me distress. That it is ill-advised. Please, Clair, do this for me.'

'But what good would it do? Why should the *senhor* listen to me?'

'Because he has listened all along, that has been very obvious. Look how he has left the children in your hands. He is extremely fond of Juanita and Amalia. Whom else would he have trusted like he has trusted you?'

'I still can't see how he would heed me in this instance.'

'In every instance he would, Clair. You have been ill, so have not seen the worry he has had for you. I do believe he has lost weight in his deep concern. I do believe something else: That you, and only you, could get this result from him, the result of my not having to attend this wretched house of Francesco Fuccilli after all.'

Except that Rosita was so deadly serious, Clair could have laughed, but she realized that for Rico's future wife to declare openly that her children's companion was the only one who could get anything from her fiancé, declare it without reserve or envy, showed the deep extent of her concern. Poor Rosita, she was near-hysterical in her objection to visiting this person, it had become almost an obsession with her. Clair opened her mouth to urge Rosita to be strong again, to defy Rico. Then she closed it. Rosita had not the strength, she realized, to refuse – the man she loved. That was natural. When you loved someone you hated to refuse.

'You will try for me, Clair dear?'

'Rosita, I—'

'Please, oh, please!'

'Very well.' Clair sighed to herself.

Her goal achieved, Rosita wasted no more time with the invalid. She gave Clair a butterfly kiss and hurried out.

Maria came in and announced that the English *signor* wished to see the *signorina*. Was she fit?

'Yes,' Clair said complacently, feeling that after the rushing waters that were Rosita, Gordon would be like a still pool.

Gordon was. He sat on the edge of the bed, and he looked very subdued.

'Don't do that again, Clair,' he begged.

'Drink that water?'

'Go sick on me. Darling, you do things properly, don't you? The ship's doctor was down here every hour. I was horribly scared.'

'What was it I had?'

'Fortunately only a heat spasm, not a water wog as we feared. *That* could have lasted for months, even years, even

355

the rest of your life. I never realized the harm a larva can do until Rico told me. No wonder he was white with rage!'

'Against you?'

'Yes. It seemed even moistening your lips could have done the evil. But, thank goodness, it wasn't that at all.'

'I told him it was my fault,' said Clair.

'Yes, but had I not given you the opportunity you would never have run the risk.'

'Well, all's well that ends well,' Clair reminded him. 'Evidently there was no taint in the water. Either that, or I'm young and strong.'

'Young and beautiful.' Gordon's eyes on Clair were full of admiration. 'Illness becomes you, sweet. Not' – hurriedly – 'that I don't want you on your feet. Look!' He took out two long coils of tickets and dangled them before her.

'Genoa to London,' he enticed.

'It sounds exciting.' Clair tried hard to feel excited.

'It will be. You'll love it. By the way, have you told the *senhor*?'

'Not yet.'

'Like me to do it, darling?'

'No.' Clair shrank from that. At least she must do the *senhor* the courtesy of telling him herself.

'Good. I wasn't looking forward to the job, not after the tongue-bashing I've had of late.'

'Was it that fierce?'

'That cold would be a better term. I've never known anyone with more capacity to freeze than the Portuguese gentleman. Even after he thawed and took the trouble to demonstrate the water larvae to me the temperature was below zero. No, Clair, I'll be happy to leave that part of the business to you.' Gordon leaned over and took up the small assegai and shield and the little Spanish lady. 'Starting a curio shop?'

'They are the twins, and this is Isabella.'

'They'd cost you a bit.'

Gordon did not ask how much but went on to say that he had a business visit in Messina, so would not be able to take Clair ashore.

'Though after the last experience, I doubt if I'd be per-mitted,' he grinned. 'Never mind, darling, once the *Firenzo* leaves Naples we won't have to refer to anyone but ourselves. You just take things easy and regain your strength.' He looked at his watch. 'Your stewardess rationed me to ten minutes only, I had better go.' He kissed Clair, threw another kiss when he reached the door, and went.

Who next? Clair thought.

The next was the doctor, who took her temperature and was well pleased. Clair was told she could leave her bed.

After he had gone she wasted no time in doing so, and had just finished dressing when Maria came in with tea, tea for two. Behind her came the *senhor*.

'You are up, Clair. Is this wise?'

'Quite, Rico. Indeed, the doctor advised it.'

'All is well, then. Do you object to my taking tea with you?'

'Of course not.'

'Perhaps, though, you would prefer to take it on the *ter-razza*, breathe the sea air?'

'I can breathe that afterwards,' Clair assured him. 'Shall I pour?'

'It will not be wearying on you?'

'Oh, *senhor!*' she laughed. 'What a wonderful husband you would make.' She did not realize what she had said until the words were out. Too late then to bite her lip in annoyance.

'That is your opinion?' Senhor Montales said it very ser-iously considering it had been only an impulsive remark. Clair flushed, reminding herself too late that this man had no humour, or at least not the bantering exchange of conversation that the British have.

'For someone, yes,' she said carelessly, unprepared for his rapier, 'Be more explicit, *senhorita.*'

'Some fair young lady,' she tossed.

'*Fair?*'

'I mean fair in the way of beauty, of course. Actually a dark young lady would be much more suitable.'

'I do not follow you, *senhorita.*'

'Fair doesn't always mean only fair, *senhor*, only blonde, it

357

can mean . . . well, what I meant was—'

'You meant that for a Portuguese a Portuguese is more in order?'

'I never said so. I said a dark young lady.' Clair added, exasperated, 'Must we continue with this absurd conversation?'

'Not at all.' He spoke stiffly. Quite ridiculously stiffly, Clair thought.

A silence fell between them.

Clair, with Rosita in mind, and with Messina only as far as tomorrow, said carefully, 'Your cousin has been very kind, she has been sitting many hours with me.'

'It will not hurt her.'

That was scarcely encouraging, but Clair still knew she must try.

'She was upset, *senhor*.' She had decided that with a man like Enrico Montales the direct approach was the best.

'Yes, *senhorita*?'

'She does not wish to visit this Italian gentleman tomorrow.'

The dark brows had met, the mouth had thinned.

'She must.'

'But, *senhor*—'

'The matter, *senhorita*, is of no concern of yours.'

'Not until I am asked to intercept.'

'She – my cousin asked this?'

'Yes.'

'What was her reason?'

'I could say formality, I could say indisposition, I could say distress at meeting a dear friend of her late husband, but I know you would realize it was not the truth.'

'Thank you.' He inclined his head slightly. 'Then?'

'It's simply that she doesn't want to go, she prefers to shop. Surely, *senhor*, that is womanly reason enough.'

'It is no reason at all,' he came back at once. 'Please, Miss Wardle, not to call evasion, reason, and please not to use womanliness as a cloak when there is no womanliness in the thought at all.'

'Very well then, she doesn't want to go. Is that enough?'

'No.'

'Why should she go if she doesn't desire it?'

'Because I desire it. Not only is it in accordance to all that Rosita has been brought up in, it is ordinary common courtesy that anyone, not just a a stuffy Portuguese' – he gave Clair a quick, furious look – 'would not hesitate to follow.'

'But who are you to order her?' Clair stopped, aghast, at herself. It not only was unpardonably rude on her part, it intruded on a personal relationship. This man was the fiancé of Signora Dal Rosa, he was to become her husband, and, as such, to the Portuguese way of thinking most assuredly to become the one in authority – if not the master already.

Coolly and accurately he read her thoughts. 'Yes, *senhorita*, that is the outmoded way we still prefer for our pattern of life. The man the leader. You disapprove?'

'Entirely, *senhor*.'

'You believe in equality?'

'I believe in equal giving and equal taking.'

'That only works when there is complete understanding, something very rare.'

'But it does occur.'

'Personally, I have never seen it.' He spoke stolidly.

'Perhaps you will.' Though Clair doubted it, with Rosita.

He darted her such a quick searching look that it was scarcely a look at all, only a flash of deep, demanding eyes, so brief, so ephemeral it was almost just a flicker.

'Shall we change the subject?' He cut into a silence that had fallen between them.

'Not until you give me your final word, *senhor*. Rosita appealed to me to ask you to withdraw your orders.'

'Orders, orders, that is all you think of me, as one who orders! Has it not occurred to you, Clair, that there could be something else behind my demand of my cousin than just a showing of authority? I have my reasons for desiring Rosita to visit the Italian *signor* tomorrow, they are long-reaching reasons, I hope.'

'Then why did you not tell her, Rico? Women will often respond to kindness when they will rebel against compulsion.'

'I had not the right, and I have not the right to explain to you. Sufficient for me to say that I wish Rosita to attend the Fuccilli home so intensely that I demand of her to go.'

'It sounds insufficient to me,' murmured Clair.

They had reached a deadlock. Clair asked the *senhor* if he would like more tea, but he refused.

'You will convey to Rosita the failure of your mission,' he said presently. 'Perhaps you would care to soften the blow by offering to accompany her and the children yourself.'

'Is that an order?' Clair's eyes flashed.

'It was a suggestion.' The dark gaze merely flickered back. 'But' – he gave his characteristic shrug – 'please yourself. Perhaps you and the Englishman already have made plans.' He paused. 'Many plans.' – Was there an innuendo in his apparently uncaring voice?

Clair half-turned away. She had a habit of flushing, and she knew already her cheeks had taken on a deeper hue. What if she answered him, 'Yes, we have made plans. They are encased in a ticket folder and the ticket reads "Genoa to London".'

But aloud she said, 'Gordon has a business conference in Messina.'

'I also, Clair. Then perhaps if you feel well enough—'

'It all depends on Rosita, Rico. She may not require me.'

They left it at that.

But Rosita did require Clair, indeed, she begged her to go.

'It is bad enough for Rico not to relent,' she pouted, 'and if you do not help me out with this boring person it will be far worse.'

So it was arranged that the four of them, Rosita, Clair, Juanita, Amalia travel to Taormina in the morning to spend the day at the home of Signor Francesco Fuccilli.

'Taormina,' enticed Clair. 'I've heard it's quite breath-takingly beautiful.'

'It had better be something,' grumbled Rosita, 'after depriving me of the little boutiques. Oh, well, it is for only a day . . .'

But it was to be for more than a day . . . for Rosita. Yet until Francesco Fuccilli stepped out of the long black Italian car parked by the Messina dock, Rosita still furiously regarded the day as a day lost.

The *Firenzo* had come into Sicily at dawn, the Strait of Messina like a bright blue watercolour, the hydrofoils already busy about their day's work.

As the big white ship had drawn into the dock, Clair had seen that the city was as early a waker as its harbour. The quaint, cobbled streets already had been hosed and swept, the little street cafés were open, and under gay umbrellas, even at this hour, lemon tea was being taken, aerated drinks and cassatas. Mamas already pushed prams, the European perambulator, very high and shaded by a small umbrella.

As the *Firenzo* threw across its giant hawsers, spun sugar stalls sprung up, gingerbread pedlars exhibited gingerbread in every shape, the balloon man with his balloons reaching ten feet high appeared – and most remarkable of all, the doll collection was put out.

Such dolls! Each as big as a small child and wonderfully dressed. Every shade of hair including the fashionable muted tints of soft rose, violet and grey. Juanita stood completely won over, and even Amalia, who never showed any maternal instinct, gasped at the display. Their mama, however, bustled them past the doll vendor to the street beside the dock where Francesco had arranged to meet them. There were disappointed tears in Juanita's eyes and a pout to Amalia's mouth – but not for long.

As they showed their landing passes to the official at the gate, the long black limousine sidled up and a man of medium height but strong build got out.

'Signora Dal Rosa?'

'*Si,*' called Amalia smartly for her mother, immediately registering the opulence of the big car.

'Franceso Fuccilli.' He presented himself. '*Signora.*' He came over to Rosita and kissed her hand, presenting her with an exquisite posy. '*Signorina.*' A deep bow to Clair. '*Bambini.*' From the back of the opulent car he produced two of the luscious dolls. He even presented the right colour to the right girl, a sweet brownette to Juanita, a pert pink-haired charmer to Amalia.

'*Grazie,*' Juanita murmured shyly.

'*Superba,*' praised Amalia.

Rosita just buried her face in the flowers and looked at Francesco with big, liquid eyes.

Francesco put the girls, the dolls and Clair in the back of the big car, and Rosita beside him. As smooth as cream the car purred off.

Between listening to the girls' delighted comments on the quality of the dolls and trying to see as much of Messina as she could in spite of Francesco's fast (though excellent) driving, Clair could catch snatches here and there of the conversation in the front seat.

'But you are young, *signore.*'

'Francesco, *signora.*'

'Rosita, Francesco.'

'I'm not so young, Rosita.'

'Younger than I thought.'

Two gay laughs.

The car climbed easily up a steep grade, descended through a sylvan glade.

'Underclothes to match,' delighted Amalia.

'Mama! It says Mama!' thrilled Juanita.

'I was a very young friend of Umberto.' Francesco negotiated a sharp bend. 'He was more a father or a big brother to me.'

Rosita responded softly, and Francesco replied to that reply in an equally soft voice. The children chattered happily, and Clair looked down on a vista of glorious coast. She was thinking of the *senhor* and what he had said. – 'Has it not occurred to you that there could be something else behind my demand of my cousin than just a showing of authority?' Could he have meant – But no, that was out of the question, *he* was Rosita's fiancé, the *senhor* was, Rosita had said so.

The loveliness of Taormina burst in on Clair like a blue shout of surprise. For a moment Francesco halted the car on a ridge for them to drink in the beauty.

'*Si,* Taormina is a joy,' he smiled proudly, 'but so is my *casa.*'

'*Casa* means house,' whispered Juanita to Clair.

But when they pulled up at the magnificent stone building rising loftily above a sickle-shaped bay, a place of spires and turrets and great bronze doors, the smell of lemon and datura breathing upward from formal sunken gardens, Clair exclaimed, 'It's not a house, it's a castle!'

'A *castello*,' nodded Amalia. 'Almost a *palazzo*.'

Rosita said nothing, but her eyes were like stars.

They went into the cool marbled hall of the *casa*, and there coffee awaited them, the most astonishing cakes that Clair had ever eaten, each one a small masterpiece of sugar and cream, and bowls of preserved figs and glazed guavas.

The girls were anxious to explore, and Clair was just as eager. Excusing herself, she took a hand of each child, the dolls having been put to bed, and ran down through the scent of lemon and datura again to stare at the almost incredible grouping of sea and cliff and graceful upthrusts of rock.

Back for a delightful luncheon of chicken macaroni, heaped wooden bowls of mandarins, medlars, nuts and pomegranates, and, of course, *vino*. Even a mild, flower-smelling *vino* for the little girls.

Rosita pleaded weariness, and said she would not climb down to the beach, and could Clair please take the children? Francesco, when Clair hesitated, not wishing to leave Rosita by herself, assured Clair that he did not mind stopping to converse with the wife of his old friend.

'I think Mama likes this Francesco,' observed Amalia, on their way down to the water-swept rocks. 'I think she may marry him.'

'Oh, darling!' laughed Clair. It was on her tongue to say that Mama was to marry Zio Rico, that Rico would be their papa, but she refrained. It was not a correct thing to gossip with children, and anyway, Amalia's interest had strayed to two boys digging for clams on the little yellow half-moon of a beach.

'I prefer the Italian *ragazzo* to the Australian,' she informed Clair. 'The Australian boy thinks only of catching balls, but ah, the Italian, he is *galante*.' She said it loud enough for the boys to hear, and they glanced across, saw the pretty pouting face and bowed, but Amalia tossed her curls and pretended at first not to see.

How like her mother she was, Clair thought, helping Juanita to scoop out a moat. She thought of Rosita's starry eyes when she had seen the rich black car, the much younger age of its owner than the age group she had anticipated, the beautiful Fuccilli *casa*. Rosita was very impressionable, and there was no harm in that – providing you were not already betrothed. But Signora Dal Rosa was betrothed, to Senhor Montales. Rico had never spoken of it, but to speak of anything so personal would have been distasteful to that aloof, proud man; also, from what Amalia had just flung, that 'I think she may marry Francesco', the children did not know the position; but most certainly Rosita had emphasized it, and in no uncertain fashion, she had said: 'Unlike many men, Rico did not turn to another woman, he remained unwed. *He waited for me.*'

All at once indignant for Rico, Rico, whose rigid principles should have inspired Rosita to be more circumspect, Clair told the girls that time was slipping by and they must return to the *casa*.

Juanita came readily, but Amalia was cross, for the boys seemed on the verge of giving up digging for clams and appeared ready to sit admiringly at her feet and listen while she talked, something that appealed to Amalia very much. However, her crossness was nothing to her mother's, when the trio returned to the house.

'Already? This is terrible, Clair! Scarcely do I begin to rest than you return.' She gave a pretty pouting look to Francesco.

'The ship leaves at nine o'clock,' Clair reminded her.

'In Francesco's fast car we have no worry.'

Francesco, impeccably courteous, assured Clair that she had done the right thing in coming up from the beach. Perhaps she would like to go upstairs and wash the *bambini* for their return to the *Firenzo*, and by that time he would have finished what he had to say to the wife of his dear friend.

Clair, because of Rosita's pique, took her time over the washing, and when the three of them came down the stairs again it was to a different young woman. She was smiling happily, and even threw her arms impetuously around her young daughters, Juanita responding eagerly, Amalia looking surprised.

They had more coffee, and then they all climbed into the big car again, and Francesco drove them a different way back to Messina. At the dock, Francesco bowed deeply to Clair once more, ruffled the girls' heads, but only gave the briefest of salutes to Rosita.

Thank heaven, Clair sighed with relief, I've returned Rosita intact, in her usual form, not just a pair of starry eyes telling the world what should not be told at all. For Rosita was quite calm, and her eyes were discreetly lowered.

The ship left on the hour, and Clair, standing beside Gordon, murmured that she would have an early night.

'I suppose you're tired, old girl; after all you're still something of an invalid.'

'We did quite a bit of climbing at Taormina. How was your day, Gordon?'

'Satisfactory. I made some good contacts. About tomorrow, Clair, if we leave Naples early in the morning we could run down to Capri. The *Firenzo* doesn't leave for Genoa until the evening.'

She nodded, suddenly finding speech impossible. She felt oddly heavy, almost as though she had a stone within her.

'Have you told the *senhor*?' yawned Gordon.

'No – but I shall, of course, and say goodbye to the *signora* and the girls.'

'Yes, do that, Clair.' He yawned again. 'I think I'll turn in, too.'

Clair had every intention of seeking out Enrico Montales right then, of informing him of her plans, but when she inquired for the Portuguese, it was to be told that he was spending the evening with the Captain.

She went along to Rosita's suite, but Sophia reported that her mistress was already asleep, and that the little girls had fallen off even on their feet, they had been so *affaticata,* so exhausted. Sophia had glared at Clair.

There was nothing to be done than leave the farewells for tomorrow, and, rather relieved, Clair went along to her room.

The climbing up and down from the Fuccilli *casa* must have taken more out of Clair than she had thought, for she did not wake up until Maria brought her tray.

'Three times I look in and you are asleep,' laughed Maria. 'The Englishman is impatient, he wishes to see Capri.'

Gordon would have to wait till she saw Rico and told him, said goodbye to Rosita and the girls, thought Clair, wishing now she had all that behind and not before her, disliking the task, but Maria called, still laughing, 'The *senhor,* too, knocked on the door, and when I said you slept he would not let me awaken you. He left this address.' She handed Clair a card. 'He said he had business in Napoli today, and afterwards would proceed there to that hotel.' Maria's voice came now through the plash of water as she ran Clair's bath, it came in fragments . . . 'see you there after he has done . . . also the *signora* and her daughters . . .'

The bath was turned off and Maria took Clair's tray and went out.

But Clair did not wait to bathe, she just flung her clothes on and hurried to Rosita's suite. At least she must explain to the *signora,* tell her to give a message to her cousin. At least she must bid goodbye to the little girls.

But nobody was there. Not even Sophia. Clair inquired, but was told that the *signora* and her children had left earlier, the *signora*'s *domestica* had also departed.

Feeling more desolate than she could have thought, Clair went back to her room, and there was Gordon, waiting impatiently as Maria had said.

He did not ask whether she had made her goodbyes, so Clair did not tell him. She gathered her things and followed him to the wharf from where their excursion to Capri was to depart.

The autobus took them to the south end of the Bay of Naples, a small launch from the Sorrento peninsula took them to the exquisite little island, with its Blue Grotto, with its vineyards, its lime and olive trees. – What had he, the *senhor,* said about olives? 'Irresistible as are the Italian olives, the Portguese—' And then, Clair remembered, he had given that characteristic gesture.

'You're quiet, Clair,' said Gordon.

'It's just that it's so beautiful,' Clair averted.

It was dusk by the time they got back to the ship. Late returners though they were, there was someone even later. Clair heard what sounded like a mild admonishment being administered at the gangplank, followed by a little repentant laugh ... a woman's laugh. She took no notice of the laugh simply because it was in a female timbre. Her eyes and her ears were straining for only one sight and one sound, and it was not the sight and sound of a woman. But Clair did not see nor hear anything of Senhor Montales. Was the Portuguese gentleman in his Naples hotel by now? Had he discovered that Miss Wardle had not come as he had expected of her? Was he on his way even now to demand in that aloof manner of his what discourteous behaviour was this? Could he reach the ship in time?

But the business conference might go on into the small hours, he might not discover her absence until the morning, unless, of course, Rosita waited up to tell him.

Rosita ... Something ticked over in Clair. That laugh just now, that small repentant laugh. It couldn't have been ... it couldn't. ...

The ship pulled out, almost an empty ship now, six hundred had left at Messina, more than that at Napoli, only a handful were stopping on to Genoa, to journey's end.

Clair lingered a while with Gordon, staring out at the glittering lights of Naples, then she said goodnight and went down.

At the corner of the corridor she collided with someone ... with a young woman. ...

'Clair!' There was instant panic in the young woman's voice. 'Clair, but you are in Napoli! With the girls! With Rico! Oh, what horror is this?'

It was Signora Dal Rosa, and Rosita's face was white with alarm.

367

ALTHOUGH Clair's impulse was to call back to Rosita in a similar strain, to ask the *signora* what she was doing in the *Firenzo* away from her family, away from her fiancé, one look at the wide, distressed eyes and trembling mouth decided her against it. So deftly, instead, she propelled Rosita into her own room.

Rosita now was wringing her hands, weeping with agitation.

'The little ones . . . oh, dear, this is terrible . . . I believed you would be with them, and here you are on the ship!'

'You, too, Rosita, why are you away from Juanita and Amalia?' Clair could not bring herself to say 'and from Rico.'

'I shall tell you, Clair, but first you must tell me. What has happened that you have proceeded on to Genoa? And what will happen now to my *bambini*?' Again Rosita began to weep.

As Clair comforted her, made her sit down, rang for Maria to bring her a glass of warm milk, she could not help feeling a little relieved that at least Rosita was not entirely the uncaring mother she always made out to be. The *signora* now was almost hysterical with worry.

'The girls, oh, the girls!'

'They have Sophia.'

'They have not. That person left me at Napoli, and she was no loss either. Always giving orders but never taking them; I was glad to see her go, not thinking, never dreaming—' The tears welled again.

'Well, at least the *senhor* will take care of them. They are with him, Rosita?'

'Yes, but he has many business engagements . . . much to do.'

'He will arrange for someone to take Sophia's place.'

'Perhaps, but something else he will do, too.' Rosita paused pathetically. 'He will send for me.'

'But, Rosita, isn't with your children your right place?'

'Yes, Clair, but not just now, not just at this oh – so important time, this moment of my *fidanzamento,* my' – she blushed,
and Clair thought how like a scarlet poppy she was – 'my be-
trothal.'

'But you've been betrothed all along.' At Rosita's puzzled
face, she said, 'To your cousin.'

'Enrico?' Oh, no, that was just the word of a naughty girl,
Clair. This naughty girl.' Rosita indicated herself and tried to
look contrite. 'I was angry because you were young and having fun yet I was young, too, but obliged to remain in my
suite and do correct, dull things.'

'But, Rosita, you not only told me that Rico belonged to
you, your eyes said it as well.'

'Perhaps, Clair, and perhaps I thought I meant it, but it
was only useless wishing. I never really loved Rico, not like—'
Her face glowed and her eyes softened. 'My cousin Rico's
riches always impressed me, his grand bearing, and tell me,
Clair, where is the girl who could resist being the wife of a
Marqués?'

'Marqués?' gasped Clair.

'Surely you knew? I think it was the prospect of being
called Your Excellency that made me believe I loved him in
the beginning,' she laughed.

But Clair did not even smile, she was thinking hard, realizing how undiscerning she had been. His Highness, Gordon
had said, the grandee, other titles, and she had taken it as banter, not knowing there had been a basis to the taunting address.

Then there had been the *palacio* Rico had spoken of, cutting
it short in self-annoyance before he finished the word.

'Palacio . . . palace!' She barely breathed it to herself.

'Yes. His home. Oh, it is beautiful, Clair, though' – a toss of
dark curls – 'not so lovely, I think, as the *castello.*'

'You mean—'

'Yes, the *castello* of Francesco Fuccilli. And a wonderful
thing, Clair, imagine it: Francesco is a Count! Also, unlike
foolish Rico, he enjoys it. I would be a—' The eyes danced.

'Wait,' said Clair, 'you go too fast. Italy and Portugal are no longer sovereign states.'

'Of course. Everyone knows that. But tradition dies hard, Clair, and in little strongholds as Enrico and Francesco still possess, a Marqués remained a Marqués and a Count a Count. That was what used to annoy me with Rico. He wanted nothing to do with a title. He would not answer to it, the foolish one. Although he could have stayed in the Palacio and done nothing at all except visit the farms of his tenants, he insisted on taking a position, an absurd one with of all things wool, and in travelling round the world.' She sighed and rolled her black eyes in scorn.

Clair waited for her to go on, and presently – contritely – she did.

'Particularly did my cousin rebel against the peasant garb of his tenants, Clair, and when I got you to dress as you did for the *ballo mascherade* I knew he would be enraged. But alas' – ruefully – 'the joke turned on me. Rico questioned me until I admitted I had insisted you wear those clothes ... he even took me out to dinner at Colombo (and what a miserable dinner it was!) with only that questioning in view. He said he could not do the probing on the *Firenzo,* for either the *domestica* or the children would disturb us. Oh, but he is a *mostro,* a monster, that one, very pleasant when it pleases him, but such a *direttore.* Now, Francesco—'

'Rosita,' Clair said firmly, 'we're not getting very far in this problem. If I can help you, and I don't see how I can, I must know everything. You tell me in all seriousness you don't love the *senhor*?'

'No.'

'But you loved him once. You had a little quarrel, and in pique you went away and married someone else.'

'It is the time for truth,' sighed Rosita. 'When I go to Francesco – oh, yes, Clair, I am going to marry my husband's dear friend – I would like to go with a clear conscience.

'At seventeen, I thought Rico was the sun, moon and stars. I adored the way he frowned on me, told me what and what not to do. I took it for an intention on his part, and when one

370

day I spoke of our future life together and he answered very kindly but very firmly that he regarded me only as a relation on whom he must keep a fatherly eye, I was so enraged I raced off unaccompanied, and for a Portuguese lady to do that was a rather terrible thing, to Cannes, and there I met Umberto.

'When you are seventeen, Clair, maturity attracts much more than youth. Umberto had far more maturity even than Rico, and he was very comfortably situated and extremely kind. When he told me of his sugar mills in Northern Queensland I thought what fun to spite Rico, to marry Umberto and go right away.'

'And that's what you did.'

'Yes, and it was a success. I loved Australia, and I had much affection for Umberto who did everything in his power for me, and I would have remained a very good wife had he lived. But he was so much older, Clair, and he died, and though I look back with gratefulness and respect, it was not such a grand affair of the heart – do you understand me? – that I could not also look forward.'

'So you looked first of all at Rico?'

'Perhaps, but oh, so briefly when I saw he did not look at me, but at a fair Australian girl.'

'Rosita, this is absurd, you are absurd—'

'No, you are, my child, if you did not know the way he looked. Oh, you British, very clever, perhaps, but still so stupid. I would have recognized that look at Amalia's age.

'Rico loved you, I could see it clearly, and because everything was going well for you and badly for me I was very naughty.' Rosita turned and smiled radiantly at Clair. 'But it is all over now, I have found my own love. Perhaps you wish me to speak of that?'

'Please.' Clair felt a little dizzy with Rosita's quick change of moods.

'As soon as I saw Francesco I *knew*. You British would not understand that.' She looked inquiringly but a little pityingly at Clair.

For a long time Clair did not reply. 'As soon as I saw Francesco I knew ....' What of the first moment Clair had seen

Enrico Montales?

She sat very still, reaching back, reaching to Fremantle, to where she had been standing in front of a wool display – and he had been there, too.

Very tall, very dark, black brows, olive skin, high planes of cheekbones, a ducal manner. *And she had loved him at once.*

'Yes, Rosita,' she said softly, 'I understand.'

'Francesco has two boys from a first marriage, his dear wife died last year. It was an arranged marriage ... occasionally European families do arrange these marriages even now ... and though it was a success, it also was not, as I said before, Clair, a grand affair of the heart. Not like now.' Rosita's eyes dreamed.

'We knew at once, and in the short time you were down on the beach with the children, we made our plans. Francesco's boys are at school, and he stopped over to make arrangements for them, the agreement being that I remained on the *Firenzo* to Genoa and that he flew to Genoa from Messina to claim me. We would be married, and go to one of those charming Riviera places for our *luna di miele,* our honeymoon.' Rosita stopped smiling and looked sad. 'And now what!'

'But, Rosita, what prevented you from telling Rico? I'm sure he would have been pleased.' Clair was thinking of the far-seeing look in the *senhor*'s eyes when she had questioned his wisdom in insisting on Rosita visiting her husband's friend.

'Ah, now, you are very British, very correct, for how sweet is a *segreto*, a secret, how romantic is an intrigue.'

'Oh, Rosita!' Clair had to laugh.

At once, seeing Clair's happy mood, Rosita pressed for an advantage.

'You are in sympathy with me, you will help.'

'How can I?'

'You will go back to look after the girls.'

'I have my ticket to London.'

'Fuff!' Rosita shrugged.

'I would not know where to go,' refused Clair. 'Gordon and I went straight down to Capri, we saw little of Naples.'

'Naples? They will be in Rome. We were only to remain this

night in Napoli, and then proceed to Rico's favourite hotel in Roma. It is situated in a little *piazza* not far from the Quirinale and but a few steps to the Via Settembre.'

'September Street.'

'*Si*,' Rosita said.

Something was nagging at Clair, something that had to be voiced.

'You were with Rico once in September Street?'

'Yes, and he was oh, so cross.' Rosita pouted. 'I suppose I had annoyed him with my foolishness ... you see it was yet another time I had run away by myself and my family had sent my cousin Enrico after me ... but, anyway, we were walking down this street and I was wishing loudly instead to see the big shops and little boutiques, since the Via Settembre is more a way of offices, churches and parks. Rico said something about spring, which was quite silly, since the season was winter and the boutiques full of knitteds. Oh, these Italian knitteds!' Rosita rolled her eyes. 'That's all,' she shrugged, 'I can tell you of the Via Settembre, except that Rico's hotel, the Fiamma, is in the small *piazza* that leads to that street.' She looked anxiously at Clair. 'You will help me, please?'

'How can I?' Again Clair said it.

'Go back to my girls. Oh, Clair, how can I have a happy honeymoon if I am worrying over them?'

Clair retorted, 'How can I go to them, Rosita, when it means I will be going as well – to Rico?'

'I have been honest with you, Clair, so be honest with me. You love Enrico?'

'Yes, but – but, Rosita, I couldn't *go* to him.'

'British women make me tired,' scorned Rosita. 'Am I not going to Francesco? Has not my cousin made all the advances so far?'

'I wouldn't say that.'

'Then I would, and I know Rico. He is proud and withdrawn, and to do what he has done, Clair, taken you from the Turistica and set you up here, escorted you formally and before all eyes, is, for a Portuguese gentleman, as good as a declaration. Anyhow—' There was a certain note in Rosita's voice, a note not to be ignored, and Clair did not ignore it.

'Anyhow—?'

'I, personally,' declared Rosita thrillingly, 'would go all the way for the man I love.' After which she closed her lips.

Clair got Rosita to her room while the silence was still on her, she felt she could not listen to any more pleas tonight.

She herself did not sleep at all. The children, she kept thinking, I never said good-bye to them. Rico, she kept grieving, I never explained. But how can I say good-bye, explain, with Gordon, dear, kind, understanding Gordon, with my ticket from Genoa to London?

But it was not to be London. Gordon, who arrived with Maria and Clair's breakfast tray the next morning, pointed this out.

'It was no use, old girl, I knew it all along but kept kidding myself. Even had Rosita not got at me last night—'

'Rosita?' she gasped.

'After you'd sent her to bed,' he grinned. 'Even then, I wouldn't have gone ahead. It wasn't just Capri and your polite enthusiasms that damned me, darling, it was – well, everything. No man, unless he was a fool, could have failed to see you were only offering a threadbare heart, and, my sweet, I am not a fool.'

'But, Gordon, I'm so unsure. I mean I know how I feel, but how can I know, even though Rosita insists it's unmistakable, how Rico feels?'

'I saw it as unmistakable, too,' Gordon said soberly.

'But if you both saw wrongly?'

'Then it's easy,' he smiled. 'You simply came down to see the girls.'

'But how?' she persisted.

'By express train, leaving twenty minutes after we disembark, which is in one hour, so you'll have to step on it, sweet.'

'But my ticket—'

'You have it in your hand.'

'Genoa to London?'

'I changed it.' There was a rueful note in Gordon's voice,

a rueful smile on his good-looking young face. 'I know when I'm beaten, Clair.' As she still stared at him he added, 'You better check.'

Clair lowered her eyes and read 'Genoa . . . Roma' through a prickling of tears.

CHAPTER NINE

THE Via Settembre was a long street. As it journeyed across Rome it changed its name several times, but where the little lane from the small *piazza* emerged it was simply Settembre ... September, and it was just as Clair had imagined, a place of old brown churches and old gnarled trees. The churches sent solid slabs of purple shadows and the trees sent frilly slats of leafy shade. It was cool and quiet, and Clair could imagine Rosita's dismay at seeing no bright boutiques.

Only the sun came brightly here between the stone walls of worship and between the thick branches of elms. Clair stood beneath one old elm and saw, with Rico's eyes, the intense green that he had seen through the *Firenzo* porthole. 'This is the only green,' he had said that day of the peak of the monsoon, 'apart from the avenue to my *palacio,* that I can liken to September Street.'

How he had loved the Via Settembre! Had stood in it in the winter and known spring!

'My spring!'

Clair echoed it, echoed Rico's voice that day.

The journey down from Genoa had seemed a lifetime ... and yet, paradoxically, it had gone too fast. She had wanted time to plan her words, rehearse them, but all the time in the world had not been time enough. She had seen none of the exquisite scenery. Never once had her eyes strayed from her hands folded in front of her, flexing, unflexing, sometimes the nails biting into her flesh.

Disembarkation had been made easy by Gordon – but it hadn't been as easy to say good-bye. Only when the train had been pulling out had Clair managed it. 'Thank you for every-thing, I'll never forget you.'

'I won't let you. When I find the right one, I'll call on you to do the same.'

His face growing blurred, then unrecognizable, then not

376

there at all.

She had not seen Rosita again ... no doubt she had met Francesco and they were now making their wedding plans.

Gordon off to London, Rosita and Francesco arranging their future, everybody doing something progressive – except Clair. She was going back.

For a while in the train the nails had bitten deeply. What am I doing? I must be mad. You don't run after a man – especially when you are uncertain about him. Not uncertain about yourself, but about him, for all Rosita's and Gordon's words. Words are so easy. But they don't establish anything. How do I know, how could I know if Rico cared?

Then there's that title of his to make things difficult. I'm an Australian girl from a little obscure island. He comes from an old, old family of an old, old country, not a new, raw land like mine.

We couldn't match. I don't understand any of his ways. Australians don't click their heels, don't kiss the hand. These gallantries are expected by the European women. Down under we would never understand.

Food, dress, outlook, temperament, everything is different, so why, *why* am I sitting in a train from Genoa to Rome?

But it had been too late then. She had burned, if not her bridges, her passage to London, behind her.

There had been nothing else she could do when she alighted at the terminal than to direct the taxi-driver to the Hotel Fiamma.

The inn had been a surprise. Clair had expected something formal, with much mahogany, dark red carpet, velvet drapes. But it was rather small and distinctly chintzy, hung in wisteria that even pushed through the window of her bedroom on the second floor.

That had been another surprise. The season was at its peak, the eternal city was full of tourists and the Fiamma was an appealing hotel, and yet there had been room for Clair. Not only room but a reserved suite.

'Senhor Montales told us to expect you, *signorina*.'

Oh, had he? had been Clair's reaction. Instead of feeling

377

pleased, she had found herself resenting him for taking her for granted. He had expected her to come to Rome, to September Street. Perhaps it was the Portuguese tradition for a woman to go all the way, as Rosita had said, to her man.

'Is the *senhor* in the hotel now?' she had asked the receptionist, who, like most Italians, understood English and spoke it well.

'No, he takes the small girls for a walk down the Via Settembre. Undoubtedly to the Trevi Fountain. It is very popular to throw coins there. If the *signorina* turns left from the *piazza* lane, then goes straight ahead . . .'

That was what Clair was doing now – between pausing to ask herself if she was quite mad or to stand and look up through the leaves of a tree.

'I'm mad. Only a fool would throw herself at a man like this, and only a very vain man would expect it. I don't like vanity. I must stop this nonsense before it's too late, before – before—'

It was then that she saw the trio just a little in front of her, three black heads reaching various heights, up to the lowest branch for Rico, up to his top button for Amalia, the next button for Juanita.

A butterfly came through the leafy haze, and Juanita, turning to watch it, saw Clair and cried out in pleasure.

The next moment the two little girls . . . Amalia as well, realized Clair happily . . . were throwing themselves on her.

'It is Clair! Dear Clair!' That was Juanita.

'Your travelling dress is quite chic.' Amalia, of course.

Rico came behind them and he was smiling, but it seemed to Clair it was a perfunctory smile.

'You are well, *senhorita*? You did not have a tiring journey?'

'Oh, Clair, wait till you hear the amazing things that Zio Rico tells us. It is as I said – remember? – Mama will marry Francesco!'

Clair glanced at Rico and he said quite unemotionally, 'My cousin telephoned from the *Firenzo* this morning.'

'She also told Zio Rico that you were coming down.'

'To look after you,' Clair said quickly – too quickly. The

378

senhor's brows rose in that old, steep manner, but he did not comment.

'It will be fun. We will live in that *castello*. I shall get to know those boys on the beach.'

'And then,' Juanita reminded him, 'there are our new papa's boys, too.'

'Fuff,' dismissed Amalia, 'six years, and five.'

'I like small boys.'

'I like big ones.'

'Hush,' said the *senhor*. 'Be quiet, you two!' He turned to Clair, and he looked concerned. 'You must be weary, child, it is quite a journey.'

'But not too tired to walk on to Trevi,' the girls begged. 'Oh, please, Clair, you are not too tired for that. It is fun, you throw in a coin so that you come back to Rome one day.'

'Assuredly I will come,' said Amalia, 'for I find the styles very good.'

'Then go now and make certain of it.' The *senhor* took a handful of coins from his pocket. 'It is down that little cobbled way, you must know, for you have done it often enough.'

'Oh, Zio Rico, can we really go alone?'

'We will be behind you, little rabbits, though not too close to spoil your spirit of adventure. Now off you go.'

'Will they be all right?' worried Clair after the girls had run ahead.

'You forget they are Italian children in Italy. They need no looking after in their own country, and Italy is their country, Clair.'

'Then I needn't have come, *senhor*, for it was because of the children that I – that I—' Her words trailed off.

He had stopped walking, and had stopped Clair with him. They stood beneath the tallest, widest elm of the lot.

The Marqués was not looking at Clair but at the tree. 'Such green . . . even in the winter you still see it in memory in the bare branches . . . the only other green to compare is the green avenue of my *pal*— a street in my town in Portugal'

'The green avenue to your *palacio*, your palace, you meant to say,' said Clair.

'You know?'

'Yes.'

'Does it make a difference — but you are laughing.' He seemed confused.

'I'm laughing because it's generally the other way about. Does it make a difference to you what I am?'

'A big difference.' Now he was more sober than she had ever seen this sober man. 'The differences of laughter, of life. Oh, Clair, little Clair, I cannot wait to parry words with you, however sweet the exchange. I love you too much, my dear.'

Rosita had said he loved her. Gordon had said it was unmistakable. The fact that he had expected her, booked a hotel room for her, underlined it all.

But his own words were what Clair had wanted, and now they sang anthems in her ears.

He was talking — talking excitedly for the grave, self-contained Enrico — telling her his plans.

'We shall be married in Portugal, darling, from the Palacio Montales.'

'What is it like, Rico?'

'Oh, big, and much mosaic set in marble, a large hall rather dim and cloistral. Baroque ceilings and fluted pillars and a lot of fretted oak. But don't let that worry you, my sweet.

'I have left its high walls — I told you — and I shall continue the business I now carry on — with a difference.'

'A difference?' she queried.

'My wife shall accompany me. The East, the West, the old countries, the new. And then, ever so often, back to Portugal again. But only if that pleases you, Clair.'

'Pleases me? But it's your home, Rico.'

'It still makes no difference if it is not your pleasure to come.'

'You would put me before — Oh, Rico!'

She was looking around her, at the violet slabs of shadow, at the frilly slats of shade, at the bright sun beween. It would be like this at the *palacio*, green and more green.

And when they were away from Portugal, the green would be in their hearts, for spring had begun, a spring for two, a spring that would grow into summer, do the whole lovely complete cycle. They would live. They would begin other lives. The seasons would grow into years.

But here it was where it was beginning, and Clair suddenly knew that she was not dreaming but *being*, for never in a dream would Senhor Montales kiss her in public, never the Marqués, yet that was what he was doing now.

A Victoria clopped by, the driver cracking his whip when he saw the lovers, for Rome loves lovers and always recognizes them.

The children were turning the corner of the cobbled lane once more, they had thrown their coins to assure their return.

Their voices were coming nearer. In a moment Rico and Clair would be four, not two.

'Clair!'

'Rico!'

A leaf left the big elm and drifted between them down to September Street.

NICKEL WIFE

Nickel Wife

"Wanted," the ad had said, "a female who can take it." And Sandy Lawford, used to working on isolated mining projects before her father's death, had applied.

At the Australian desert campsite she found the job ill-defined and the boss obviously displeased with her lack of feminine charm. She tried to leave immediately.

But Sandy was reminded of her signed contract and was forced to endure the taunts of Stone Wetherill, a man as hard as his name implied.

CHAPTER ONE

Two miles from the small village, which consisted only of a hotel, garage, store and post office, and bore the incredible name of Busy Acres, the meagre allotment of bitumen ran out and a stone-strewn, stick-dry track took over. Now, Sandy's driver informed her, they were back in the gibber again after the shopping centre ... shopping centre? ... brush against a mulga, he said, and it would snap off, everything was brittle and dead as old bones. Lots of people, he went on, used to say to give the gibber back to where it belongs, only they weren't saying it now, they were watching the finance columns, following the stock market, they were waiting for a pointer from the diamond drill. For when it finally came down to it, Sandy's driver, who had introduced himself as Cleve, finished, it all depended on the diamond drill.

Alexandra Lawford, looking eagerly around her, for even a sophisticated person must look eagerly around at a strange place that is to be their new home, and Sandy had never been sophisticated, nodded, then asked about a distant, rather strange white peak.

'Quartz Hill,' said Cleve. 'There are old gold workings at its foot, but it's not gold that's the boom now, eh? Hang on.' He took the jeep carefully over a very big gibber.

No, thought Sandy, it was not gold, which had a romantic sound, and which had had a small but interesting ... sometimes dramatic ... part in her previous projects, it was nickel. Nickel was the message the winds whispered now, and it was the reason she was bumping along in this rough mail waggon to the Oasis.

She smiled privately at the Oasis, just as she had smiled privately, very privately, at Busy Acres, for the owner of the hotel had been proud of his town, of his town's future. 'It only stands to reason,' he had told Sandy, 'that there has to be a pivot for the nickel, and geography must make it Busy Acres, the same as geography made B.A. the gold centre seventy years ago. There were four hotels then, and three thousand people. It's going to be the same again. The Palatial' ... that was the hotel's equally incredible name ... 'was finished before this new mining started, the wind was ready to knock what was left of it down, but now there's a second chance, it looks certain there'll be bigger and better nickel mines, and the Palatial will be IT. Look' ... he had put a plan in front of Sandy ... 'this is how I see us. Power, all facilities, proper staff, not just me and one of the boys standing around for someone to blow in. Six deep at the bar ... three, anyway, I reckon ... no parking space left outside. Busy Acres will be back where it was.'

Sandy had said she sincerely hoped so, and had taken up her bags because through the window she had seen the mail car coming down the bitumen to pick her up. Yesterday she had been flown to the nearest strip to Busy Acres, then collected there by Cleve who was the local transporter as well as the private contract mail man, then brought into the Palatial Hotel. The accommodation had been scarcely palatial, but what could you expect, the hotelier had said, without a feminine touch. He was married, but Shirley wouldn't come up to B.A. because there were no women, but that would all be over soon; there would be the nickel wives.

Sandy had needed no explanation of that; it was undoubtedly because of a nickel wife, she thought, that she was here now.

'Wanted,' the *Australian Miner* had advertised . . . the *Miner*, the *Engineering News*, the *Oil Recorder* were the only magazines that had found their way into the Lawford place and they had continued to do so after Sandy's father had died . . . 'a female who can take it.' After adding that what would have to be taken was roughness, toughness, remote locality, no entertainment, it had given a number to ring.

Sandy had rung and had learned that it was a nickel project that had advertised, which had interested her, for she had inherited her father's enthusiasm for such things. She had been pleased that the owner of the voice that answered her remembered the Professor and had believed she might do. 'For after all,' he recalled, 'you were with the Prof at the Snowy, weren't you, when it wasn't the luxury tourist attraction it is today. It wasn't easy then. I stayed with you once at Falcon's Neck, but you wouldn't remember at such a tender age.'

'Those years spoiled me for anything else,' Sandy had admitted. 'Now Dad has gone I can't see myself settling down in some suburb, going to an office. If you could assure this nickel firm that I could fit the bill—'

'No need to. Stone Wetherill left it to me entirely and you'll do. As a matter of fact, Miss Lawford, you're our only applicant. That having-to-take-it of Stone's must have put them off.'

'Stone?' Sandy had queried, accustomed through her pioneer years to apt tags. 'Because he's hard?'

'Could be.' A short laugh. 'You need to be out

there in the gibber.' – So it was the gibber! – 'But no, Stoneleigh Wetherill is his name. If you could be ready to leave next week . . .'

She certainly could be ready. The apartment Dad had leased while he made up his mind which offer he would accept next, for an esteemed geo like Dad always had offers, the confined unit that had irked him, but not . . . still with a hurt even though the doctor had forewarned her about her father . . . for long, had been due for re-letting, and Alexandra Lawford had been politely asked to make new arrangements.

'I can leave next week,' she had answered into the telephone.

She had.

In her bags had gone the wise things experienced project people pack, the able-to-take it tough jeans, the sensible shirtmakers, for the occasional social life remote places put on, the reliable flat heels.

The pilot of the smaller inland plane she had transferred to from the nearest large centre had appreciated her few light cases, and had had her up beside him to point out the country over which they had flown, the black scars the zinc and lead had left behind them, the man-made deserts where mulga and eucalypt had been eroded through overstocking, the clay pans, the salt pans . . . then the gibber.

As near to Busy Acres as the gibber would permit, though if the diamond drills came up trumps, the pilot said, there would be a first-class strip built nearer the town, Sandy was put down, and Cleve had taken her up. From Cleve's waggon she had watched the plane take off again through the upturned white plastic buckets, then she had turned her attention to the terrain around her, the same stone-strewn, stick-dry country as now, this following day.

'Why the Oasis, Cleve?' She concealed her amusement as she asked it. An oasis here!

'Stone called it that.'

She had no need to ask next: 'Why Stone?' because she knew now he was Stoneleigh Wetherill, by the sound of that 'Could be' and the short laugh when she had asked on the telephone was it because he was hard, *hard*.

The Oasis, she thought, would be one of this Stone Wetherill's sarcasms. Looking around her at the almost unbelievable bareness, she knew it would have to be sarcasm. She had heard quite a few of this man's sayings in the Palatial last night. Evidently he was held in high repute, and only a hard tough man would be so regarded in a hard tough corner like this. Oddly, that is odd for her predilection for frontier places, she did not like such men. Her own father, though always in the midst of pioneer living, had remained a gentle, quiet person.

Stone says ... Stone reckons ... Stone thinks ... Stone did ... Even the blow-ins, as the casuals were called, and there had been several last night, had known of Stone Wetherill, and had spoken with a certain caution. He would be like this country, she decided, rocky, stick-dry. He would be gibber.

'Yes, Stone called it the Oasis when he came back from a scout up top,' Cleve said.

'Up top?'

'N.T. Northern Territory.'

'Scout?'

'To see if there were any signs.'

'Signs?'

'Of it.'

'Nickel?'

'Yes,' Cleve said evasively.

'Did he find anything?'

'Lady, up here that's a question you never answer. Too many nosey parkers. The spy planes would be around the next day.'

'Spy planes?' she queried.

'They move over the drills, then sell information sheets as to who is working where. Maybe Stone did find signs, maybe not, maybe again he's keeping it all on ice until he puts this present baby to bed. All I know is that when he came back from up top he took one look at the set-up then said, "The Oasis". And it stuck.' Cleve took one hand away from the wheel to brush at a fly. 'What's it mean, anyway?' he asked naïvely. For a man who had lived all his life, he had told her, out here, had travelled no further than B.A., he could be excused that, she thought.

'It means—' she began, then stopped short. They had rounded a bend in the track, and she stared in pleasure. Before her was grass, coarse admittedly, but something that actually grew in the hopeless red earth. There was a sprinkler with water coming out of it playing on the grass. There were caravans with gardens round them. There were shrubs and young trees. There was even a large, circular, blue plastic-lined tank made into a swimming pool.

'It means *that*,' Sandy told Cleve, who had brought the waggon to a halt and was reaching for her bags and the mail.

A rangy, pleasant-faced, red-haired man was coming across the grass to meet her, his hand outstretched. He was so different from what she had imagined Stone Wetherill would be, she could hardly believe it.

'Welcome, Miss Lawford, it's great to have a second woman here.'

She had expected that 'second'. Though she had been given no details of her job she had guessed it would be mainly for female company. She had seen women in some of the projects she had visited with Dad pack their bags because they could bear it no longer without women friends. Even the hotelier's Shirley had refused to stay at Busy Acres, yet a hotel was seldom lonely.

'I'm pleased to come,' she beamed back. 'Where is the nickel wife?'

'Never been a nickel wife yet,' he grinned. He scratched his rusty head. 'But I suppose you could say a nickel intended. She's been here almost from the kick-off.' His smile faded.

'Well,' encouraged Sandy sympathetically, 'perhaps I can hurry it on for you.'

'Reckon I wouldn't want that,' he demurred at once, 'reckon once a man is trapped the missus makes him go her way, which could be right away, even back to the bright lights, not that I can see it like that here, but it does happen, doesn't it, and Stone—'

'Stone? Then *you're* not—'

'Stone Wetherill, the boss? Lor', no. Nor a geo-chemist. Nor a geo-physicist. Any geo you name. Nor a diamond driller. Nor a rigger. Nor anything, really, though camp foreman will do. I'm the man who changed this dust bowl into something worth living in, at least I like to think it is. Stone thought so, too, when he came back from up top, so he called it what it is.'

'But I don't understand, Mr.—?'

'Call me Rusty.'

'The ad I answered was for a female who can take it. But here ...' She looked around in frank admiration.

'That would be Stone,' laughed Rusty of the ad ... but pleased with her praise. 'And that wording was certainly called for before he went scouting up top and I got to work while he was away. Why not, I thought. Even though you may not be here long you may as well put down roots.'

'Not here long?'

'Well, that's the usual nickel song.'

'You mean if what you're after is not there you move off?'

'In a way.' Cagily.

'In a way?'

'May as well tell you,' he shrugged, 'seeing you're going to be one of the family. It's like this: not all the nickel moves back and forth, hither and thither, are because of that, because of the rock. Some of the moves are to fool the spies.'

'I heard of them from Cleve. But surely the big reliable names that are said to be involved—'

'There's big reliable money, too,' Rusty reminded her grimly, 'and money puts a different slant on things. Take me. I never knew a daisy from a daffodil, but I reckoned the two hundred dollars I was getting ... you'll find you're paid well, too, they don't skimp on the nickel ... encouraged me to do more than I was asked. Though I suppose it was that sense of being in the start of something big and important and national, really, that did it.' He smiled a little shyly, slightly embarrassed, then went back to what the Oasis once was.

'Yes, you needed to be able to take it all right,' he said. 'Still need to now in a way. You wait till you see our dust. Then we recorded one hundred and thirty degrees once, and that's warm, I'd say. Also there's no life unless you go into B.A., and you saw the life there.'

'Yet evidently the nickel wife, I mean the nickel intended always could take it,' said Sandy of the 'kick-off' days. She felt a little jealous of this other woman, this first woman making her the second woman, who had beaten her to the tough part of the sequence.

Rusty did not answer that at once. He looked to one of the caravans, evidently the woman's caravan, then looked at Sandy. Up and down. Down, then up.

'Wasn't her idea to have you,' he said a little uneasily, then looked sorry he had spoken.

'I don't suppose it was Mr. Wetherill's, either,' said Sandy with determined cheerfulness, for she did not care much for Rusty's implied absence of enthusiasm on the intended's part, 'not after he found what you had done to the place. The way I see it is this: Mr. Wetherill wanted someone to help out when the going was bad, but now it's good, as it certainly is good . . .' She gave a rueful laugh and shrugged. 'However, it was too late, I'd answered the ad then and now I'm here. But don't worry, Rusty, I've had lots of project wives . . . I mean,' she amended, 'project intendeds. We've always got on. Can I see the pool?'

'It's only a large tank really.' Rusty was veering her quite purposefully away from it. 'It doubles up as a reserve for the drills, if needed.'

'Its very presence,' admired Sandy, 'would be balm to the mind out here.'

She started across, then, aware that Rusty actually

didn't want her to go, halfway there she stopped. Perhaps one of the men . . .

'I'm sorry,' she apologized.

'It's not that,' blurted Rusty, 'it's – Miss Janice. She mightn't like me presenting you while she was in the swim.'

'Then of course not,' agreed Sandy, trying to make allowances for such niceties in a place like this but secretly finding it hard.

She turned back again – but not before she had had a quick glimpse of a young woman lounging on a rubber float in the middle of the pool. She was an exceptionally beautiful young woman, even a brief glance assured that, black-haired, black-eyed, for all the burning strength of the sun very white-skinned. Sandy, who freckled until the freckles met at last and formed a tan, envied that gardenia skin.

For a moment the two girls . . . Sandy was twenty-two, this girl would be slightly older, Sandy judged . . . looked at each other. It was a fleeting look . . . yet sufficient. Sandy turned back to the foreman.

'A pity,' she said, 'that Stone Wetherill hadn't seen the Oasis before he advertised, and had a second thought. I have a feeling I'm not needed here.'

'I reckon,' proffered Rusty encouragingly, but not explaining why he said it, 'he still could have cancelled you out even then, yet didn't. Anyway, the rest of us will want you.' He crinkled up his eyes in a friendly smile. 'There's a dearth of women here.'

'Thank you.' But Sandy still felt uncertain, her small, very open face, not helped by the short-cropped, un-framing, junior boy hair, looking very young and vulnerable. Rusty, touched by her, obviously searched for more words, then thankfully gave up the search.

From one of the caravans a man had emerged and crossed over to them, and if Sandy had judged Rusty as rangy, this man was the highest mountain of all. He was broad to match, yet still hard – resilient, whip-cord, tough. He was near Red Indian-skinned, almost the same colour as the unusual red-stoned ring he wore. That ring stood out quite oddly, for he definitely was not a ring-wearing man, she judged. She knew before he reached her that he would have those narrowed, far-seeing, intensely blue inland eyes. Wrong, really, she thought a little foolishly, he should have gibber colour, whatever that was. For undoubtedly he would be the gibber she had christened him.

'The boss,' Rusty was introducing, 'and Stone, this is—'

'I think,' came in Sandy, 'Mr. Wetherill already knows.'

The boss did not answer this, he said coolly, taking out the makings of a cigarette and whispering it between large brown palms, 'Presumably you have a handle, Miss Lawford?'

'Handle?'

'Name.'

'You know it,' she reminded him.

'Your first name. Christian name.'

'A.' That would do him, she thought.

He still waited, and Sandy said irritably, 'Sandy Lawford. Alexandra. Only I'm never called it.'

'I see.' He turned to Rusty. 'You and your dearth of women, you've landed yourself another boy.'

'It's a nickname, of course,' Sandy said angrily. She was aware of her pants suit, a very utilitarian rust-brown pants suit, not at all the becoming feminine version now being worn, the gear she had considered suitable for the dusty journey out, she was aware of her cropped hair, her tanned skin— Aware of that brilliant gardenia beauty now sitting up on the float and watching with amusement.

'I see, Alexandra,' he said.

'There's no need for that!'

'Don't be ridiculous, you can't be called Miss out here.'

'At all the other projects—'

'Ah, a project lady.' He was lighting the rolled cigarette.

'I was Sandy,' she finished.

'It will be Alexandra. If you require a reason hark back to what I just told Rusty. "You've landed yourself another boy." Sandy is a boy. These diamond drillers eat holes out of the ground, but they'd sooner eat out of a woman's hand.'

'If you think I've come to—'

'I don't think. Calm down. Some of them are the gentlest of men, some are not, but all are better for a bit of femininity around the place, and' ... looking her significantly up and down ... 'seeing your correct name is all you have to offer in that line—'

'How dare you!'

'Your gear,' he pointed out.

'Makes sense.'

'Your hair.'

'I always wear it short.'

'That short, *boy*?'

'Most boys I know wear it longer.'

'Not here. It would get caught in something— Look, Alexandra, what I'm trying to say is—'

'Is you didn't get what you expected. Sorry about that, but I *am*, you know. Do you want biological

398

proof?' Her cheeks were flaming red.

He was laughing softly at her, his eyes pinpoints of amused deep blue. 'What would you say if I said yes?'

'You're beyond the limit! Because you forget to cancel the ad, you're taking it out on me.'

'What ad?'

'The one for a female who could take it.'

'Oh, that.' An easy shrug. 'Yes, I did forget.'

'Then you don't have to accept me.' She looked around for her bags.

'Wait a minute,' he said. 'I forgot to *alter the words,* that's all. I still needed the woman, and that's why I retained the ad. I needed her here before I went north and I needed her even more when I came back. Because with these conditions' . . . he spread his large hands . . . 'most certainly the first lady would stay on.'

'But naturally you would want that.' A pause. Quite a long pause. 'Oh – I see. There has to be – well—' Sandy reddened.

'I think propriety,' he said drily, 'is the word you're fumbling for. Do you always fumble like that? Haven't you a dictionary?'

She asked pertly, ignoring his criticism, quite recovered now, 'A need for propriety in a latitude where relaxation surely is the keynote!'

'Certainly, Alexandra,' he said coolly, 'that's how I like it. And now if you've finished adding up my morals I'll show you your caravan. It's no use looking around for Cleve, he's left, and he won't be here for a week.'

She *had* been looking and at his words she wheeled round.

'A week! A week before he's back! But I don't care

399

for this job, Mr. Wetherill. Can you please drive me into B.A.?'

'I can't, and none of my men can. All our conveyances right now are out on the investigation area.'

'Then I'll find them.'

'You won't, though.' He smiled blandly. 'We've all our drills and magnetometers out there, and the way we've concealed them from aerial survey, on foot, and it would have to be on foot, you wouldn't have a chance in Hades. Anyway, you'd die of heat before you got a mile. My representative told me you were a cold country girl. The Snowy, wasn't it? The Takeover? Savage Creek? Roaring Billy? Well, it can get cold in the desert, too, at night.'

'I won't be experiencing it. When will they be in? The geos and drillers, I mean?'

'In four days.'

'Then can I telephone?'

'No.'

'Pedal radio?'

'Reserved for emergency.'

'This is an emergency.'

'Like broken legs,' he continued as if she hadn't spoken. As he had been talking he had been edging her nearer the caravan that evidently had been set aside for her.

'This is you,' he said unceremoniously. 'Rusty will be along to see if you're lacking anything.'

'Like a dinner gown, you mean.'

'Heard of them, have you?' A maddening smile. 'If you feel like a dip before chow, just tumble in. Actually the water is for the project, but right now we're doing fine from our last rain, there's no restrictions so go right

ahead. As a matter of fact it saves the shower-house. A
portable one. Rusty will show you where that is. Please
abide by the notice: "Do not take away – men showering". It would be inconvenient as well as embarrassing. However, I don't think you would be able to
remove it. You're not much of a size.'

'You should have stipulated that and – and the femininity in the ad.'

'I should,' he agreed, and opened the caravan
door.

She climbed the several steps behind him, went in,
and as he moved back shut the door. She heard him
moving away, and the direction sounded like the direction of the tank pool where the intended . . . Miss
Janice, wasn't it? . . . lazed on a float. A white gardenia
in a pond.

Angrily Sandy made sure the door was fastened,
then she turned and looked around.

Rusty had painted everything cream and blue, the
blue was distinctly bright, but it was cheerful. He had
tacked a magazine flower illustration on the wall for a
picture and put a jam-jar of Salvation Jane on the
table to add a welcoming touch. The touch touched
Sandy. The camp foreman was making a real effort,
not like Mr. Nickel who seemed to deal only in words
as hard as himself. If it had not been that there had
been no way to get into B.A. she would have left at
once. But the Salvation Jane . . . strictly a weed, but a
pretty one . . . did something to Sandy. She determined
there and then to help Rusty raise a garden between
her other activities . . . if she stopped. Though certainly
she wouldn't stop. Not with a boss like that gibber. She
felt a little regretful about the garden, though. She

recalled her joy when she had persuaded up her first freesia in the few inches between their matchbox unit and the cliff-edge at the early Snowy diggings. She longed to achieve something now. Had she stopped she would have, too; she had sympathetic fingers. As one of the Snowy migrant workers once had commended . . . she had been a child at the time: 'How did you know you had to talk to flowers, *meine Liebe*? Most Australians, even the big ones, don't.'

'Most' would certainly include Stone Wetherill, a typical rock man, no buds and frondage there. Touching the Salvation Jane, she realized that the intense blue was the same as the intense blue of Mr. Nickel's eyes and she stepped back. She wondered had she stopped if she would have been required to work for him . . . office or something of the sort . . . or work for his intended— She had nearly said wife.

Intended was a cosy old-fashioned description, certainly Rusty's, never surely the gibber's. She could not imagine Mr. Wetherill introducing, 'This is my intended.' The thought of that made her giggle.

The caravan was only to sleep in, she saw; there was no provision for meals. She took out and hung up her clothes, which occupied her only a few minutes. Her upbringing had made her organized and she travelled light. Too light? She could not help wondering this as she looked at the small van wardrobe still almost vacant after she had depleted her bags. But perish the thought. She had not come here to dress up, she had come to work.

What work?— That is, hurriedly, until she left the moment any form of transport got back from the diggings and she could get in to B.A. Right away from here.

Well . . . a shrug to the wardrobe . . . everything she could do had already been done for her in this van. She would go and find out what made the place tick.

There was nothing to show, she thought, as she walked round the camp, to mark why *here* particularly a centre should have been formed. In her experience of projects a sufficiently high location to insure drainage yet not too high to be blown away had been the goal of the camp organizers, but that could not be the case here, for as far as the eye could see stretched flat barren terrain. Gibber terrain, yet in odd patches the gibber completely ceased and the red earth, that unbelievably vivid red earth of the Australian inland, showed through. She looked down to the grass coverage beneath her, meagre so far but still grass, and decided that the Oasis had had its beginning at this particular spot because at least one would not be walking on stones. The break from the gibber extended as far as the camp extended, so that must be the reason . . . unless Rusty had cleared it all up himself.

She laughed at that. It would have been a mammoth effort to shift those layers of stones. Rusty laughed, too, as he joined her in her tour, and she asked him if he had wheeled the gibber away from the site in a wheelbarrow.

'No. Nature did the clearing. When Stone saw the earth break, he said "This is it." '

'But I can't see any mining activity near the camp.' Sandy screwed up her eyes and looked out on the red landscape.

'There were a few indications around here,' Rusty said, 'so as well as earth beneath our feet instead of wall-to-wall rubble, the location for a camp was considered fairly central. If you go over the hill there' . . .

hill? ... 'you'll find a line of red flags marching to kingdom come. Well' – a grin – 'four miles, anyway.'

'A grid line?'

'I see you know a bit about it. Yes, a reference for geological work. Look' ... with pride ... 'this is an orange tree that's taken on. Reckon I'll be making marmalade if only we can stop here long enough.'

'Are you the camp cook, too?'

'Oh, no, Andy's that. But Andy's out with the boys just now. When he's there I manage in here. Then when he's back again I do the fancy extras.'

'Like marmalade?'

'More likely something to go with the steak. I hope, Miss—'

'Sandy.' She said that determinedly in spite of Mr. Wetherill's 'Alexandra'.

'I hope, Sandy, you like steak. Because here it's all steak except occasionally when we have steak instead,' he grinned.

'It sounds red-blooded, anyway. Why the steak?'

'Pastoralists to the left and the right, and all good friends. Naturally so, the team often finds water for them, and that pleases the cattle men. Also, although we're pretty cagey we don't mind sharing some of our news with these blokes, and I reckon quite a few of them are in the mineral boom.'

'From your satisfied voice, Rusty, I reckon you could be, too,' Sandy smiled.

'Could be,' he nodded. 'Well, seen enough? How about a cuppa?'

'It's what I really came out for,' Sandy admitted. Like all project people she had a tremendous respect for the tea ... or coffee when it was an American project ... break. 'I wonder,' she asked, 'could I have a pot and a cup in the caravan, seeing the light is laid on.'

'No power points as yet,' said Rusty, 'we have to go lightly and not overload. But you've only a few yards to the cookhouse, and there the tucker's always ready. Always a bubbling kettle.' He led the way.

The cookhouse was really another caravan . . . no, not a caravan, a bus. A double-decker bus. Cooking downstairs, some tables up top. Sandy looked long at the bus, thinking at first it had borrowed the red colouring of the desert. Then she clapped her hands.

'A London bus!' Sydney's were green; a few blue beginning to creep in.

'That's right. Belonged to a party of young 'uns who drove it all the way from England across Europe and Asia. But the going got too much for Matilda' . . . he showed Sandy the bus's name . . . 'after she left the Alice and tasted Aussie horror stretches. Stone bought it from the group. It's been very useful, I can tell you, though I'm thumbs down on that upstairs lark.' He scowled.

'You mean eating upstairs?'

'She – Miss Janice – started that. Oh, not for the mob, of course, just for—' He shrugged.

'Then where do the mob eat?'

'Mostly outside. They'd sooner their chow cafeteria style. But not—' A disgruntled glance to the upper floor of the converted bus.

He began pouring tea, black with a plentiful presence of leaves, holding up a jug of reconstituted milk. Unperturbed, for she had been practically reared on this unadvised liquid, unadvised, anyway, for the very young as she had been young then, Sandy leaned over and took a spoonful of the coarse, unrefined sugar. 'It

405

doesn't get so lumpy,' Rusty explained of it.

A big slab of project cake . . . that's what they had always called the yellow yard-long block of vanilla-flavoured sawdust . . . and she was back again in her memories with Dad. At Falcon's Neck with its soaring mountains and its pre-fab matchbox houses. At the Takeover with its thick afforestation and its canvas accommodation. At Savage Creek in dormitories. At—

Suddenly . . . unwillingly but inevitably, inevitable because she really had known no other scenes after her mother had died when she was very small and her father had taken her with him than these frontier ones, because instinctively she loved them, Sandy knew she was happy.

She drank more tea, then told Rusty she'd explore some more. She left the cookhouse behind, then circled the other caravans, finally walked to the 'hill' Rusty had pointed out, only some three or four hundred yards away. She had smiled when he had said hill, but walking to it she realized it was a higher level, very little higher but in the burning heat and stumbling over the gibbers it might have been a lesser Mount Everest.

When she reached the hill, marked by a larger collection of gibbers than what Nature had flung around, she looked out on the red landscape and saw the line of red flags Rusty had told her about . . . in such a red terrain yellow would have been better she thought . . . marching as far as the eye could see. This would be the grid line, set out by surveyors to act as reference points for geological work.

She turned her eyes from the grid line and looked at the rest of this particular corner of the world. A very big corner, it stretched and stretched. And the longer you looked at it the less featureless it became, You started to see hills. Not mere rises like this one on which she stood, but red and purple ones, rocks sticking out of them like bare bones, and catching the glittering sun. A sun that sparkled down from a sky of heraldic blue. Not one whisper of a cloud. Just blue. Very blue. It's a blue world, she thought, in spite of all the red. Blue sky. A jam-jar of blue Salvation Jane in my caravan that's painted cream and blue. And that man's, that boss's blue eyes.

She turned quickly back, feeling a little trapped, trying to think of getting into Busy Acres again, from there to some other place than here, for she certainly would not stop here, she didn't like it. *She wasn't going to like it.* She liked mountains. And dams to be cradled in them. Causeways over bubbling water. She liked afforestation. Anything but gibber desert like this with a gibber boss to order you around. Anyway, who wanted such terrain? Who needed it? Only nickel men who lost no time in getting out of it as soon as they had found what they were after and cashed in on their find. Then they got out.

This was what she kept telling herself as she stumbled back over the stones; she had to say it, because already her traitorous heart was saying something else, that heart that, like it or not and she certainly didn't like it, had already embraced this rough, tough place. She was remembering unwillingly how one of the new boys on the Takeover had said of the timbered country they were working on that he didn't take to it here, that he couldn't see far enough. She felt like that now, as though she was seeing far enough for the first time in her life, and she tried to fight the feeling. Like a place like this? Never. She hurried, stumbled, fell, scrambled up, hurried again. She was unbearably hot by the time she got to the camp, and she made for her caravan with one urgent purpose in mind, climbed at once into her swimsuit, then crossed to the converted tank, every bit of her hot and yearning for cool impact.

The pool was empty, thank goodness, and it proved quite delightful. The large circular galvanized receptacle had been lined in blue plastic that made the water, already blue from the sky, a deeper blue still. Almost forgetmenot. She put her toe into it and found it more refreshing than she had thought with that hot sun beaming down on it.

She dived in.

Down there ... what it lacked in circumference it made up for in depth ... in the sparkling depths she did not hear the second impact on the water. The first she knew of Stone Wetherill were his eyes only inches from hers. She saw his water-waving grin.

She did not smile back. A good water girl, she was still not this good, not good enough to stop down too long to exchange smiles with another swimmer. Anyway, she had no smile to exchange with him.

She began to surface. He impeded her by swimming over and under her. He did it several times, and it was quite a few seconds before she spluttered to the top. She was out of breath and she was annoyed.

'I might have drowned!' she said angrily as he surfaced, too.

'I wouldn't have done it had I not seen that you knew what you were about. I really was accustoming you to what you'll undoubtedly get when the boys get back from the diggings, that is after they've recovered from the imposition of having to wear trunks. You'll be dive-bombed. You'll be pulled down, pushed in, made one of the polo team. If you splutter like you're sputtering now, duly resuscitated. Are you experienced in the kiss of life?'

'There's no need for any rehearsal of that,' she said coldly as she swam to the side and hauled herself up. It was quite a big haul, a man-size haul, and he had to give her a hitch. Furiously, and ungracefully, she knew, she struggled over the edge on her stomach. She heard him laughing softly and hatefully behind her, and righted herself quickly to see him lift himself with remarkable ease for such a big man from the water.

'About that imposition of trunks,' he said, 'I think you should make a note that besides not removing the shower tent while men are showering, you should whistle before you take a dip.'

'No need to instruct me, I won't be here.'

'In the pool?'

'*Here*. As soon as a conveyance is available I'll be leaving, Mr. Wetherill.'

He leaned over to his towelling robe flung carelessly by the tank pool and took out paper and makings. He performed that previous ritual of shaping and rolling. Only when he was licking the edges of the cigarette paper together did he look at her. He kept on looking while he lit up. He puffed out a blue wave of smoke, then spoke at last.

'Reckon,' he said, 'you never read the small print. You, a project girl!'

'There was no contract. There was nothing to sign. I mean ...' Her voice trailed off. All she had put her name to had been a paper that she had thought was a travel warrant; the man who had accepted her on behalf of Stone Wetherill being an old compatriot of

Dad's it hadn't seemed necessary to go into details. She sat vexed and shamed. This was the first thing you urged upon a project employee, to read the small print, but she, who should have known better, even though such things had been Dad's concern, for she had just tagged along, had not practised what was preached.

'How – how long?' she asked. She meant for what duration of time was she legally bound to stop.

'Six months.'

'He – Mr. Winslow never told me six months.'

'Had you bothered to look at the contract you would have seen that it was written there.'

'But why? *Why?*'

'I like things done properly,' he answered.

'Not that. Why did you want me?'

'Not you particularly,' he reminded her.

'You wanted someone, otherwise you wouldn't have advertised.'

'I wanted quite a few, as a matter of fact,' he said coolly.

'A few? But the ad said: "Wanted: Female". Singular.'

'Presumably you wouldn't be the only female to read that,' he reminded her succinctly.

'But the only one who answered,' she flashed. When there was no comment, rather a pointed no comment, she considered moodily, she asked, 'Why did you want quite a few.'

'There are a few men here.'

'Were you intending starting a matrimonial agency?' she asked impertinently.

She knew from his thinned lips that he had not missed the impertinence, but he answered seriously, 'I believe in balance. I'm not one of those stern bosses

410

who decree men only, women stay out. I believe any camp is the better for normal living.'

'Male and female created He them,' said Sandy.

He looked at her sharply, but she was too quick for him, she returned his gaze with an innocent gaze of her own.

'How old are you?' he asked abruptly. 'You look like a boy of sixteen.'

'I'm a woman of twenty-two. It must be my hair.'

'Lack of,' he came in. He exhaled. 'Anyway,' he resumed, 'my scheme didn't bear fruit.'

'Except me.'

'Except you.'

'And you still want me?'

'I said so when you arrived.'

'Oh, yes, propriety.'

'Don't be a fool,' he said, annoyed. 'Do I look the kind who would demand that?'

'You said it yourself.'

'*Do I look the kind?*'

'I don't know your kind.'

He eyed her coolly. 'Care to discover?'

'I hardly think female-one would approve. Look' . . . before he could comment on that . . . 'Look, Mr. Wetherill—'

'Stone. You can't stand on ceremony out here.'

'Then you can't call me Alexandra.'

'I was hoping to.' A sigh. 'I was hoping for a woman.'

'Are we to go through all that again?'

'No – Sandy.' He shrugged his defeat – something, she guessed shrewdly, he did not encounter much. He asked, 'You were saying?'

'Stone' . . . she had to gulp and he saw the gulp and

grinned . . . 'What am I to do here?'

'What can you do?'

'The usual woman things.' She went brick-red and this time he laughed outright.

'Sorry, kid, I'll give it to you straight, no more baiting. What I said about a mixed camp was true, but it hasn't come off. Not yet. Perhaps it's just as well in a way, life to date is much harder here; in spite of Rusty's "oasis" it's tougher than even the toughest of our gang has ever experienced. Once the boys leave the camp for the nickel traps they're in the gibber, and—' Again he gave a shrug. 'They're a good mob, and they stick it, so I try to help by making the necessary term a mere three months. I'm proud to say they've stopped twenty-three.'

'Three months,' pounced Sandy, 'yet I get six months.'

'You would be in the Oasis, not in the blistering desert. Let me tell you about that desert. Rusty likes to quote us once reaching one hundred and thirty degrees here, but out there *nearly all the time* it's around one hundred and fifteen. The corrugated tin walls of any huts we find time to erect glow, the roof if you touched it would burn your fingers to the bone. Under canvas you're in a turkish bath. The only way to cool off is to jump into baths that are carted along. Not exactly Olympic size,' he laughed. 'Still, they help. At night stretchers have to be pulled out into the open for air. And you complain about their three months!'

'I complain about my six months.' A pause. 'What are they doing there?'

'What do you think?'

'Oh, I know they're looking for carbonated rock—'

He raised his brows at that, but he did not say as

Rusty had of her grid line that she seemed to know something about it. He must have mentally recorded it, though, for later he remarked—

'They're looking for signs of nickel,' he said shortly now. 'Signs of anything else likely.' He grinned. 'They should be called the likely lads.'

'I see,' she nodded.

He had finished the cigarette, but he did not roll another.

'The bugle will ring for tucker fairly soon.

'Are you putting on your dinner suit?'

'I will, if you can produce something else than trews.'

'You're beaten, then. I have two dresses.'

'One: a shirtwaist with buttons. One: a shirtwaist with a tie. The first brown, the second navy blue.'

She could have cried with rage. She had exactly that. It was incredible. Even the tie on the navy was correct. Those dresses had seemed so suitable when she had packed them, so—

'At least, though, it will be a skirt.' He got to his feet and leaned forward to help Sandy up.

'You haven't told me what I'm to do,' she reminded him.

'Just now I feel like telling you to dry up.'

'The dishes?'

'Smart, aren't you? You could try that, but when the gang get in they attend to their own.'

'As well as eating cafeteria style. Rusty said—'

'Rusty says too much. I'll chew over your chores, Sandy, inform you later. By the way, was that carbonated rock of yours just a stab in the dark?'

'Of course not!' indignantly.

'Then something from an article you've read?'

'My father was Professor Lawford.'

'I'm aware of that, but it doesn't mean you inherited any brains.'

'You are—'

'Impossible. We've had all that. I was just asking, that's all. There's the bugle now. Don't bother about the dinner gown after all. Rusty isn't such a good cook, Andy's our one for tucker, and if you're not there when it's on it's ruined.'

He said the last to air. Sandy had taken the bugle seriously. It was something she had learned in her project days, you always obeyed the cook on the dot.

Besides, she was hungry.

CHAPTER TWO

JANICE said, 'Steak!'

They were sitting on the top deck of the bus at a small table – only the three of them. Rusty, after carrying up the essentials, had disappeared to eat his own meal downstairs. Probably by now he knew that whatever he took to the upper deck would not be the right thing, so wisely ate alone. Already Sandy had gone down twice for something Janice suddenly fancied.

'Steak,' deplored Janice, but Sandy noted that for all her small, bored, delicate forkfuls she made a good inroad. As for herself, she could have wolfed it. It tasted entirely different from town steak. It needed no embellishment.

'Of course,' said Stone Wetherill when she remarked this, Janice meanwhile looking pityingly at Sandy's unmistakably robust appetite, 'no cellophane has ever encased it. It's straight from the hoof.'

'Ugh!' said Janice, still making the dainty but telling inroads.

Sandy tried not to be so noticeably appreciative and to avoid Stone Wetherill's amused glance. What a disgustingly healthy pig she must seem compared to the gardenia girl!

She could have amused herself over Janice's clothes, for they were the trews Stone Wetherill had disparaged. But she was deprived of that amusement, for they were also trews of a very different persuasion – flowing satin culottes, as feminine as Janice herself. Beside them Sandy's own skirts . . . the brown skirt to the brown buttoned shirtwaist, and he had raised a reminding brow at that ... looked almost boy's garb.

There was beer with the steak, and Janice pouted prettily at Stone.

'Always beer!'

'It's the only drink for out here.'

'I would like,' said Janice dreamily, 'a lemon sole and a Chablis.' She looked up at Stone through long lashes, so long that Sandy ... uncharitably ... decided they must be false. 'Candlelight and soft music,' Janice added.

'One day,' smiled Stone with a tolerance that maddened Sandy. If *she* had said that. . . .

He not only said the pleasant thing, he put out a pleasant hand and patted Janice's shoulder. Janice almost purred, or so Sandy considered the near noise that went with that cat-who-got-the cream look. The girl flicked a sidelong glance at Sandy.

'No dessert?' asked Janice. 'Not that it matters, it's always something steamed.'

'Project Pud,' nodded Sandy knowledgeably. 'I like it.'

'I think,' said Janice sweetly, 'you like food.'

You couldn't answer back sweetness, so Sandy just sat and thought things. Why was this girl here was part of what she thought ... that is, not counting the obvious reason. She was certainly beautiful, and men are clay when there is beauty, but somehow she could not imagine Stone Wetherill as clay. He was deeply interested in Janice, though. That was unmistakable. Every few moments he looked across at her and smiled. Often he touched her shoulder or her hand, and the touch was gentle.

'Can I find you a sweet?' Sandy asked. She offered because Stone was being attentive again and for some mad reason it irritated her. 'Perhaps a tin of fruit—'

'I thought of a crêpe suzette, but one of your cigarettes will do, Stone.' Janice smiled across to the man. 'Next to my Turkish, your specially rolled are best.'

'Thanks, Janice, it must be the flavour of my fingers. Sandy, can I persuade you to taste my fingers?'

'No. I mean – no, thank you.'

'I wash them,' he said mildly.

Sandy said only a little short of truculently, 'I don't smoke.'

'Well, that's something,' said Janice, fixing her eyes on Sandy's empty plate. It was too much. Sandy got up and collected the dishes.

'I'll wash up.'

'Dry up was my suggestion.' It was so low and non-committal that it missed Janice, but Sandy burned. She stamped downstairs to find Rusty already on the washing-up chore so that her job was drying up after all.

After that, the way it is in the higher Australian latitudes, especially in the desert, the night came instantly. One moment there was brilliant sunlight, the next moment it was dark. But what a night! Sandy had thought she had given her heart to Snowy nights, cold, clear, pale, the moon and stars cut out with silver scissors, but here night blossomed. You felt if you stood on tiptoe you could take down one of those star-flowers, fold your arms round a fat moon.

'There's a common-room.' Janice and Stone had come down the steps, and Stone addressed Sandy. 'It's actually several caravans grouped together and joined by an elevated walk. The men read or write there or have a game of chess. You' ... magnanimously ... 'would be in bounds.'

The magnanimity annoyed Sandy. She said, 'Thanks, I'll have an early night.'

'It will be very early,' he commented. 'The nights here are as dark at eight as your nights were in the small a.m.'

'I'll still have an early night.'

'I'll see you across.'

'I'll be all right.' She started off before he could put that big hand that had been patting Janice's shoulder under her elbow – and fell over one of the new shrubs.

Stone came forward at once and said, 'I hope to Betsy nothing's happened,' and bent over the shrub. Infuriated, Sandy darted off again, and this time fell over her own shadow – or so he said, catching her up, and delivering the aged joke very heavy-handedly as he steadied her.

'Are you always so clumsy?' he inquired.

'Yes. I drop plates. I burn toast. I spill milk. I fumble.'

'Annoyed, aren't you?'

'Nothing of the sort! I'm – I'm—'

'Yes?' She could see him grinning at her in the more-than-darkness. For some reason she suddenly had to laugh back at this hateful man.

'I'm not annoyed,' she admitted, 'I'm furious'.

'Good on you.' He patted *her* shoulder. 'I hate half measures. I also like honesty. Here's home now. In the cupboard drawer you'll find a torch, a very necessary piece of equipment out here. Always take it with you at night. You should have brought it over when you came across to dinner.'

'And saved you the trouble of bringing me back,' she nodded.

'As well as maiming Rusty's plant.'

'Have I?'

'I think it will survive, you're not much weight.' He opened the caravan door and switched on the light. 'Don't be afraid if the warrigals howl.'

'I won't, but are there dingoes here?'

'Sometimes.'

'I thought there was a kind of fence.'

'That's Queensland, and it's thousands of miles long, not a kind of fence.'

'Sorry.'

He accepted that. 'All the same there is a fence ... kind of ... here. But we're in the part that keeps the other part intact. Or so it's hoped. Apart from the exploratory mining and the opal fields, it's mostly pastoral here, cattle variety. No sheep. So we're on the dingo side, you could say, for it's the sheep that the dingo is after. See?'

She nodded, then put one hand on the door, waiting for him to go.

He took his time.

'Tomorrow I'll have worked something out for you, Sandy.'

She nodded again.

Still he did not go. Almost she could have taken it that he did not want to go, but then for her age of twenty-two she was rather inexperienced in such things. She had made so many moves with Dad, never putting down roots, never beginning close associations, that she had never ... well ... When she had learned a little, always the opposite necessary character had been a different nationality from her own for the reason of the remote background. There had been Karl, the young German at—. Then Antonio. Then—

'Why are you looking at me like that?' he demanded unexpectedly.

'I wasn't . . . I mean . . . Good night, Mr. – good night, Stone.' She shut the door definitely. For she *had* been looking at him, and she had been thinking: 'I've had very few Australian male acquaintances, in fact this is the first Australian male I've really properly encountered, but that's the way in project life.'

The first Australian . . . tough as they come . . . nickel dedicated. And already claimed. Well, she's welcome, Sandy said aloud, undressing quickly and getting into bed.

It was a very comfortable bed. Coolness had come with the darkness, and the temperature was just right for sleep. Why then couldn't she sleep? Was it because this was the first time she had been out on a project without Dad? No, she had come now to accept Dad as gone on. To be glad that he had had no lingering illness to stop him doing the things he loved and lived to do, those careful assiduous geo things in high places, in dangerous places, in distant places. Dear old Professor, you had a full life, she thought. No, it was not Dad, it was – it was—

The desert? She had got up now to stand by the little window and stare out at velvet obscurity. It was all plush out there, but . . . a smile . . . if you walked on it, that is walk beyond the camp confines, you would find the plush-hard gibber that tripped you up, bruised your feet. Yet seen like this it had almost a faerie quality, as though you could lift up your skirts and dance over its softness. She looked up at the extravagant sky, for extravagant was the only adjective. *Too* deep blue.

Too starry. *Too* much gold to the moon.

She knew she loved it.

She went back to bed, but half an hour afterwards she admitted he had been right . . . as usual? . . . and she had been wrong. It was too early to sleep. Perhaps a book . . . There might be a stray one in the common-room, for she had none herself. If she pulled over her dress . . . she was in a shortie nightie . . . and took the torch and went carefully across . . .

She did it successfully, no stumbling this time. But she did not go into the common-room for a book. Through a window some yards from the group of caravans with their connecting ways she saw Stone and Janice sitting closely together. It had to be close, for his arm to be around the gardenia girl like that.

Sandy went silently back, the torch held low, only lighting what was strictly needed to see her to her caravan again. Once there she went straight to bed, no looking up again at the night sky, no staring out at the velvet obscurity. Anyway, it was all rock, all gibber, all desert.

. . . Some time, hours after, she slept.

She awoke early, even though it had taken a long time for her to drop off. She pulled on her dressing gown and ran across Rusty's lawn to the shower-house painted: 'Do not take away – men showering.' The portable three by three, surely no bigger, was in use; someone's voice singing above the splash of the water proclaimed that. She supposed she could take a plunge in the tank pool instead, but she felt she needed soaping. So she waited.

Stone Wetherill came out in the towelling gown he had used merely to carry his makings to the pool yesterday, for he hadn't bothered to put the gown on. His black hair was slicked back. He seemed more Red Indian than ever.

'No, don't go in.' He stopped her. 'I'll find you a dry spot.' He turned and lifted up the shower-house and deposited it some yards away. 'It's all yours, Sandy. Don't forget to sing.'

'Sing?'

'How otherwise does anyone know it's occupied?'

'You could hang out a sign,' she suggested.

'Where?'

He was right. The instruction not to take away took up all of the small space.

Sandy went in and sang loudly as she soaped and rinsed. She towelled herself, gowned herself, scuttled across to her caravan and put on jeans and shirt. She wondered as she combed her short dark hair what the gardenia would wear this morning. Even a hothouse flower like Janice couldn't turn up for breakfast in floral satin culottes.

But Janice didn't turn up at all, and evidently never did. When Sandy, deciding to be helpful ... she was also curious ... offered to take across a tray, Stone laughed.

'She's a late riser. We may see her at noon. Now I thought today—'

'I could at least take her coffee.'

'Leave her alone.' He had raised his voice. 'Do you hear?' A pause. 'I mean that, Sandy.'

'You sound as though you do.' Sandy had stopped in her tracks at his sharp note.

He did not climb down. He repeated, 'Just keep out of it, do you understand?'

'No.'

422

'Then still keep out.' There was no laughter in him now as there had been previously, not even a faint amusement. She stared at him, not comprehending. He must have read her confusion, for he said, 'No need for my explanations and no need for your wonder. It's just none of your business, so accept that. Now I thought today—'

'Mr. Wetherill, do I still have to stop here?' She burst out rebelliously, for her last night's acceptance was gone, she wanted to leave the place again.

'Here?' he misunderstood. 'You mean right here?'

'I mean the Oasis.'

'But I thought I told you—'

'Yes, but that was yesterday. It's today now, and I want to go more than ever. Isn't there *some* way around that small print? Couldn't I forfeit—'

'Forfeit what? You haven't done anything yet, not even' . . . sarcastically . . . 'dry up. Unless you count those dishes last night.'

'I could pay you something for the ad. Return the fare money.'

In answer he advised: 'Don't sulk.' He added, as her lip instinctively went out, 'For that's what you're doing, isn't it, sulking. Sulking because you're not in-cluded in something. Well, you're *not*. Also, you *stop*. Now, I thought today—'

She sat down beside him. What was the use of fight-ing? There was no escape from here unless she walked, and that was out of the question. A few miles in this climate, a climate much more intensified out there in the middle of nothing, with no shade, no cover, and she would be mistaking that faint indentation in the gibber that was all to mark the track for a wind ripple, finding another . . . imagined . . . track, she would be lost, and she would be doing those things she had read about . . . clutching at her collar, piece by piece discarding her clothes, losing her senses. No, she would have to wait at least till the gang came in. Undoubtedly some of them would be going on to B.A., and she would go, too, small print or not. She couldn't, and wouldn't, stick this place.

'It was me bawling you out, wasn't it?' His voice cut into her thoughts, cut quite amiably. 'It was the idea of being left out of something, yet Janice being left in. All right then, be big enough to accept it, Sandy, *because that's how it is and will be.* And for heaven's sake don't trip over that bottom lip. Now today—'

'Yes?' she said, beaten for the moment. 'Today?'

'That's better,' he awarded quite kindly . . . what a crosscurrent and a contradiction he was! . . . 'keep it up. Well, today you can earn your keep.'

'The garden? Help Rusty?'

'How about something more scientific to suit the daughter of Professor Lawford? How about some field-work? Or at least a field survey?'

'Really?' She looked up eagerly as children look, and he smiled to himself.

'Actually I'm anxious to see if you're all steam,' he admitted whimsically, 'merely bursting out what little knowledge you do have. Carbonated rock indeed!'

'I've no university training,' she admitted.

'Only the hard facts. That's what I want. We'll leave at once.'

'On foot?'

'Lor' no!'

'But there's no conveyance.'

'There's my helicopter.'

'Helicopter!' she gasped.

424

'Very essential out here.'

'And you actually have one?'

'Had you snooped around a bit more on your explorations yesterday ... oh, yes, I was watching you ... you would have discovered it.'

'A helicopter? But you told me there was no way for me to get into Busy Acres.'

'There wasn't. This is strictly a project 'copter, no unessential flights like that. Now hurry up, you've wasted enough time. Don't stand gaping, I'm starting a count-down. Ten. Nine. Eight—'

She was back by four with her hat and her sunglasses. Breathless. Excited. A little resentful still, but ready to go.

He led the way across the camp to a shelter at the extreme end of the break from the gibber, almost on the gibber, and wheeled out the craft, the smallest type available, she estimated.

'Ever been in a chaffcutter?' he asked.

'No.'

'This actually is one.' He grinned. 'No hope of any spying with a clangour like Betsy sets up. Hang on to your ears.' He added as the noise he had warned her about lived up to the warning: 'Poor Janice, that's the end of her siesta.'

Yes, poor Janice, thought Sandy, still lying in bed, while she, Sandy Lawford, became part of that heraldic blue upturned basin of cloudless sky, even if it was a noisy part. She looked down and rejoiced.

'Like it, eh?' He shouted to her above the chaffcutter's clangour. He was smiling at her enthusiasm. He pointed out a distant road that went as far as the eye could see – narrow, bouldered, straight as a gun barrel, but for all its roughness still a road. 'It catches

425

up with the Bitumen eventually,' he shouted, 'and in time you can get to Alice Springs.'

A camp beside a drilling plant caught Sandy's eye and she asked Stone if it was his.

'No. Rivals. But friendly rivals ever since I helped them out once with a mad cook. The heat got him . . . it had been one hundred and twenty for three weeks . . . and he ran around with a meat cleaver. I happened to be going over, and I saw, so I put Betsy down at once, and helped. Since then I've been a welcome visitor so long as I don't snoop too near. Like to see the general layout? No closer, mind you . . . may as well, for I've had news that our own gang are shifting around to beat the spies, so we won't be seeing them today.' Without waiting for Sandy's answer, he began to lower Betsy.

'Any women here?' she asked as the craft sank down.

'Never on the drilling. You as a Snowy girl should realize that.'

'Oh, I know that a diamond driller is sensitive to being watched, but I thought that that might only refer to high places, dangerous places.'

'And don't you think it can be dangerous here? Don't forget there's blistering heat as well to contend with, it is not an unusual thing for a driller to collapse from exhaustion and fall off a rig.'

She nodded. She did not have to be told about drilling hazards.

'Also,' he went on, 'you must know about drillers and women.'

'I know,' she agreed . . . for everyone who had been on a project knew that when a diamond driller was hard on the job women were strictly taboo. They had been taboo at Falcon, at the Takeover, at Savage,

Roaring Billy.

Stone Wetherill was looking around the plant, and he said, 'You're in luck. Maggie and Brenda have driven out from the home camp to give their men a meal. Now you can meet *real* nickel wives.' He began leading her across to where a jeep was pulled up, but before they got there two women eagerly approached. They were in shorts, shirts and boots, the last, Sandy mentally noted, much more suitable out here than her own thin rubbers. They greeted her with the enthusiasm of women who long for another woman to talk to, and while they talked Stone Wetherill got with the men.

Maggie, the taller woman, had been with mining all her married years.

'Long ago it was copper,' she related. 'I followed Bill like a gipsy, except that I drove a utility and towed a caravan. Then this other started, and it's been rocks ever since. We've moved after the "signs" six times this year.' She did not say the nickel and Sandy was careful not to ask any questions.

Brenda admitted the life here was hard. When it got really hot . . . no, this was a cool day, only a hundred . . . their two men, both drillers, would work right through the night instead and sleep, or try to, through the day. Their wives would lead the same life. Then when it was mild weather like now . . . mild? . . . the wives would come out to the trap and boil a billy, as they were doing this moment. The men looked forward to it, they both said, and you knew at least that they had knocked off for a bite. 'You're just in time for a cup,' they invited.

It was the usual strong sweet cup, but there were corned beef sandwiches and pickles instead of slab

427

cake.

'We come out all the time now with tucker,' they told Sandy, 'ever since the cooky went berserk with the cleaver the boys haven't bothered to have someone on the spot.'

The conversation left the camp, and Brenda said how she missed suburban shops and Maggie how she hated the dust. 'Put a coffee cup down and in an hour you think you never emptied out the dregs. Oh, well, it won't last for ever, and the money is all right.'

Stone was signalling for Sandy to leave. She said goodbye to the women, waved to the men, then got into the 'copter again.

'I hope you never said anything out of place.' He shouted it because the chaffcutter was setting up its clangour again.

'Not a word. Our conversation was mostly dust like coffee dregs.'

'They're wonderful women. They're the real nickel wives.' He turned his attention to the helicopter and presently she saw he was putting down again. She looked around, but could see no reason.

'I've had my eye on this part,' he told her. 'I did think of pegging a claim. But I've too many eggs in the basket just now, and pegging isn't exactly cheap, not when you get up in numbers. Also, it's fairly near to a station here. Cattle, of course. Mainly, and for good reason, the pastoralists are friendly, we find them water, let them in on a strike. But we also occasionally mess them up with holes that can possibly break a brumby's leg.' He sat Betsy down and nodded for Sandy to get out.

'Now show me what you know,' he demanded.

She looked around her, considered the rocks, then

did. It wasn't much, but it made sense, proved she was no greenhorn. Taking out his makings, he conceded her that.

He finished the rolling, licked and lit up, then brought out what looked like a schoolboy's magnet on a piece of elastic. 'I carry it like you would carry a lipstick,' he grinned. 'If a rock is magnetic it could contain nickel. That's only a rough indication, but it's worth following. Mainly I look for outcrops where subterranean rocks have come to the surface. That's the start. Later on the technocrats come in with their magnetometers, polarization, what-have-you, and then come the first percussion drills, then the delicate drilling that brings out the core that reveals the structure of the ground. Then . . . perhaps! . . . nickel.'

She was listening to him . . . yet not listening. She was interested, *really* interested, but somehow she could not concentrate, somehow he kept on becoming a blur, then clearing, then blurring again.

Then the blur remained, it did not flicker away and reality return. It just stopped dark and dizzy and obscure. When awareness did return, not long afterwards, but it could have been a lifetime for Sandy, she was flat on the ground under a sparse mulga, her shirt was loosened and Stone Wetherill was fanning her with the wide brim of the ten-gallon that he had evidently put in the helicopter in case shade would be needed, for mostly, she knew, he would wear a helmet.

'How did that come about?' He sounded angry.

Sandy was *very* angry . . . at herself for fainting, she never fainted, but more at him for being annoyed about it. Anyone would think she had staged it.

'How did it come about?' he repeated doggedly.

'How would I know?'

'You haven't missed out on your salt tablets, have you?'

'Salt tablets?'

'Oh, lor', salt tablets, she asks! Yes, *salt tablets*. Surely a woman who knows about carbonated rock would know that.'

'I know about other things besides rock, but I don't know salt tablets.'

'Up here,' he almost yelled, 'you have to replace what you lose in sweat. Being a lady I suppose you say perspiration. But it still has to be replaced. Four tabs a day at least. The drillers take up to ten.'

'But how would—'

'Look, don't question me, just do as I say, and get this into you now.' He produced a rather large tablet, put it into her mouth and waited till she swallowed. 'Four a day. While I'm in the Oasis you can come to the office and get them. I can see that you actually take them then.'

'I'm not a fool.'

'You must be to come out here without that precaution, it's not so essential in at the camp. Well, do you think you can get to the 'copter or will I carry you?'

'I can walk, of course.'

In answer he bent over and picked her up, carried her firmly across to the craft. Because he held her so rigidly she could not struggle free, but she made her anger apparent by remaining stiff and aloof.

'Hate it, don't you,' he grinned, 'but I'm doing it to drive home a point. Don't ever forget those tablets or this happens. See?'

'I never knew about the tablets, how could I do

something I knew nothing about? But I won't miss out, I assure you.' She sprang away from him the moment he put her down. She ignored his helping hand as she climbed into the craft again.

They avoided an overlanding mob some time later, cattle were touchy things, Stone said, and the noise of Betsy could start a rush. Overlanding was growing steadily rarer now, he told her, road-training or air-beefing taking its place. They aroused a herd of brumbies, which were wild horses, and soon after a herd of scrubbers, which were cattle gone bush, then they rimmed an opal field, and that was all he intended to do, just rim it, Stone grinned. There was trouble down there. Big trouble. Since the Mines Department had granted new exploration leases the opal men, rightly or wrongly, were feeling they were being squeezed out. 'For it's still free country,' Stone said, 'free for all, not just the pastoralists, the opal men, us. It's still an open go for every trier, it's still all-Australian.'

'What would happen if two conflicting interests co-incided?' Sandy asked.

'War.' At her look of disbelief he explained, 'Gelignite war. In other words a few sticks of gelignite shoved into expensive equipment.'

'They wouldn't!'

'They have.'

'Someone could be killed,' she protested.

'They have.'

'It's . . . it's a barbarian part of the world.'

'I agree.'

But she could see his expression as he looked down on the vast terrain beneath them, that great red terrain where you could gaze almost for ever, for there was nothing to stop you seeing, even the mulga was bent

431

low to help you, and she knew he did *not* think that.

'It's tough, rough, dry, dead, harsh, savage, primitive, impossible country,' he said. Then: 'Want to leave it?'

He took her by surprise, but she recovered quick enough to ask at once: 'When?'

He laughed at that, then answered, 'Remember the small print? I was only tantalizing you, of course.'

They were hovering over the Oasis again, then sitting carefully down, coming to a halt. The quiet when the engine was cut off was bliss.

But — *quiet*? Somewhere a baritone voice boomed quite musically, but evidently unappreciated, for there was an impact as something was thrown, accompanied by the thrower's vivid shushing language, obviously intending to shush the song. From the tank pool came splashing and yelling. Someone was trying out drums. A thick plume of steam rose from the cookhouse chimney. Everywhere there was the sound of . . . *noise*.

Stone Wetherill put two fingers in his mouth and emitted noise of his own, an ear-splitting whistle that actually succeeded in breaking through. 'Two of you blokes,' he shouted, 'can knock off whatever you're doing and put Betsy to bed, and no argument either, seeing you're back three days earlier than you should be. And I'll want to know about *that*!'

The rabble paused, then continued, but it became a closer rabble. From the caravans men were emerging to greet Stone and stare at Sandy. Heads were appearing over the tank top, but evidently it was not a trunks job, for only the heads remained in sight.

Stone looked keenly around at them, and Sandy would not have put it past that man with those keen blue eyes, those almost *drilling* eyes, to be counting them.

Then: 'The gang's back,' he said unnecessarily to her. That he *had* been counting them was proven in his next brief: 'But only thirteen of them.'

CHAPTER THREE

'WHERE in tarnation is Bevis?'

Typical of this Stone Wetherill, Sandy seethed, he, the big boss, had to be informed on things first. The expected civilized courtesies ... like presenting the men to her, presenting her to the men ... came afterwards. Though perhaps he had no intention of presenting her, perhaps for all that 'balance' of his, that 'normal living', male and female, the female was to be ignored. That the gang was not with him in this was obvious from the interested looks Sandy was collecting. The men, that is the ones not confined through necessity to the tank pool, were circled around them, but most of the circle was near Sandy.

'Why isn't Bevis here?' demanded Stone Wetherill. 'Did he come in from the traps?'

'He came and went straight into B.A. Must have had a white collar thirst.'

'He can damn well fix that here, and he knows it.'

'Perhaps he wanted women and song as well as the wine,' offered one of the men whom Sandy, from hearing his name, now sorted out as Barry. Stone Wetherill looked ready to explode at that, so Sandy ducked away to the nearest shelter, which happened to be the cookhouse.

Rusty beckoned her across as soon as she reached the door to join himself and Andy over the eternal cuppa at the big working table – at least Sandy supposed the other man was Andrew the cook. He was. Already he was floury from the evening meal preparations, he was making—

'Project Pud.' Sandy beat him to it, and he grinned broadly and put out the big floury hand. 'Reckon you're one of us camp mob.'

'I used to be.'

The cook raised his brows at that 'used to be', and Sandy, taking the large cup of tea that Rusty handed her, said with dislike: 'That man—'

'Bevis?'

'*That* man. Mr. Wetherill. Anyone would think he owned the place!'

They looked at each other in surprise. 'He does.'

'But – but isn't this a company? I mean a – well—' What she meant was this nickel thing was such a big thing, a national thing . . . often a world thing . . . it surely must entail a lot of big names, a lot of big wealth, big backing. There couldn't just be one boss, Stoneleigh Wetherill.

'It's entirely his show,' the two men said together. 'He's up against all the big companies – English, American, French, the rest. There's Consolidated, Ventures Incorporated, Universal Mining, some other bumper concerns, and Stone is pitting himself against the lot.'

'He must be a millionaire.'

'He's not. He's got some, of course, he'd have to, but more than that he's got know-how and guts.'

'And a loud voice. I know something of undertakings, and you can't, you simply can't rule men's lives. This Bevis—'

'Is a young idiot,' said Rusty frankly. 'I wouldn't put it past Stone to go into B.A. after him and boot him right out.'

'Just for going in for a drink!'

'There's enough here.'

'But in a man's spare time!'

'It isn't, though. You see we're all in this, too, and that's why Stone did his block. Not only are we paid top wages, higher than any that the big projects are paying, but we're *in* this.'

'A kind of company?'

'Yes. So Bevis was a fool.'

'I still think a man's entitled—'

'Not until he's been briefed. The gang's come in before they were expected. That means either of two things: there was a failure, or there was something bigger than they thought. The geos have the answer there, but they'll only report it to Stone. If it was just the result that Stone had expected, the gang would have stopped the arranged days. But they're *in*, and that means something. It also means no one leaves the camp until it has been talked over, thrashed out. The very last thing it does mean is scoot into the Palatial and spill the beans.'

'But would Bevis?'

'Not briefed and full of cheer very likely he could. He's young and fairly new. Yep, I reckon he could be booted out after this. More tea?'

'No,' said Sandy a little faintly. She went and stood at the door.

The men had left the tank pool in her absence and got into shorts. They were lined up in front of Stone Wetherill and he was conferring with them in a more controlled voice. He saw her at the door and beckoned her across.

'The four good-lookers there are miscellaneous geos and one engineer,' he presented, 'you can work their particular specialities and names out later yourself, though they're Barry, Leo, Hunt and Paul. These tough boys here are our drillers, the ones I told you eat holes out of the ground, so watch your step. Jim and Alf are the roughriders of the quartet, John and Jeff the more delicate core bringers-up. There are also six riggers, but one of them, as you may have heard' . . . he gave her a hard look, . . . 'is missing. Not gone with the wind but gone in a company jeep into B.A. I won't say "He'll keep" because I'm going in after him. Boys, this is Alexandra Lawford. But she has other ideas about that name.' He turned on his heel and went.

Sandy found herself surrounded by men, but she was used to that . . . yet not used, and she realized it now, to Australians. All her previous project associates had been European, imported mainly for their snow country skill, which mostly Australians had not, for all her projects up to now had been cold climate ones. Even the Takeover had had climate challenges, and as for the Snowy – and Savage— She had liked those other men, got on well with them. How would she get on with her own sort? Not very satisfactorily if they were like . . .

They were not. If she had been fair Sandy would have acknowledged that it could have been because they did not carry the responsibility, but Sandy could not be fair somehow. Not when it came to Stone Wetherill.

The engineer knew of her father.

'Professor Lawford? I grew up on a thesis of his.'

The geos she didn't sort out at once, but she instantly liked them. The diamond drillers . . . well, diamond drillers were the same, she now found, whether it was here, the arid centre of a continent, or a continent's

437

loftiest top. They were tough . . . yet sensitive. Ruthless
. . . yet delicately-strung. They were uncaring yet vulnerable. How could they not be like this when they
dealt with something that no one else dealt with? The
core, the mysterious heart of the earth.

One of them knew Anton Wolhar who had been
their prize driller at Sandy's last project. They talked
reminiscently about Anton.

The riggers . . . finally . . . were happy and friendly.
Had Sandy a singing voice? they asked. They were
getting a group together, Bill here on the drums and—

'No voice,' admitted Sandy. 'I only sing in the
shower.'

'Thanks for that reminder.' Stone Wetherill had
come out of his caravan and joined them. 'I want you
boys to take one of the baths you brought back across to
Miss Lawford's van, put it near the tap and rig round a
shelter.'

'But—' began Sandy.

'No portable showers now,' he said, 'not with a camp
waiting for you to finish your song. Private facilities
instead. How long do you think a bath will take?'

She looked at him confused, and he said, 'I'm going
into B.A. I thought you might like to come, too.'

'No, thanks.'

'A change of mind? You were pestering me before.'

'To get *away* to B.A. Not just to visit.'

'All right, please yourself, but most women like to
shop.'

'At Busy Acres?'

'There's a store, you should remember, the usual
undertaking mixed store, but if you know these
businesses—'

Of course she knew them. She had shopped all her

life at them. The prospect now was irresistible. Anyone who has ever gone into a project store wanted to go again. From then on they were hooked for all time.

'Please yourself, as I said.' He was turning away.

She hesitated. 'I was thinking of boots. The nickel wives wore them, I noticed. Rubbers are too thin here. But the store would be closed by now.'

'Closed while there's someone around?' he scoffed, and she knew he was right. Project stores did not abide by shopping regulations as to time of opening and shutting, they opened . . . and shut . . . according to the customer. Only when the last one left did the bolts shoot home.

'Perhaps Janice . . .' She had to say that; after all she was female-one.

'Janice is already in there.' He said it so expressionlessly she could not have judged whether it meant anything, or not.

'I do feel grubby.'

'Then your bath awaits.' He pointed to the tub that had been carried across to her van, quickly enclosed in a concealing rig. As ordered it had been placed near a tap, for Rusty had taps handy to each of the caravans. 'Be ready in half an hour,' Stone called.

She was, though she would have liked to have lingered longer in the tub after the day's dust. It was sheer bliss to lie in the bath, which was outsize, to relax in the water from the tap that was still comfortably warm from the exposed pipes that entrapped the solar rays. But she forced herself out, encased herself in a large towel, and climbed the van steps to get dressed.

That part offered no problem; one thing lack of clothes solved the vexing question of choice. She put on the *other* dress, the navy shirtwaist with the tie. She was out before he could call.

He beckoned her to a jeep, and waved away by those of the men who were not relaxing now in the common-room, they started bumping over the track into Busy Acres. It was not so much a track, Sandy noted now, for her attention last time had been on everything around her and not on the road, as twin lines of flat-tened gibbers, flattened by jeeps such as this, or Cleve's mail van, all passing over the same ground. Not so much flattened, perhaps, as pressed down. You had to pass over the two lines, she smiled to herself, or really bump. She wasn't counting the continuous bumping now, but anticipating how, if the jeep left the indents, the wheels would rise and fall. Skid, too. Some of the gibbers were as smooth and slippery as ice. But Stone was an experienced driver. Never once did they leave their own flattened rocks for bigger rocks. Assured by now, Sandy looked around.

A reverse trip, she had always found, revealed different aspects in a terrain. But this terrain was the same wherever you looked. Stone-strewn, stick-dry, dead as old bones. There was a moon-country quality about it, a sort of unearthliness ... also an agelessness in spite of its age. Why, she thought with an odd excite-ment, it's the beginning and the end, it's basic, fun-damental. It's dead ... and yet it pulsates.

She saw that between keeping the jeep to the track he was watching her, judging her reactions. In spite of his expressionlessness as he did so, she knew he was sensitive to what she thought, and that he was pleased. He loves it, she knew. He wants others to feel some-thing about it as well, not just a distaste because it is not green and fruitful.

Then actually he was showing her a fruitful corner.

Here, in the stone-strewn, stick-dry land he found a 'wurlie' for her to marvel at, dabble her fingers in. A wurlie was an aboriginal watering place. This one had not been in use for years: the natives had been provided a camp further north, she learned, in a more favourable aspect.

But the animals had taken over the narrow deep cleft in the large rock, obscured from the sun so that the water was deliciously cold. Stone showed Sandy the pad-marks of warrigals, kangaroos, other animal footprints. There was evidence of birds. If one was quiet enough one might even see, at sundown, snakes coming to drink.

'It's easier to observe them then than you'd think, there must be a law in nature that no attack on each other is ever made at watering time, so that a watcher is not suspected as he ordinarily would be.'

'I'd love to see that,' she said eagerly.

'Yes.' A quick bare sigh. 'But not now.'

She caught the sigh, and questioned him, 'Is it so important to get this man back from B.A.?'

'Who said I was getting him back?' Stone's voice was grim, all the regret gone. 'I might be giving him a shove on.'

'Then why the hurry?' For, if speed was possible on this track, they were hurrying now.

'Bevis is fairly new to me, I don't know how many beers will open his mouth.'

'You mean he could say more than he should say?'

'Yes.'

'Then the men had something to tell you today?'

He took his eyes off the track a moment to glance obliquely and coldly at her. 'Are you a spy, grilling me like that? If you are, you're not doing it very well. You

441

want much more finesse.'

'If I was, would I be fool enough to ask you straight out?'

'I don't know,' he said a little futilely. He seemed to grow tired and disillusioned. 'I don't know what ticks in a woman.'

'Janice—' she began.

'Janice too. Janice particularly.' There was a note now in his voice she couldn't understand. 'Do me a favour,' he said presently before she could comment, 'drop it. You're here for the ride. Or to shop. Or – or something. But don't needle me, spy or not.'

'*Not*,' she impressed on him. 'And I didn't mean to needle you. Will you drop me at the shop?' They were nearing the meagre bitumen now, the narrow strip that ran into the town.

'Will be done,' he nodded. 'When you're finished, see me at the pub.'

Sandy was surprised when they came down Busy Acres' Main Street, which was its only street, that it was much busier than when she had been here before. There were cars in front of the Palatial; the host would be pleased, she thought, he would be adding extra rooms to that plan of his. The inn parlour must have been filled, for there was a small crowd drinking outside.

'Blow-ins,' said Stone, and he cursed.

'Why?' She forgot she was not to participate, that she was to 'drop it'. 'Why do the blow-ins annoy you?'

He must have forgotten his order also, for he answered, 'There's talk that Ventures Incorporated struck rock out at the Gulch. All the leeches' . . . he indicated the cars of the blow-ins . . . 'are in town with

442

their ears open. And to think that Bevis is here, too!'

'And Janice?' Sandy could not have said why she added that.

He gave her a sharp look. 'Women can't resist coming in. You've come yourself.'

'I never said otherwise,' she defended herself.

'Undoubtedly,' he went on, 'Janice saw Bevis leaving and couldn't stop herself reaching for a bit of life.' He paused. 'Poor kid!'

'Poor kid?' The last Sandy would have said of Janice was poor kid. She looked in surprise at Stone Wetherill, but he was bringing the jeep to a halt now and pointing out the shop. Not that there was any need, she smiled to herself. Its crowd almost rivalled the crowd at the Palatial.

'Twenty minutes,' he called.

She went into the rough store, feeling at once that same atmosphere of all stores that serve project camps. Though here the speech was Australian, she had no need to trot out her *merci bien, danke, grazie* as she had had need before, the voices were drawled, slurred, they took short cuts . . . more often than not they were over-vivid. She was the pivot of attention for a while, but shopping was such a serious business when weeks of inconvenience could be caused by forgetting to include a simple purchase, that eyes and attention were soon on lists again, and Sandy could look round and enjoy herself.

For there was nothing, she thought, simply nothing to compare to the *everything* that these places offered. Just as Alaskan trading posts and Pacific Island markets have their magic, so did this gibber store, and just as she had been enthralled before at Falcon's Neck, at the Takeover, Savage, Roaring Billy, Sandy was enthralled again.

She stood revelling in the unbelievable confusion of everything. The dress materials . . . other women here? . . . bacon, tins of fruit, ties, hats, rugs, blankets, billies. There was lingerie and perfume, but she knew about these now, for she had seen men send up things to Sydney, or down to Melbourne, from high remote places, just for the *feeling* of sending such things, even though the woman to receive them could have bought with more choice where she lived.

She smiled at umbrellas. Umbrellas in this rainless world? At room-warmers . . . though she had been told that the desert grew cold.

She turned over handkerchiefs, scarves, fish paste and strawberry jam. No one seemed to mind the confusion, in fact they appeared to like to jumble around.

A cool voice greeted her. Janice, trying out a lipstick colour. 'You here?'

'Mr. Wetherill brought me in.'

'You're quick, aren't you?'

'No, I don't think so. We left at—'

'I mean quick at getting a lift into B.A. from none other than the big boss. What's brought him, anyway?' Janice's dark eyes were narrowed slightly on Sandy. 'Celebrating a find?'

'How would I know?'

'Taught you to be cagey already! It's something we all have to learn out here. Did he say anything, though?' The dark eyes were still narrowed.

'I told you I know nothing. He was coming in and seeing I wanted a pair of boots—'

'Where is he now?'

'At the hotel. He came for Bevis.' Sandy did not

444

know whether it was to extricate Bevis or put Bevis on his way, so she left it at that.

'He needn't have worried,' said Janice scornfully, 'he knows nothing, Tim Bevis. Evidently they left him at the depot.' She gave a short laugh. 'All that boy has is a thirst.'

'That is the worry, I think.'

Janice shrugged and said something that Sandy could not catch. She did not address Sandy any more. She put down the lipstick and went out of the shop.

Sandy turned back again, then turned over goods until she came to the shoe corner. As she rather had anticipated, there were no boots for women. But boots were still what she wanted, boots to walk on the gibber, and eventually she found a boy's pair, strong and stout if not exactly glamorous. She bought them, then looked around again.

She fingered each of a row of dresses, and was amazed at the style and quality, yet not amazed really, for she recalled the trade Mr. Eisokovits had done at the Takeover. Always a woman's dress was being bought by some nostalgic project worker. Mr. Eisokovits had often asked Sandy to fold them in tissue paper ready for mail.

The store owner came across now and she remarked on the surprising variety.

'Yes,' he said, 'we try to keep in touch. Don't go past us for your next buy.'

Sandy felt like buying now. There was a flame-coloured linen, straight and simple, that would have lit up that stone-strewn background, a green sheath with spring in it that would have brought a season to the place that it appeared never to allow, but to buy these would have been to acknowledge defeat to Stone

Wetherill, to admit her bare two dresses and two dresses alone. She heard again his taunting words ... taunting to *her* really, not Rusty, to whom he had addressed: 'You and your dearth of women, you've landed yourself another boy.'

One brown dress, one navy blue, he later had said. She resisted the temptation and stopped her purchase at the boots. She went out of the store, then up the street to stand by the furthest post of the hotel. She had not been there long when a man sauntered across.

He spoke pleasantly to her, and she answered civilly back. After all, she thought, you can't, at a remote place like this, at a latitude like this, turn away and wait until you're formally introduced.

'From the Oasis, aren't you?'

'Yes.'

'Been busy boys out there, I hear.'

'I wouldn't know.'

'I suppose not. Hush-hush, eh? Still, you do get ideas, don't you? Look, can't I buy you a drink?'

'No, thank you, I'm waiting.'

'For Wetherill. He doesn't seem in such a happy mood. Wasn't it all he thought today?'

'I really don't know. I know nothing at all. I— Here's Stone now.' She stepped eagerly forward, relieved he was coming. Then stopped.

Stone was not by himself. A man, a young man, evidently Bevis, was with him, and the man was being frog-marched rather brutally out of the swinging doors. Or brutally, Sandy considered it. She had no doubt that Bevis did not feel the iron grasp on him, the compulsion forward, for he was too convivial and relaxed for that, but Sandy could see Wetherill's whitened knucklebones, whitened from the strain of forcing

446

Bevis, who was large and lumbering and with all a young giant's strength, to where *he* wanted him to go, not Bevis. The direction was plainly the jeep, so Bevis was not being shoved out but pulled out, out of the Palatial. He was being taken back to the Oasis. Had Sandy been in the boy's place, for his smooth young skin was that of a boy still, she did not think she would have preferred the reprieve, not with a frog-marcher with a set expression like Stone Wetherill's.

Bevis must have suddenly decided that he did not like it. His cheerfulness left him and he began to protest, pull back. Especially did he pull back when some of the men, blow-ins, Sandy decided, for they were wearing town clothes, held up bottles.

Stone Wetherill wasted no time. He simply turned round and flattened Bevis with a single sharp blow strategically placed. Then lifting up the young giant with what appeared effortlessness but must have been considerable effort with as big a weight as himself made weightier still by the resultant inertness, he carried him to the jeep Bevis had purloined, and fairly flung him into the seat. Here the boy remained, falling instantly asleep. Or perhaps he was unconscious, Sandy fumed.

Unaware that she was doing so, she had followed the pair. Indeed, she saw, looking around her, that all the hotel had followed. Including Janice.

Stone Wetherill looked around him, then unerringly saw her, and threw across some keys. By some miracle, for she was taken by surprise, she caught them.

'Drive?' He did not waste any more than that.

'Yes.'

'Follow behind with Janice.' He nodded to the girl.

'But—' But I've never driven over such country, Sandy started to protest, I've never driven a jeep like this. She did not say it, though. She had no time. He simply nodded for her to get in the other vehicle, then got in his own and started off.

'Janice!' called Sandy, but Janice was already in the waggon and waiting for Sandy to take over. Sandy noted, and was surprised, that the girl looked a little nervous, a little pinched around the lips. It's him, she thought, he scares us all.

Scares *us*? No, she corrected grimly ... turning the key and finding to her vast relief that the engine responded in the usual way, for she had no wish to remain here without the protective presence of Stone Wetherill even though he was a brute, for she hadn't liked that man who had come across and questioned her ... no, he doesn't scare *me*.

But the track scared her for a while. One yard from the indents and that gibber could turn you over, she knew. Besides, it was getting dark now, the twin lines becoming fainter. The only thing to do was follow the tail light in front of her. Sandy did, glad that Janice made no attempt to divert her by beginning a conversation.

She did not dare a glance at Janice, driving took all her concentration, but she knew by the girl's hunched stillness that she was not very happy with herself.

At last the journey was over, the lights of the Oasis coming up. Men were hurrying out to help Stone Wetherill with his burden, a dead weight now that Bevis was sound asleep and snoring stertorously.

'Just deposit him as he is,' tossed Stone, 'let him sleep it off.' A grim note. 'I'll see him when he sobers up.'

But the voice he used on Janice was so different,

Sandy found herself biting her tongue to stop herself from remarking on the change.

'Are you all right, Janice? Can you make it? It's a hard journey from B.A. Not a pleasant trip.'

Not a pleasant trip! All the girl had had to do was sit, she hadn't had to strain her eyes through the dusk, grab the wheel, concentrate . . .

In anger she heard Stone advising gently an early night for Janice, tea in bed. *He* would bring it across.

Bring it across! Sandy seethed. Would he bring tea across, too, to her?

It didn't appear so. Janice gone wearily . . . *over-wearily*, Sandy uncharitably judged, noting the girl's exaggerated progress . . . Stone Wetherill turned next to Sandy.

'Bugle call's over, but Andy will have chow put aside. I'll see you in the cookhouse as soon as you've washed up.'

And as soon, Sandy added a few minutes later as she sluiced her face in cold water, ran a comb through her boy's hair, as you've taken Janice her tray. Or is that for afterwards, Mr. Wetherill? In a more romantic time of the night, when camp responsibilities have been dispensed, when you can relax?

Not changing, though in that brief time the dress was already dirty, the navy blue a drab, dusty less-than navy from its coating of desert grit, Sandy went across to the cookhouse, entered and sat at the table.

Andy was throwing three large steaks on to the huge grid. (So Janice was to have her tray at once after all.) But following the few necessary turns for the rare he then served without asking first . . . evidently Stone had rare, resented Sandy, who took medium, so what the boss said went . . . he dished two of the steaks, with vegetables he had kept hot, to Wetherill and one steak to Sandy. (So Janice was to be attended in the relaxed mood later.)

Stone, who had come in washed and slicked, nodded for Sandy to start eating. He began himself.

The steaks, Sandy knew from last night, were excellent. She knew that Stone Wetherill would tolerate no less than a perfect chef. But she wasn't hungry. Indeed, she had never been less hungry in her life. But she did not dare play with her meal. Not with *that* table companion beside her, silently, intently consuming, almost showing her *how* he wanted it done. For there was none of the gourmet about him, he simply ate to replenish. And heaven help her, his silence seemed to indicate, if she didn't deplete her plate as well.

As she did so she thought that here life was demanding, strenuous, food as well as a necessity almost an ammunition. She left some of the steak on her plate . . . really it was too much.

'Eat it.' He looked across and advised it briefly. 'No room for finicky appetites here.'

'I—'

'Eat it.'

She did, but sulkily. 'What about Janice?' she asked.

'What about her?' He had finished and pushed aside the plate, he was shaking his head at Andy who was proffering sweets.

'Well, doesn't she eat?' She does, you know, Sandy felt like adding, small forkfuls that do an astonishingly diminishing job.

'She ate in at B.A. I'll take her a tray later.'

'Yes. You said so.'

450

He flicked her a quick look at that.

Andy was removing and rinsing the dishes. As soon as he had done, Stone nodded for him to go.

'Tea?' the cook asked attentively.

'I'll attend to that if I want it. You've had a long day, Andy, two meals at the traps, then back to serve dinner here. Best grab some kip.'

The cook said good night to Sandy and went out. There was silence as Stone reached for his makings, silence as he performed the rolling ritual, that whisper of dry weed against a large palm. The cigarette was moulded, licked together. He lit up.

'Well,' he invited, 'shoot.'

'I beg your pardon?'

'Don't keep it in. Let it out. You were shocked in there at B.A., weren't you? It showed in your face like a flag. And yet you, a project woman, must have witnessed discipline previously.'

'Yes,' she agreed, 'but not violence before today.'

'Violence?' He put down his cigarette and began to laugh. 'Violence! That love tap!'

'If that's love, keep me from it!' she snapped.

'The tap is scaled, of course, for the different sexes.' He was looking at her through the blue weave of smoke, his Salvation Jane blue eyes narrowed to the size of diamond drill points. She could not tell whether the points were amused or hostile, or both.

'You thought I should go over to Bevis and say, "Look, old chap, it's time you knocked off," ' he said conversationally.

'Nothing of the sort. I'm not a fool. But – but you needn't have marched him out like that, hit him, thrown him in the waggon like you did.'

'What else?' he invited.

She tried to think, tried desperately, but nothing came. Childishly at last she flung, 'It was horrible! Also I think more than handling the boy you were – were showing off.'

'What?'

'There was an audience today, wasn't there, you wanted to show them how tough the Oasis boss was.'

His face had darkened, its Red Indian deepness was shades deeper, and that should have warned her. But recklessly she went on.

'When I stopped that first time at the Palatial it was Stone Wetherill this, Stone Wetherill that. I could see you were a bit of a legend. This evening I saw you were determined to keep the fable in circulation. Please!' For he had leaned across and taken her wrist in his. The grasp was uncomfortably tight.

'I could break it in the fraction of a minute,' he said almost speculatively, looking at her slim brown wrist. He released her hand. 'I won't.'

'Thank you.'

He finished, 'That is, for the present I won't. For those' . . . he began smoking again . . . 'were dangerous words, and call for a reckoning. I have never "showed off", as you put it. I have never needed to. I am what I am. Good lord, the last I would want to impress would be that scum. They live on a hint, a nod, an innuendo. They go from place to place hoping to hear the right word, see the green light, find something to peddle. They have never . . . never, I tell you . . . rolled up their sleeves, climbed a rig like young Bevis has.'

'For which Bevis gets the reward he did.'

'If you would care to look the boy over you would see no skin break, not even the first discolouring sign of a bruise.'

'You're experienced in punishment?'

Again the oblique look through the weave of smoke. 'Experienced,' he concurred.

Andy had a clock in his cookhouse and it ticked clumsily. Sandy counted sixty ticks and knew a minute had passed.

'Actually' ... Stone Wetherill broke the silence ... 'I did the boy a service.'

'Yes, I know. By bringing him back you're keeping him in the company, the remarkable company where men are not only paid bigger wages than at other similar workings, they participate in the project itself as well.'

'Rusty or Andy been briefing you?'

'Both. You have devoted henchmen.'

'Then you do see I did the boy a service?' he appealed, if this big man could appeal.

'Yes. It was ... it was just the method, that's all. It did seem to me that you were warning the blow-ins at the same time, telling them to stand off.'

She waited for his anger again, but to her surprise none came.

'Well, maybe there was something like that behind my strong arm,' he admitted wryly at last. 'If they got such a message I wouldn't object. But I do assure you it was the only way to kill what had to be killed in a short time.'

He waited for her question and when she did not ask it, asked it for her.

'Kill what? Aren't you burning over that?'

'No. It doesn't concern me. Even if it did I was advised before I got here never to be a nosey parker, not among the nickel.'

'It *does* concern you, you *have* to be involved. Even

453

on the coast, even in other countries, there is involvement with this thing. And I challenge you to look beyond that door and not feel a participation now. Come.' Before she could protest he had her on her feet, impelled her to the threshold, tilted her chin up. The vastness of the sky almost accosted her with its endlessness of stars, but it was not that upturned blue and silver bowl that caught her breath so painfully, it was his fingers under her chin. Cool fingers . . . yet where they touched her she felt a strange, disturbing heat.

He had impelled her back. 'Involvement,' he repeated, 'and though I admire your prudence, Alexandra, in not asking questions, you added also just now "not among the nickel". Well' . . . a shrug . . . 'we are *not*.'

'And you raced in after young Bevis to stop him from saying that!'

'And to stop him from saying that deeper down than we've gone the geos feel there might be a strike to kill all the big 'uns that have ever happened.' A pause. 'No, Bevis wasn't there to participate, he was left at the depot, but he'd know all right. Only' . . . he ashed his cigarette . . . 'we're not sure yet, not anything like sure. For one thing we haven't the delicate equipment, nor the man to man it if we got it.'

'Then what can you do?'

He grinned. 'Get the equipment and the man. I'll be gone south before you wake up in the morning, Sandy.'

'Could I go with you? I mean could I have a lift into B.A.?'

'You were in today.'

'Yes, but . . . Mr. Wetherill, why *am* I here? Oh, I know you had a dream of balanced living, male and female, or so you say, but it just doesn't make sense, for in another breath you told me that none of these men work more than three months, and any man and woman can be parted for—'

'*Can they?*' he came in before she could finish. 'Is that your pattern?' He was rolling another cigarette now. 'I work from a different book.'

'Well, the book was wrong, wasn't it? You didn't get the women.'

'Only you.'

'And Janice.'

'I never advertised for her.' There was a definite note in his voice that cut her out of any discussion, and she winced at the cool exclusion. She hoped he had not seen.

'If men participate in a company,' she went on, 'as you have told me these men do, would they only remain on the job for a matter of three months?'

'Yes, because it's so costly, proportionally to them as well, so rigorous that if we can't get a show in that period they would do better to move out and on to somewhere and someone else. I tell them that in all fairness . . . though if they *want* to stop, then of course . . .' He smiled. Presently he said, 'It's different for me. I'm—'

'The boss.'

'I was going to say dedicated, but I suppose that's overdone. Well, any questions?'

'The one you never answered. Why am I here?'

'Why did you answer the advertisement?' he said for reply.

'Because like the mountain there to be climbed it was there to be answered.'

'Well, I'm keeping you on because like the mountain

there to be climbed you're here to be worked. So I may as well work you. The engineer will have a few reports for you to bash out tomorrow. Do you type?'

'Yes.'

'The geos might have some charts you can copy.'

'Then there's Rusty and the garden. Andy and the kitchen.' She said it brightly ... too brightly. 'And Janice,' she finished.

'Janice?' He gave her that sharp look he had once before when she had spoken of the girl.

'Propriety,' Sandy reminded him blandly. 'Your word in the beginning even though you scoffed later on. As well as the typing, charting, weeding, cooking, I can play chaperon.' She expected a sarcasm, but, like her accusation that his episode at B.A. with Bevis had had other things in view as well, he passed it over.

'Get your boots today?' he asked quite casually.

'Yes. Boy's.'

'Why not?' A grin. He got up, his head almost touching the top of the converted London bus. 'Think I'll turn in.'

'Isn't there a tray to be carried across?' she reminded.

'I hadn't forgotten. If you were thinking of doing me out of a job, no go, Sandy.'

'I wasn't thinking.' She got up angrily, went to the door.

'Better take my torch,' he offered.

'I don't need it.' As she said it she tripped over the same shrub that she had last night. She heard him chuckle. Getting up at once she ran, not tripping this time but more from luck, for she was running blind ... from temper as well as the dark night.

When she reached her van she stood a moment look-

456

ing back at the lighted cookhouse. She saw him standing at the door. Then she saw him take a tray and start across to Janice's van. She heard the door of the girl's van open, heard it close once more.

CHAPTER FOUR

SOMEWHERE in the blurred small hours she heard a jeep's engine springing to life, no opening or shutting of doors, for those long legs stepped over at will, then the waggon leaving the Oasis and starting along the gibber track.

So the big boss was gone.

Lying in her van bed, Sandy wondered drowsily what the place would be like without him. She had not experienced it without him. He had not been present when she first had arrived, only Rusty had been here (and Janice floating like a white gardenia in a flower bowl in the pool), but he had emerged from his van soon afterwards and the place had changed in some subtle, unexplainable way. It had been like a water-colour, she thought whimsically, for the Oasis had seemed like that after the dramatic oils of the desert, that had stopped being merely a painted scene to become something that moved and breathed instead.

Movement and breath. These, too, comprised that tough, rough, hard, vital man. Movement as he leaned over her when she had flipped out in the desert because she had taken no salt tablets, strong movement as he effortlessly carried her to the helicopter . . . of course it would be effortless to anyone who could carry Bevis. Then breath. His breath on her neck as he bore her, none too gently, to the craft, deep made breath sending warm eddies down her back.

Movement and breath. Had Janice got up to wave

him good-bye from the door of her van? Janice in something pink and feminine and just what this camp needed? Normal living. Balance. Male and female created He them. 'Rusty, you've landed yourself another boy.'

Like the facets of a kaleidoscope, everything was spinning round.

In the jumble, Sandy slept.

It was bright hard daylight when she awakened. One morning, she yawned, running water from the tap into the rigged-in bath, she must get up early and see what the young hours were like here. Surely there must be some preparation for that heraldic blue sky ... a tentative grey, a lilac daub, perhaps. It couldn't just burst blue like that shouting blue above her now. Also the air ... would there be a cool breeze before the burning heat set in? The dazzle of the red earth where the gibber did not spread more a pinky smudge?

She lay in the cool bath, completely encased but seeing the sky above her. She heard, then saw a small plane pass over.

When she finished, got into her jeans and shirt and went over to the cookhouse, Andy asked her if she had seen the spies.

'Was that a spy plane?' she asked.

'Who else would go over here in a Cherokee?'

'But what would be the use of going over a camp?'

'They'd see the gang was in again. Oh, yes' ... at a question on Sandy's lips ... 'they'd know we'd been out. They would put two and two together, or try to, anyway.'

Drinking tea, Sandy asked, 'How could they tell the gang was in?'

'Lots of ways – waggons back, clothes on lines, more smoke from the cookhouse chimney. Oh, there's enough signs.'

'But they wouldn't *know* anything. Not about the—'

'They'd know our result was one of two things: nothing doing – or the reverse. With Stone gone down south, and I tell you it would be impossible in B.A. to hide *that*, you can take it from me we'll be in today's sheets.'

'Information sheets?'

'Yes.'

'But does it really matter? I mean it seems cheap snooping like that and then selling what you see, but after all, isn't that the way of all press? A perfectly legitimate process?'

'That's not it, it's the hummers and hangers-on with no guts of their own to find what they want who come knuckling in on someone else's blood and sweat.' Andy tossed a pancake on to her plate and growled: 'Get that into you.'

Sandy felt she had been accepted, what with nickel talk and food offered camp style. She reached for the sugar.

Breakfast over, she asked Andy if she could help him in the kitchen, but she could see he was one of those jealous cooks, jealous of his own domain, so she accepted his thanks and polite refusal, then tried Rusty.

There was little she could help Rusty with, though. He was a handyman, and odd jobs and carpentering were not among Sandy's skills. The gardens as yet were not ready for weeding, and the watering was done by a cunningly contrived spray.

She collected a few mending jobs from the boys, but their clothes were tough and didn't wear much. Or at least, as Hunt said, they either stood up to it or wore right out. Hunt was an engineer, and he had some typing for Sandy. She went into the office ... and could have stepped into the office in any of the undertakings she had lived at. A table, a chair, walls of blueprints, charts with legends and maps. It was like Falcon. Takeover. Savage. Except, she noted, that the maps were very different. No dam-sites, no river diversions, no pressure shafts, surge chambers, underground power stations, almost bare evidence except hierographic marks here and there.

Hunt told her what he wanted, and she typed happily until lunch, which she had, cafeteria style, with the boys. She asked about Janice, but they were either vague or non-committal. Probably in her van, they shrugged. Probably still asleep. They were men and Janice was a beautiful girl. It puzzled Sandy. Either *such* a beautiful girl made them hang back or Janice had let them know right from the beginning she was not interested. Or ... and this was *most* likely ... Big Boss had established Janice as his property, obliquely warned them there was to be no trespass. Being the man he was he would see that he was heeded.

In the afternoon she did some copying work for the geos, mapping, structural interpretation, pit sampling, then, the sun on the tin roof becoming too unbearable even though no less than four fans whirred at her from every corner, she accepted an invitation to meet the boys in the pool ... 'strictly a neck-to-knee job, Sandy,' they laughingly assured her ... and was grateful, after the preliminary polite swimming around, that Stone Wetherill had prepared her for the horseplay that in-

461

variably goes on, the dive-bombing, ducking, pushing, then afterwards the water polo for which the two sides tossed up to see which of them would get a new player.

'I'll be no asset,' she warned.

'Then you can be a lucky mascot. You've won, Tim' ... Tim Bevis was the B.A. episode boy, now duly chastened and accepted to the bosom of the camp once more. He was an excellent swimmer, so, although the junior, had been voted the captain of his side. There was also, Sandy suspected, a determination in the rest of the gang to keep him from Janice, for he alone seemed interested in the lovely girl. Successfully diverted, Tim beamed at Sandy and told her what he expected in her play. It was a riotous game. Sandy had to be pulled out when it ended, she would not have had the energy to lift herself from a child's wading pool, and the sides of this tank were steep. She remembered, still with mortification, how Stone Wetherill had had to shove her up on her first swim. She didn't mind being shoved now, though, not by all those hands, and she slid over the top panting and waterlogged, her short hair that needed no cap streaked in dark tendrils across her head. Even her eyelashes stuck together with water. As she blinked her excess moisture away and looked up she saw that Janice was standing watching. She gave Sandy an amused look, but she paid no attention to the boys, except for a swift smile to Tim. The boys, Sandy noticed, paid no attention to her.

She looked so beautiful, so feminine there in her lotus pink culottes that it didn't seem feasible to Sandy that the gang could direct their attention to a rather skinny, crop-headed girl. Especially a girl of whom it had been said: 'Rusty, you've landed yourself another boy.'

But— 'See you at tucker, Sandy' . . . 'If you've nothing to do I'm playing some records, Sandy' . . . 'Sandy—' One by one they moved from the tank back to their vans, leaving their new polo team-mate alone with Janice.

'Sandy is very popular,' said Janice . . . but her voice was not so much taunting as thoughtful.

'Come and have a cup with me in my van,' Janice invited. 'It's awful being among the mob.'

'I don't mind it, and I do think they like having a woman, I mean' . . . hastily . . . 'women around.'

Janice let that pass. She was leading the way to her caravan, and because this was the first time she had made a friendly overture, Sandy, though she would have preferred to have listened to the records, followed the girl.

The van was untidy, but it would be difficult, excused Sandy, to keep it in order if one had brought many clothes. Janice had brought many clothes. They spilled everywhere – from the small wardrobe, over the chair, across the table, which Janice cleared slightly now to make room for two cups. She had what Sandy had not, her own tea equipment. Seeing Sandy's eyes on it, she said, 'Stone insisted. He keeps me away from the boys.' There was a note in her voice that Sandy could not place. Instead of triumph at Stone's protectiveness, it sounded more like resentment, frustration, disappointment. But why?

'Naturally, I should think,' Sandy offered.

Janice pouted, but said, 'Oh, yes, with me it would be natural enough.' She was very vain, Sandy decided, but with beauty like that . . .

She made a bad cup and poured it sloppily; domesticity would not be in her veins. But she was making a distinct effort to be nice, so Sandy tried to be nice back.

'Settled in?' Janice asked.

'More or less. I'm used to this kind of life, so I should shake down.' Sandy never mentioned how up to last night she had been clamouring to get away.

'Stone's gone down to Sydney,' said Janice next.

'I believe so.'

'Do you know why he's gone? I mean' . . . at Sandy's surprised look . . . 'he and I, well . . . we never talk shop. Or' . . . a little giggle . . . 'nickel, as it should be. There are cosier things to say.'

'No doubt.'

A short silence. Then: 'What did he go for, did you say?'

'I didn't say, because I don't know.'

'Oh.' Another pause. 'The gang were back early this time.'

'Yes . . . though really once again I don't know. I'm a greenhorn here. Entirely new to this stuff.'

'They go out for four, five or even more days. This time they came home long before they should. I wonder . . . You say you never heard?'

'No. I wouldn't understand it, anyway, if I did.'

A longer silence this time, Sandy wondering if Janice had done with her. She half rose.

'Don't go,' said Janice, refilling the cup with the indifferent brew. 'Girls together.' She smiled. 'But you also get along with the boys, don't you?'

'As I said, I'm used to this sort of life.'

'And you're just the type they'd warm to. I'm . . . well . . .' She spread her hands in a graceful gesture.

'I think maybe they are over-awed with you,' Sandy

proffered. 'You're very glamorous, Janice.'

Janice smiled a little absently. She had probably been on the receiving end of so many compliments that one more didn't matter. 'Yes, they like you,' she mused of Sandy. 'That's very obvious. I suppose you get lots of confidences.'

'I haven't had any to date.'

'Oh, I don't mean personal ones . . . they take time. But . . . well, camp talk. How the work is going. All that.'

'No,' Sandy said.

'Yet you were working for them today, weren't you? You were busy on reports and charts.'

'Yes, but that wouldn't mean anything unless you could understand or read them, otherwise' . . . a laugh . . . 'I probably wouldn't have been trusted.'

Janice laughed with her.

'You want to borrow a chart,' she said, 'and do some homework on it. Surprise them. I thought of doing it myself, I mean I'm tired of being the unattainable, I'd like to be included like you are, only' . . . a shrug . . . 'the office is always locked. But you with your work could easily—'

'Not so easily. Anyway, I still wouldn't follow what I was working on. Also' . . . a pause . . . 'I wouldn't do it.'

'Of course. I was having fun. If one doesn't have fun here one goes berserk – which gives me an idea. You drive wonderfully. Oh, yes, you do. Not everyone can handle a jeep across a gibber track like you did from B.A. Perhaps we could go out some time.'

'Go out! But where?' As she said it, Sandy felt ashamed. She was making the desert sound as at first it had seemed, red, barren, featureless. But it wasn't like that. She thought of the 'wurlie' Stone had shown her. How the longer you looked at this hinterland the fuller and richer . . . and even beautiful . . it became.

'Yes,' she said before Janice could reply, 'I'd like that.' Before more of the indifferent brew could be pressed on her, Sandy escaped to the mess . . . and beer and steak. 'Steak, always steak, except occasionally when there's steak instead.'

Guiltily, for she always had believed that women should stick together, she knew she preferred the men's company. Well, at her age that was understandable, but what was not understandable, and Sandy frowned, was the men's avoidance . . . it could almost be called that . . . of Janice. Yet wasn't it understandable with a boss like Stone, a man in whom possession would be a jealous and very present thing?

She listened to records after dinner . . . listened to the group the riggers were trying to form. Then Hunt was cornering her, remarking in an offhand kind of way that emphasized what he had to say much more than if he had not understated it: 'Sandy, I see you've been getting better acquainted with Janice.'

'Yes.'

'You two matey?'

'Well, we're not quarrelling.'

'Good. That is . . . I mean . . .'

'What on earth do you mean?'

'Could you . . . well, take her out of our hair?'

'Take Janice out of your hair!' disbelieved Sandy. 'Already you ignore her, as she does you.'

'Well – *socially* she does.'

Again Sandy asked, 'What do you mean?'

But Hunt would not say precisely. He skirted around by saying the geos couldn't work with perfume; that

Janice must have been in the office.

'It's locked.'

'Well, you know locks and keys.'

'Hunt, what are you trying to say?'

But he wouldn't say it. He substituted lamely, 'If you could keep her occupied—'

'Well, she's asked me to go out with her.'

'That would be fine.'

It would have been no use probing Hunt, so Sandy didn't, and she could reach no solution puzzling, so instead she shrugged and left it at that. When Janice suggested a run the next morning, she agreed.

'But where?' Sandy asked.

Janice had no idea, but once on the track to Quartz Hill, which Sandy considered should be interesting as well as safe driving, for no one could lose that remarkable hill, she talked incessantly. Girl chatter. But always the small inserted question. Did Sandy know if . . . Did she know where . . . Had she heard . . .

The old diggings at the foot of Quartz Hill had been long deserted. Janice sat on a stone as Sandy rooted around for interesting specimens, even, she said brightly, a lump of overlooked gold. Only that, of course, would start a boom here, something the nickel men did not want. They seemed to have enough on their plates already with evacuated natives . . . evacuated to more suitable grounds though many of them continually called for the old grounds . . . with yet to be fully convinced pastoralists, with resentful opal men.

Sandy looked up at the hill above her, the white peak where the sun touched it almost a tender pink. She wondered how many it had beckoned to it in the search for gold.

There was no gold now, but she did find a tiny hesitant stream, and, seeing that Janice was becoming bored, she called her over to tell her about alluvial gold, of which she knew a little, having panned with occasional success for it at other undertakings.

'You need a dish and a dolly pot. It's great fun. You get a queer, priceless, subconscious sort of feeling when it's actually close to you, like . . . why, good gracious!' For there was a grain of gold. Not mica, but gold. Gold was always gold, warm, unmistakable. She told this to Janice as she fished it carefully out. She saw that Janice was diverted. The girl looked at the grain in fascination. Would there be more?

Sandy told her she believed not, or if there was very little. 'Only a dentist job,' she laughed.

'Dentist?'

'The grains go to the dentist after you fill up a bottle, and a bottle holds a lot, but a pellet, that's an assayer's job.'

Janice's eyes were shining. She was more animated than Sandy had imagined she could be. She watched her as she put a tentative finger on the glistening gold.—Gold fever? Some people reacted like this to gold. But no, it wasn't the precious stuff, for Janice said breathlessly, 'Sometimes where there's gold there are gems, aren't there?'

'Rhodenite, blue agate, carnelian,' remembered Sandy of her own gemming days.

'Sapphires?' Janice gave a shiver of delight. 'Oh, I'm crazy about jewels; always have been.' She stopped abruptly, her face a study . . . until she turned triumphantly to Sandy. 'We'll go there. You'll take me. Oh, say you will!'

'Go where, Janice?'

'Thunder Arm.'

468

'Thunder Arm? But that's—'

'Opals. And it's not far, either, I mean not impossibly far.'

'We did fly over an opal field,' nodded Sandy.

'Yes, that would be Thunder,' said Janice. She looked eagerly at Sandy.

It certainly hadn't seemed far, thought Sandy, though in a helicopter . . .

'It's no distance,' persisted Janice, 'only twice the ground we've done this morning, and if we started early . . . Oh, it's fascinating, Sandy. You'd love it. They live underground there the same as they do at Coober Pedy. And the opals have been assessed as more than Coober's value. I adore opals – the flame in them, the gleaming blue, the green and scarlet.' She shivered with joy.

'But we couldn't get any, Janice,' Sandy smiled.

Janice hesitated, then said, 'Seeing them in the rough would be fascinating.'

'Yes,' agreed Sandy, 'it would but—' She found she had nothing to add to the 'but'. She had been asked to occupy Janice and certainly those shining eyes even at the mention of opals promised more than mere occupation. Again if it was only the distance to Thunder Arm that Janice claimed, then there was no reason they should not go across. Also . . . she quite looked forward to it herself.

She was cautious, though. She checked up that night. She asked Rusty the mileage, as she had asked him before they went the mileage to Quartz Hill. It was as Janice had said.

'Straight as the crow flies,' said Rusty, and pounced on a grub on one of his shrubs. 'Hard enough to get the flaming thing to grow without you taking your supper off one of the two leaves,' he said angrily to the offender. He began to spray.

There was no need to ask which track. Sandy recalled that there was a signpost of sorts several miles from the Oasis, one of the fingers pointing to Quartz Hill, one finger to A.S., meaning Alice Springs, with a formidable distance beneath it, and a third to Thunder Arm.

When Janice came across to her van that night Sandy told her they would get away at sun-up.

'If you can make it.' She smiled a little doubtfully, for Janice was never seen until noon.

'For jewels ... for opals, I would stay awake for ever. Don't you feel like that?'

'Not really. They're beautiful, but to me beauty is something else.' That somehow biblical landscape, for instance, Sandy thought, going to the door of the van, the age-old mystery of it, the savagery and yet at the same time the almost aching tenderness.

'I'll be ready,' Janice promised.

She was.

Now at last Sandy experienced desert dawn. The temperature in the sweet low eighties, a soft breeze that rippled the red earth where the gibber cut out, the tenderness of a pink, beige and violet-smudged sky that would turn into that cloudless heraldic day-long blue until the dramatic crimsons and purples of dusk took over.

'It's a white opal,' said Sandy of the morning gentleness, for white opals were like that.

But Janice was eager for her fiery gems of Thunder Arm, for the black ... and scarlet, indigo, crimson ... opals.

They reached the fingerpost and set out along the

arrow-straight track. It dipped down slightly into a pan, and Sandy was glad she was not travelling in wet weather, though that was very unlikely with the less than a tenth of an inch annual rainfall.

The track showed little usage . . . if any. The popular entry to Thunder Arm would be from the west, including as it did a larger opal field as well as the rim of a national rocket range.

There was little to see on the journey, but, unlike yesterday when she had grumbled persistently, Janice now did not complain. When, after several hours, dug-ins began to occur, the girl could hardly contain her excitement.

By the time they reached Thunder Arm, comprising a store and a water tank, Sandy felt an excitement, too. The track had become alternately dusty and rocky, with some very corrugated stretches. But even if you skidded, there was plenty to skid to. Right to the horizon if you wished. Sandy didn't wish, so she went carefully, which was hard because Janice was growing progressively more excited. She kept on saying 'Look—!' and grasping at Sandy. At last Sandy stopped and said they would walk the rest.

Janice, who hated walking, jumped down eagerly, and the two girls strolled past dug-ins and workings.

Most of the men were down their workings, but there are always moments for smokes, and those who had come up stared frankly at Janice, looking, with her dark beauty, almost an opal herself.

They went into the store . . . underground like all the camp was . . . and the proprietor showed them how comfortable and cool he had made himself.

'As well,' said Henrik Bruder . . . most of the miners were from Europe . . . 'I am cosy in winter. It's a good life in this little shop.'

'Paying?' asked Sandy.

'Well, not so much as a miner when he has a good strike,' smiled Henrik without envy, 'but when he hasn't, when he is only mining potch, I am better then.'

As they examined Henrik's comfortable quarters, all underground, Henrik, who had dug before he turned to shopkeeping, told them about opal mining . . . or at least Sandy believed he was telling both Janice and herself. It was not until they returned to the shop-post office . . . Henrik also ran the post office . . . that she saw that Janice had left.

She could not have gone far, though, so Sandy listened to Henrik with deep interest.

It all started off with a miner's right, Henrik continued from the post office end of the store, also underground. You decided where you wanted to work, put in your four pegs thereby marking out your claim, measuring one hundred and fifty feet square. Then . . . a grin . . . you dug. The top-soil could be one to two feet, and then there would be dirt and loose stones for a few feet more. You would be lucky if one of those stones didn't break your pick, Henrik said with joy. 'I sell picks,' he told Sandy.

Next came sandstone, loose stuff, then about six feet down real sandstone, solid and tough. If you had the money you could use gelignite here to help crash through. 'I sell it.' But you had to be careful and give yourself enough time to get out of the shaft. 'I don't,' said Henrik this time, 'sell coffins.' But nothing, he added, had happened like that yet, though slow climbers-out had got sore ears.

When you got right down you had to shift out the

dirt on a windlass. You could be lucky and strike straight away . . . it rarely happened . . . but if you did you couldn't miss it, it was like sinking your pick in glass.

When you finally got your opal you cleaned the sandstone off it, you followed the colour to see how far the colour ran. You classed what you had into firsts, seconds, thirds if you were experienced, but of course it wasn't you who finally set how much per ounce, not when two hundred dollars the ounce was only a medium sum.

It was an unpredictable life, mining, said Henrik, one might make as big a find 'noodling', which was going through the dirt after miners had discarded it, as sweating blood. For himself, he was pleased to be selling tins of fruit, stamps and souvenirs.

That reminded Sandy to buy a souvenir . . . and she looked round and realized that Janice was gone.

'Can't go far,' shrugged the shopkeeper, 'she's more interested in the finished product, that one.'

Sandy had a lemonade, bought an opal paperweight and an opal penhandle, then went out to look for Janice. She could not see her, but that meant nothing, as soon as you entered a dug-in you were an invisible person.

She went back to the jeep. She hoped Janice would not be too long. They had plenty of time, it was early afternoon, but Sandy wanted to be on the safe side. It was hours to dusk, but inland nights were instant nights, no pale preliminaries, no warning dove-grey, just fiery red one minute then all the extravagant voluptuousness of too many stars, too bright a moon . . . too much of everything. Sandy wanted to be home by then.

She reached the jeep and sat down. It seemed a long time before Janice came out of one of the dug-ins, but Sandy supposed it was just sitting there and waiting that made it seem like that.

She watched the girl cross over the rough earth. She seemed exhilarated, stimulated. 'Find something special?' she called to her, then laughed at the idea, for Henrik had told her how rare that was.

Janice hesitated . . . then laughed, too. 'No such luck.'

'Ready to push off? Because I'd like to now, Janice. I prefer to be on the safe side.'

'Of course,' Janice agreed.

Sandy reversed carefully, got back on to the wheel tracks, and they started for home. Janice did not talk much, but she seemed very pleased, still exhilarated and stimulated, so the day's outing had done her good. Sandy felt satisfied.

But her satisfaction went some time later when the jeep spluttered and stopped.

'What on earth's wrong with it?' asked Janice, coming out of her happy trance.

'It won't be anything. The boys keep it in good order.' That was true. Never on any project had Sandy seen vehicles afforded such meticulous care. Sandy pressed the ignition again, then again. Still nothing happened.

She got out and peered at the engine; she knew a little, enough, anyway, to see if anything was obviously wrong. As far as she could judge it was in good efficient order.

She came back and tried once more, adjusted several knobs, pulled, pushed, rotated.

'It could be a blockage,' she said. 'If I could roar the

474

engine, really accelerate it to its utmost—' She shrugged. 'But it won't even tick over.'

'Try again.'

The harsh scraping was repeated, with no result.

'Get out and help me shake it, Janice, sometimes that helps.'

Janice got out sulkily, all her previous elation gone. Together they shook the jeep.

Then Sandy gave the ignition another try ... with the same result.

'If you run it downhill—' suggested Janice.

'There is no downhill.' There was a slight decline off the track, but Sandy was nervous at trying that. If the engine still did not come to life they would be worse off than before.

'Well, I'm not the driver,' said Janice irritably, 'I should think at least you'd know why it won't go. It's hot here.' She dabbed at her brow.

It was very hot, and it would grow hotter. They were now approaching mid-afternoon, the hottest time in a centralian day. Even midday did not gather the heat that the afternoon gathered. It seemed that the sun, sensing its approaching decline, summoned its forces to show what it really could do before it finally bowed out.

Slackly, but not knowing what else to try, Sandy went through everything again.

'Is there any petrol?' asked Janice cuttingly, and Sandy answered that she herself had watched the tank being filled.

'Perhaps it eats up more than you estimated and you should have carried a spare can.'

'It couldn't be the petrol, there was ample pumped in for twice the distance. But just to satisfy you . . .' She found a dipstick.

She only did it to show Janice, so that the result shocked her more than it would have had she eventually come to this investigation on her own accord. For the dipstick came out dry: It wasn't possible! She had supervised the filling very assiduously, it was something she always took care over. Perhaps one of the gibbers had pierced the tank and they had lost their supply. She went down on her stomach to examine the tank, but found it intact.

'You forgot to fill it.' There was a slightly hysterical edge to Janice's voice. Sandy, experienced in this condition from other projects, experienced in the terror that can engulf some people when they are put in an unaccustomed position, when they are faced with an unaccustomed issue, bit back the retort that she had *not* forgotten, that they had started off with a full tank.

Instead she said nothing; it wouldn't help, anyway. What could have happened, though? she wondered; could – oh, *could—*

'Janice,' she said, 'while I was with Henrik, where were you?'

'You saw me come out, didn't you?' A furtive note had ousted the hysteria. Instinctively Janice's hand tightened on something.

'Look,' said Sandy, 'I don't care what you did, I just want to know whether you were in sight of the jeep.'

'I was underground like you were. Everything is underground here.'

'Then that's it,' sighed Sandy. 'We've been milked.'

'What?'

'Our petrol has been stolen. Oh, it happens everywhere. Even in the best centres it can happen, and at Thunder Arm with its petrol almost twice the price as elsewhere . . .' She shrugged.

'You – you mean they've taken it?'

'Yes.'

'We can't go on?'

'Not without gas, Janice.'

'But what can we do? We can't stop here.'

'Someone might come along. This is a public road after all.' But even as she said it Sandy knew how remote that possibility was; she had noticed coming in how unused the track was. Most of the travellers would take the rocket road.

'We never saw a soul on our way to Thunder,' cried Janice, growing agitated.

'That's not to say we won't now.'

'Can we go back?'

'You mean walk back? It would have to be walk, you know. No, Janice, it's too far. Also it's too far to walk forward to the Oasis. On the mileage we have covered I reckon we're midway.'

'What'll we do then? What'll we do if nothing comes?'

'I'm hoping something does, but if it doesn't . . . well, Rusty knows where we are.' But *did* Rusty? She had not told him where they were going, she simply had asked him a distance and Rusty had told her . . . and immediately channelled the conversation to his shrubs. *Did* Rusty know?

'I can't stop here,' said Janice. 'It's so empty.'

'It's just as empty either direction, at least we have shelter here.'

'I think the car attracts the heat.'

'In that case we can lie under it.'

477

'There could be things crawl over us . . . centipedes, scorpions.'

'Oh, don't look for trouble, Janice.'

'You mean don't look for it when it's already here,' Janice came back. Then she said the thing that shattered Sandy most of all. She said: 'I'm thirsty.'

Sandy looked at her quickly. Surely the girl had refreshed herself, as she had, before she had left Thunder. For a few moments she could not bring herself to ask.

Then . . . 'Janice, when did you last have a drink?'

'Oh, I don't know . . . at the Oasis, I guess.'

'This morning?'

'Yes.'

'Didn't you drink anything before you left that dugin?'

'No.' Janice actually giggled. 'I had something much more important to think of.' Once more, as before, her fingers tightened on a small article.

Sandy had a fair idea what it was; only one thing would tighten Janice's fingers like that. The girl had gained herself an opal.

An opal! For a brief moment hysterical laughter ached in Sandy's throat. An opal! What Janice needed was water. She needed water herself, or she would need it, but at least she had not started off as Janice had started.

The thing to do, she knew, was to divert Janice for as long as possible. Once the girl knew there was no water . . . and Sandy would never forgive herself for that, for even though the predicament they found themselves in was an unlikely one she should have been prepared . . . there would be *real* hysteria to deal with.

She said persuasively, 'Can I see your opal, Janice?'

'How did you know ... oh, all right.' Tenderly, almost with worship, certainly with obsession, Janice unwrapped the gem. Sandy stared at it, shocked. Entranced, should have been the word, but the undoubted value of it, undoubted even to inexperienced eyes like Sandy's, shocked her.

'Janice, this is really an outstanding stone.'

'Yes,' Janice breathed.

Well, this was no time to worry over the opal, how Janice had got it, for Sandy had a fair idea that no money had been passed over. The only way to regard the opal was to be glad it had filled in an awkward moment, though sooner or later, in this heat, in this burning-down heat ...

'I'm thirsty,' said Janice again. 'Where is the water?'

'I thought we should ration it. It's always advised.' Sandy tried to say it casually.

'I'll have my ration now.'

'I think it would be wiser not to. When night comes there'll be condensation.'—Sandy had read that, but she had no idea as to how one preserved that condensation.

'Tonight!' Janice was aghast. 'We can't be here then.'

'We might have to be.'

'I can't. I can't. I hate the desert by day. By night I think I'd go mad. Give me my ration and I'll start to walk. I'm sure we're more than halfway.'

'We're not, Janice. Also we're stopping here. It's the only thing to do.'

'You can do what you like. Where is the water? ...

Oh, I see now . . . you're keeping it for yourself.'

'I am not. I don't need it . . . not yet. I drank before I left.'

'I didn't, and I want mine now. Where is it? Where?'

Sandy said: 'There's none.'

'What?'

'There's none, Janice. I'm sorry. Janice, that won't help!' For Janice had crossed to her and slapped her stingingly across the face.

'There must be water,' she was crying, 'there must be!'

'There's none. But tonight' . . . hopefully . . . 'there will be. Janice!' For now Janice was picking up sand and throwing it at her. Never very emotionally strong, Sandy judged, the real thirst that already was taking possession of the girl was unbalancing her long before Sandy had expected it. 'Don't waste your energy, Janice,' she said as sharply and clearly as she could, and she was relieved to see that the words reached Janice.

She stopped grabbing at the earth and began crying. Sandy let her cry for a while, then she said, 'It's possible I could find an animal pad leading to a hole . . . even a disused wurlie. If I left you here under the car in the shade, would you stop, Janice?' She added appealingly, '*Please*, Janice, because in your dehydrated state it would be disastrous to venture out while the sun is so high.'

Janice nodded dully and allowed Sandy to make her as comfortable as possible on cushions under the car.

'I won't be long,' Sandy promised. 'I'll just scout around.'

She looked back many times to see if Janice was still resting. The girl was, and Sandy believed she would remain there; she was not an active type.

She marked her own way very carefully; a lot could depend on this.

Failing a waterhole or wurlie, for she had the feeling they were rare, she was looking for a seepage, however unattractive, she was searching for somewhere at least to dig.

At one time she believed she had found an oozing, and certainly a nauseous yellow trickle, glutinous with age and filth, threaded into the hole she burrowed, but she sensed that it was undrinkable.

She got up, still determined to discover something, but a dusty wind had risen, as desert gusts do and then depart again both without warning, so she decided she had better get back to the jeep before it was obscured.

She was wind-burned and red-eyed by the time she reached it, but ... thank heaven ... Janice was still there.

She sat down beside her, grateful that the girl dozed. She did some serious thinking. She had never been placed in a position like this before, her experiences had been where there was too much water, but she still knew that eight hours in such country without liquid could cost a man his life. She herself had drunk amply only hours ago, but Janice ...

She stayed very still, fearful of disturbing Janice. If only her sleep would extend to nightfall, the lowered temperature should help considerably.

She tried to remember the things one should do ... like plugging mouths and ears to preserve any moisture content. But she could not recall about condensation,

481

the very fact she should have stored away.

She looked ceaselessly for birds, for if birds hovered, somewhere there must be a source.

She was alarmed, when she opened her eyes again after closing them to shut out the glitter, to see a mirage. A mirage so soon? It was a large stretch of blue water, and it was so real she nearly cried out. By some miracle she stopped herself, then shut her eyes to shut out the tantalizing vision.

She felt dizzy and vague, and she knew afterwards that for a brief period she was either unconscious or she slept. But whichever it was, when she opened her eyes Janice was gone.

Gone. Gone where? Sandy was on her feet now and looking urgently along the flat, seemingly endless track to the Oasis, then along the flat, seemingly endless track back to Thunder Arm. But Janice also could have taken neither tracks, she could have veered out to either side. The radius that might be involved defeated Sandy. She stood there in frightening disbelief.

Then she cried.

Afterwards, when it was all over, she was angry with herself for those weak tears. They could have obscured her vision just as the dust storm had obscured it, only much more dangerously, for the dust merely drew a veil, it did not conceal like tears did. *Those tears could have concealed Janice's discarded head-scarf*. But, by some miracle, by some wonderful chance, Sandy saw the scarf between her hopeless weeping, and she knew at once that she must find Janice in a very short time.

The girl had not left the track . . . a subsequent hanky of Janice's told her that . . . she had started back to Thunder, changed her mind, then turned to the Oasis, gone back towards Thunder again. All this was established by Janice's neckerchief . . . then her silk cardigan . . . then her blouse.

Sandy might never have lived in a desert, understood its demands . . . why, she hadn't even known about salt tablets! . . . but she had heard of this calamitous effect of heat and thirst, and she knew now that she had to reach Janice very quickly or lose her for ever.

The dust fortunately was almost settled. There was still a haze in the air, but the wind that had whipped the red-grey grains into an obliterating curtain had dropped, and soon there would be glittering light again. She would see further ahead. She did not think Janice would have the strength to go far, not in her present prostration, but if she had stumbled off the track, or gone off deliberately in the mistaken idea that it was the right way, then . . . then heaven help *both* of them. For she would never, Sandy knew for herself, get back to the jeep again.

Meanwhile all she could do was stumble on, and hope, hope that that slight bend she was approaching now round the only drooping mulga she had encountered so far, in fact the only vegetation, for there was not even a show of spinifex, would reveal the girl. Because if it didn't, the rest of the track appeared gunbarrel straight, just as Rusty had said. Rusty! Would he remember what she had asked him last night?

Choking a sob that kept rising up, Sandy rounded the mulga. There was no one there. She let out a cry of distress . . . but changed it as she came nearer, almost in disbelief, not trusting her burning eyes, to a throaty gasp of joy. She *was* there! Janice *was*. Prone beneath the other side of the impoverished tree. Very little shade, but better than nothing. Instinct must have prompted her feet around to the shaded side before she collapsed.

She was beside her in a moment, lifting the dark head on to her lap, remembering before she was in no state to remember any more to cover the girl's ears and mouth for preservation of moisture. But before she covered the mouth she wet the lips with a minute, very minute remainder of skin freshener she had not known she had carried until she had groped for a handkerchief to tear up. What dampness was left after she finished she wiped on her own lips.

. . . And that was the last thing Sandy remembered.

CHAPTER FIVE

IT was like the swirl and withdrawal of a wave, Sandy thought vaguely. She was part of that wave and when it came into the beach she felt and she heard things around her ... felt a supporting arm ... heard that laboured chug that waggons grind out when the going is tough. When the wave withdrew, she withdrew ... from awareness ... too.

But while the wave was in she was conscious of an ordeal over, and of Rusty ... for it would be Rusty who had remembered and then saved them ... holding her gently. Once she reached up and kissed him gratefully.

He kissed her back, and she thought drowsily, for the wave was receding again, that it *wasn't* the sort of kiss that she had expected from Rusty.

When Sandy woke up, woke up fully, it was not in her own van. A van, admittedly, but not hers.

'At last!' smiled a woman she slowly focused, then remembered as Maggie, Maggie the nickel wife she had met on that friendly rival project the day Stone had taken her on a tour of inspection in the helicopter.

'Welcome back,' said another woman. – Brenda, the other nickel wife, and standing beside Maggie.

'How's Janice?' Sandy asked first.

'All right. Stone rang Air Ambulance and got her taken into Minta-Minta Base Hospital. She was badly dehydrated and needed expert attention.'

'But you,' came in Brenda, 'were tough. Mostly, Stone reported, you were conscious as he brought you here.'

'Stone brought me?'

'Yes, dear. Do you think you could drink a cup of tea?'

'Thank you. Stone drove while Rusty looked after me, you mean?'

'Rusty drove while Stone looked after you. A bite of breakfast, dear?'

'Thank you, Brenda.' That kiss. Not Rusty's. *His.*

'She still looks confused,' pitied Maggie. 'We'll tell her all.'

She propped Sandy up with pillows, and while Brenda brewed tea at the other end of the van, for evidently there was no separate cookhouse here as at the Oasis, told.

'When you didn't arrive home . . . Stone had arrived back meanwhile . . . everyone started to worry. Everyone debated where you could have gone, but Stone said that seeing Janice was in it, it would have to be one of two places.'

'Two places?'

Maggie and Brenda exchanged quick looks, then Maggie corrected, 'I should have said that Janice being Janice, it would be gems, of course. The opal fields. Thunder Arm.'

'Then,' took up Brenda, 'Rusty recalled you asking him about the direction and the distance to Thunder. So the two jeeps set off.'

'Why two?'

'Out here one never knows what one is going to find, it's better to have two back seats in case more than one is needed if there's more than one casualty. Janice was put in one jeep and rushed back to Thunder and air ambulance contacted to pick her up there. As I told you she's in Minta Base now and doing fine. But you' . . . a smile . . . 'were more of a problem.'

'But why? You just said I was tough.'

'But where to put you, Sandy? You see, you had to be put to bed, and being put to bed means – well, put to bed.'

'Something that at last our Stone couldn't do,' mused Maggie.

'Could,' suggested Brenda drily, 'but being the camp example . . .'

'So dear,' they both finished, 'you were brought here.'

'I'm all right,' protested Sandy.

'Are we that unattractive?' they laughed, and Sandy laughed back and apologized. She was still thinking of a kiss in answer to a kiss given, and her cheeks reddened.

'She's a little flushed,' Maggie said quietly to Brenda.

'Yes. Stone was wise to have us watch her for a few days.'

A few days! Sandy almost said that protestingly, but stopped herself in time. These women were doing her a kindness, or at least Stone a kindness . . . for no doubt that man would be glad to be rid of her for a while. She drank the tea and ate the toast.

But it was nice, she soon found, to talk to your own sex. Talking to Janice had meant talking *of* Janice, her looks, her clothes, everything about her . . . except the why of Janice. That angle, Sandy puzzled, had always been discouraged by the girl. Why, when she obviously hated project life, was she here? The answer naturally was Stone Wetherill ... but wasn't there something else?

Sandy stopped docilely in bed the next day. It was no hardship; she felt flattened out. But the following day she got up, and found the camp very inferior to the Oasis, a fact that the two nickel wifes proffered themselves.

'Our husbands are working for a big company, and mostly big companies believe that where nickel is, or might be, action is, or should be, but certainly not action wasted on establishing any amenities.'

'Here today but could be gone tomorrow is their motto,' took up Brenda, 'and in a way it's to be expected when they're so remote from the scene – Sydney, London, even New York. Never right *here*, like Stone. They see things differently in their air-conditioned city offices, they think "Why waste time and money on doing up a temporary camp?"'

'Also,' said Maggie, 'we're not officially recognized here, I mean not like you at the Oasis, Sandy. A paid, legitimate employee. We just tagged along after our men.'

That it had been a difficult tag Sandy found when Maggie showed her photos of her two young sons at boarding school in Adelaide. 'I miss them terribly,' Maggie sighed.

Brenda, little more than a new wife, missed the little home she and her Ron had built and then lived in so briefly before Ron had joined the company and been sent out here.

'It's a gipsy life,' she admitted, 'going with the drills. I shouldn't complain, we're in the money, but often I think of nice houses in nice avenues with shops around the corner.'

'White washing instead of brick red,' added Maggie, who told Sandy she had had eight moves in two years.

'Bill drives the rig, and I come with the utility towing the caravan.'

'Nickel wives are fools,' said Brenda cheerfully. Her voice made it evident she intended to remain a fool.

While she was at the camp Sandy went out one day to the drills with the girls. They regularly travelled over the sand and gibber to their men to cook them a midday meal. 'They're filthy and exhausted, too much so to do it themselves, so it's worth while.'

Sandy, remembering how Stone had come near to the activity but not too near, also remained a distance away, though ... as she told Brenda ... none of it would have made sense to her.

'Thanks for the consideration all the same,' smiled Brenda in appreciation. 'Naturally we're grateful for that, for everything here is hush-hush. But if there's one who *is* acceptable, it's Stone. So you, too, Sandy.'

It was pleasant sitting under a canvas umbrella eating barbecued steak. ... 'Here it's all steak except occasionally when we have steak instead' must be the general rule, Sandy thought ... drinking black tea ... feeling the red-gold burn of the sun.

Brenda sat up suddenly and drew attention to a rising haze in the distance. Sandy, who had been absorbed in the absolute quiet of a gecko lizard pretending he wasn't there, looked up, too. The lizard scuttled away. Sandy asked with feeling, because of what she herself recently had gone through, if it was a dust storm on the way.

'No,' said Ron, 'a herd. This is almost purely pastoral here, not like the Oasis that edges into the opals as well, so you can expect a bunch to go by. No one complains, unless it's the pastoralist when a beast breaks a leg in one of our holes. Like to watch, Sandy?'

Sandy was eager to, and they drove across. Not too near, for the cattle could be edgy, and even the ignition of a match to light a cigarette could start a rush.

They found a slight rise and stood silently fascinated as the great beasts lumbered by, clouds of dust lifting and wreathing around them, a rippling river of bodies that looked rather intimidating to Sandy but that Ron assured was jogging along quite sweetly.

In the far distance they heard the whirr of a helicopter and Bill said it would be Stone. 'Only 'copter around here. But Stone won't come any nearer. He's been in the Inside all his life and knows how things have to tick. He'll have seen the mob and will stand off accordingly.'

'But not,' came in Ron angrily, '*that* fool.'

'*That* fool' was a small approaching plane ... a Cherokee ... from the south-east, the same direction from which Stone had flown, only unlike the helicopter the plane was not standing off.

'He's been scouting after Stone's 'copter,' said Bill furiously, 'spying for his information sheet, which he'll print and sell, as to who is digging where. He must have thought Stone was on to something, so he followed. The sheet's bad enough, but that damfool thing kicking up that row is worse.'

For the damfool thing was flying over the mob now, the mob that had been proceeding quite sweetly, as the boys had said. That the drovers were unhappy was evident in their changed seat on the saddle. No longer they jogged along looking as relaxed as a Sunday after-

490

noon . . . Bill had said that . . . they went up and down the ranks, obviously alert for the first beat of a restless hoof.

'Nervy,' grunted Bill laconically to Ron, and Ron nodded uneasily.

'Reckon we'd better get the girls back.'

But before the girls could reach the jeep, it was on. It only took one beast to change his mind about his direction and the entire mob altered course. Thick palls of dust rose up as they wheeled round, no mere wreathing clouds now; the great press turned the other way.

The stockmen were on to them at once, the boss drover fairly flying along the ranks, the dogs racing up and down and doing their bit, but the great medley of horned beasts had started, and they were trampling ground that had not been planned. Countless hooves churned by in a wrong direction . . . at one time it seemed they were swinging towards the jeep . . . but the stockmen and the dogs turned them in time, and eventually they calmed down again, began moving once more in the orderly rhythm. But . . . and Sandy saw Ron bite his lip . . . the episode had cost a beast.

'There'll be trouble,' Ron said in a low angry voice to Bill. 'That idiot!' He was looking at the receding plane.

'Stone will take the beast loss as his responsibility,' said Bill. 'But there'll be a reckoning, you'll see.'

'He's landed back at the drill,' nodded Ron, starting up the jeep. 'Yes, he'll be wild all right. There'll be that reckoning.'

A reckoning. That was what Stone Wetherill had told Sandy he demanded. It had been on the occasion of Bevis. She had said coldly back to him: 'You're experienced in punishment.'

He had nodded and concurred: 'Experienced.'

Now she gave a little shiver, not for the spy pilot whom Bill and Ron saw Stone reckoning with . . . but for herself. At no time had she believed that she would go scot free as regarded the opal incident, but she had hoped the time and the place would soften any impact. But it seemed the time was to be now, with Stone's fury, for another reason, at its peak. And the place would be the drill at which they were pulling up at this very moment . . . Stone beside his 'copter some tactful fifty yards away.

He didn't come up to the drill, even in his anger he was still careful over that, but the distance between them did not diminish his white-hot fury.

'I'll deal with the fellow,' he called across. 'Leave it to me, boys.'

'Right, Stone,' they nodded.

There were a few more words between them, a few friendly words from Stone to Maggie and Brenda . . . remarkable how the man could alter his tone, Sandy thought; could the friendliness mean he would spare her?

Then – 'Miss Lawford' . . . there was absolutely no expression in his voice . . . 'can I see you a moment?'

She hesitated, knew she couldn't refuse, then walked across to where he stood in the shade of the helicopter. Perhaps he had used up his rage.

His rage, yes, but not his displeasure, disapproval and eventual reprimand. He was rolling a cigarette, not beginning what he had to say, as he always practised, until the smoke was ready.

'So our project woman,' he began, 'hadn't even the elementary sense to carry a flask of water.'

492

'Janice—' she began, feeling in all fairness that the girl could have thought of it as well, but he put up his big hand and brushed that aside.

'I'm not dealing with Janice but with *you*, Alexandra. You, reared for emergency, one could say, slipping up on a thing like that.'

'In the Snowy and the Takeover we didn't need to think of water, only how to get rid of it,' she excused herself lamely, and saw the anger flaring up in him again. Yet he was right, she knew with honesty, she had failed badly. She should never have left the camp without checking up first, making sure of that precaution. She had done something very foolish, even dangerous, and it was pigheaded now to fight back. Miserably but fairly she admitted this to Stone Wetherill.

He stood looking at her for a long moment, then he said, 'That must have hurt, but you still went through with it Good marks, Alexandra.'

'So you award marks as well as punish.'

'You remember what I say!' He said it in mock pleasure, and she flushed.

'Am I finished now?' she asked him.

'No One good mark doesn't wipe away several bad ones that I have to mention. Like going over to Thunder Arm opal fields and not telling the camp.'

'I did . . . in a way.'

'Yes, you asked Rusty the direction and distance, and luckily he remembered.'

'What else, Mr. Wetherill?'

'Oil check, gas check, engine check – did you go into all that before you ventured over the gibber?'

'I think you know I didn't.'

'Then say it.'

'I didn't check,' sullenly.

493

'Right. Now for the credits.'

'Credits? Have I any?'

'I just gave you one for admitting a discrepancy,' he reminded her. 'Here's another for having the sense to cover Janice's mouth and ears, to spare her all you could. You did a good job.'

'Thank you.' She said it a little dazedly. Really – this man—

'Well, that's done,' he dismissed. 'How are you feeling, girl?'

'Quite well.' She was more dazed still.

'Ready to come back?'

'Do you want me?'

'I certainly don't intend to keep paying you a salary that you don't earn.'

'You needn't pay me for this week,' she flashed.

'Drop it,' he shrugged. 'You're needed back. I'm expecting Janice.'

'Do you think that's wise?' she asked impetuously. 'I mean couldn't she stop somewhere – well, more like Janice – I mean—' What she meant but could not express was that Janice was not suited for this life, that he might be able to place her somewhere on the coast where he could fly across.

'Janice is not leaving me.' He said it so certainly and so intensely that Sandy flinched. To be loved, she thought with a sudden emptiness, to be loved like that . . .

'What did you think of Thunder Arm?' He changed the subject abruptly.

'Interesting. That underground living!'

'There are some tough types there. Sterling ones, too, but the opal gets the blow-ins the same as the nickel, and they're not always the best. Did you en-

494

counter any?'

'I only met Henrik.'

'Bruder. Yes, I know him. No harm there. Bring home any opals?'

Sandy thought of Janice's spoil, that perfect black ... and red, blue, fire and emerald ... stone, but decided that was her affair.

'No,' she answered.

'Nothing?' His eyes had narrowed slightly.

'A paperweight and a penhandle.'

He shrugged and dismissed that subject, too.

'When can you come back?'

'Whenever you wish.'

'Now,' he said.

'Well, I haven't any of my things back at the camp,' she admitted, 'for the reason that I hadn't anything there, but I still would like to thank the girls.'

'Then thank them here.'

'You don't think it seems – chary?'

He shook his head. 'These four are as sterling as they come, if I can expand enough to win them over to the Oasis ... they're on a top screw here now, so for their own benefit I'd have to better it ... I'll do it like a flash. No, Sandy, they'll understand.'

Sandy went back, shook hands with Bill and Rón, kissed Maggie and Brenda.

'See you, dear,' they called.

She nodded, a lump in her throat at these two brave smiling women, one with part of her heart with her two boys in boarding school, and one who had left some of her heart in a new house in an avenue with shops round the corner. Nickel wives are fools, they had said.

Wonderful fools.

Up in the 'copter this time Sandy found she could

orientate herself much better. Stone climbed higher than he had before so she could see how the different terrains overlapped each other ... the cattle stations, the opal fields, the gibber ... and future nickel? ... stretches. They seemed almost neighbourly from the air, but she knew now the hot dry miles between.

She had an enthusiastic welcome home at the Oasis, more, Stone said caustically, than she deserved after worrying them all like that. Probably though, he added, they were short of a man in the water polo team.

'I am not!' she snapped.

'No. You even once offered biological proof,' he grinned hatefully, and went to his van.

Sandy, after talking back to the boys, went across to the cookhouse and sat for a while with Rusty and Andy over a pot of tea and yellow cake. She thanked Rusty for remembering her asking him the direction to Thunder Arm. If he hadn't, she said, she and Janice surely would have perished.

'It's happened before,' nodded the two men soberly. 'You never take the Inside lightly.'

'If it had happened to Janice, I wouldn't like to think what Stone would have done,' said Andy.

'No,' Rusty agreed gravely. 'Not Janice.'

Sandy suddenly wanted to call out, 'What about me? What about something happening to me?' She managed not to.

Rusty said, 'No doubt Stone won't have Janice away a moment longer than he can help.'

'No,' agreed Andy, 'you can bet on that.'

All at once the slab cake ... vanilla sawdust, they used to call it at the Takeover ... choked her. The tea would not go down. Mumbling something and hoping

496

it sounded like an apology, Sandy rose and crossed to her van.

She lay down on her bed and tried to think of anything, anything at all . . . save Janice and Stone. I'm a fool, she told herself, as her train of thought kept coming back to them, *I* am the lucky one, I'm independent, uninvolved. I'm free. The ones like Janice and Stone are bound. Who wants to be bound? But she felt a hot sting of tears and turned her head to the wall.

Some time later she heard one of the jeeps roaring out of the camp, and almost at once there was a tap on the door. It was Barry . . . Hunt behind him, and Sandy was asked would she like a run into B.A.

'What for?'

'Good grief, here's a woman questioning the chance to browse round a shop!'

'I'm not, but my intuition tells me there's something else.'

'There is,' admitted Hunt. 'Stone has just left.'

'For Busy Acres?'

'Yes.'

'Go on,' she urged.

'He wouldn't take any of us, but there's nothing to prevent us going on our own.'

'Be explicit, Hunt.'

'Well, you saw what happened today? I'm referring to what Stone has told us.'

'You mean the cattle rush after the plane went over?'

'Yes. Stone was furious, and good reason to be, with beef the price it is that beast will cost him some hundred—'

'All right, Hunt, go on from there.'

497

'He would have had a reckoning, anyway, when he went in, but after the radio call—'

'What call?'

'Engleton . . . he's the pastoralist concerned who was having the mob moved . . . got through pedal radio to us and blamed Stone.'

'Blamed him?' she echoed.

'Indirectly. He said if Stone hadn't come out as he did the plane wouldn't have followed. He wasn't accusing Stone of being responsible for the loss of the beast, but he certainly was making him a kind of accessory. The small chance he knew he had of identifying the spy, for a plane is a different thing from a helicopter, only left him Stone to blame. And in the understandably filthy mood he was, Stone fitted the bill.'

'Yes?'

'Stone promised recompense, of course, but that's not the thing. In this mining business you can't afford to quarrel with the land, for that's what a cattleman boils down to, the land. No, the two elements, the *above* and the *below*, meaning the pastoralist and the miner, must relate. As it is, although Engleton will get a cheque for the beast, the bad feeling will be there, and that's why Stone left just now.'

'I see. And what do you want me to do?'

'We thought that perhaps a woman—'

'I'm not Janice.' They looked at her in surprise at that, but Sandy had no time to question the surprise, she went on, 'My presence would only inflame Stone Wetherill. Though perhaps that's what's required, an extra burst of savagery, for it is something like that, isn't it, that you fear?'

'Never *fear*. Not with Stone Wetherill. But yes,

Sandy, we do feel there could be an incident. Will you come?'

'To badger or bandage?' she asked coldly.

'Oh, come off it,' appealed Barry. 'You're the Oasis the same as us, aren't you, you have to stand behind Stone.'

'If it's force you want—'

'Not wanted. Anything that's done in that line will be done and done efficiently by Stone alone. We just feel that you should be there. You needn't even be seen. You can shop in the store. It's just a feeling, Sandy, that we both have. Will you come?'

She thought for a minute, then said yes.

This time there was no looking around as they travelled in, no discovering wurlies and watering holes. Barry drove quickly and silently, and Hunt barely spoke. When they reached B.A. they took her straight to the store, saying they would pick her up there again.

The store was different today – not the goods, they were as varied and remarkable as ever, but, in spite of the fact that there was a crowd in town . . . Sandy had noticed the number of blow-ins . . . the shop was practically empty. Only a few customers picked over the commodities, and the proprietor was most obviously preoccupied *outside* his shop. He frequently crossed to the door and peered up the street.

Sandy turned over the things with the others until the proprietor, noting and then recognizing her, came across.

'You're from the Oasis.'

'Yes. Did you get in any more boots? Women's boots?'

'Are all the boys in?'

499

'You said you might be getting some.' Sandy found herself being as close-lipped as any of the gang.

'What's going on?' went on the proprietor. 'We heard about the cattle incident and how Wetherill was going to stand the cost. Grapevine works quickly here, when you consider the miles between. But it's not like Wetherill to be so meek. And it's not like him not to get that cost out of the right party. He's in town, isn't he? Did he come for that?'

'I'd like a high-laced style, I think. If you haven't any, could you try for me?'

'How many came with you?'

'A black boot, or at least something dark.'

'I wonder if they've flown in the law yet.'

'The what?' That did put Sandy off.

'Sergeant Withers from Winfield Downs. He does the district. It certainly looks like he could be needed.' The man was right outside his shop by now and staring up the street. Sandy joined him. She saw that in front of the Palatial a larger crowd had gathered than on the occasion of Bevis.

'It's a barbarian place,' she said disgustedly.

'Sure is,' agreed the proprietor with relish. He turned back to his store. 'Did you folk intend buying anything? Then make up your mind. I'm closing shop.'

'Closing shop?' But it was only Sandy who said that; the browsers seemed to have experienced it before and not to be surprised. They concluded their purchases, and, with Sandy, were shown the door. The proprietor shot home a bolt, then fairly shot up the street. Already the other shoppers had gone in that direction; it appeared the only direction anyone was taking. Disgustedly, but curiously . . . though she wouldn't have

500

admitted it ... Sandy went, too. She did not know what she expected; there was no Bevis to be pulled out this time. She went and stood on the other side of the street so as to be out of reach of any nosey parkers, as Cleve the mailman had called them, for, recalling her last B.A. visit, she knew they were around.

But no one worried her on this occasion. All eyes were on the front of the hotel where a fan of men had formed a half ring. Behind the ring, and watching keenly, were Barry and Hunt. She also recognized several others ... the host of the hotel, the pilot of the small plane who had brought her to B.A. and who was evidently stopping the night and taking someone out tomorrow, Cleve, the contract mailman, the shop-keeper ... others she had seen before. There were also the blow-ins, unmistakable by their town clothes and their foxy looks ... foxy, anyway, Sandy considered them.

Finally there was the rival group; Sandy could not have said why she considered them that, but rival they must be, and not friendly rival like Maggie's Bill and Brenda's Ron, for Stone had emerged from the hotel, and he was confronting them.

She could not hear what he said because she was on the other side of the street and he spoke very quietly. But she could tell without words what was happening. Stone Wetherill was demanding which project had had a plane spy on him, and in that spying had started a rush in Engleton's mob for which Wetherill's were now being blamed.

She heard a low sneering laugh from one of the rival crowd; she saw another of them lean forward and tauntingly offer Stone a dollar note towards re-payment.

Both the laugh and the payment were mistimed, for Stone Wetherill's quick feint forward with his right hand as he hit out once but hard with his left, then repeated the action for another's benefit, both before either could take a second breath, was perfectly timed. The two men were as big as he was, one perhaps bigger, but it was all over in an instant.

'Like taking candy off a baby,' said Barry un-originally and breathlessly as he excitedly collected Sandy and began bustling her to the jeep.

'I think it was horrible! I think it was disgusting! I think it was—'

'Yes, Alexandra, you think it was—?'

'Oh, it's you, Boss.' Barry was looking almost dog-like at Stone Wetherill, and Sandy wanted to stand and stamp her foot, call out, 'What *is* this? What is this violence?'

She must have said some of it aloud, for Stone Wetherill answered, 'Violence for violence. That fool could have caused a stampede, all of you could have been trampled to death.'

'There are other ways.'

'Out here they would be redundant.'

'You really mean, don't you, that you only know one way.'

'Perhaps I do.' He looked at her levelly. 'Keep that in mind, Miss Lawford, for the next time you feel tempted to misbehave.'

'You . . . why, you . . .'

'Yes, Sandy,' he agreed, 'but not here. We appear to be gathering as interested a crowd as the skirmish did. Get into the waggon quicksmart.'

'I'm with Barry and Hunt.'

'You were, but you're not now. Get in, I say, unless

502

you want me to throw you in.'

'Like you threw Bevis?'

'Oh, no, the spectators wouldn't like that. They've had their blood, now they want some tenderness.' He had come nearer to Sandy. 'Get in, Alexandra,' he said in a low voice, 'or I'll lift you up very gently and place you in.'

'You said throw.'

'But *lover-wise*,' he taunted, 'for which these people will go overboard. Under their tough exteriors beat soft hearts. They'll delight in some tender play.'

'You're—' she began.

'Tell me on the track. I'm not joking. In one moment there'll be action.' He flicked her a warning look.

Sandy climbed in. She looked around and saw that Barry and Hunt had left. The crowd were nodding benevolently on them, and Sandy fumed at the kindly faces.

'They're imbeciles!' she seethed.

'Don't be so harsh on them, they're just love-starved until the next movie night, which, incidentally, you must see.'

'I'll be gone,' she announced coldly.

'I don't think so. The small print on a contract, remember.' He set off along the road, and the faces blurred out.

'I only came in because Barry and Hunt said I was a woman,' Sandy blurted defensively, then was angry with herself and her ridiculous words because she knew he would pick her up on that.

He did, of course. He drawled, 'They were wrong, weren't they?'

'I'm tired of your banter, Mr. Wetherill.'

He said wearily, 'I'm just tired, period.' He drove in silence until the bitumen stopped and the indented track in the gibber began, and then he drew up the waggon.

'Alexandra . . .'

'Yes?'

'Once I kissed you to make you better.'

'Had I known it was you supporting me that day,' she came in angrily, 'I wouldn't have acted as I did. I thought it was Rusty.'

'That's not the point. I repeat that I kissed you to make you better. How about a reversal now?'

'A. . . . Why, you're mad!'

'No, tired, that's all. And in need of a recuperating kiss.' The Salvation Jane blue eyes were near hers, and coming nearer. Sandy leaned back, then raising both hands pushed back hard against his chest. It was the work of a pygmy on a giant, and he laughed scornfully. But he did not try again.

'I'm not really interested, anyway,' he grinned. 'I have enough on my plate.'

'Yes – Janice.'

'Why not?'

'No reason at all, except you could wait till she returns, couldn't you, for that recuperation.'

'The wait will only be till the Oasis. She'll be home tonight.'

'Tonight?'

'Oh, yes, she'll be back when we get back. You can stand at your van door and watch me cross to Janice's. You've done it before, haven't you?' He smiled thinly. 'Do you want me to go on?'

'I want you to drive on.'

'You're in such a hurry to see the tender reunion?'

'I – I just want to shut my door on you, on this whole, violent, barbarian, primitive place!'

'It will be done,' he agreed, and he touched the ignition again. He drove so fast they were back almost on the heels of Barry and Hunt.

Stone got out, snapped an order to the boys to garage his waggon, then with a curt 'Good night, Miss Lawford,' strode across Rusty's lawn.

To Janice's van.

CHAPTER SIX

THE next morning things returned to the same routine as they had been prior to the opal and the stampede incident. Other incidents. Janice took on her elegant lady role once more, only emerging from her van at noon, ignoring the boys and practically ignoring Sandy. Sandy could understand the position as regarded herself; Janice was anything but a woman's woman, and this type of girl never got on with other girls, but she could not understand Janice's attitude to the boys. Those of them who were not good-looking were at least manly, even ruggedly attractive, or so Sandy considered, yet Janice still ignored them.

She mentioned this to Barry, and he gave a wry grin. 'You might have noticed our attitudes are mutual ... with the exception of young Tim Bevis, but he's new, and he'll catch on in time. All the same I think Stone should have a word with Tim.'

'Private property, hands off,' interpreted Sandy.

'Oh, no, not that,' said Barry. 'It's ... well, you'll catch on yourself.'

'I don't know how,' shrugged Sandy. 'Janice barely speaks to me.'

'It's not the speaking, it's the listening,' said Barry ... quite incomprehensibly, Sandy thought. Barry then said that the engineer and the geos wanted her to help them out as before.

Sandy was glad to be occupied the next day, glad to be sought after at the pool as a member of the water polo team. But not so glad one afternoon when Stone

506

took over one of the other side's positions. . . . Paul had a sore throat . . . and, playing directly opposite to Sandy, drove her so relentlessly that when the final whistle went she could hardly drag herself out of the tank.

'Need a heave up?' he grinned.

'No, thank you,' she said haughtily . . . then promptly dropped back in the water again.

He gave that hateful amused laugh of his and heaved her up in spite of her protestations. 'Don't be a fool,' he advised, 'and let your pride cause you to drown.'

'I had no intention of drowning.'

'Then you must have meant to hang on to the side of the tank all night. You're quite exhausted. Admit it.'

'Then it's your fault, you concentrated on me.'

'That's what the game is for. Also, I had other reasons. I thought I might make you tuckered up enough to stay still for a while and listen to me. You've avoided me all the week.'

'Did you have something particular to say?'

'Do I have to? Can't I just ad lib like the rest? No, I see I can't. So I'll say it all at once. This is it: When I was in Sydney I got the special drill I was after.'

'Nice for you!'

'I sincerely hope so.' His face was sober. 'Because it would be very nice as well for a lot of others if that was so.'

'Anything else, Mr. Wetherill?' Sandy went to get up from the pool edge . . . the rest of the gang had gone to the portable showers.

'No. But at least let me finish, can't you?'

'I'm sorry. You got up to the drill.'

'I also signed on a new driller. He'll arrive next week.'

'Do I say nice for you or nice for him?'

'Just say nothing, Sandy, if you can't do better than that.'

'I'm sorry,' she said again, stiffly, 'I just can't see the point of all this. After all, I'm only employed here. As soon as the small print doesn't detain me any longer I'll be gone.'

'You really mean the place does nothing to you.'

'Does a place of employment have to?'

'And that's all it is to you, isn't it? A place of employment. Oh, no ... I forgot. It's primitive, barbarian, quite disgusting as well.'

She did not answer him; she turned her head away. She did not want him to see the instinctive denial in her eyes, the bright evidence that the place *did* mean something, that the strangely moving, almost biblical purity of the empty vastnesses, that the harshness made soft by incredibly beautiful colours, had already seeped into her as high country places never had done.

He waited ... then when she did not correct him she heard him give a slight sigh.

'All right,' he dismissed, 'you don't like it, so we can't help that. But even feeling detached, I thought you might be interested in the new drill and the new driller. To be more explicit I thought you might *know* of the driller. Name of Ralph Hudson ... but that could also be Rolf Hartwig ... or Raoul Harber ... or—'

'What do you mean?'

'I don't know about the fellow, his nationality, anything, except what he says, what he tells me. That's the trouble. I've always handpicked my men before, but this time the men could pick their boss. There was overemployment offering. Good jobs, too. I was lucky to get this Hudson.'

'Then what's wrong?'

'I don't know, as I said. I mean there's nothing concrete, of course. I just thought I'd ask our project lady if she'd ever run into a Ralph Hudson.'

'No,' said Sandy, 'never.'

'Your answer came promptly.' He had taken out his makings and was busy on a cigarette. 'You were always closely in touch, I'd say.'

'Which way are you saying it, Mr. Wetherill?' This time Sandy *did* get up. She felt she had got in the last word, and went proudly to her van.

The boys went out on the field the next day, Stone with them, and the camp was lonely without the gang. Sandy worked with Rusty on the lawn, with Rusty again, for he stood in for Andy when the fieldworkers were busy, in the kitchen. But the time still dragged. Especially it dragged with no one else but Rusty to talk to, for Janice never bothered to exchange any words with her, until . . .

Janice came across to Sandy's van soon after lunch on the second day the men were out. Sandy, repleted with Rusty's large helpings which she had not the heart to refuse, was lying on the camp bed.

'Sandy! Are you there, Sandy?'

Sandy got up and opened the van door. She was shocked by the girl's drained face. Janice actually looked apprehensive.

'Have you seen my opal?' she burst out at once.

'Your opal, Janice? The opal you bought at Thunder?'

For a moment Janice did not speak, if possible she went even whiter, then she mumbled, 'Yes.'

509

'Have you lost it?'

'I don't know. I mean I had it. But it's not there now.'

'Not where?'

'Oh, how should I know? The van is so small, so cluttered—' Sandy could well believe that, the girl was incredibly untidy.

'Perhaps it's only mislaid,' she tried to soothe.

'That's what I'm afraid of.' Janice gave a little shiver. 'I think I'd sooner have it lost.'

'Janice, what do you mean?'

'Nothing. Nothing, of course. Well, if you haven't seen it . . .' She half-turned away.

'I'll help you look if you like.'

'Will you? It's terribly important.'

'Of course it is. A stone like that.'

'It's not the stone so much, it's . . . it's . . . Sandy . . .' Janice moistened her lips.

'Yes, Janice?'

'Will you do something for me? Will you promise not to tell Stone that I brought it back?'

'But why, Janice?' Yet even as she asked, Sandy felt she had a fair idea. Stone Wetherill would naturally resent such a beautiful gem when *he* had not bought it for Janice himself. Any man in Stone's position with Janice would feel the same. Yet if the girl had paid for it out of her own money surely that would help. But – *had* Janice?

Sandy stared extractingly at the lovely face, but was met with such misery, such entreaty, that she could not continue the probing look.

'All right, Janice,' she promised.

'Thanks. Thanks awfully.' Janice hurried away, leaving Sandy to muse over the strange position of a girl less unhappy over the loss of an exceptionally beautiful gem than over the possibility of being discovered to be the owner. It was, Sandy decided, distinctly odd.

She hunted around the camp for the opal with no success, but when she reported this to Janice, Janice was much less upset than she had thought.

'Just forget it,' she said, 'forget I brought it back. You promised. Remember?'

'I promised.'

The geos had left work for Sandy to do, and she found herself enjoying the hours in the office. Also, she found herself understanding her background much better, she who had only known water deviation, as at the Snowy, the changing of erosion into abundance to form a vast national reserve, as at the Takeover, similar experiences at Savage, at Roaring Billy, now discovered fascination in the nickel traps, as they were known, as reported in the geo books that she dealt with.

She read the unofficial comments the boys had written ... Boomerang Limited: 'Reasonable chance of commercial establishment' ... North United: 'Significant finds but needing further enhancement' ... Ebbsworth ... Vigil ... others. But there was never any report on their own Oasis among all the sheets. That, Sandy deduced, was kept carefully under lock and key.

On the morning of the fieldworkers' return, Sandy finished her copying and put it in a neat pile ready for the engineer and geologists. Then she went across to help Rusty in the cookhouse, Rusty having told her he wanted to take the first few meals off Andy's hands. 'He's on his own on the nickel traps, and it's no fun to feed that crowd when you have to do it over a fire and have only your own two hands.' Now Rusty, not a born cook, was glad to have Sandy's hands as well, and together they turned on a reasonable meal.

The camp, the same as before, suddenly sprung to life with the return of the gang. The engineer, geos, drillers and riggers, girl-hungry after a desert of men (even though the girl wore those Stone-despised boyish jeans and shirt) sought out Sandy, and soon she was swimming with them, giving them back as good as they gave her.

In the middle of the riotous horseplay afterwards, Sandy at the master end of the hose, Stone Wetherill crossed the lawn, stood looking at the scene for a brief, unenlightening moment, then went on to Janice's van.

'Pax!' Sandy was shouting exhaustedly, and they all took a rest on the struggling grass.

'Have to tidy up before the pikshers,' said Barry presently, getting up and hurrying across to be the first in the portable shower. The others who evidently had forgotten about the event jumped up, too, calling out to Sandy that the utility was leaving promptly at seven.

'Where are they being shown?' she asked.

'This time it's at Ten Mile, which is forty minutes' run from the Oasis. Are you going to wear a dress?'

'I don't think I'm even going,' Sandy said a little thickly. That dress inquiry had touched her. She realized for the first time how deprived were these men. Though she hated giving in to Stone Wetherill she knew that after her next visit into B.A. there was going to be something more hanging in her van wardrobe than a navy and brown shirtwaist.

'Of course you're going,' they said, aghast. 'Every-one goes to the pikshers.'

'Even the boss?' she asked.

'Not always, and never after a spell on the field, too much writing-up to do. But Her Ladyship goes.' A nod to Janice's van.

Sandy was surprised. Somehow the pikshers didn't sound like Janice.

The men didn't wait to persuade Sandy, they just took it for granted she was coming. She watched them queueing up at the showers, calling abuse if the one inside the hessian took longer than it took for him to finish a song. Strictly a verse and a chorus was the duration. A little excited herself, she started off for her van, remembering half-way there she had left the office door open when the gang had descended on them from the desert. She ran across to shut the door, looking with professional pride at the neatly piled work she had finished for the geos . . . or at least the first flick of her glance held pride. But something was different. It didn't seem the same as she had left it. She advanced a few steps, puzzled, and was about to pick up the last sheet she had done to check it when she saw Stone Wetherill walking across. The hose was still where the jokers had left it, and he bent over to coil and replace it. Not wanting to be admonished for her part in the revelry, Sandy took the opportunity to hurry out of the office and to escape to her van by skirting around the back of the adjoining cookhouse.

As she bathed she thought wonderingly again about those papers . . . they had looked differently placed somehow. But perhaps Stone Wetherill had been in-specting them while the boys swam and played. Yes, that would be it, she dismissed, towelling herself, then

513

scuttling into the van to examine her two dresses. The brown? The navy? Whichever she chose it would look dowdy beside Janice.

In the end she found a ribbon to put in her hair, and did so a little self-consciously, but keeping in mind the boys' wistful looks.

It was just her luck, she thought disgustedly afterwards, to run straight into Stone, whose quick blue eyes noted at once her pink Alice band.

'Who is marked down for the tender trap?' he said hatefully.

'I . . . well, you see . . . well, the boys . . .'

'It does nothing, Alexandra. I'm afraid you'll have to do better than that. All the same, enjoy yourself.' He strode off.

Enjoy herself! As though she could. She would have torn the band off then and there, only it was too late, the utility was tooting impatiently for her. Angry at that man for spoiling everything, for still seeing the boy in her and never the woman, Sandy joined the gang – and Janice, Janice not helping at all by looking even lovelier than ever in a very feminine cream crêpe. Though . . . and as before Sandy wondered over this . . . the gang were polite but never personally attentive. With the exception of Bevis, of whom Barry had said: 'Tim's new. He'll catch on in time. All the same I think Stone should have a word with Tim.'

About what? Anyway, it certainly hadn't been said, for Tim couldn't take his eyes off the lovely girl.

Once away from the lights of the Oasis the desert enfolded them in almost Arabian Nights plush darkness, the beam of the ute cutting a golden swathe in the black black gibber, for it was early evening, and the

514

stars only new slivers as yet, not up to their blossoming best.

As they approached Ten Mile they could see that many others had journeyed over for the piksher night.

'Why piksher?' had inquired Sandy.

The aborigines always called the one-night stand that, she had been told, and the name had been adopted by all. Mostly the programmes consisted of twelve year-old newsreels, ancient cartoons and silent films chosen either for their action or emotion.

The piksher man had put up his screen and the audience were settling themselves on rugs, cushions, deck-chairs or stools on the hard ground. Sandy found herself on both cushion and rug and thanked the boys for their forethought. She looked around to see if Janice had been similarly pampered, but Janice had left the Oasis group, and in this early evening less-than-starlight Sandy could not pinpoint her.

The piksher man began operating ... the twelve-year-old newsreel about which Sandy had been warned. The children, both brown and white, sitting together in the front row, voiced their boredom at once. They approved the cartoons, though, evidently not minding the flickers, but when the main attraction 'Broken Heart' came on, they began clapping their bitter disappointment, joined in by the male audience, and the piksher man put on the lights and said, 'Sorry, folks, I'll keep that for the ward at Minta Minta Hospital. We'll change to "Blood Gulch".'

'Blood Gulch' flickered on accompanied by loud cheers. It was a very old, wavery Western, older than the newsreel and with more trembles than the cartoons, but it was enjoyed by all, for even cowboys have their tender moments, and since they were brief, the children and the males allowed the females to enjoy themselves with a minimum of guffaws.

Interval found the piksher man augmenting his income by selling popcorn that had popped a long time ago and potato crisps no longer crisp. No one minded.

The lights went off again for the rest of 'Blood Gulch,' and in the last flicker of acetylene Sandy noticed Janice, far to the right, standing near a man she felt she had seen before. She frowned, then remembered him at Busy Acres. He had come up to her on that first occasion when they had gone in to get Bevis, and he had probed her, pleasantly of course, and offered to buy her a drink.

Now, as she watched briefly, she saw two things change hands, a small envelope from the man to Janice, a larger envelope . . . very like the ones in the Oasis office . . . from Janice in return.

'Howdy, pardner,' reported the lettering under the picture of two cowboys in Blood Gulch meeting up together again, but the entertainment, and for all its flickers and age it had been entertainment, was gone for Sandy.

That envelope that Janice had handed over. . . . That small envelope she had accepted back. . . . But most of all *her* side of the exchange, Janice's. The envelope had looked like . . . like . . .

The rest of the piksher night was torment for Sandy, even the riotous corpse-ridden end. She did not enjoy the journey home, which she should have, for the moon and the stars were at their exaggerated best now, the background purple velvet. The desert was no longer gibber, but silver stones.

The utility bounced into the Oasis, and after coffee in the cookhouse where Sandy fretted with every minute but knew she must not leave first, the party broke up, the men, after a long day out on the nickel traps followed by an eighty-minute journey there and back to the pictures, several hours on hard ground only partially helped by pillows, now ready for their cots.

But Sandy had never been more alert. She went across to her van, waited for a while, then put out her light, then waited again before she ventured out. She knew the ground now, there was no fear of falling over one of Rusty's trees. She went round by the back of the cookhouse, then quickly and carefully to the office door. No doors at the Oasis really locked, that is securely locked, only contents considered important were carefully concealed away, and Sandy just wanted to satisfy herself on a pile of papers she had left for the geos, papers she had thought . . . fleetingly . . . earlier in the evening had not seemed the same as she had left them. They meant nothing, otherwise they would have been put away, but had they been touched . . . removed? Had she only thought Janice had handed something over out there, received something in return? Not daring to put on a light, trusting to her memory, Sandy went forward to the desk and put down her hand. . . . *On another hand.*

The little scream she started was killed in its infancy by a large hand over her mouth.

'Be quiet,' ordered a low voice, and the hand remained there until its owner was satisfied she meant to obey.

Then Stone Wetherill released her.

She watched as he closed the door again, pulled on the light.

'Keep away from the window,' he advised shortly. 'Any of the boys not already asleep might see your shadow and take this for an assignation.'

As she did not comment on that, though there were many things that Sandy would have liked to have said, Stone drawled: 'Though perhaps rendezvous would make a more romantic word. Did you creep over to see me, Alexandra?'

'Of course I didn't. What do you think I am?'

'Frankly I don't know. I'm waiting to hear.'

'Then wait.' She turned to go, but his big hand shot out like a flash and whirled her back.

'What do you think you are?' Stone Wetherill demanded angrily, 'trespassing like this then believing you have the right to toss your head and walk out.'

'It isn't trespass. The office isn't properly locked.'

'Neither is the cookhouse, but you're not creeping in that direction. Neither' . . . a pause while he took out his makings . . . 'is my van.'

'I wouldn't be creeping there.'

'No?' he said deliberately, with a lazy amusement that infuriated her.

Angrily she came back, 'I'd leave that to Janice!'

'Jealous?'

'Jealous? Jealous of—'

'Yes, Sandy, jealous of Janice?'

'No.' She put everything into it, everything . . . but was appalled by its hollow sound when it emerged.

He waited a moment, then rolling and moulding, he lit up and exhaled. In the darkness the less dark weave of smoke rose bluely.

'Yes,' he mused, 'Janice. Janice would come creeping. But then, of course, she has a goal.'

Sandy echoed bitterly, 'Of course.'

'Why are you here?' He said it quite calmly, but the calmness she knew was deceptive, he had every intention of being told.

Loathing him for the position he had placed her in, that of informing him that the papers earlier had seemed in a different position and she had thought she would check, she told *part* of the story.

He listened intently. 'So you thought they'd been touched?'

'I didn't say so. They just seemed different, that's all.'

'You never bothered to find out, then?'

'Well – it didn't really occur that much to me until later.'

'How was that, Alexandra?'

But this time she would not tell him. She simply shrugged and said, 'My mind was wandering ... the picture wasn't very good.'

'It never is. Are you telling me the truth?'

'Yes.'

He waited a moment, his eyes trying to extract something from hers, then he smiled slightly.

'You worried unnecessarily. You must have gathered by working here that nothing of any importance is left around.'

'I just did my work,' she said virtuously.

'Pigs,' he disbelieved.

'Are you finished with me, Mr. Wetherill? It's late.'

'There's nothing doing tomorrow: we all can sleep in.'

'You're not going out?'

'Neither I nor the gang. We're expecting the new drill and the new driller. I'll be looking the fellow over before I take him out to the traps.'

'Are you always so suspicious?'

'Always. Suspicion, direct action and brute force are things that come with a frontier, and this is a frontier, Sandy, the last perhaps in this over-civilized, over-pampered world. The last, I should say, of its kind.' He mused on that a moment. 'Tonight you saw the last of the American West . . . "Blood Gulch", the boys told me . . . but now, this very moment, it's all being played out here, Australian style. You might criticize us for being the barbarians, the primitive ones, but there has to be the start, and this is it. Give us time and we'll level out, find in us all the niceties civilization demands. But until then there's a different order.'

'*Dis*order,' she flung.

'Ah!' He fairly pounced it. 'You admit then what you've brought about?'

She looked at him stupidly; what on earth was he talking about?

He looked narrowly at her as he withdrew something from his pocket then placed it on the desk.

It was Janice's opal.

'The souvenir paperweight,' he sneered. 'The pen-handle.'

She was staring at the beautiful thing. 'Where did you find it?'

'Around. Does it matter? So long as you've got it back.'

'But it wasn't—' She stopped herself in time.

'Yes, Alexandra?'

'It wasn't lost,' she said instead. 'I really mean—'

'What do you mean? What do you mean *exactly*?'

'That it's none of your business. After all, it's not your stone.'

'But it's my unfortunate result. This gem' ... he picked it up and looked squint eyed at it ... 'is valuable. How much did you pay?'

'I—'

'How much, Miss Lawford?'

'I—'

'Two hundred? More? Or' ... a long pause ... 'the location of a drill so that a few tough men in Thunder Arm could get busy with gelignite, which is cheap and doesn't leave fingerprints?'

'What on earth do you mean?'

'Just that. You never bought this opal, you wouldn't have the cash, I think. There's another way besides spilling a few harmless beans, because they would be harmless, Alexandra. Our real expectations would never be revealed to you, they would stop with us, but that other way I don't think you adopted. Or' ... an estimating pause ... 'did you?'

'What other way?' she asked.

'The oldest way on earth.' He gave a low laugh as, infuriated, she raised her hand at him.

'Sorry,' he apologized, stopping her first, 'I said that I *didn't* think that.

'You see,' he went on, 'we're continually arguing with the gem men. They believe we're trespassing with the nickel search. So do the pastoralists, though to a lesser degree, for they're more open to reason, knowing we can benefit them so often, put them on to water they didn't know they had. But some of the gem men are tough, they fight back. It might interest you, Alexandra Lawford, to learn that just after you left for Blood Gulch tonight I had a bloody time myself. Even back here I heard the explosion. A few sticks of gelignite lobbed into my field equipment was as good as a

521

letter to say Push Off.'

'Was – was anything harmed?'

'Everything. Gelignite just doesn't make a noise. Luckily it was lesser equipment – a rig or so. But the real stuff isn't left round for a woman to clap her eyes on and then sell for an opal.'

'I didn't!' she protested.

'Who then? You were with me when we went out that day, no one else.'

'This is all unbelievable. It's . . . it's . . .'

'Far-fetched? Yes. But it still exists. A lot of the gem men feel that we nickel boys are squeezing them out. A few of the tough ones are fighting back. I've been very unlucky in this. I've never encroached on their fields, not at any time, I've had no need to. However, because someone wants an opal, and deliberately or stupidly – for yes, Alexandra, I'm giving you that benefit of a doubt – shoots her mouth off, I have to suffer.'

'Will you fight back?'

'No. But I'll let them know they made a damn mistake.'

'Will they . . . will they recompense you?'

'When they've already let go a valuable opal? Not a chance.'

There was silence in the room. Stone Wetherill finished and ashed his cigarette.

'Here it is, Alexandra.' He handed her the beautiful stone.

'I don't want it.'

'Then get the thing out of my sight, for I don't want it either. Women! Damn chattering women!' He went across and flung open the door.

'The light,' she reminded him tautly, 'remember the rendezvous.'

'With you?' He gave a short laugh. 'And yet' . . . with estimation . . . 'it's not a bad idea at that, though it has an old-world sound, hasn't it, that rendezvous, more in keeping with lavender and lace, not gibber and canvas. But perhaps we could try it.' He was taking her with a contemptuous gentleness in his big arms.

The taunting in the Salvation Jane blue eyes so near now to hers angered Sandy. 'Get away!' she said.

'No lavender and lace, then? You prefer primitive approach? Like this?'

If ever she had been in a man's arms before, and Sandy had, those other arms from this moment were nothing, from now on she would never even faintly remember them. For there was no love and softness here, no gentleness, no consideration, no protection . . . there was hardness, passion, mastery, fire, savage demand instead. Challenge. A little amusement. – But never tenderness.

The next morning Barry told Sandy about the gelignite incident. It was true, she learned, that a few sticks had been lobbed into one of their equipments. Not an important one, otherwise Thunder Arm would never have known its existence, the real thing was kept as close-shut as an oyster. However, this digging, said Barry, though certainly not advertised was certainly also no secret, and fairly easy to find.

'Then you don't blame me?' she asked.

He looked at her in surprise. 'No one does.'

'Your boss does.'

'Not really,' he grinned.

'He pointed out to me that I was the only one who had been out on the nickel . . . I mean, of course, apart from the staff.'

'He was having a bark. All dogs have to bark some-time, and he's a dog if I ever knew one.'

'Native variety? Warrigal? Dingo?'

'Now come off it, Sandy, you're being too tough on him.'

'Isn't that what we're all supposed to be here? Tough?' Sandy said feelingly, remembering that hard ruthless mouth last night.

'Not entirely. There has to be a balance, a softness somewhere.'

'Then he missed out.'

'That's where you're wrong, entirely wrong. I'd like to tell you, only it's his story, his and Janice's.'

'Obviously!'

'No, not that way at all.'

'We were speaking,' came in Sandy, 'of the gelig-nite incident. I just can't believe such a thing could happen.'

'It's happened before. Will again, unless the gem fields succeed in ridding themselves of their rougher members. Mainly the opal blokes are good blokes, and that's saying a lot, for heaven knows no one puts up with a rougher life. Not even nickel fools' . . . he gave a wry laugh . . . 'have such heart-straining, back-break-ing battles, not only against the weather, and the con-ditions, and the loneliness, but actually with the work itself. You think the gibber's tough? Well, you should see the hard going on opal digging when the shaft turns stubborn.'

'It all seems very unruly to me. Surely there's a boundary line saying which belongs to whom?'

'It's all leasehold,' said Barry, 'pastoral, nickel, opal, what-have-you, and our present trouble began when the gem grants were issued this last time when some of the miners were in Adelaide in the high summer to escape the worst of the heat. They missed out by being absent and are now unable to peg new claims. It isn't so bad when they keep equal pace on their old claims, but when someone on a new claim makes a find they're angry. They see the claims they've missed out on, they see others operating these imaginary claims . . . nickel men included . . . and they finally see red, not opal.'

'And they act accordingly?'

'Yes. But only occasionally, thank heaven. Anyway, this is the first time for us. For one thing this area is not really good opal potential, and they know it. For another thing even though gelignite leaves no finger-prints, there's still a risk.'

'What about the Government?' she asked.

'Oh, no, they're not brought in.' Barry gave a small smile.

'Then – reprisal?' Sandy said in horror. What kind of a land was this?

'Let's say that Stone Wetherill will be visiting Thunder today, after which I don't think we'll be bothered any more, thank you.'

'It's unbelievable! It's right back to the bad old days.'

Barry said, just as Stone Wetherill had said last night, 'Give us time and we'll level out.'

'This place will never be better than it is now – primitive, barbarian, only for ruffians.'

'I say, Sandy—' protested Barry, but Sandy swept by him and made for Janice's van. She had just seen Janice at the window, and she was going to return her opal.

Janice went into squeals of joy as she held the gem in her hands once more.

'My glorious darling again!' She kissed the stone. 'Where did you find it?'

'I didn't. Mr. Wetherill did.'

Janice stopped caressing the opal. She went pale. 'Did – did you tell him it was mine?'

'He never asked.'

'Then you didn't tell him?'

'No.'

'Oh, thank you, Sandy, thank you!'

'Why were you frightened of him knowing, Janice?'

'I ... well ... well, you know how it is. He mightn't have liked me having such a lovely thing.' Janice had a sudden inspiration. 'I mean when *he* didn't give it to me,' she added.

Sandy had thought on the same lines herself, but now Janice's confirmation came raw and biting.

'I suppose so,' she conceded with a difficulty she despised. She was silent a moment. 'You knew that they blew up a rig, Janice?'

'No,' Janice said briefly.

'Well, they did. Stone has gone over.' At least, Sandy thought maliciously, if the rig being treated to gelignite didn't particularly affect Janice, the fact that Stone Wetherill was over there did. For the girl went ghastly white this time.

'Stone has gone over ... do you think he'll find out?'

'Find out what?'

'That ... well, that I spent as much as I did.'

'*Did* you, Janice?' Sandy looked hard at the girl, then turned and went out.

Janice did not appear all day, not even when the jeep, with Stone at the wheel, came out of the desert.

From Thunder? Sandy wondered.

Wherever he had come from, Stone Wetherill looked satisfied with things. He called out to the men, 'She's jake,' and they nodded back.

Sandy was standing near them, her mouth a little parted from the questions that were fairly aching to come out. What had happened? Had there been a reckoning? Had he learned the truth? What was the truth?

He looked consideringly at her, rolling and lighting his cigarette as he did so, then he nodded to Janice's van. 'In?'

'Yes.'

He crossed over.

It was half an hour before he emerged again, and when he did it was with Janice, his arm on her shoulder. The girl flashed Sandy a quick triumphant look.

Stone Wetherill looked at her, too, a hard, narrowed, challenging glance. Challenging her to begin something.

Sandy stood and looked back, but she could not stare out those slits of brilliant blue eyes, and she turned away. She heard him give a soft laugh, that evidently Janice believed she should join in, too. The pair of them laughed quietly . . . significantly? . . . together.

Sandy went rather blindly towards her caravan, but before she reached it another vehicle came into the Oasis. From B.A. direction this time. Cleve, the contract mail and transport man, and beside him another man . . . the new driller presumably, Ralph Hudson.

Across Rusty's struggling lawn Sandy looked at him. She had never seen him before, and yet . . .

The man looked back at her without recognition.

Between the two of them Stone Wetherill looked at

both of them in turn, looked quietly but keenly. Then he came forward and took the newcomer's hand.

'Name of Hudson,' he announced to the camp. 'He'll be on the new drill. Hudson, meet Goddard, Brent, Smith, Willis . . .' He went on through the engineer, geos, drillers, riggers. He presented Andy and Rusty. 'Janice Ferris,' he said next. Finally: 'Alexandra Lawford.'

No, Sandy decided once more, she had never seen him before.

Yet . . .

CHAPTER SEVEN

In the several days that followed Sandy brushed aside any small cobweb of wonder she had felt regarding the new driller, for Ralph Hudson proved a quiet, agreeable person, and appeared to fit easily into the Oasis regime.

Half of the gang had returned to the nickel traps again, but Hudson was being introduced to the camp and its surroundings, briefed on the new drill that had arrived and what this new deeper drilling would entail. Stone Wetherill had stayed behind to instruct him about this. Among the others who were in camp was young Tim Bevis, and the boy did not conceal his delight at having more of the company of Janice than he had anticipated.

On the second morning, Sandy, working in the outer office, heard Barry, also staying behind at the camp, speaking in the inner office to Stone Wetherill about this. Or at least she gathered that it could be the matter under discussion.

'He's seeing a lot of her, boss,' Sandy heard Barry intone a trifle uneasily.

'Then that's good,' came back Stone Wetherill. 'It's always better to form your own opinion. It counts more when it needs to count.'

'But is it – wise?'

'Why not? We've never had him anywhere that really adds up.'

'Yet in time—'

'By that time,' Stone Wetherill came in confidently,

'there'll be no need for us to consider whether we should speak or not, he'll have decided things on his own account. I've watched him. The lad's all right.'

Barry must have decided to accept this, for he started next on their new driller.

'Is Hudson the right man?' he asked directly.

'Why do you say that?' Stone's answer came sharply.

'I was wondering why you were keeping him in here.'

'You're here, aren't you? Half the gang is here.'

'Yes, but Hudson's case is different, he's to be a key man, isn't he? Oh, I know there's been some gen to give him, but—'

'We're all key men here,' said Stone, 'different size keys perhaps, but just as necessary when it comes to an opening up. But I see your trend. You're thinking of time lost, of the big companies that never sleep, and you're dead right, but Hudson came with a list of merits as long as your arm, and I had to make sure those merits *were* his. You might have noticed the hours the two of us have been cloistered together.'

'I noticed. Does Hudson pass?'

'He does.' Stone's voice betrayed nothing at all. 'The fellow knows drilling all right. It's just . . .'

But at that juncture Stone must have noticed a shadow in the outer office, for he started on a different topic. Not wanting the men to know she had over-heard, yet actually she had heard very little, Sandy went quietly out.

As she crossed Rusty's lawn she refused to ponder on that first topic the men had spoken about, the one that could have referred to Janice and Tim Bevis. After all, no names had been mentioned, and Sandy had not

530

lived in projects all her life not to know the pitfalls of jumping to conclusions regarding identities. The circle of living was so small, so confined, things became exaggerated, blown-up, where they should have remained postcard size.

Hudson, though, *had* been named, and she found herself estimating that hesitant 'It's just . . .' of Wetherill's regarding the new man and measuring it against her own previous uncertain 'And yet . . .'

However, passing Ralph Hudson at that moment, she found herself smiling back at his amiable grin, and reproving herself for indulging in 'camp-itis', a well-known (in camps) affliction that made campers see more in things than existed.

But one thing, Sandy progressively decided next, by this time passing Janice's van, Tim Bevis's infatuation with Janice was *not* 'camp-itis', *not* imagination. Whenever Tim was not detailed to a job he was hanging around obviously in the hope of seeing the girl. He was there now, and Janice was graciously leaning out of the window and allotting the boy some of her attention. (The rest, Sandy noted, was on the receding Hudson.) In spite of her previous refusal to consider this topic of Janice and Tim, Sandy found now that she had to wonder at the answer that Stone had given to Barry when Barry had said, 'He's seeing a lot of her.' She found she had to wonder at that 'Why not?' with which Wetherill had come back. It seemed an odd answer when the girl was . . . *his* girl. Well, she was, wasn't she? His girl! Sandy tasted that, and, in spite of herself, of her better judgment, found it bitter.

The next morning Stone tapped on her caravan door and when she opened up handed in a tray of breakfast.

'Why, thank you,' she said, confused, 'but you shouldn't have . . . I mean . . .'

'It's a matter of expedition,' he dismissed briefly. 'I'm driving Hudson out to see the lie of the land.'

'Then don't let me stop you.'

'I decided you could see it, too.'

'I've seen it,' she reminded him. 'Several times into B.A. Over to Thunder Arm. Quartz Hill. Also from your helicopter.'

'This time we're going in a different direction. North-west.'

'I hope Mr. Hudson finds it interesting.'

'You have fifteen minutes. That's why I brought a tray. You can grab a mouthful as you dress.'

'You're very considerate, but no.'

'No what?' he asked baldly.

'No, I'm not coming. I have some typing to do for Barry.'

'That can wait.'

'I prefer to do it this morning.'

He came right into the van, and all at once Sandy was aware of the short pink cover she wore over her short pink pyjamas. She drew it closer to her.

'You seem to have the wrong idea,' he said. 'This is not an invitation, this is an order. Now stop making excuses I don't intend to listen to, and get dressed.'

'*When* you leave, Mr. Wetherill,' said Sandy icily, and without another word he turned and went.

'Pig!' she said, inflamed, stuffing toast into her mouth after she had skipped her bath and made do with a sluice from a dipper of water. She shoved a plaid cotton shirt into her hipster jeans, took up a large-brimmed hat.

'Five minutes!' he called from the jeep. He had a

penetrating voice.

Not 'Whistle my lad and I'll come' seethed Sandy as she crossed to where he and Hudson were waiting, but 'Shout and I'll run'. Deliberately she made herself take her time, and knew from his narrowed eyes and thinnéd mouth as she eventually reached the two men that her insolence had not escaped his notice.

'You'll keep,' he said softly for her ears alone as she quickly took in the seating position and promptly put herself in the back of the jeep. Ralph Hudson sat himself beside Stone Wetherill, and they bounced out of the Oasis into the vast red terrain.

Sandy could see no road at all. The one into B.A. had fair indentations, the Quartz Hill and Thunder Arm tracks at least could not have been mistaken for wind ripples, but now there seemed nothing at all. However, one look at the back of that proudly-held head of Wetherill's and you knew he was aware of every inch he travelled, that even on a moonless, starless night, if this interior ever had such nights, he would unwaveringly find his way dead on target.

Sandy regarded the head with dislike. What an autocrat it belonged to! Having finished her critical scrutiny of hair, ears, neck and straight broad back, she turned her attention to Ralph Hudson, almost as tall, as large, as dark-haired ... and somehow, *somehow* familiar. I've never seen him before, she remembered thinking on Hudson's arrival, and yet ...

And yet ...

Stone Wetherill was pulling up the jeep. No need to pull aside out here, for there would be no traffic. He stopped just where he wished to stop, and began pointing out items of interest to the new driller.

'You haven't been to the opal fields, Hudson' .. . he

called him Hudson, and it interested Sandy; every other man at the Oasis went by his first name.

'No,' Ralph said.

'Our passenger has.' Stone did not turn his head. 'This stretch here is identical to Thunder Arm terrain, I always think. It's not only my opinion' . . . he waved a hand to a shaft some hundred yards away that Sandy noticed for the first time . . . 'it looks as though we have a lone prospector. A pity, Miss Lawford, you didn't come out here for your opal. I think you may have got a better deal as well as causing a deal less trouble. Happen to have the prize with you, by the way? I could ask our friend about slicing it for you.'

'No,' Sandy said shortly, and Wetherill hunched his shoulders.

'Not much use in its present form,' he reminded her, and got lazily out and crossed over to the rig to speak to the prospector.

As she watched him go, covering the clay and gibber with long practised strides, practised in the rough impact of hard stones and crusted earth, Sandy said angrily, 'It never was my stone.'

'No?' Ralph Hudson said almost idly. He had got out of the jeep to pick up a piece of matrix, which was a mixture of silicone and sand. He tossed it idly in his hand as he smiled and suggested, 'Miss Ferris's, I would say.'

'Yes, she—' Sandy stopped herself. She had learned very early in her project life that a still tongue, or still, anyway, as regarded others, was a very wise thing in a camp.

Hudson had come back to his seat in the front of the jeep, and for a moment, as before, Sandy felt she had known him once. She was grateful to him that he did not press her as to what she had started to say. He *is* nice, she decided firmly . . . wondering at once why she could not really *feel* that. For she wasn't feeling it. Exasperation with herself at her unreasonable attitude was expended in a studied lack of interest when Stone returned from the rig with some potch for Hudson to examine. She turned her head away as Stone told Ralph that semi-précious finds usually went with opals. For instance, topaz, jasper, also gems suitable for tumbling and polishing. Also, he added significantly, often it lived next door to the beckoning nickel.

There was no difficulty if you wished to try your opal luck, Stone continued, depths could vary from eighteen inches to eighty feet, and no timbering or shoring necessary, as opal potential was always located on solid beds of sandstone. Yes, sandstone, he nodded, it didn't look like sandstone here, but under that broken clay and gibber it was there all right. Opal mining was almost pure hazard, Stone added, the geos couldn't help you find it as with nickel.

Sandy, still looking impertinently away, stole a quick glance back to see what effect her rudeness was making on Wetherill, and was chagrined to find that her pose had passed Stone by, that his attention was solely on Hudson. His Salvation Jane eyes were those blue slits again, his mouth unrevealing.

'Odd to think,' he was intoning to Ralph, 'that a serpentine belt, or intrusive, in other words the host rock, host to what we're all after, could also relate to sandstone. For instance there's no blackbutt trees here, which can be a nickel indication, there's no trees at all, but yet—'

'But yet there is gossan,' Hudson said impulsively. He was staring at a group of light brown iron silica rocks not many yards away from where Wetherill had pulled up the jeep. Before he could look up at Stone to laugh and shrug, 'The one thing I *do* know, Wetherill, and supplied to me by the Mines Department before I came up here,' Sandy's and Stone's eyes met . . .

That look was over in an instant. Ralph was now apologizing for being the complete greenhorn and Wetherill was telling him of his own early experiences, first in gold . . . 'we all had our minds fixed on gold, we didn't know the significance of nickel nor what to look for then' . . . then, after the fabulous Kambalda find out of Kalgoorlie, that new message the wind carried. Nickel.

'I was no learned geo.' Now Stone was looking levelly instead at Sandy almost as if to establish something. 'I was just a stubborn rock man who wanted to beat the big companies with all their wealthy equipment and know-how. So I worked for them and their experts and I picked their brains.' Still he looked challengingly at Sandy. 'I lived and I breathed maps. I did without everything . . . three hundred dollars to peg a claim and seven dollars a foot to drill it makes you do without.'

'And finally you won through.' Sandy came in with that sarcastically. She felt she could not bear this poor-boy-makes-good story any longer.

'Not really,' he said coolly, 'but I have hopes.'

'Then good for you,' she smiled thinly.

'And you, too. You enjoy employment.'

'I am employed,' she amended.

Stone Wetherill turned to Ralph Hudson. 'In case all this perplexes you, Hudson, in an otherwise willing camp is an unwilling camper. Miss Lawford here did not read the contract's small print.'

Hudson smiled politely, and Stone got into the jeep and they continued the tour.

They passed a waterhole with a carcass protruding out of it, and Stone stopped the jeep abruptly, and told Hudson to help him pull it out. 'The beast must have got bogged there in the last rain ... a few drops out here and it's a bogging matter. If we don't remove it the remaining water will be polluted and lives could be lost.'

Ralph did not look enthusiastic, and Sandy did not blame him. She looked the other way, and was still staring into that heat-dancing distance when the men returned to the jeep.

'An object lesson here, Miss Lawford,' Stone said. He was drying his big hands on his handkerchief. 'If this waterhole was your last hope and you found it polluted, what then?'

'It wouldn't happen. I wouldn't be out here.'

He made a gesture of impatience and said, 'Look, girl, it could possibly save your life, so don't turn away. You attend, too, Hudson. This is it: always carry a sheet of plastic. Dig a hole about a yard square and half of that deep in dry soil. That' ... a short laugh ... 'shouldn't be hard to find. In the hole place a small container and surround it with any desert shrubbery you can find. Oh, yes, there is some if you look for it. Now place your plastic loosely over the hole, with a small stone in the centre to make it sag towards the container. The sun shining through the plastic heats the soil and plant material, and draws moisture on the underside of the sheet in small drops. They'll drip into the container.'

'And a life is saved,' said Sandy pertly.

'Thank you, Miss Lawford, though you could have

537

put worthless in front of that life if you referred to yourself.' Stone turned to Hudson. 'It makes a kind of solar still,' he explained. 'You should enlarge the hole and add fresh material every day. But even the three feet square will produce a daily pint.' They set out again, and Sandy saw that they were approaching the other side of Quartz Hill, that is the side not visible to the Oasis, and the side behind which she and Janice had ventured. The men were talking about quartz, and how where quartz was could be gold, and how where gold was could be something else.

It was pretty here after the barren plain, and Sandy was glad that Stone pulled up and actually produced a flask and a hamper.

The tea was black, sweet and strong. The sandwiches were beef. 'Health is good in the hinterland,' Stone said, 'it might be a case of steak and more steak but occasionally steak instead, but it's still the highest protein intake in the world.'

'Which makes for strong men,' Sandy said slyly.

'And strong women, Miss Lawford. Did you eat the breakfast I brought you?'

'Only the toast. I only take toast.'

'You'll eat full breakfasts in future.'

'Is that also in the small print?'

'It's in the name of common sense. You're not living an ordinary life out here. A doctor isn't just around the corner. So naturally you try to maintain a very good standard.'

'Oh, I do,' she inserted.

'Of health,' he continued.

'Then,' said Sandy, 'I must certainly eat another sandwich.'

The snack finished, Sandy left the packing up to

Stone, and began poking around the dry creek. Once she glanced back to the jeep and saw that Ralph Hudson was looking around as well. Also that Stone Wetherill was watching him.

A little puzzled, though she could not have told what puzzled her, she returned to her stick pushing, in the hope of finding some moisture to prove that this was indeed an old creek. In her absorption she did not hear the man until he was by her side.

It was Stone. 'Do you know,' he said, 'that underneath all this there's a river? Yes, that's true. Australian hinterland rivers flow underneath, not on top like respectable watercourses. Only when the Wet comes do they appear as rivers should.'

She was fascinated, and listened to him tell other tales of what happened when the Wet came. Of a gouging, swirling, muddy beast that once had leapt to life after twenty-eight inches in twenty-eight days and come roaring across the plains, washing away fences (where there were fences) and widening on one occasion to seventy miles across.

'And seventy miles across is some river,' Stone said.

She liked him like this, the Salvation Jane blue eyes telling the story at the same time as the long sensuous mouth told it. She listened eagerly. But abruptly in the middle of his recounting he turned and looked to the jeep. Hudson was not there. Without a word of explanation he left Sandy.

She began her reconnoitring again, but abstractedly now. Why had Stone Wetherill left her like that? But soon she became absorbed in her probing, her satisfaction at finding a wet stick at last turning to sheer delight when she actually discovered a drip of water making a crystal impact on a rock beneath a small overhang near the base of the Quartz Hill.

It was at that moment she heard a slight sound, almost like something falling. She waited, then heard nothing more, so concluded it was a stone that had dislodged. She followed up the crystal drop, almost dropping herself in a narrow cleft that opened up without any warning. There was a cluster of growth at the bottom of the chasm, some rough sagebush, a surprisingly delicate green fern . . . and there was also a man's sleeve.

About to step back out of danger, Sandy now edged carefully forward instead. She looked at the sleeve. She looked at the hand emerging from the cuff of the sleeve, large, brown, capable. Though Mr. Stone Wetherill, she thought, was not so capable now. For Sandy had recognized the ring he wore. Upon her arrival at the Oasis she had wondered at a ring on such a male male. She did not know the stone, but it was large and dark red, nearly the same colour as his Red Indian skin.

But what was she doing thinking of rings now? The man could be concussed.

She had slid to the bottom by this, and was kneeling down beside him. Yes, it was Stone Wetherill, and he was unconscious, but, thank heaven, he was nowhere near rock, so there should have been no damaging impact.

But others things could happen. Sandy, accustomed to such emergencies, made sure that his neck was not turned unnaturally, arms not entwined, legs not twisted. That everything was fairly normal.

She had his head on her lap now. Mouth-to-mouth resuscitation, she thought, and bent her head to his.

He let her do it, and only when he changed the kiss

of life to a kiss of something else did Sandy realize he was laughing at her.

'You're horrible!' She jumped up and away from him.

'I couldn't resist it,' he grinned, 'you looked so serious.'

'If this is your idea of a joke . . .'

'I wasn't joking, Alexandra, I did actually knock myself out for a moment or so. Not looking where I was going, or rather looking elsewhere, I walked right into this cleft. I was genuinely out to it until you applied the kiss of life, or started to, and then – well, I came to life myself.'

'It's a pity,' Sandy said, 'you hadn't stopped dead.'

'And deprived you of this?' he laughed softly. He had got up, too, and he put his arms around her. He held her so tight she couldn't move, couldn't even bring her hands together to push him back as she had . . . or tried to . . . that other time.

But when he had her imprisoned, he did nothing at all about it. He just smiled lazily and let her go.

And that, thought Sandy, climbing up unaided behind him, following him back to the jeep where Hudson was waiting, was the most withering of all.

When they got back to the Oasis the working party was home, and, as only to be expected after days of stone, sand, unrelentless heat, nights of no other company than their own, Busy Acres, with its proud strip of bitumen, with its cool saloon, some of the ensuing conversation (with luck) gloriously feminine . . . most of all its long glasses with inches of white collar . . . beckoned, and all went in. All, that is, with the exception of Stone.

'But don't let that keep you from going,' Wetherill said tauntingly as he himself opened one of the jeep doors for Sandy to climb in. Tim Bevis was already there, and looking disappointed that he had not won himself Janice for the miles into B.A.

'I had no intention of letting it keep me here,' Sandy returned coolly.

'What's the attraction for you today?' Stone asked, and he began his rolling ritual. 'A white collar thirst like the gang?'

'More boots were coming in,' she answered without interest. 'I'm tired of these boy's ones.'

'You tired of being a boy!'

'Also,' she said deliberately, 'I might splash on some new dresses. I noticed the store had quite a variety last time.'

'You slay me. But then that's the intention, isn't it, that's why the female adorns herself, to slay the male.'

'Perhaps, but I can assure you that in my case, Mr. Wetherill, I didn't have anyone particular in view.'

'You really mean you weren't thinking of me, don't you?'

She smiled thinly at that and settled herself beside the frankly bewildered Tim, who only got sweet words from Janice, and had come to believe that all love ran smoothly . . . even though Janice was in some other car now.

But perhaps this could be an advantage. During the ride in Tim produced a bundle of dollars and asked Sandy to do some shopping for him.

'What kind of shopping, Tim?'

'Oh, you know . . . something she'll like.'

'For Janice?'

'Yes.'

'She has a lot of things already.'

'But a girl always likes pretty things and I want to give them to her.'

This was something that Sandy certainly understood; at every undertaking at which she had lived with her father there always had been among the umbrellas, loofahs, paperbacks, bacon, soap and other normal store offerings, pretty boxes of lingerie, frivolous slippers, stoppered phials of French perfume, frothy blouses. They had sold well. Seldom had a man bought even a plug of tobacco without buying something, if only a tin of talc, for the little woman . . . it didn't matter that she was not there, nor (as Sandy sometimes sympathetically had thought) that she did not as yet exist. That 'balance' that Stone had spoken about had urged along the small transaction, and the purchaser had gone out with a bulge in his pocket and a smile on his face.

But Tim was not quite in this category, the idea was not occurring to him as he bought something for himself and noticed a pile of pretties; he had come to B.A. with a certain intention, and he was asking Sandy's aid. It would benefit neither of them for her to refuse, so . . . though unenthusiastically . . . she asked, 'What did you have in mind, Tim?'

'Something that you as a girl would very much like yourself.'

Sandy felt like saying, 'Thank you, but I'm not. Not a girl. Hasn't your boss told you that?'

Instead she smiled, 'I'll look around and let you know. I'm calling in at the store, anyway, to see their new boots.'

But Sandy, upon arrival at B.A., found herself

claimed by the nickel wives Maggie and Brenda, who were also in town, and eager to talk. While they stood chattering eagerly in the middle of the street, cars carefully edging around them, for women were precious out here, the host of the Palatial-saw them, and let out a cry of joy. Shirl had come up, he informed, but was about to pack up and leave again, but with crowds of her own sex around . . .

'How do we make three look a crowd?' giggled Brenda, as they followed the hotelier into the inn, but Shirl was so pleased to see them that the next hour went past without Sandy realizing it.

Then she saw Tim looking plaintively from the bar door at her, and rose and excused herself, after first assuring Shirley she would call again, and not to dare leave before she came in.

'Not her, she's one of the club,' laughed Maggie. At Sandy's inquiring look she said, 'The Nickel Wives. When are you joining, dear?'

As Sandy went through the bar she saw that by this time the sand and gibber thirst the Oasis boys had brought in from the desert was being suitably attended to. Several of the gang called cheerily to her to join them, then when she declined held up their glasses in a toast.

Reaching the swinging doors, someone spoke to her, and looking up at the man Sandy recognized him from her first visit to B.A., later at the piksher night. He had tried to pump her, she remembered. He had stood beside Janice and the pair had exchanged envelopes. She prepared herself now to refuse that offer of a drink with which he would probably preface his probing.

But the question when it came surprised her.

'Since when has the Oasis been dealing in matrix?'

'Matrix!' That was the result of silicone and sand, found among opals, and of very little value.

She had not realized she had answered this aloud until the man smiled thinly and said, 'Once, perhaps, but not now. They're processing them these days, and it takes an expert, after they've been boiled and baked in sugar and sulphur, to tell them from a top grade stone. I should have thought that your boss had had his fingers burnt enough over the Thunder episode without antagonizing those opal cookies any further. What I mean is they're not going to like him trading in substitutes, are they?'

'He is not!' she retorted.

'Then why did one of your men unload some matrix just now?'

'None of them did.'

'The new one,' smiled the man, 'I saw him.'

'He wouldn't even know what it was. He's our new driller, but he's never been in the Centre, only in high country places ...' Yes, thought Sandy, and that's where I met him. Only I can't remember ...

'So he doesn't know matrix,' the man was laughing. 'Probably doesn't know opal, either. And as for nickel ...' A sly grin.

'If you'll excuse me, I want to get out.' The man was blocking the doorway.

'Certainly.' He moved aside. 'But don't forget, will you, who gave you the drum on that matrix. It should be worth an appreciation. After all, your boss doesn't want more gelignite served up.'

'Excuse me, please.' Sandy pushed past him and went along the street to the store.

Here she was joined by Tim, and because Tim was so desirous to get something really remarkable for

Janice, and because in such a conglomeration of goods that took some doing, Sandy had no opportunity to think about what had just taken place, the words the fellow had said. But of one thing she was certain: the man must be mistaken regarding Ralph and any matrix. Hudson had certainly picked some up, but carelessly, without knowledge, and she felt she had no reason to disbelieve that action even though that first faint feeling of knowing Ralph previously still persisted. On the other hand she had every reason to *dis*believe the informer, especially since that episode on the night of the pictures at Ten Mile. So disbelieve him she would.

Putting the episode aside, she looked for the new boots, found they still hadn't arrived, settled Tim in a corner with some exciting ... to girls, anyway ... boxes to examine, then made for the dress racks. She was remembering her determination this time to have something more than two dull shirtwaists hanging from her caravan wardrobe.

She dithered happily between a sky blue button-through and a straight tangerine crepe that would be sure to win a whistle from the gang ... but she bought neither. For, coming to a space in the rack which was probably the storekeeper's idea of differentiating the sizes, Tim, holding something up for her opinion, close behind her, she came upon Janice ... with Ralph Hudson.

Well, that was nothing. One struck everybody at some time or other at the shop. It would be unusual not to.

They did not stand really close together. Not even their hands touched. There was nothing at all, *nothing*, to make Sandy feel sick at heart as she was ... at once

. . . for Tim. She wondered about it afterwards, wondered why Tim also felt the same at that pair standing there. It was only natural that a man and a woman meeting in a store like B.A.'s should stand and talk, it would be unnatural if they didn't. But she knew before Tim turned blindly and went to the door that he had felt as she had. And she knew she had no need to ask if he *still* wanted her to choose something for Janice.

The odd thing about it, she thought later, was her sickness for Tim, never for Stone, and yet it was Stone Wetherill, not Tim Bevis, to whom this girl belonged.

Catching Tim up, walking beside him, she tried to think of things to say. Like: 'Don't take it badly.' Like: 'It mightn't be as you think.' Like—

But everything she thought of was trivial, the whole episode appeared trivial . . . everything that is except the boy-hurt in Tim's face. He was young. First job, probably. First girl . . . or at least he had thought she was his girl.

She came behind him as he turned into the bar. The place now was a riot, a crowd of blow-ins had arrived since she had left to go up to the store, and not having done too well with the present cagey company, they greeted Tim eagerly. Eagerly . . . too eagerly . . . Tim greeted them in return.

Over their heads Sandy could see Hunt and Barry using sign language to each other. It didn't take much reading to know that they were considering which way it would be best to extricate Tim from the nosey parkers.

She pushed through to Barry's side, and said, '*No.*'

'I never asked you, Sandy. We've finished, anyway.'

547

Barry was still frowning over the boy.

'No, don't stop him, Barry, leave him be. After all, he can't do any damage, I mean he hasn't been out on the traps, not *really*, so there's nothing he can tell. Just let him be.'

'Boss won't like it, Sandy. Not with a kid like Tim.'

'*Leave him be*. He . . . well, he's been hurt.'

Barry looked hard at her, guessed what she was *not* saying, but was still unsure.

'The boss—' he began.

'*I* will take the responsibility. Now tell Hunt . . . tell the others . . . to leave him alone.' Before he could argue Sandy went out to wait in the jeep.

It was an hour before the Oasis party left B.A. for home. Mostly they had got beyond cheerfulness and reached the weary stage. Some of them were almost asleep on their feet.

'All right, smartie,' said Barry unhappily to Sandy, 'seeing you're responsible for all this you'll have to drive.'

'I will. Everyone here?'

'Yes. Janice and the new bloke went some time ago. I'll say this for him, Hudson wasn't sticking his neck out for trouble like us.'

'I told you, Barry, *I* will be responsible. Anyway, Tim's asleep.'

'But he's no featherweight, and we'll have to get him to his cot.'

'Surely between you—'

'Between us?' Barry looked around at the ranks, those not asleep certainly not looking very able.

'We'll meet trouble when it comes,' Sandy said, releasing the brake to follow behind Hunt who was in the first jeep.

Driving took all her concentration, but between the effort she still thought confidently that she should encounter no difficulty. It was fairly late, and if Stone Wetherill was not already in bed, having assumed by the return earlier of Janice and Ralph that the others were coming close behind, he would be working in the office, and work always absorbing him as it did, not bother to come out. With any ordinary sort of luck if she drew the jeep close to Tim's van . . .

But ordinary luck was not Sandy's luck, in fact no variety of luck at all.

Stone Wetherill was standing at the cookhouse door, and there was that pervading aroma of strong coffee.

'We're off first thing!' he called as first Hunt pulled up, then Sandy, then the others. 'I was going to say first thing in the morning, but' . . . a look at his watch . . . 'it's that now. You can all get some sobering brew into you. Hudson was the only sane member. He's in bed already. Step lively and follow him. It's going to be a really tough try this go.'

As he was talking he was approaching them from the cookhouse, and those quick blue eyes at once set on Tim.

'How did the kid get like that?' he fairly hissed at Barry.

'Sorry, boss, but you know how it goes.'

'Yes, I know. But I also thought *you* knew. Seeing you didn't, then you better find somewhere where knowing or not knowing isn't so important.'

Sandy looked incredulously at the man's furious face. Actually he was discharging one of his best friends, one of his prized geos, and, according to what she had been told, an investor in his company.

549

'You're mad!' She stepped in front of Barry.

'Keep out of this, Miss Lawford.'

'Barry did nothing,' she persisted.

'Nothing?' Stone wheeled round. 'Look at the boy. If he'd known anything of value . . .'

'Known anything! *Known* anything! That's all you can think about. If – if you were affronted because of his morals, or his health, or – or— But no, it's just "if he'd known anything".'

'And if he had, he would have spilled it, and I and all these men would be right back where we started, to taws. Doesn't sound much when you say it like that, you don't feel the blistering heat, the backache, the blood, the sweat, and all for nothing. But that's what it means, Miss Lawford, and what it could have meant had Tim Bevis had anything to spill, as undoubtedly he would have spilled in such a condition. It would have been the end for the boys and me.'

'But particularly,' she said cuttingly, 'for you.'

Across the ring of men, suddenly sobered, the two stared furiously at each other.

'Get coffee, all of you,' Stone Wetherill called, 'I'll see to Bevis.'

Sandy saw Barry and Hunt rather nervously offer to help and get brushed aside. Had she had any sense she would have taken their brushing aside as her own as well, have crept thankfully to her van.

But Sandy was inflamed. Running after Stone Wetherill who had picked Tim up like a sack of potatoes and was carrying him effortlessly to his cot, she said, 'Make sure you *throw* him in, won't you, like you threw him before.'

He did not answer. He climbed the van steps, put the boy down on the mattress, then turned and looked down on her as she stood on the strip in front of the caravan.

Then: 'You next,' he said.

She turned and hurried away, but he jumped down the several steps and overtook her, then, lifting her bodily he carried her as he had carried Tim, only this time not over his shoulder. Though certainly, Sandy thought, half choked by his shirt, half stifled by his big encroaching arm, she also could have been a sack of potatoes.

He climbed the van steps and crossed to her bed.

'Now do I throw you . . . or do I do this?' he asked. 'After all, I let you get off easy at the creek.'

His arms around her were whipcord. There was no escaping from them, so she just stood rigid in the hard embrace.

He finished at last. He said, 'No wonder you had to have that opal from Thunder, for there's no fire in you, is there, Alexandra, no flame at all.'

He put her down so abruptly she rocked a little, but he did not steady her.

'The high mountains lady,' he taunted, 'the cold country girl. Look what it's done, it's put ice in your veins.' He turned up the collar of his plaid shirt. He pretended to blow on chilled hands.

'If you've finished, Mr. Wetherill . . .'

'Finished! I've not even started.' As she stepped nervously away from him, he laughed, 'Not *that*, although that's not started either, but your explanation regarding Bevis, why you took upon yourself the role that you did.'

'I can tell you.'

'And I can guess it. Puppy love comes to a touching close. Am I right? Well, he would have got over that

551

just as well and with no headache had you let Barry bring him home.'

'He was emotionally upset,' she persisted.

'He'll be more physically upset on the job tomorrow. Oh, yes, I'm taking him out at last. Out to the *big* stuff, Miss Lawford, the stuff that will make or down us. Who knows? Only the assayer when we take the sample in. But after last night Tim won't need to stop in the nursery any more, he'll know how to keep his tongue quiet like the rest of us. For which knowledge let us all thank woman. Woman, I thank you.' Stone bowed.

The backward action took him to the door of the van, and Sandy promptly shut and locked it on him.

He did not attempt to try to come back, though she knew that strength like his could have forced the door with ease. she heard him laugh softly as he went down the steps and over Rusty's lawn.

Sandy did not know if the rest of the camp slept that night . . . certainly all the lights were out.

She did not sleep herself.

CHAPTER EIGHT

Towards morning Sandy must have slept, for she did not hear the departure of the gang, and seeing that everyone went, that is everyone with the exception of the camp foreman and, of course, Janice, something should have penetrated that eventual uneasy rest.

But it didn't. The jeeps roared out, one after the other, the tabletop with the necessary equipment, Andy in his four-wheel drive utility with his pots and pans and provisions, the riggers, the drillers, the geos, the engineer. The boss.

By the time Sandy opened her eyes there was silence in the camp. But somehow not a peaceful silence, she thought uneasily as she bathed. Silence should be calm, fortifying. This one was not calm and she was not fortified.

She dressed dispiritedly and went across to the cookhouse. Rusty poured two cups of tea and sat down beside her. He looked troubled. They drank for a while, then Sandy asked, 'What is it, Rusty?'

'Blowed if I know.' Rusty ran his fingers through his sparse red hair. 'Here we are,' he said presently, 'nearly there .. or so the feeling goes ... but what do I think of? I'll tell you, Sandy. I think it will never be the same again.'

'It needn't be different,' she tried to cheer him.

'Never saw a concern that prospered *not* change, girl. I look at my lawn. I look at my trees.' He sighed.

'It's said there's a blessing on everyone who plants a

553

tree. I mean, Rusty, you don't have to *live* near the tree. The very fact you grew it—'

'How far do you think any of these trees will grow without care?' grumbled Rusty.

'Anyone would think you were leaving,' she tried to reason. 'Oh, I know the projects shift around to cheat the spies, but the Oasis is a base, and—'

'Whose base?' gloomed Rusty next. 'Whichever way it goes on this trip I reckon it's the end for us. If it turns up like Stone hopes it will, the camp won't be big enough. If it doesn't, and we're skinned out, it'll be too big and we'll have to quit.'

'But those who come after you will look after your garden,' endeavoured Sandy. 'Well, not as you do, perhaps, but—'

But Rusty was not to be cheered up.

'I'm Sinbad today,' he admitted over a second cup. 'I haven't had that Old Man of the Sea feeling—'

'The sea out here?' she tried to jolly him.

'Since young Roge went.' He put down his cup of tea, his face crumpling. 'Yes, Roge, and the feeling now is just the same.'

'What do you mean, Rusty?' But the camp foreman was wiping his hands . . . and his face . . . on the roller towel behind the door. He had not wet them, so Sandy knew he was wiping away something else. She slipped out of the cookhouse.

Never had the camp seemed so lonely, so isolated. Still, she tried to reason, actually it was lonely and isolated, it was miles from Busy Acres and B.A. was miles from anywhere. Apart from B.A. there was only heat-dancing horizons and stretches of gibber and sand. But ordinarily you did not feel the isolation, even when the gang was out someone was left behind. An air remained in the place. This time the whole troop had gone and there was no air. Even the blue-lined pool did not entice her. Sandy sat beside it and ruffled the undisturbed water with her finger. Who had been Rogé? she wondered. Was Rogé short for Roger, and had he been related to Rusty for Rusty to crumple up like that? Yet Rusty had compared that feeling with the feeling he had now, so Rogé could have belonged to this camp.

How little she knew, she sighed, how little she really knew of anything that had occurred before she came here . . .

All that day her unease persisted. Sandy woke up with it again the next morning, woke up to that feeling of isolation, to a hollowness of not knowing what was going to take place, what was taking place. What had taken place once.

A fragment came back to her of something that had been said. It had been after the opal incident when Rusty (or had it been Andy?) had told her that what almost had happened to her in the desert had happened before.

Then . . . and clearly this time, almost as though it was spoken beside her . . . she heard Andy say: 'If it happened to Janice I wouldn't like to think what Stone would have done.'

Janice. There was her only source of information, and all at once it became imperative to Sandy that she learn something . . . anything at all.

She waited till mid-morning, then she left her van and crossed to Janice's, thinking that as usual the girl was lying in. Well, it was late enough now to have a reason for rousing her.

'Janice,' she called, 'shall I bring you some tea? Jan—' She stopped in surprise at Janice, fully dressed,

555

and standing beside several large bags at her van door. It seemed redundant to ask. 'Are you going away?'

'There are no cars,' she said instead a little stupid-ly.

'There's Cleve,' shrugged Janice. 'It's mail-day today.'

'Does – does Mr. Wetherill know?'

Janice gave a pitying little laugh. 'He doesn't have to know. *I'm* not an employee, remember.'

'But you – but he—'

'You thought that, did you? Perhaps I might have thought about it myself had I not thought, too, about this place. Because this place *is* that man, and always will be. Whoever marries Stone will marry stone. Stone and all the rest of the wretched things that make up this wretched interior. I hate it, and I've wasted all these months in it. But I'm not wasting any more. Not now that—'

'Does he know?'

'Stone? No. Why should he?'

'Because you and he—'

A sly smile flickered over Janice's beautiful face. She seemed amused, diverted. 'Leave it at *he*,' she suggested carelessly.

'You mean that you never – that you—'

'No, I never. But Stone? Well' ... she looked significantly down at herself, at her outstanding beauty. 'Poor Stone,' she smiled.

'Why did you come here, Janice?'

The girl glanced at her for a searching moment, then, wearing the amused look again, she shrugged.

'The usual reason,' she said. '*His*. But it's finished now. At least I am. He's all yours, darling. Do you object to hand-me-downs?'

Words rushed to Sandy, fumbling, defensive words, disbelieving words, yet how could she disbelieve? She recalled the patience and the care Stone Wetherill had always given Janice ... impatience and challenge had been her lot. She remembered again that: 'If it had happened to Janice I wouldn't like to think what Stone would have done.'

Janice was standing outside the van door now, narrowing her eyes at the distance. Sandy looked, too, and saw the first red cloud of dust. It would be Cleve. Bringing the mail.

'Before you go, Janice, tell me,' she appealed.

The little amused smile again. 'I think you already know.'

'Then tell me who was Roge?'

That stopped Janice. She stood on the first step down for a long moment. She went quite pale.

'I don't know what you're talking about,' she said.

'Roge. For Roger, I think.'

'How should I know?'

'Because you do,' Sandy said. 'And I want to know, Janice, before you go.'

'Then find out,' Janice advised, 'for I'm leaving with Cleve. I'm catching the plane from B.A., and Ralph—'

'Ralph?'

'Oh, forget it.' Janice gave a little click of annoyance at herself. 'Thank heaven,' she said, 'this is my exit.'

'I don't think it is,' Sandy said slowly, troublously, something closing up her throat. 'Because it's not Cleve.'

'Not the mail-car?'

'No ... it's one of ours, and it's travelling fast. There's a couple of the gang in it. It's Barry and—' She screwed up her eyes. 'And I think it's Stone.'

'Stone.' Janice stepped into the van again. 'What's wrong, do you think? Why are he and Barry back?'

'There's someone else there. Stretched out. I think something's happened. I think someone's hurt!' Sandy pushed past the girl and ran down the steps.

She and Rusty reached the jeep together, but Stone Wetherill did not speak to either of them. He didn't even seem to see them. He fairly leapt from the waggon and ran across to where he kept his small helicopter. Rusty ran after him to help him wheel it out.

Sandy turned to Barry, still behind the wheel of the jeep, and asked him silently.

'Tim,' he replied, 'he fell from the rig. It's bad, Sandy. I don't think—'

'What's Stone going to do?'

'Air Ambulance could never have landed there, nor here, so he'll have to be taken to the nearest strip.'

'Can we do anything now?' Sandy asked urgently.

'No,' said Barry bluntly, blunt from emotion, 'you see I think . . . and I know Stone thinks . . .'

All the same Sandy climbed into the waggon, knelt beside the boy. He had been laid down tenderly on every rug and cushion the camp could muster. He was not unconscious, though he could not speak. He looked up at her and she knew what he wanted. She knew she shouldn't disturb him, but he would be disturbed, anyway, when Stone transferred him to the 'copter. Gently she crouched down and tenderly she put his head in her lap.

It was such a slight wound in his boyish forehead, such an unimportant-looking injury, such a small oblong of congealing blood that she could not believe that—

Then she saw the blurring gaze, the stiffening lips. The eyes beginning to glaze.

She knew he couldn't see now. When he blurted painfully at last after much effort, much reaching, 'Jan-ice?' she answered, 'Yes, it's Janice. Tim.' Then she bent over and kissed him.

Before the others came back he died.

Sandy still sat with his head in her lap. She was aware of nothing, neither sorrow, pain, relief that he hadn't had time to suffer, resentment that he was so young. She stared at the camp, the glittering sun dancing on Rusty's shrubs and plants, but could not have said what she saw.

She listened unheeding, too. To the quiet sounds of the desert. The small, idle plains breeze lazing through the new blades of grass. The pool water slapping the tank sides now and then. Somewhere high up a hinterland bird. She would have liked to have cried, but there were no tears. She would have liked even to *feel*, but she seemed to be apart.

Then the mists cleared and she saw the 'copter being wheeled out. She raised her hand to the men and they came across.

'It doesn't matter,' she said expressionlessly, and nodded to Stone's small craft.

They understood.

Afterwards she could not remember Rusty holding Tim's head in gentle hands as she slipped away from him on to her feet. She could hear voices, but she could not understand what they said, but she must have followed an impulsion, because presently she was in her own van and sitting on her bed.

She sat there a long time. She heard the 'copter

being wheeled back. The jeep ... with Tim ... being driven to Stone's own quarters. Later she heard the mail-van arriving and Cleve's cheerful whistle being hushed by Rusty. Rusty must have taken Cleve to the cookhouse for coffee, for there was silence ... to be broken only minutes before Cleve left again by Janice.

The girl knocked and came in. She stood against the door and looked at Sandy and moved her lips in a dull 'Good-bye.'

'Good-bye, Janice.'

But still Janice paused.

'I *know*, Sandy,' she said.

'Yes.'

'It wasn't my fault ... at least I didn't mean it to be. I didn't really lead him on, that is I didn't lead him on any more than I lead anyone. It was just him, I think. It was Tim. He took things so seriously. Some of them do. Roge did.'

'Will you tell me, Janice?'

'Roger came up here to make a fortune, because that's what I wanted. I can't help it, I always went without when I was a child, so I wanted things later on. Can you understand?'

'Go on,' answered Sandy.

'But there wasn't a fortune here ... or if there was it was going to take a long time. I wrote up to say it was all off, though really it had never been on. Roge was like Tim, young and serious and – and—'

'Intense.'

'Yes. Well, he just walked out into the desert and didn't come back. They didn't find him in time.' Janice put a hand over her eyes. 'But it wasn't my fault, Sandy, I never dreamed it would be like that, just like I

560

never dreamed that Tim— But I'm finished now, finished up here. And next time I'll be careful. I never mean to hurt, I suppose it's because I'm like I am, and men—'

'Yes, you're beautiful, Janice.'

'But it will be different, and if it helps anyone at all I will *not* be meeting Ralph, starting what I started before.'

'I don't think it could ever be like that, not with him. He hasn't that capacity.' Even as she said it Sandy was remembering at last . . . remembering *Rolf Hudlut*.

It had been at the Snowy. She had been only a schoolgirl. She remembered the Professor telling her about it.

'Other men,' he had sighed, 'you could appeal to, but never this man.'

Rolf Hudlut had found gold tracings in the tunnel he had been drilling, and his ultimate price for keeping that quiet had ruined the small company that had won the contract, yet they had had no alternative, for a boom that was gold would have ruined even more than a tunnel, it would have tumbled the entire national undertaking.

'Yet what,' the professor had said, 'could the company do but bribe the fellow? This was no man to whom one could point out a decade of hard work, suffering, sweat and blood. He had no ears for the wealth of harnessed waters, only for the wealth, *personal* wealth that was gold. So the fellow got what he asked and a gallant little group of men had to cancel their own contract and start off again.'

Other advantageous happenings, advantageous to Hudlut, or Hudson, probably more aliases, had come to the man, but after he had left the project Sandy had never seen him. Until, though unrecognized, now.

'Were you joining up with him, Janice?' she asked.

'Yes. He has the money, you see . . . and he expected a lot more.'

'A lot more?'

'He wasn't as new here as you all thought. He was feeling out the way things would go. He knew that something big had started out in the traps and — and—'

'Yes?'

'He was going to beat Stone to it.'

'Only,' said Sandy softly, 'Tim stopped that.'

'Never Ralph,' said Janice . . . and she put her hand over her trembling mouth.

When she took it down again it was to whisper, 'Good-bye.'

Sandy heard her steps, heard the mail van engine springing to life. Then all was silent again.

Around dusk the gang got in. How little we know what we possess until it is gone, Sandy ached. She longed to hold yesterday again in her hand . . . the dive-bombing, ducking, leg-pulling, the crazy horse-play. The water polo team of which Tim was captain of the side she swam with. The noise.

Now everything was quiet. Men shod in silence moved about their tasks. Rusty brought over a tray and later took it back untouched. The lights that had come on went off again very early. Sandy never puts hers on; she just slipped into bed.

She crossed over to the cookhouse the next morning to save Rusty bringing a tray. She noticed that the camp was moving again, hands waved to her, heads nodded. Life was going on.

Only not for Tim, and because she had to know she asked Rusty.

'Stone and some of the boys have taken him into B.A., there's a little acre there.'

'Not down to Sydney?'

'Didn't come from Sydney ... Melbourne ... anywhere particular. He just got around. Well, he could, he had no relations, no ties. Stone reckoned he was *ours*, so we'd keep him here. Only' ... Rusty frowned ... 'I don't know whether that's wise. We won't be here.'

'The results were not what they thought?'

'Even better. But— Well, you see this go was all only exploratory. Nothing official, Sandy. It's a thing Stone has never done, he always pegs a claim first. But funds were going down and he was worried. You see it wasn't as if they were all his funds, they were ours as well, and Stone is like that. So he took a risk for the first time. He did what he shouldn't do, legal-wise as well. He looked before he bought ... or so he thought. He saved three hundred dollars ... and lost that many thousand.'

'But how? *How*. Rusty?'

'Hudson.'

'But Hudson wouldn't ... not with Tim ... not with him—'

'He did. It's over the grapevine already. The pedal radio hasn't stopped. Hudson's sold out to one of the big companies ... Quickcats. He's sold our blood.'

'But how?' Sandy asked again.

'You might have noticed how he never returned to the Oasis. At no time did he have any intention of returning ... we know that now. He had one of the

563

rival Cherokees ready to pick him up. It was to be a race between him and Stone if the rock came up what they hoped . . . oh, yes, he knew rock all right.'

'Opal, too,' murmured Sandy. 'Matrix.' She paused. 'But surely after Tim . . .'

'Tim was an advantage he hadn't anticipated . . . yes, I say that, Sandy, the man has no heart. While the gang did what they could for Tim, he did what he could for himself. According to the talk he did it pretty well.'

'I see.' Sandy took up her cup, put it down again. 'What happens now?'

'What I told you. Others come in. Well' – a shrug – 'we would have had to shift on, anyway, if we'd been rich. Out here there's no half-way.'

'Tell me about Tim, Rusty, I'd sooner you say it.'

'He was doing all right. Any depression he had the first day was pushed aside by a heck of a hangover. But after that he could talk about it, and when you can talk about a thing, Sandy, you're O.K. Tim was O.K., otherwise Stone never would have let him man the rig like he did. He was working well, the gang told me. Things were going fine. Then—'

'What was it – the heat?' She remembered Stone telling her how men collapsed on the job.

'No. The simplest thing really. He tripped. Maybe it was the footing, maybe it was his shoes, maybe he misjudged, or lost his balance. What's it matter, anyway?' Rusty put his head in his hands. 'It can't help.'

'Then – it wasn't Janice?'

'No.'

'I'm glad for her,' Sandy said quietly, and Rusty looked up from his hands.

'You see I know now about Roger,' Sandy told him.

'How he was here . . . how he walked into the desert because of Janice. I know all that, but what I don't know is *why* Stone had Janice here.'

'Well, how do you think he felt,' demanded Rusty, 'a man like Stone?'

'Responsible, I suppose.'

'Yes. And it ate him up, Sandy, it plagued him. He went down to Sydney himself and got her. He brought her back and treated her like something rare and precious . . . which he knew she wasn't.' Rusty looked grim.

'Because of the letter?' asked Sandy.

'Letter?'

'The letter to Roge telling him it was over.'

'I never knew about that. Stone, either. We all thought Roger had been working too hard and missed his girl and walked farther than he should.'

'Then why did you say just now that Stone treated Janice like something rare and precious . . . which she wasn't?'

'Because she wasn't here for a week before she tried to pry. In no time she was on the pay list of every dirty competitor who would give her a hand-out for anything she heard. Only she heard nothing. Stone saw to that. He picked her at once, and the boys soon cottoned on. Anything that lady ever passed along wouldn't have done any harm.'

'Yet you still retained her?'

'She'd been that boy's girl . . . at least that was what we thought. What Stone believed. But now you say—?'

'*Janice* said,' said Sandy. At a sound outside she went to the cookhouse door. Andy and Rusty were there already, watching the jeeps come back again from B.A.

Stone got out and nodded to the gang that he wanted to speak with them. After they had followed him to his quarters, Sandy returned to her own caravan. She supposed she had better pack, for whatever happened, and according to Rusty it already had happened, the Oasis would be closing down. As she folded her few things she wondered about the small print on her contract, whether there were penalties against anyone else if they broke it against her. Not . . . drearily . . . that it mattered.

Rusty came over with a tray again, it seemed to have become a habit, but Sandy sensed that the man needed something to do.

He saw her bags and commended her for them. 'Must have known you were going into B.A.'

'I didn't know . . . though, of course, B.A. is on the way home.' Home! Where was home? Since Father had died there had been no home. Like Tim, she had been alone.

'The reason to stop at B.A. was the funeral,' said Rusty. 'Stone thought you'd like to go as well. It's a nice little corner, Sandy.' Rusty looked pleased about that. 'Pioneers there. Real men. Tim would be proud.'

'Yes, and I'm glad to go,' Sandy answered.

She half-waited for Rusty to say, 'But you won't need both bags.'

He didn't say it. So she was on the way out.

All the jeeps, all the camp went into Busy Acres. The Palatial accommodated them.

Sandy spent the evening with Shirley, a quiet, subdued Shirley, but a Shirley who admitted to Sandy that she was coming to like the place.

'And with nickel wives like Maggie and Brenda and—' She looked at Sandy.

'It finishes there,' Sandy said. 'I'm not one, Shirley.'

'Oh, I don't mean married, I mean ... well, *here.*'

'But I won't be here.'

'But I heard—'

'Shirley, I've lived in places like this all my life and you always hear.'

The little corner was all that Rusty had said of it. Sandy wandered away after the simple service and looked at the stones. There were few, because very few had lived here. Among the pioneers there was a man who had been speared working on the first telegraph line, and at his side a black brother rested. He had given his life saving the small child of a pastoralist from a rearing horse. Yes, Sandy thought, Tim would have been proud.

The gang stopped on at the Palatial that night ... now that it was breaking up Sandy supposed there was no hurry to get back.

She had better make a move herself, though ... book a flight back to Sydney ... start taking the *Australian Miner* again, the *Engineering News*, the *Oil Recorder*. But she found herself shrinking at the thought of another project. Perhaps she had better become a suburban nine-to-five girl.

But whatever she did it had to be out of here, away from B.A. The first thing was to find out when the small feeder plane was expected.

Shirley, very important behind the desk, a role she

had taken upon herself, said, 'But the store's handling it now. What with increased business it got too much for us. Want me to ring?' The telephone was new, and Shirley was proud of it, but Sandy smiled and said she would walk the few yards.

She went down the bitumen . . . it was quite deserted today, no blow-ins . . . then turned into the store.

As before, as always in these places, the interior caught her imagination with its trading-post tumblings of dress bolts, umbrellas, bacon, ties, hats, billies.

Out of a corner of her eye she saw the boot and shoe section, and, yes, new boots were in. But she was no longer interested . . . though the city was wearing boots she could get them there if she still wanted them, no need to carry them down.

She went up to the desk the store had erected for its fare business now that the Palatial had grown too big to handle it, and said, 'Can you tell me, please—'

'Yes?' Stone Wetherill asked.

She looked at him in complete surprise. She had supposed he was in the bar at the Palatial with the boys . . . or cloistered in his room with the boys . . . anywhere where they could lick their wounds. The last place she had expected to find him was the store.

'I . . .' she stammered, 'well, you see . . .'

'Mr. Watson has slipped out for a moment. I'm holding the fort. What was it you wanted, Miss Lawford, a dictionary?'

He had said that when she first had arrived at the Oasis, and it had enraged her, but now it proved something astringent to buck her up . . . astringency was something you could always get from Stone Wetherill . . . and she tilted her chin.

'I want a ticket to Sydney.'

568

'Can't do.'

'Oh, I'm aware it's a feeder plane to—'

'Still can't do.'

'But Shirley said they're not handling it any more, that the store is.'

'You still can't have it, and if Shirley wants to know why tell her that she also hasn't read the small print.'

'Oh, that small print!' Sandy was exasperated. 'I know that can't hold me.'

'So you knew all along there never was a real contract,' he mused. 'Does this mean you *wanted* to stay?'

'I knew no such thing, I took your word that there was.'

'Then why did you just say the contract couldn't hold you?'

'Because there's no project to warrant a contract, and – and— Oh, Stone, Stone, I'm sorry. I'm terribly sorry.' A pause. '*Now* please can I have a ticket?'

'No.' Someone was coming forward with a shoulder of bacon, and Stone wrapped it and took the money. He directed a man to the ten-gallon hats.

'No,' he said again.

'But—'

'You see there's still to be a project, as you always call it. The Oasis remains.'

'Then – then Hudson didn't get that claim and sell it?'

'Oh, yes' . . . grimly . . . 'he did.'

'But—'

'But I'd previously pegged further claims . . . that was why I was chary on this last one, I was using the gang's money, and I felt I'd spent enough.'

'And these other claims, are they as rich?'

569

'No. But I think a whole deal steadier. I can be almost certain on a good resultant two per cent nickel ore, a steady ore, Sandy, I know this country of mine, and I reckon that what we've got this time is the enduring if not the showy stuff. There's a serpentine belt that makes me certain ... more certain than Quickcat with Hudson's goods will ever be. Oh, we're not going to be rich, far from it, but we're going to have enough in our pockets. So' ... a grin ... 'pick yourself out some boots.'

'Oh, don't be stupid, Stone! I won't be here.'

'Don't *you* be stupid, Alexandra ... or are you being coy? Hard to get? At least hard to *keep*? Only woman in the camp now and going all prima donna about it. Then let me spoil your little act: there's going to be at least two other nickel wives.'

'Other wives?' she echoed.

'Maggie and Brenda. Yes, the boys are joining the gang. Not that big screw I hoped to offer them, but much better expectations. They're happy, anyway. Then some of the gang are getting the marrying itch. I reckon it won't be any time before we're an equal balance. Remember how I wanted that?'

'Yes, I remember. I thought you were holding Janice to begin that balance.'

'There was never a thought like that. I kept the girl because I had to. I'd taken everything away from her ... at least I believed I had.'

'Rusty told you'?

'About her letter, yes. And I suppose he told you how we soon found discrepancies in Janice, but bore with her because of what had happened, or so we thought.'

'And then it happened again with Tim.'

'Yes.' He was looking down at his big hands, no words now, nothing at all.

But she felt the rawness of his pain, the amputation of it as though it was hers.

'It goes with places like this, Stone,' she whispered, 'it goes with toughness and roughness and the beginnings of new ventures.'

'I know,' he said gruffly, 'I know. But . . . oh, help me, Alexandra. Help me.'

Afterwards she knew that that had done it, that big, rough western man appealing to her.

The storekeeper had come back and they had edged behind the dress racks.

'I love you,' Stone Wetherill said . . . he could probably think of no other way to say it except this basic, fundamental, elemental way. 'I love you.'

'You never showed it,' she reproached.

'I kissed you, Sandy.'

'Roughly. Like a barbarian.'

He was taking out his makings, rolling, lighting up, looking at her through the smoke. 'That is Wetherill,' he reminded her bluntly.

'But I can't quite believe that,' she protested, then, as he raised his brows, 'You wear a ring, not a signet ring, a ring. You don't seem a ring man.' She was looking at the red stone that she had noticed the first day she had met him . . . recognized on his hand that time he had fallen down the cleft.

'Yes,' he said. 'Here is Love. For that is actually what the natives call it, in their own language, of course. Here is Love. It's of no value . . . no commercial value. It was given to me at . . . but that doesn't matter. What does matter is I was told to wear it.' He paused,

571

then said: 'Until.'

'Until?' she took up.

'Until I knew I had to give it away. I'm not asking you to have it instead of a diamond ... or would you sooner an opal?'

'I'd sooner a red stone, Stone,' Sandy said, 'but are you – are you asking me—'

'No,' he denied, '*demanding*. For that's what barbarians do. Your word, Alexandra.'

...'And yet,' said Sandy some minutes afterwards, 'surely barbarians don't propose in a dress section?'

'They do when their girl is a boy,' he reminded her, and grinned. 'You're having this one, Sandy' ... he took a frock from the rack ... 'this one' ... he took another ... 'this. If I don't make a woman of you, my woman—'

'Then you'll take back Here is Love?' she asked, turning it round her finger, for it was much too large.

'Never. *Never*. Look, we're going to dodge the gang and go out to the gibber. Dust and red earth, Sandy, I know what I'm doing there.'

'But, Stone ...'

For he had whirled her round to him, picked her up, enfolded her, and it was on her tongue to say he did this often ... until she suddenly and sweetly knew by the tender, the very tender harbouring, that he really had never done it before.

He carried her out. And being an uncivilized, barbarian, primitive corner of the world, no one took any notice.

... Except the storekeeper who saw a sale escaping and called: 'Miss Lawford, I got in those boots!'

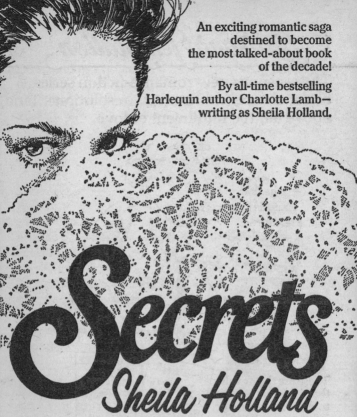